In

The

Shadow

Sherian

McInerney

CONTENTS

PART ONE

Adrienne Albanese, age 13, was born and raised in Paris; her mother Jezalee was born and raised in Manhattan. Her mothers' parents moved to Greenwich, Connecticut while her mom was in college. Her family would visit them usually during summer and on special occasions. Adrienne's mother was an only child of an Irish mother, and an Italian father, last name being Marino. After graduating from Harvard University in 1968, she attended Yale University for two years. Every time Adrienne and her family visited America, she thought one day she would want to attend college there. Adrienne's father, Paul, who was born and raised in Pisa, Italy, had one brother a couple years older than him, named Peter. Their parents were Italian and lived in Pisa all their life. Paul attended Harvard University the same time her mother did; that is where they met and fell in love.

Adrienne loved the school she attended, and they had many Foreign Exchange students from the United States. She made friends with a few of the students and could speak fluent English with them. Thanks to both her parents speaking English, Italian and French at home, she and her siblings were fluent in all three languages. Adrienne's younger sister Jessica was 12, and her younger brother Alexander was 10. She was close to her siblings; but Adrienne had become attached to one girl in her classes by the name of Morgan O`Malley, who was born and raised in San Francisco. So, like most teenagers, her siblings were pushed aside when her friends would come over; especially when Morgan was there.

When Adrienne and Morgan met in school, they hit it off instantly; they were like any other teen in the 1980's, they liked the same music, boys, literature, food, and fashion. Morgan was her best friend from America and the two became inseparable. Adrienne's parents, Paul and Jezalee, had asked their daughter to get Morgan's parents phone number because they wanted to meet her friend's parents, particularly since they hung out so much together. Adrienne and Morgan were either talking on the phone, going over to each other's home, or being dropped off at the nearest movie theater; it was time her parents met Morgan's family. After Jezalee spoke with Morgan's mom, she invited their family over for dinner.

It did not take long for Paul and Jezalee to connect with Morgan's parents, David, and Mallory, they had a lot in common and enjoyed one another's company. Both sets of parents were the same age, each had three children, both men were highly educated, successful businessmen, David being a self-made millionaire, and Paul being a self-made billionaire. The wives were highly educated as well and helped their husbands build their businesses to the success they currently were. Both Jezalee and Mallory were involved in numerous charities, non-profit organizations and were philanthropists.

Mallory worked with David to build up his worldwide import-export business over the years. She was an executive officer handling the United States portion of their business. They exported cars, exotic fashions, plastic products, light fixtures and at least thirty other items. They imported cars, furniture, medical equipment, gems, and precious metals to name a few more things, Mallory worked tirelessly alongside her husband until the youngest child, their second daughter, Erica, was five.

Jezalee worked her way up in the Louvre as an art museum director, and curator. She also worked part-time as an art historian at the Cathedral of Notre Dame, only a fifteen-minute walk from both historical landmarks in Paris. Paul encouraged his wife with her love for the arts and wanted to do something in that field. He wanted Jezalee to follow her lifelong dream. She was fortunate and talented enough to have the career that fulfilled that passion. Jezalee had also been instrumental in Albanese's International Italian Sauces, which was the leading company in the world for over ten years.

Before she started working in the Museum and the Cathedral in 1972, she was an intricate part in their businesses, which they were able to start from the ground up due to Paul investing in the stock market with some of his earnings from Paul A. Designs. He had studied a lot about the stock market while he was in college and made a considerable amount of money. Due to his income from his designing business and his investments he earned enough money to start Albanese's International Italian Sauces in 1971; the recipes were from his ancestors dating back to the 17th Century; Jezalee added her Italian American versions as well. Paul and Jezalee owned Vineyards-Wineries in Italy, Argentina, Spain, France, and California; which produced some of the highest quality of fine wines in the world; Jezalee worked diligently in these business venture with Paul as well.

Even though they were living in Italy, running all their businesses from there, Paul knew how much his wife wanted to work at the Louvre and the Notre-Dame Cathedral; so, he decided to keep the Corporation in Italy; but move an office to Paris in 1972, and run their businesses from there. Later, Paul branched out with offices in London, California, and New York.

Jezalee was proud of Paul for having an entrepreneurial mind and especially, as a young boy; he was always drawing baseball, rugby and soccer uniforms while watching the games on television or going to the games with his brother and father. He never liked what they wore so he would draw players and design what he thought would look best on them, and more comfortable in. His father knew a few people in the sports world and took his son's drawings to Milan and the rest was history. Before Paul went off to America to attend college, he became an overnight success as a designer of athletic uniforms for every type of sport in Europe. He named his company Paul A. Designs. He had been designing for several leagues from the ages of seventeen to currently. His children always got a kick out their dad designing uniforms for athletes and had been commissioned by the Olympic Committee to design the Italian athlete's uniforms and street wear for the opening ceremonies. He made quite a name for himself in the sports world with his designs and it was quite a lucrative field to be a part of for almost thirty years.

The O'Malley children, Morgan 13 years old, Erica was 10, and Adam was 9. They started taking French lessons as soon as their parents mentioned they would probably live in Paris for one school year. After a year of French lessons, the children spoke French half the time at home. Their parents spoke French fluently and were impressed how the children learned to adapt to the language so well.

Jezalee could not believe the O'Malley family packed up what they needed, brought their household staff and family, and settled in so nicely to Parisian society. Mallory was back in the throes of the business because she wanted to help David in any way she could.

Morgan and her siblings did not mind coming to Paris and attending new schools; sure, they would miss all their friend's, but they were up for the adventure and kept in constant contact with them. They knew they could call or write to their friends anytime, so that made it easier living abroad for the school year.

The girls were relieved that their parents had become close friends in a short period of time and all six of the children got along splendidly. The children were close in age, so they had a lot in common.

Jezalee could not wait to give the O'Malley's a private tour at the Louvre where she had worked since 1972. After being there for over thirteen years, she knew every inch of the 73,000 square foot Museum. They were especially excited to have a tour of the private areas of Notre Dame since they went to Mass at the Cathedral every Sunday.

During weekends of the school year, the O'Malley's, and the Albanese's toured all of France, Italy, Spain, Switzerland, and Belgium. The children would visit Paul's parents, Antonio, and Elene while they would tour some areas that David and Mallory had not seen before. Paul and Jezalee took them on a tour to their Vineyard-Wineries in Italy, Spain, France, and Argentina. In each Country, Paul and Jezalee would enhance David and Mallory's travel experiences taking them to out of the way restaurants, and unique boutiques in each country, which most tourists never got to experience, with having limited time when traveling. David and Mallory had done a lot of traveling over the years but not to intimate, out of the way little gems that Paul and Jezalee had been adventurous enough to find over the years. While they were in Italy, David and Mallory got to spend a few weekends with Paul's parents, in Pisa, Tuscany. Anytime they went to visit them, they went to Mass at his brother Peter's Church. Antonio was known for his Italian and French cuisine; so, he loved to get in the kitchen right along with his wife, Elene. He would challenge Mallory and Jezalee to cook-offs and he always thought he was the best cook. They would make so much food, Elene would call the neighbors and invite them over for a grand feast. Antonio always bragged that his dishes were better than the girls, so they let him believe it. The senior Albanese's, lived in the same house for over 40 years, they raised Paul and Peter there and had never changed their rooms from when they were teenagers. Paul's children always bunked in their dad's old room; they got a kick out of looking through his old yearbooks, prom photos, his report cards, and his first sketches as an artist.

Paul's brother, Fr. Peter had been a priest for twenty years and had been at the same Parish for over fifteen. His Parishioners had loved him from the first time he stepped foot on the altar. He was 6 feet 3 inches, coal black hair, cocoa-colored eyes, athletic body, was charismatic, with a great sense of humor. Everyone at his Parish called him, "their dreamy, Priest" because he was so handsome and looked like he was a movie star. Fr. Peter had an open-door policy whenever anyone needed him to lend an ear. He was an artist and hung up his paintings throughout the rectory, the parish office and in the gift store; he even had some in the local eateries, his paintings were popular and sold out as quickly as they displayed them. All the money they made went for donations for the less fortunate; he knew that the more he painted, the more the Church could help the local people. He had always been close to his family but knew being a Priest would lessen the times he would have with them. Whenever he did see them, they made up for lost time and he cherished those moments. Peter knew that his family, including his brother Paul were not initially happy with his decision; only because he could not always be around at family functions and trips; but, once they went to his first Mass, they could see he had chosen what he was called upon to do in his life. They became proud of Peter, and they made every effort to let him know how they felt. He finally felt at peace and knew that his parents and the rest of his family understood what it meant for him to be in the Priesthood.

David and Mallory loved the fact Paul and Jezalee had three children as they did. All six children got along famously; and they were always delighted when they got the chance to do things together. Adrienne and Morgan would hang out with the younger ones but most of the time they were off in another room of the house, talking about stuff that did not interest their younger siblings. Usually, the four younger children hung out together and were always trying to sneak close to whatever room the older ones were in so they could listen in on their conversations. The foursome would invariably start giggling and the girls would catch them listening in. They would inform their siblings when they became teenager's they would want some privacy too. The four of them would just laugh and went on their way.

Both families had the most fun at the Albanese's country chateau in Saint-Germain-en-Laye, 35 miles from Paris. The younger four would go down by the river and swim, try to catch a few fish, which rarely ever happened; when they did, they would rush up to the main house to deliver their fresh fish and ask their moms to fry up the fish for dinner.

Adrienne and Morgan loved to spend most of their time going on long walks on the massive land the Albanese's owned. The topic of conversation was usually Adrienne wanting to ask her parents one more time if she could go live with the O'Malley's for her first year in high school. Adrienne knew it was just a matter of months that Morgan would be going back to San Francisco, and she yearned for the opportunity to have that experience of living somewhere else. She might have been hesitant if she had not grown up, speaking French, Italian and English; she knew she had the advantages of knowing three languages and it would make for an easy transition from her Paris upbringing to the American culture.

While Morgan had lived in Paris, Adrienne's parents had seen first-hand that both girls were always respectful to others, well-mannered and did not sneak around or hang out with the wrong crowd and they were religious. After dinner that night, Morgan commented on how staying with her was like being in her own home, she could not get over the fact that her parents were so much like Adrienne's parents. Both girls knew that their families were very wealthy; and had been raised around families of the same prominence; but they both knew that other families did not treat their staff as part of their family. Both girls had lived with the staff all their lives and they were a part of the family and they loved them. None of their other friends had a closeness with any of the people that lived and worked for them.

They knew they were missing out on knowing the people that helped take care of them; how sad and pathetic, and they considerate them complete snobs.

The months flew by, and Adrienne had constantly asked her parents if she could live abroad for one year and go to school with Morgan. She let her mom know that Morgan had discussed it with her parents, and they were on board with the idea. Jezalee discussed it with Paul and they both agreed it was out of the question. She called Mallory the next day and apologized for Adrienne's insistence on spending a school year in San Francisco. Mallory said there was no need to apologize and to be assured that it was an open invitation for Adrienne if they changed their mind.

One night at dinner with their children, Mallory and David discussed Adrienne's wishes in coming to San Francisco and relayed the conversation their mom had with Jezalee. Her parents are not willing to let her lave, Paris. Mallory said she nor David would not be asking the Albanese's anymore. "We have extended an olive branch for Adrienne to live with us for the school year; her parents are saying no, so we need to respect their answer and move on," Mallory regretfully said. Morgan walked away sad after dinner was over; but understood what her mom was explaining to her.

Morgan went to her room to do the rest of her homework and called Adrienne later that night. Adrienne was upset; after she got off the phone with Morgan, she went in to talk to both parents. Adrienne rushed out of the room in a furor and went straight to her room and cried herself to sleep thinking what horrible parents she had.

There were two weeks before their 8th grade graduation. Adrienne was not speaking to her parents as much as she usually did; they knew she was upset so they left her alone and hoped her anger would lessen in time. They had a suggestion they ran by David and Mallory; Jezalee called them and asked if Morgan could stay after graduation until Adrienne started summer school. They thought that was a grand gesture and they knew Morgan would be ecstatic. The next day at breakfast, Paul told Adrienne that Morgan would be spending time with them until the day before she started summer school. She silently thought to herself, if they think that is going to make up for her not being able to go to school in San Francisco, they are very much mistaken. She put a fake smile on and said that was great news and left it at that. Her parents knew her well enough to know she was not jumping for joy.

Graduation from 8th grade had been fun but Adrienne still had a black cloud over her because she was not getting her way. Both families got together and had a graduation party for the girls and invited a few of their classmates and parents over to celebrate. David, Mallory, Adam, and Erica left the next day with their entourage back to America.

Morgan was filled with jubilance being able to spend two weeks with Adrienne and her family. She told Adrienne, let us plan to have lots of fun and make the most of it. She agreed, but after a week, Adrienne started burdening her parents once again. Jezalee and Paul kept telling her she would not be going to San Francisco and informed her the answers were not going to change. One day, after the girls woke up, Morgan finally pleaded with Adrienne to not ask her parents anymore about going to San Francisco because she was feeling uncomfortable being there under the circumstances. So, Adrienne promised she would not bring it up again.

When it was time for bed, the two girls would go to Adrienne's room and gossip, listen to music, then they would talk about how cool it would be for them to go to high school together; at least a year. Adrienne pulled out a crystal ball one night and shook it; she and Morgan made a wish that they would be friends forever, no matter what. As time closed in on them, they were both becoming sad, knowing that it was just a couple of days and Morgan would be jetting off to her family.

The night before Morgan was to leave, they asked her where she would like to go for dinner. They ended up at her favorite pizza place, Parisian Pizza Palace, they had a karaoke machine on stage and the girls happily participated. The girls did not want the evening to end and got up several times and sang duets. The Albanese family were astonished that the girls were great singers! They kept yelling out from the audience; sing some more and they did. It was a fun-filled evening all around.

Jezalee and the children took Morgan to the airport because Paul had left early for a business trip to London. Adrienne had dreaded the ride in the car because she knew what it would be like once they saw Morgan off. The four of them watched the plane take off and Jezalee turned to Adrienne, and she could see the tears had already started. She felt a pang in her heart and for a fleeting moment, had second thoughts about what she and Paul had decided. On the way. back home, no one said a word, Alexander and Jessica were tight-lipped for the first time in their lives and their mom knew they were afraid to say a word for fear Adrienne would have an attitude. The Albanese's asked Mallory to call them as soon as Morgan landed; they wanted to make sure she got home safe. Adrienne went to her room as soon as they arrived home; she did not want to see or talk to anyone.

Mallory and David were so happy to see Morgan. Erica and Adam had made a welcome home sign with all her favorite colors, and she was so happy to see everyone. Even though she had fun with Adrienne and her family, she had missed hers. It had only been two weeks, but they had a huge celebration for her homecoming. It was a big deal because she had never been away from home. in another country, without her family. Nell, the cook, her mom, and her siblings had worked all day cooking and baking. She was quite impressed that Erica and Adam had helped their mom bake a beautiful cake. Nell, Linda, their housekeeper and Bob, their caretaker and driver, and Bob and Linda's son, Manny were all there as well. "I should go away more often, this is quite a celebration, thank you all so, much," Morgan happily said. They stayed up late that night; except for her dad, he had an emergency in Morocco and needed to fly there immediately, he said his goodnights to everyone and apologized to Morgan.

After Morgan had left for the states, Adrienne argued every day with her parents, and she realized she was not getting anywhere; but she was not going to stop. Adrienne even tried to convince her parents that by living in the states for at least one year, it would enrich her life tremendously. She said she would be exposed to more culture, and it would enhance her teen years and gain maturity. Jezalee spoke with Adrienne; to let her know that the O'Malley's would not have let Morgan come over to Paris by herself; so, she hoped Adrienne understand. "You know that don't you?" Jezalee. asked. Adrienne did not say a word, she was too stubborn to listen to anything that sounded even remotely true or made sense. She just wanted to fulfill a dream of hers, by gong to California. Sure, she had been to America many times with her family; but she wanted to go on her own and experience living away from home.

Jezalee was getting exhausted over Adrienne's attitude, she had other pressing things on her mind, and it certainly was much worse than dealing with a daughter that wanted to go to America. Jezalee had struggled for over six months and kept up a brave face and now dealing with the constant arguing with her daughter, kept her from dealing with what she needed to take care of. Jezalee had taken a sabbatical at both the Louvre and Notre Dame, she had too much on her mind and she had to take a break.

Adrienne stayed close to her bedroom, other than going to summer school; she was not participating in any family functions. Her brother, and sister, had always been close to her and were disappointed in how she was handling things. They were always able to make her laugh; she would play games with them and spent the weekends doing all sorts of fun things. Now they could see that their sister was too sad to do anything with them; so, they pretty much left her alone. No matter what, Adrienne made it through each day but her last thoughts before going to sleep were wishing she could attend high school with Morgan. A lot of tears were shed on her pillows at night but she kept quiet so she would not upset the household anymore.

Paul and Jezalee tried everything; but Adrienne just was not herself. Here she was in summer school, barely wanting to attend classes, then she had to think about high school in France. Sure, she had tons of friends and they were great, she had known most of them since the first day she started school at five; It was not the same, she was close to her friends but not like she was with Morgan; they were kindred spirits.

Alexander and Jessica were constantly aggravated with Adrienne. They felt rejected and knew they were losing the closeness they once had with her. They adored Morgan and her siblings, but here they came into their lives as strangers then Adrienne wanted to go live with them on the other side of the Continent. None of it made sense to them but they told one another they would always stick together.

Adrienne had been attending summer school for her third year in a row and had always done exceptionally well; this year, the headmistress could see a major change in Adrienne, and it was not for the better. Miss Boreal had contacted Jezalee and they discussed Adrienne's behavior and lack of good workmanship. Jezalee was not happy and knew she would have to discuss the matter with Paul. She knew Adrienne's potential and was very displeased at her all-around attitude because she was not going to America and now failing in summer school. That night when Paul arrived home Jezalee confronted him, and he was incensed with Adrienne. They both knew how much school had always meant to her and she was at the top in all her classes. They could certainly see she was not acting like a student who cared. Later that night, after dinner, the two younger children were excused, and they told Adrienne they needed to speak with her. They asked her to go into Paul's study because they needed to have a serious talk with her. She reluctantly sat down on her father's favorite leather sofa, across from her parents and froze. Paul handed her the progress report from Juliana's school; he questioned her reasons for doing so poorly. While he was asking her, Nina, their housekeeper motioned for Jezalee, she informed her she had an important phone call from the Louvre and asked her if she wanted to take it and she said yes. She excused herself and left Paul and Adrienne in the study. While Jezalee stepped out, Adrienne explained to her dad that she could not concentrate on school and did not care about her classes anymore. Her father had always been a reasonable man with the patience of a saint. "You have pushed us too far you have deliberately gotten bad grades because you did not get your way. Let me tell you, this is not hurting your mother and me, it is a reflection on you," Paul looked at his daughter, glaring over his glasses, embowed at the end of his nose, and said. "I no longer care," Adrienne interrupted him and said. She hit a nerve in her father that she had never seen before. He told her she was jeopardizing her entrance into a university because of her current actions. He began to tell her he thought it would be a marvelous experience for her to go abroad, especially at her young age; but he had agreed with her mom, this was not the right time. He explicitly told her he was not impressed at how she handled the situation. Paul grimly pursued the conversation by informing his daughter she had taken the wrong road to get what she wanted; getting lower grades is not acceptable. Adrienne frowned and explained that she had no other alternative because no one was listening to her demands. He was astounded at how she was talking to him; he never thought he would ever have such a conversation with her like this one. Paul turned away but abruptly announced to her, she was not to demand anything from them. He expressed how ashamed he was of her intolerable actions, and he was not sure that she really understood what she had done. Adrienne started to stand up, he sternly told her to sit back down, I am not done. She sank back into the sofa and stared her dad. "I have always had pride in our family and thought we were close but the mere idea that you would alienate yourself from all of us is very hurtful and I will not tolerate it," Paul sternly said. Adrienne and she was sorry but could not stop crying. He looked down at her face and suggested that they have a family meeting about all of this and see what conclusion they could come up with.

Later that night everyone reluctantly assembled into the family room to have a discussion if Adrienne should be able to go to America for her freshman year in high school. As she walked into the room, she felt as if she was going to her execution. When Adrienne looked around the room, she saw four sullen faces and felt the end-result was not going to be good. Everyone had their moment to say how they felt about her going away to school; each expressed how distant she had been and how hurt they were that she wanted to leave her family. They discussed things for nearly two hours, and they took a vote. The outcome was one that would change not only Adrienne's destiny; but also, the entire family, they just did not know how much yet. Before Adrienne went to sleep that night, she went into her parent's bedroom and apologized for everything she had said and done. She promised to be the best student in school and would behave properly at the O'Malley's. Her parents would call the O'Malley's and she could call Morgan in the morning.

Adrienne was in shock! She was going to school in America; she could not believe her wish was coming true. She was thrilled, over excited and could barely contain her enthusiasm. When Adrienne got in bed that night she smiled, thought to herself, what a great family she had and knew how much she would miss everyone. Now, that Adrienne knew she was leaving, it was settling in, she would be so far away from the family and staff she loved more than anything; and she would miss going to her grandparents and other relatives during the summer in Italy.

After Adrienne left her parent's bedroom, Jezalee told her husband she could not believe they had a daughter getting ready for high school. They discussed how beautiful she had become. She was tall, 5' 10", slender, olive skin, emerald-green eyes, her raven hair was as thick as velvet with each strand shining like a piece of pure satin. Adrienne had never had her hair cut, only trimmed and it beautifully cascaded down her back. Paul commented that their daughter could easily be a runway model with her height, bone structure, high cheek bones, and natural beauty. Jezalee agreed but their daughter from a young age said she was interested in being a psychologist and never wavered away from that field. Her father said he was just waiting for her to do a one-eighty and surprise them one day. He looked over at Jezalee in bed; and commented on how much Adrienne looked like her; she is almost as beautiful as you are. Jezalee thanked him for the compliment; but had much more on her mind.

It was 7:00 a.m. on a beautiful Saturday morning, the sun out with a slight breeze whispering through the forest of trees throughout their lush estate. Adrienne could smell the aroma of bacon sizzling, coffee brewing and hopefully, that was homemade cinnamon rolls baking in the oven. Adrienne flew out of bed, put on her favorite blue chenille robe, slid on her fluffy white and very worn bunny slippers, and darted into the kitchen like it was her last meal. Helga was just taking the rolls out of the oven when Adrienne approached her to give her a good morning kiss on her pretty face. "I know why you love me! It's my cinnamon rolls," Helga said as she set the pan down and hugged Adrienne. "That is just one f many reasons, there are at least a hundred more," Adrienne said. "You are so sweet, thank you, my dear," Helga gave her another hug and kiss and said. Now, please wake up your parents for breakfast; but do not disturb Alexander or Jessica because they want them to sleep in a little longer. Just as Adrienne was getting ready to knock on her parents' door, they were walking out to come to breakfast.

Jezalee let their daughter know that they had called the O'Malley's at 6:00 a.m. Paris time, 9:00 p.m. San Francisco time and they were not going to tell Morgan. They wanted you to be the one to call her; so, we will wait to have breakfast after you call her. "Honey, please make the call short and sweet then you can get your brother and sister down here to eat with us," Jezalee asked. "Sure mom," Adrienne said, I promise. A few minutes later Paul and Jezalee heard screams of joy coming from his study. By that time, the other two children were up; the three children headed for the kitchen for a delightful breakfast; Helga sat down with them and wanted to know what they wanted for lunch and dinner.

It was an exceptional morning for Adrienne and after breakfast she asked her parents if she could call Morgan back to talk longer. They both agreed she could; but not more than fifteen minutes. The girls were over the moon excited about Adrienne coming to stay with the O'Malley's. She let Morgan know she had a lot to do with getting her clothes packed and shopping for a few more items and saying her goodbyes to all her family and friends. Morgan said her mom was taking care of things at her end and her room would be ready when she arrived.

Adrienne spent the next week mostly on the telephone saying her goodbyes to her friends and relatives. She got together with some close friends from her school but had no idea that she would see them again soon. Her parents decided to throw her a huge surprise going-away party. Three of her close female friends from school, had volunteered their services and Jezalee welcomed them with open arms. They had invited Adrienne's teachers from kindergarten through eighth grade, the entire junior high school class, custodians, everyone from the school office, their grandma and grandpa from Italy, and their household staff. Everyone attended the send-off, some people brought lovely going away gifts and some gave her money to buy some new things in America. Adrienne's parents were so happy that everyone came to her party and knew that she was completely surprised. Jessica and Alexander even kept the party a secret; that was a fete-in-itself.

Everyone knew that Adrienne had a fire beneath her feet, and it was mostly caused by a desire to travel; now she was finally getting the opportunity to go to America solo. It had been a whirlwind for Adrienne two weeks prior to her trip. She made up the assignments she had done poorly in, ones she had not done, and some extra credit, she walked away with an A+ average and her parents were pleased she did so well. It was long last the day for her departure to America. She had made up with her siblings and the three were thick as thieves once again. She was not going to leave until the three of them were back to their old selves and that was accomplished so she felt great. Adrienne had not realized how emotional it was going to be saying her goodbyes to her family and the people that helped raise her. They were at the airport and Adrienne knew she would be forever grateful for their undying love and support for her. Helga and the rest of the staff bought her a beautiful light blue nightgown, a robe and a new pair of white, fluffy bunny slippers, Helga had also made her favorite chocolate chip cookies and had packed them in a very elegant carry-on case that she could use as a makeup holder. They had wanted to wait and give her the gift at the airport instead of at the party. Everyone took lots of photos before Adrienne boarded her flight and wished her a safe journey. Even though she was living one of her dreams, tears were streaming down her young, beautiful face. As Adrienne was saying her goodbyes, Paul put his strong and comforting arms around her and started sobbing too. Jezalee tried to hold back the tears; but was unsuccessful at her attempt. Everyone gathered around Adrienne and knew it was time for her to board the plane.

Adrienne met a few interesting people on her flight across the Atlantic and this helped her contain her excitement to a minimum, she still could barely keep her composure at best. She was getting rather sleepy after socializing, reading, then jotting down her thoughts in her journal. The next thing she knew the plane was circling the runway and it was time to freshen up to get ready for her arrival in the Big Apple. When she opened her new purse, she saw a tube of blush pink lipstick, she had mentioned to her mom she was hoping she would be able to start wearing a light pink lipstick in high school. Adrienne opened the tube, and it was the perfect color for her. She got out a small jewel adorned mirror and applied the beautiful color to her pretty lips. This brought back wonderful memories of the many times her mom let her wear her lipstick and clothes for dress-up. After applying her lipstick, she brushed her long thick strands of hair. By this time, the stewardesses were letting the passengers off. Adrienne had been relieved that Morgan had flown to New York to spend a week with her grandparents and was meeting her at the JFK airport, and they would be able to enjoy the flight from New York to San Francisco together.

As Adrienne departed the plane, she looked around and spotted her welcoming committee with their overly indulgent signs. She laughed and thought, from what Adrienne had been told about David's parents, they were surely the pranksters that made the signs. She blushed the color of her lipstick and looked around hoping no one was staring.

As she got closer, she could not believe she was in America. Morgan laughed as she gave her a big hug; she quickly informed Adrienne she had no idea her grandparents hid the huge signs in the trunk of their car. "Guilty as charged," Morgan's grandparents, Patrick and Kathleen said. They took the girls to eat in one of the restaurants at the airport while they waited for their flight to depart for San Francisco.

Adrienne did not know about the surprise vacation the O'Malley's and Albanese's, were about to go on. Morgan filled her in on the surprise as they ate their meal. Her parents mentioned it would be a great idea for the two families to go on a two-week vacation before school started; this way they could also see where Adrienne would be living for the next school year. "Why didn't my parents have me come with them?" Adrienne asked. "They wanted you to get acclimated to our place, I think it was a good idea," Morgan answered. Adrienne Agreed.

Adrienne and Morgan had finally arrived in San Francisco and the entire family, with-the-exception of David, who was on a business trip, met them. The family knew that this trip to America was a big deal to Adrienne because it was her first trip alone. Adrienne called her parents to say she arrived there safely. Afterward, they went to one of their favorite places to eat, Bunny's 24-hour Diner in San Francisco. Needless to say! that evening the girls slept in Morgan's room and tried to catch up on a few subjects; one being boys. Morgan expressed excitement telling Adrienne about the cute guys that attended Saint Mary's on Saturday, and Sundays. There were six weeks left until the girls would be freshman in high school. In the meantime, they were more than ready to embark on going shopping, blasting music, running into some cute guys at the local mall and going to the beach with a group of Morgan's friends.

The next morning the children slept in. Mallory managed to get up around 8:00 and went out to get the Sunday newspaper. She went to the kitchen where Nell was waiting for her favorite section of the Sunday paper. It was her weekly ritual with the O'Malley's. Nell started the coffee brewing for her and Mallory; Sunday was usually a big breakfast day, before Mass or they waited after Mass to have brunch. She had finished cooking the potatoes and onions together and made chicken fried steaks with country gravy to go along with the homemade biscuits. Mallory set out the bacon, and eggs which would not be cooked until the children came downstairs for breakfast and then start preparing a fruit bowl. Mallory insisted Nell sit down and enjoy the peace and quiet because it was not going to last once the children woke up, as she well knew. The ladies sat at the oversized kitchen table, classical music playing in the background, and talked a while. Morgan had called from her bedroom intercom to say they would all be down in fifteen minutes. Mallory started the bacon and eggs while Nell heated up the rest of the food that had been cooked earlier. Bob, Linda, and Manny arrived at the same time the children came down at 8:45 in their Sunday best clothes and took their places at the table. Mallory had just finished cooking the bacon and eggs. It was Erica's turn to set the table and get the drinks for everyone. Adrienne looked around the table and thought how familiar sitting around the kitchen table reminded her of being home; she missed her family so much and could not wait for them to get there. Morgan and Adrienne were discussing boys while they ate breakfast and Adam overheard them; he was pretending he was reading the sports section of the newspaper; he had a crush on Adrienne and wanted to hear everything she was saying about what kind of boy she was interested in. He knew he had to keep his crush a secret or Morgan and Erica would not only tell Adrienne; they would incessantly tease him.

Mallory let the children know that they would be leaving in thirty minutes for Mass. The staff always went to Mass with the O'Malley family; Manny always liked sitting between his dad and David and when David was out of town, Adam took his place. Adrienne was introduced to a few Nuns, the presiding Priest that gave the Mass, and several friends of the O'Malley's. Adam kept his eye on Adrienne because he noticed a few of Morgan's male friends looking gaga over her and he did not like it one bit.

David had arrived three days later from his business trip in Spain; he was anxious to arrive home and discuss their itinerary for their two-week trip with the Albanese's. He and Mallory had called the Albanese's and put their thoughts together, to decide what states they wanted to visit. They decided on Colorado, Wyoming, and Montana. Neither family had ever been to those three states so they were gearing up for quite an adventure; especially since the children found out they would be saddling up on some horses and staying at a Dude Ranch, where they would be learning how to live on a working ranch.

One night after a late dinner, David and Mallory were discussing how the years had gone by so quickly; they could not believe their oldest daughter was going to high school. Morgan was this magnificent, 5'7" tall, slender figured, gorgeous, thick, shoulder-length chestnut brown-haired beauty, with eyes as black as the night, with a beautiful face that lit up any room.

Between the O'Malley's and Albanese parents, they had raised three children each, at a fairly young age. The two couples had great educations and knew how fortunate and privileged they were. Wealth was a part of their lives; but make no mistake! They never took their social standing for granted nor the money they had acquired on their own or what they had inherited along the way. Their parents had instilled in them to honor what they had; but to honor the less fortunate in the same way. They were taught that everyone was their equal whether rich or poor, any racial or religious differences and political affiliation. Both sets of parents were in sync the way they raised their children; that is one of the reasons they liked one another so much and got along so well. They informed their children know that people have different lives and do the best they can; some just have a harder life and have many struggles to bare, this did not mean they were not their equals. No matter who the person was they were to always treat them with the highest level of respect and dignity.

Adrienne's family was missing her and was counting the days until they would see her. Alexander and Jessica called her nearly every day to say hi and how much they loved and missed her. After Adrienne had left, Jezalee knew it was time to confront Paul about her London trip she went on six months earlier. Even though she had fought the idea of Adrienne going to school in America for one school year, she knew what she had to do at home, and it was going to be easier with her away.

Jezalee had made sleep over arrangements for Alexander and Jessica at their best friend's homes so she could speak with Paul without the children being around. She was finding it more difficult keeping the secret she knew about her husband. Six excruciating months Jezalee had held onto a very ill-gotten secret, and she could no longer keep it locked up inside her. All those months she had to pretend she was still the happy, loving wife to an extraordinary man, she had been devoted to and admired for over twenty years. They had an amazing life with their three children and Paul was her friend. Jezalee was in so much agony but for the sake of her innocent children, she knew she had to wait it out until school was over. She really did not know if she was being scared, brave or ignorant in waiting as long, as she had.

It was Friday evening and Jezalee was a nervous wreck waiting for Paul to come home from his office. She had kept herself busy all day to keep her mind occupied; Jezalee made homemade pasta and bread, put together an antipasto salad and got out a jar of her homemade marinara sauce. She had time left over so she decided to bake a few batches of cookies so the children would have a treat when they came home on Saturday night. Jezalee loved baking and cooking, and this got her through so many days and nights with what she had endured for six months. Their cook Helga had been with them since Jezalee got her job at the Louvre; a year later she added on more work when she started working at Notre Dame. During the first couple of years, her work schedule did not give her the opportunity to be in the kitchen that often, with-the-exception of the weekends; but she knew how precious time was, so she wanted to give Paul and their children her undivided attention. Helga living in the main house, had been the only one that noticed there was something different about Jezalee; but when she asked her about it, she would always say she was fine. Jezalee decided to finally confront Paul about what had been gnawing at her. Helga would be away for the weekend, and she would have the children go to their friends' houses for a sleepover.

Paul arrived home promptly at 6:00 p.m. asked where the children were, and she said at a sleepover. Dinner was ready and Jezalee was unusually quiet while they ate. Paul asked her if something was wrong, and she said she needed to talk to him about something after dinner. Before they finished their meal, he had complimented her as he always did on what an incredible cook she was; she thanked him and went on eating. Paul helped Jezalee clear off the table and said he would load the dishwasher; she immediately told him the dishes can sit until after her talk. Paul looked quite concerned and asked her if everything was okay. She gave him a glare that he had never seen on her beautiful face before, and she sternly said, "No! Actually, I am far from okay." Jezalee had him worried; he put his arms around her, but she instantly walked away from him and said, "Just let me talk.'' Paul asked her where she wanted to be while she talked, and Jezalee said in their living room; she followed in behind him. As soon as they sat across from one another, she had tears in her eyes; he looked at her and his heart was racing. All Paul could think of was that one of the children or she was ill, and it was too difficult for her to tell him. He was getting scared and just wanted Jezalee to hurry up and tell him no matter what it was. Jezalee rehearsed what she was going to say to him a dozen times, now the moment was there, she was having second thoughts. She knew it had to come out and they were the only ones at home, this was the time to face him with what she knew. Jezalee folded her arms together, looked him in the eyes and knew it was time.

Paul, for six months I have lived with knowing something I never thought would be possible to have to bear witness to. I should have brought it to your attention when I found out. He still could not figure out what she had kept from him that was so important. Paul tried to sit next to her, and she said, ''stop!'' please do not come near me; he was baffled! He asked her if one of the children was ill. "No!

What would ever possess you to think I could keep something like that from you for even a day, must less six months?'' Jezalee irritatingly said. "Then what is it that you had to wait six months to tell me?" Paul impatiently said.

As Jezalee listened to him, she knew it was time to tell him everything she knew. "Paul, do you remember when I went to London to meet up with Annabella?" Jezalee asked. "Yes, I do recall that," Paul answered. "That day started out beautifully, we went shopping in our favorite boutiques, went to Harrods then went for a late lunch at a nearby restaurant," Jezalee informed him. While Jezalee was talking, all Paul could think of was how distant she seemed and what could have happened that day. She told him they had lunch first then decided to talk a little longer over a cup of tea; unfortunately, Annabelle got an emergency call from the hospital and one of her patients took a turn for the worse; so, she suddenly had to leave. Jezalee decided to stay and finish her tea, then she would be on her way back home.

There were two women seated at a table beside her and she could not help but overhear their conversation. The undisciplined, garishly dressed woman, loudly began to tell her friend that she liked the arrangement she had with her man. Her friend commented and asked her if she was going to marry him, and the woman laughed out loud and said he is married with three brats. Her friend asked her if he gave her enough money to help raise their son and she said he was loaded. Her friend also asked if his other children knew about their son Jonathan, and she said she could care less if they know or not. How old are his other children? I am not interested in their ages or anything about those rich brats. Her friend then commented she could hardly believe Jonathan was almost six years old, time goes by so quickly. Her friend asked the names of his other kids, and she said she overheard him talking to someone named Adrienne but didn't know who she was and couldn't give a rats-ass one way or the other. Jezalee is telling this to Paul as he turns ashen, becomes anxious, tense and feels as if he would throw up at any given moment. He wanted to interrupt her and tell her the truth why he had a six-year-old son with this demonic woman; but he could tell that Jezalee needed to tell him everything she heard that grim day. She was in tears as she kept talking; he just wanted to put his arms around her but from her body language, he knew he needed to stay put. As the tears continuously kept streaming down her face, she told him how difficult it was to keep this secret for such a long time and was disgusted to be near him; but for the sake of the children, she knew she had no alternative because she did not want to disturb them while they were in school. She emphatically let him know how excruciating it was to fake wanting to be in the same bed with him all those months knowing he not only slept with another woman but got her pregnant as well. Paul tried to intervene so he could tell her the true story of what happened, but she was not going to listen to anything he had to say. Jezalee gave him a nasty look as she asked him what it was like to have an illegitimate son? She also wanted to know when he had planned to tell her and their children about his double life. "I am not leading a double life! I have nothing to do with that despicable, wretch of a low-life woman," he blatantly said. He did let Jezalee know he sees his son whenever he is in London, which she knew was once a month when he went there on business. "I want details of your sordid affair," Jezalee yelled out! Just as he was getting ready to tell her the truth, she stopped him in his tracks; she stood up, cried out in high volume some more, and said she knew enough, and she did not want to know anything else. He still tried to talk, and she ran out of the room shaking and hysterically crying. Paul went after her and said he needed to tell her everything. She looked at him in disgust and warned him if he got any closer or said another word, she would call Adrienne, then inform Jessica and Alexander when she picked them up tomorrow of his other woman and child. Paul was devastated! His first thoughts when he found out Gloria was pregnant; was to tell Jezalee how it happened. He was now at his boiling point and told her under no circumstances would he ever tell their children they have a brother. "You will tell them right after our group vacation is over; in fact, after we get back to the O'Malley's we will tell them in private that we are getting a divorce. When you are alone with the children you have no alternative; but to tell them you have an illegitimate son; if you do not have the guts to do it, I will be forced to. Jezalee added, you are going to let them know the reason I am divorcing you," Jezalee yelled out. As she walked away from him, his whole life passed in front of him; he could not fathom life without the woman he loved. She went into Adrienne's bedroom, got into her night gown, and sobbed under the covers. Before Jezalee could fall asleep she kept thinking that she could not stay in this house where once there was so much love, respect, devotion and three beautiful children she and Paul had created and raised. Her life with him had been extraordinary, up until six months ago and that fatal day in London changed her life forever. She was not looking forward to telling their children; but she was forced to do so; she could not live another moment sleeping in the same bed with a man that had cheated on her or stay in the house where there were too many great memories. She knew what she had to do and unfortunately, she had to be in the house with Paul for two more weeks then off to San Francisco the four of them would go. Jezalee was forced to keep up the facade as if everything were wonderful for a little longer, which would feel like an eternity to her. She had suffered for six months, another two weeks in their home and two weeks on a vacation, she would have to endure. After six months of keeping his secret, Jezalee would be forced to make the best of it for the next four weeks.

Paul walked past Adrienne's room and saw from under the door that the lights were out; he decided not to disturb Jezalee. He went on to their bedroom they had shared for many years and felt his life crumbling before him; he knew from her reaction she would never believe his story; he knew it was over. One minute he had this amazing, beautiful, and incredible wife, the next minute, she was leaving him over something he had no control over. Paul tossed and turned all night; thinking what happened to him that night in London almost seven years ago. He went on monthly business trips to London, usually having to spend one night in the city. Once and a while Jezalee joined him, and they made a weekend out of it. He had his favorite place in London where he would grab a quick meal, have one glass of wine then go straight to his hotel. Well, the woman to whom Paul had a son with, had seen him come into the restaurant once a month for nearly three years; she knew he was very wealthy and kept an eye on him every time he came to the city. Gloria had been a waitress there for five years and barely made ends meet so she had a plan to change her financial status.

. One night after Paul had his meal, he asked for his usual one glass of wine; but, this time Gloria, the waitress bribed the bartender and one of the bouncers to put something in Paul's drink that would knock him out all night. As he was drinking his wine Gloria made sure the bouncer was close by and the bartender was making sure he was getting woozy. As the bouncer got closer to him, he pretended Paul was too drunk and he would assist him to the exit door. He looked around and wanted to make sure that a few people saw Paul and that he indeed looked as if he had passed out from drinking too much. The bartender needed to help the bouncer get him in the car and they both would have to get Paul into Gloria's dingy little flea bag of a flat. Normally the bouncer could handle one person by himself, but Paul was very tall and a good size build; the bartender had to help. He informed the owner they were having trouble with a drunk and he needed to help the bouncer get him to his apartment and he needed to have someone take over his shift. The owner did not have a problem with that and said he would cover for him; he told the guys to handle Paul gently because he is a very wealthy man and wants to make sure that his guys took good care of him being so drunk, the owner gave them the name of the hotel where Paul always stayed, while on business. Gloria had informed the bouncer and bartender in advance that she was going to make it worth their while for doing her this favor. She let them know that she would be coming into some money in a few months and would reward them for their services. Once they had him outside, Gloria went out the back way like she always did to go home; this time she would meet up with the bouncer and bartender to give them their instructions. They trusted her; because she had worked with them for years, and they were glad to help her out. They had no idea what she had planned for Paul until she handed the bartender a camera and asked him to take a few photos once she had the bouncer strip him and situate him in her bed. As he was doing that, she began to take off all her clothes and slipped in next to him. She had them take some very provocative images and was quite pleased that they went along with it. They left and she began to take advantage of him being unconscious and was pleased that her plan was working just as she hoped it would.

On the way home, Paul really did not know how to tell Jezalee and was completely humiliated that a woman raped him; he certainly did not agree with the current law, and he would look-into the prospect of having it changed. He was drugged and raped, and two men helped her get away with it. Once he got to the front door he tried to put on a smile before he entered the house. The children ran towards him and gave him hugs and kisses and Jezalee followed right in behind them. After they happily greeted their dad, he looked at his wife differently that night and knew that he was never going to be able to tell her what happened. He knew he could not lose his family. He meant every word he had said to Gloria; if she tried to come near his family, he would leave the country, and no one would find them. If this scenario played out, he would be forced to erroneously make up something so bizarre and scary and make his family believe him.

Paul had his mind racing over the event that had happened almost seven years ago; he wept and felt a chill come over him. He got up out of bed and slowly walked down to Adrienne's room. He opened the door and Jezalee turned on a lamp by the bedside. Jezalee looked at him and told him he should not be disturbing her and next time he needed to knock on the door first. He apologized and said he had forgotten to ask her what time would the children be coming back home from their sleepover. She indicated they would be returning around 7:00 PM the next day. By this time, she sat up in the bed and said that after they go on this vacation with the O'Malley's she would be filing for a divorce. She had already gotten an attorney and she suggested he do the same. They were extremely wealthy; there was the Paris estate they lived in, the Country Chateau the children dearly loved; a penthouse in New York they rented out, a villa on the Winery property in Napa, stocks, bonds, their retirement and buildings in Paris, London, Rome, Spain, and New York; they owned two Diamond mines, five Vineyards-Wineries, Paul A. Designs, Albanese's International Italian Sauces; which was the world's leading supplier of sauces and had life insurance policies. There was a lot of money at stake. Paul asked her why she had not gone to their attorney, Marvell they had together? She said she was informed it was not such a great idea. "I understand you do not want to be married anymore; however, you certainly do not need a different attorney. Why don't you forget about your new attorney and call our, attorney? I really do not care about any of the money, our homes, buildings, our businesses, you can have it all. "None of the material things we have gotten over the years mean nothing to me without you and the children. I just wish we could talk more about this," Paul sadly looked at her and said. She point-blank said it was never going to happen and if he kept pressuring her, she would make sure he did not get to see the children. He was devastated at what just came out of his wife's mouth. All of this was too much for him to take in. He could not understand what he had done in his life to deserve what Gloria had put him through. He had always been an honest man, never hurt one person and had met and married the love of his life and had the greatest children that he loved beyond words. He felt so powerless, and he knew he had been had in the worst way possible.

As he stood in the doorway of Adrienne's room talking to Jezalee, he asked her when the children come home tomorrow, we still have almost two weeks until we leave for San Francisco. She interrupted him and asked him; "So, what is your point?" "What about our sleeping arrangements for the next two weeks and at David and Mallory's?" Paul questioned her. "Unfortunately, it looks like we are going to be forced to sleep in the same bed until we inform the children we are filing for divorce," Jezalee smartly answered. "No! You are the one filing for divorce, not me!" Paul said adamantly. "I am telling the children that you want the divorce," Paul said. "You caused me to want a divorce, on the grounds you slept with another woman, and I use that word loosely, for that piece of trash, and I want you out of my sight, now get out." She fired back! Paul turned around and walked out of the room with the nightmare he was facing as tears welted up in his normally light chocolate brown eyes beginning to become blood shot.

After Paul shut the door Jezalee felt freed from the angst of telling him what she had found out. She cried herself to sleep that night as she thought of what the divorce would do to their children. The five of them had been so close and had lived a very charmed life. THEY HAD ALWAYS HAD SO MUCH FUN DOING THINGS as A FAMILY UNIT AND IT MEANT SO MUCH TO PAUL AND HER TO KNOW HOW CLOSE THEY WERE. Jezalee knew all that was about to come to a halt. She knew it was not right for her to keep that secret as-long-as she did; but she was not about to disturb the children's school time; she was hoping if they were told in the summer, by the time they went back to school they would be hopefully over the shock of their parent's divorce. Jezalee had carried that burden for so long and many times she had wished she had never found out about his sordid affair; knowing he had another child out there. She asked herself, why should her and the children live with someone with no scruples and was filled with deception for all those years.

Paul went to bed a different man that night and knew his life would be forever changed. He knew when he woke up the next morning the love of his life would not be next to him. From the moment he had met his Jezalee, every day had been the best days of his life. He had been in bed for about fifteen minutes, felt sick, rushed to the bathroom, and threw up. He made his way over to the sink to wash his face and hands to get rid of the putrid stench, looked up in the mirror and saw himself as a person he did not know anymore. He kept staring at his reflection and knew he had been very weak how he handled the rape and wanted the nightmare to go away. If only Jezalee had not gone to London that day, if only he had gone to the police, if only he had told Jezalee that he was drugged and raped. All he knew now was they would never be living the life they had made for themselves and the happiness they created would forever be a faded memory. That night, all he could wrap his brain around was the fact when he walked through the door to have dinner with his beloved Jezalee, it was the end of a life with his wife and children as he knew it to be. When Paul got up in the morning, he was exhausted, and was hoping when Alexander and Jessica came home, they would not notice anything different about their mom and dad. He felt he was having an out of body experience and there was no way he could come back from it. Jezalee had a miserable night as well, but she was not going to weaken at this point. After divulging to Paul what she knew, it gave her strength that she did not know she had. Jezalee decided to leave for the entire day and would call the children to see when she could come pick them up.

Paul had stayed home in anticipation of seeing Alexander and Jessica later in the evening. He had no idea where Jezalee was or what she was doing all day. At this point he knew he had to stop thinking about her and put all his energy into seeing his children. He had not asked Jezalee what friends they had spent the night with; so, he knew he had to keep himself busy until they got home. He had some work to look over; but his mind could not concentrate on anything for any length of time.

It was 7:30 p.m., the children were still not home; he was mad that he did not know where they were. He thought he would start calling some of their closest friends but thought it would be strange calling the families. He had no idea where his children spent the night because Jezalee had not informed him of what friend's homes the children had gone to. Suddenly he saw Jezalee's car, and the children were with her. They ran in the house, came over to their dad to give him a hug and kiss like usual; he already felt better. He made sure he did not look at Jezalee when she entered the room. They had stopped at one of their favorite restaurants and brought dinner home for the four of them.

As the four ate dinner there was some conversation while they ate but most of it was coming from the children. Paul asked the children what they did while they were at their friends and that was about the extent of the conversation. After dinner Paul asked the children if they would like to go for ice cream and they could not jump up fast enough. Jessica asked their mom if she wanted to join them, and she said she did not feel that great and wanted to go lay down for a while. Paul asked if they could bring her anything from the pharmacy and would she like her favorite ice cream. She said she had something in the house to take for her upset stomach and would be okay and would pass on the ice cream.

After dinner, Paul asked Alexander if he would play a few pieces on the piano, and he was always ready to perform. He played Sebastian Mia Theme, Moonlight Sonata, and Turkish March. Alexander was a natural and no one else in the family came close to trying some of the pieces he played. Paul could see this had put everyone in a great mood and that is what he was going for.

The next two weeks Paul could not sleep, eat, or keep his mind on anything but was very worried about the outcome of how his children would take the news of their parents divorcing. He had always been such a religious man and his brother being a Priest, he thought he would be able to confess to him what happened; but he just did not have the heart to ever tell him. He now thought differently since Jezalee was filing for divorce; his brother would have insisted he go to the police; but Paul said that was out of the question. Just the thoughts of that filthy piece of trash having sex with him while he was unconscious was inconceivable to him. He could still smell her cheap, stinking cologne; his body shivered every time he flashed back to when he woke up in Gloria's bed.

The O'Malley's had an enormous estate and they made Adrienne feel right at home. The day Adrienne walked into her bedroom at their home, she could not believe how beautiful it was and could see all the love and hard work that went into making her feel so welcome. Morgan had given her mom ideas how Adrienne's room looked in Paris. She had her favorite colors, pale green, peach, and ivory with rich woods for furniture. She liked things that were more feminine than Morgan whereas her room was in red, white, and black with modern lacquered furniture. She was excited to show her room to her family when they would arrive for the two-week vacation. Mallory had framed photos of Adrienne and her family for the finishing touches.

The O'Malley's cook, Nell, the housekeeper, Linda and her husband, Bob, who was the caretaker and chauffeur, had been with them for twelve years. They were as much a part of the family as any of their children and their relatives. They adored their staff and were always treated as family. The children got along splendidly with them and loved hanging out with Manny, who was Bob and Linda's 5-year-old son; it was one big happy and extended family.

While Adrienne was talking with Nell, she found out that Mallory and she both had relatives in Ireland and were neighbors who became close friends. The O'Malley's went to Ireland quite often and would take Nell with them and have a great time with all their relatives. Nell explained the kitchen rules and Mallory was strict about them, Adrienne was all ears and hoped it was not something weird. "The rule is each person gets to choose a favorite meal at least once a week and it is served at dinner. Now, you will have a day also!" Nell said. Adrienne grinned and expressed to Nell that she loved that idea and when her mom comes, she is going to ask her to implement that rule also.

The O'Malley children did volunteer work at the local Boys and Girls Club and Adrienne wanted to help-out as well. The Albanese children especially missed going to the family center in Paris and was glad to be able to help wherever they lived. She especially missed going to the family center in Paris; but was glad to be able to help wherever she lived.

One day after they finished volunteering Bob picked them up and drove them to Pier 39 at Fisherman's Wharf; Adrienne was head over heels loving the area; especially when they went to Ghirardelli Square where she could get as much chocolate as she wanted. Her parents had given her a weekly allowance and she could either save it or spend it on whatever she wanted. That day she stocked up on all things chocolate and promised to share it with everyone. "Now you know that you are not going to share that with us, you are too much a chocoholic and will keep it all to yourself; and probably eat it all at once!" Adam said. Adrienne laughed and said she loved chocolate; but she would never indulge much of it at one time and she always shared her treats. "Can she be any sweeter?" Adam thought to himself.

Two weeks flew by, during that time Paul and Jezalee pretended all was wonderful; but it was difficult on them. They always flew first class and the children usually sat together but Jezalee said she wanted to change things up since it was the four of them; so, she suggested that Paul and Alexander sit together, and the two gals would sit together. They thought that was a great idea and Jezalee was so relieved because she did not want to be any closer than she had to be with Paul. They would be boarding the plane tomorrow and Paul knew that it was getting closer for he and Jezalee to tell the children, they were getting a divorce. At least he would have one more vacation with them as a family and he was going to make the best of it.

The evening prior to the Albanese's arrival; everyone at the O'Malley's were gathered around the dinner table discussing their up-and-coming vacation. The children were still unsure if they thought it would be fun going all-Western for a vacation; but knew that is what their parents had settled on. "Yippee Ki yay, get along little doggie," all Adam could say. "You just wait until you are roping the steers, in that wide-open country of Wyoming and Montana!" They all Laughed, and Morgan responded.

Everyone woke up considerably earlier than usual for a Saturday only because they were anticipating the arrival of Adrienne's family. While David and Bob drove to the San Francisco Airport to pick them up, the children hung out in the game room until their arrival.

Once the men arrived with the Albanese's everyone ran outside to welcome them. David had the children take all the luggage to whatever room Mallory had assigned to them. Mallory had Paul and Jezalee join she and David in the family room and had set out some appetizers and cold drinks to have before dinner was served. The children went up to the game room and Mallory had set up snacks for them as well.

After everyone filled up on a delicious meal, Jezalee helped Mallory clear the dining room table; Jezalee was taking the dirty dishes to the kitchen. Mallory could always sense when someone was distant, had something on their mind or was not a hundred per cent themselves. When the Albanese's, first arrived, she noticed a difference in Jezalee and for that matter, in Paul as well. Mallory turned around to take the dirty dishes out of Jezalee's trembling hands and as she handed the dishes over to Mallory she burst into tears. "Would you like to go somewhere private to talk?" Mallory asked. "I would like that very much" Jezalee said. They rode up in the elevator and they would go to her master suite where no one would disturb them.

When they entered the room, Mallory motioned for Jezalee to have a seat on the overstuffed, down-feathered plush sofa. Mallory sat across from her and told her she had her undivided attention. Jezalee took a deep breath and told Mallory she was filing for divorce. Mallory looked as if she had been hit with a sledgehammer and was certainly caught off guard. As Mallory attentively listened, Jezalee began to tell her how difficult it was going to be to tell their children. She indicated to Mallory they were both going to tell the children when the vacation was over. At one-point Jezalee had decided it was best to wait and divorce Paul after their children had finished high school; but that was no longer an option. "Anytime we were ever around you and Paul, you appeared to be the ideal couple, I am truly devastated, what happened?" Mallory said.

Jezalee said she had been in the same bed with her husband for six months carrying a secret about his indiscretions; without him knowing she knew about it. The six months were filled with torchier, agony, and sadness beyond comprehension. She first, blamed herself thinking she was not giving Paul the attention every spouse deserves from the other. Secondly, Jezalee thought he lost his lust for her and the more she thought about that scenario, she got madder. Jezalee had a lot to think about for six months, and her thoughts were all over the place. When he wanted to be intimate with her, she had so much pent-up anger that she faked it when they were making love. Jezalee was fine during the day because she was either busy at work or scheduling functions with the family, and when she arrived home, she was busy with the children. There were times Jezalee faked intimacy with Paul because she was not ready to tell him she knew about his other life. Waiting all those months to finally let him know that she knew about his sordid affair and his son was the most difficult conversation Jezalee hoped to ever have in her lifetime.

There were times Jezalee wished she had never gone to London that day and would never have known about Paul's second son. The longer she listened to that dreadful, illiterate woman, Jezalee could not get up, she literally could not catch her breath and her mind would not stop racing at high speeds. What hurts most is the fact Paul and I have always been such close friends. He was the love of my life, and we always had such respect for one another. He had the audacity to inform me he would never tell the children he has another son. Jezalee told him the two of them would tell the children they are getting a divorce and he would be telling the children the reason when she was not in the room. He said he could not do it and Jezalee told him he did not have a choice because they were going to question why we are divorcing. Paul was going to tell them he did not want a divorce and it was all her.

Currently, Jezalee felt he did not deserve anything from her or the children anymore. She drowned in sorrow that day in London, blaming herself, not him. Jezalee kept telling herself she was not pretty enough or maybe not sexually attractive anymore. When she looked at her, she could see the ill-spoken woman was not attractive and could not picture Paul with her; she was unkempt and to be quite honest, disheveled. Every other word out of her mouth was a four-letter word! Anyone that uses swear words as much as that woman did, usually has a limited vocabulary, and uses those words to fill in the blanks. From where I sat, she appeared to be an uneducated woman; a true broad in the worst-case scenario; which it boggles my mind that Paul would ever have an attraction to someone like that. Jezalee wanted answers; but knew she had to wait to find out. Mallory was still in shock, and she asked her if he ever gave her a reason. Jezalee said the bottom line! She did not care one way or the other if they have a relationship or not; they have a son together and Paul broke their marriage vows. None of this is ever going to change; Jezalee said she would not accept a man, where she had constantly given all her love to, turn around and cheat on her; must less, have a child with her. It is completely over!

"Jezalee, did Paul really think you would not eventually find out about his kept woman, his child, and the London flat?" Mallory asked. "I may never have known if I had not gone to the same café his lover was at. It has already been seven years and there are no signs of him treating me and the children any differently. He is a darn good actor; I can tell you that! His infidelity has changed the course of mine and our children's lives. I cannot believe I blamed myself in the beginning and not saying anything to Paul. The difficult part is the love I always had for Paul; has been destroyed. Our marriage that we built on trust and respect is over for good!" Jezalee remarked.

Jezalee thanked Mallory for listening to her devastating news and expressed what a true friend she had become. Mallory got up and went to sit next to her on the other sofa and gave her a big hug and told her that no matter what, she and David would always be just a phone call away any time she needed them. Mallory said she was very worried over how the children would react over a divorce. Jezalee said it is going to be life changing for them and the worst part is the fact the children have the utmost respect for their father; he has always been their rock! What is so ironic is the fact that Paul taught the children to have respect, good morals, lots of ambition, always tell the truth, treat everyone as equals and most importantly, always love your family and friends.

After dinner, the children went for a swim and the adults headed for the living room to visit awhile. Mallory and Jezalee mainly discussed what they would pack for their trip. David and Paul were in their own zone discussing sports and what teams they favored in the US. After the men finished with their sports talk, they began discussing their trip with the wives about their cowboy-cowgirl adventure. "Guys, whatever happened to the East Coast trip?" Mallory asked. "Oh! We thought you ladies would like to experience a real western adventure and have an excuse for buying some of those tight jeans and fancy boots; and learning to rough it a little," David answered with a grin on his face. "I am up for the adventure as long as I do not have to rope a steer, ride side saddle on a horse, or milk a cow," Jezalee laughing remarked. It was getting late and Jezalee said she needed to get some sleep and Mallory said she would walk up with her and retire too.

When Jezalee opened the bedroom door, she gazed over at the bed and knew she was not going to sleep with Paul anymore. She was not happy being in the same room with him much less having to feel his body in the same bed anymore. Jezalee felt like going to Mallory and asking for another bedroom because she could not be in the same bedroom with him. She decided not to disturb her and left a note for Paul to sleep on the oversized sofa in the sitting area of the bedroom. Jezalee wrote a PS, Sheets, blankets, and a pillow in the walk-in closet. When Paul finally came up to go to bed, Jezalee pretended to be asleep. He never said a word and went directly to the closet to get his bedding. Paul had a difficult time falling asleep because he was so used to being next to her in bed. He was trying to settle down and had one extra prayer; that Jezalee would give him just ten minutes of her time to explain what happened in London seven years ago. So far, every time he tried, she either walked away or told him under no circumstances was she going to listen to anything he had to say. Jezalee tossed and turned all night and knew there was no way she would be able to go on a vacation with Paul for two weeks.

After David had taken his nightly shower, got into his pajamas, he slid into bed close to Mallory. They were both going to sit up and read for a while; Mallory sat her book down, looked at David with a painful look in her eyes; he knew something was wrong. "What is wrong dear?" David asked with concern. "Well! It's Paul and Jezalee, they are regretfully getting a divorce," Mallory sadly answered. David fell back into his oversized satin covered pillows behind him, looked up at the vaulted ceiling and was stunned to say the least. "Are you as shocked, as I was when I first heard it," Mallory asked. "Of course, I am! Who would not be, they have always seemed as happy as we are?" David remarked, it would never have entered my mind with them. Mallory began to fill him in on how and when Jezalee found out about the affair. "Do you think they should be in the same room?" David said. Mallory explained that she did not know about the divorce when she assigned them a room. She told David she would not put Paul in a different room until Jezalee gave her the go ahead because their kids would be suspicious if their parents had separate rooms. David thought that was the only way to handle it, until further notice.

The next morning Jezalee quietly snick out of the bedroom and went downstairs before Paul woke up. Mallory and Nell were already preparing for a huge breakfast for everyone. Mallory asked Jezalee how she slept; and she said she needed to talk with her if it was not an inconvenience. Mallory asked Nell if it was okay if she finished preparing breakfast and she said of course! Mallory led Jezalee into David's den for privacy in case the kids or Paul came down. She closed the door behind them and asked Jezalee what was going on? She began to break down and sob and told Mallory there was no way she could go on vacation with Paul. Mallory said she understood completely and would never suggest that she put herself through anymore agony. "I thought I could have the strength for a couple more weeks; but I can barely stand being in the same room with him," Jezalee sadly admitted. "Oh! My goodness! Now do not worry, you will just need to tell the children sooner than later," Mallory said. As Jezalee tried to talk between her sobs, she admitted it had been a bad idea having Paul come to San Francisco with them. Mallory spoke up! I discussed your situation with David last night and he was appalled at Paul's behavior and believe me! The only reason Paul is even welcome here is our love for you and the children. Jezalee let Mallory know she would be telling the children once Paul was gone to his satellite office in the city; he wanted to set up a few meetings prior to our vacation and needed to set things up with his secretary here and give her his itinerary for the next two weeks. Paul will be gone most the afternoon and I will pack up his things and take them to his office. Jezalee said she had changed her mind because she wanted him gone now! I cannot fathom going on a vacation with him. "Dear, I do not blame you, just let us know when you are ready to talk the children, we will make sure you have the utmost privacy," Mallory said with a sadness in her heart. Jezalee said she would have them come to her bedroom and that would be enough privacy; she did not want to put them out because of her family drama. Mallory, you, and David have been such true and loyal friends ever since we met in Paris and I am so grateful for your love and support, I love you both dearly. The feelings are mutual, my friend, and we feel horrible about this whole situation, and it is quite devastating at the least, said Mallory.

While Mallory and Jezalee were in the den, Paul had gotten up, came downstairs and made his way to Nells delicious croissants and coffee and left for his morning meetings. Little did he know he would not be coming back to the O'Malley household. He had ordered a taxi without anyone knowing he had left, other than Nell. He wanted to get an early start in the office so he could get back early and play some games with all the children and maybe get some swimming in. He was really looking forward to the vacation with both families and knew what was in store for him after the vacation which he was not looking forward to telling the children about the divorce.

Mallory and Jezalee went into the kitchen to have a cup of coffee. "Jezalee, you just missed Paul, he went to his office and said he would be back in a few hours," Nell said. She thanked Nell for telling her, and decided she had to go wake up the children and get her talk over with. She got up from her chair and Mallory asked her where she was going, and she said to talk to the children. "Please wake up the children and we will have a great breakfast then you can talk to them; you four are going to need to be nourished and anyway, Nell has made a delicious meal for us," Mallory insisted. "In that case, how can I refuse?" Jezalee said. Mallory informed her that Bob would drive her downtown whenever she was ready. Jezalee thanked her for all her help!

After breakfast with Mallory, Nell, and the children, Jezalee asked her three to follow her upstairs to her bedroom before they started going in all different directions. Adrienne said sure! What's up mom? Well! I have something important I need to discuss with you, it will not wait any longer. The three looked puzzled at why their mom would need to talk to them. The children followed her upstairs and they sat on the elegant sofa and were ready to listen to their mom. Jezalee was trying to hold back the tears as she looked at them. Adrienne looked at her siblings and was now worried that one of their parents was ill. Jessica shouted out! Jezalee, in between the tears, proceeded to say that she was getting a divorce. The children were motionless! Stunned beyond belief with what their mom had just said. The three of them broke down in tears and grabbed one another's hands. "Why would you think of divorcing dad?" Alexander questioned his mom. "I wanted your father to be here to tell you in had an affair,' Jezalee could hardly get the words out, she was sobbing uncontrollably. She told herself, she would only divulge the affair but say nothing about him having a child; she would leave that to Paul. Adrienne stood up and rushed toward her mom and put her arms around her; it is going to be okay you can tell us anything. Jezalee sat down across from them and began to tell them what happened when she went to London over six months ago. The only detail she left out was his affair led him to becoming a father; she was going to leave that to Paul. After Jezalee finished, the children gathered around her and the four of them cried. Ten minutes later the children sat back down on the sofa and started asking her questions and she said she was not up to answering them. Jezalee said she had pretty much told them everything she knew; and the rest of their questions would need to be answered by their father.

Jezalee said since their vacation starts tomorrow; she was leaving the decision up to them if they wanted their dad to come or ask him to go back to Paris. She explained how sorry she was that she did not wait until after the trip but once she got to the O'Malley's she knew she could not pretend anymore. Adrienne got up off the sofa and knelt on the floor next to her mom. "Mom, you have nothing to be sorry about, he cheated on you; I can hardly believe you were able to keep this inside you all these months and we never suspected anything was wrong," Adrienne commented. Jessica started hysterically crying and Jezalee got up from the chair and asked the three siblings to lay down on the bed with her and cuddle for a few minutes. A few minutes led to over an hour, and they clung to one another the entire time. Before they got up, Adrienne asked her mom one more thing! "Mom why didn't you let dad and us know as soon as you found out?" She sadly said because she did not want to let them know until school was out; she knew it would have disturb their concentration and not be able to focus one hundred percent on their studies. "You carried this burden all that time! How horrible it must have been for you," Adrienne sadly remarked. "It was dear! But look at it this way, you got through school unscathed, you three had so much fun the last six months and I did not want to take any of that away from you. Your dad and I had fun too; I will always hold that dear to my heart. Your happiness was worth the torment and anguish I was feeling. I was not ready to admit to him I knew his secret; but I did come close at times wanting to abruptly shout it out and get it over with. When I look back and it was worth the sacrifice just knowing we had that time together as a family unit. Jezalee admitted she needed time to adjust herself; telling them as soon as she found out, would have been disastrous for her because she could barely deal with it alone, much less have three children traumatized while she was trying to heal. It was an impossible situation; but she had to do what she thought was best for all of them," Jezalee explained.

Before they got up out of her cozy bed Jessica cuddled closer to her mom and said how much she loved her; but to never ever keep a secret like that to herself again. Alexander sat up, pushed his mom's hair out of her face and kissed her cheek then proceeded to tell her he was the man of the house now. She looked at him, made it clear, she would never impose that burden on him. "I want you to live a young life with no adult concerns or responsibilities towards the household," Jezalee said. There are many trials and tribulations we go through in our daily lives and those will be dealt with at my discretion. "Are we a burden on you mom," Jessica asked. "My goodness no! I did not mean it that way! Being a parent is a privilege. A child having to deal with adult matters would certainly place a burden on him or her and I would never let that happen. The only responsibility I want the three of you having is working hard in school to get the education you need to go on to college and become what you are going to be happy doing. I also want the rest of your childhood and teen years to be great, have lots of friends, love one another and know how much your dad and I will always love you unconditionally," Jezalee adamantly said. "Does that mean we will not be burdened with chores anymore?" Alexander quipped. "I am sorry! But you are not that great of a comedian and you three will still be responsible for your chores, they will help build your character," Jezalee responded. "Oh! Mom! I have been told by many that I am already quite a character," Alexander remarked. "Yes, I will agree with that, and you are a character that will have chores until you go off to college," Jezalee laughed and said. "Darn it," Alexander says laughingly.

Before the four of them left their moms bedroom, Adrienne made it clear, "I am glad you told us about dad's affair before we went on vacation because the three of us do not want him to come with us, and personally, I do not want to see or talk to him right now and I really do not know when I will." Alexander and Jessica spoke up as well and said they felt the same way. Suddenly Jezalee felt sick to her stomach and was upset she told the children before their trip. Jezalee thought to herself, what did I just do? Why didn't I keep the divorce to myself and Paul? She knew she had ruined the children's vacation and was upset at herself. She should have waited another two weeks; she went six months without telling them and she had to do it now!

Now children! Listen to me! I think I have been a little too harsh and made a huge mistake in telling you about the divorce without your father present. He and I made a deal, and I did not stick to it. I should have kept quiet! I did not want you three not to see your father. I am the one married to him and I am the one that will not be seeing that much of him. You three have his blood running through your veins and you will always be his children. Alexander impulsively said! He should have thought about that before he cheated on you! Adrienne agreed and said he cheated on them too and as it stands, it was unanimous, they did not want to be near their father at this time.

I knew I should not have told you before the vacation! Mom, you have suffered enough, just send him packing and do not let him come back here. It has been decided, we do not want to see or hear from him. Jezalee informed them that they will think differently once the dust has settled. I do not think so, said Adrienne, right now

I feel like I have been hit by a speeding semi-truck, and it has thrown me over a cliff. "Mom, you must remember how you felt the moment you heard he was cheating on you!" Adrienne remarked. "Yes! I do remember vividly; an emptiness that I thought would never go away; but enough time has gone by that I do not feel as the three of you do right now. Do not get me wrong, it still hurts deeply; I keep hoping in time there will be less pain and resentment. It will take a good deal of time for all four of us to make a new life for ourselves and we will work on it a day at a time," Jezalee said as she walked closer to her children and extended her arms out to give them a group hug. She explained to them even though she was getting a divorce from their father she knew that he loved them more than anything in the world. Jezalee wanted to ensure her children that they will understand in time that things like this happen in the best of families. Your father made a huge mistake and will live with that the rest of his life; it will just, not be with me. I hope you three will begin to understand and realize anyone can fall from grace. I have prayed for six months, once you knew about the divorce, the three of you would make your way back to your father and carry on a great relationship with him. I do not want the dissolution of our marriage to ever be a factor, and you three will always have the same love and respect for your father. I know this is difficult to understand now but trust me! Things will get better as time passes on. This divorce is between your dad and I and we will not let you three be in the crosshairs because of us. Now, let us go downstairs, you three need to go have some fun with the O'Malley children; while I take your father's luggage to him; I will be back after that, and Mallory and I may join you all in the pool later.

Jezalee called Bob to let him know she was ready to go whenever he was available. He set aside what he was doing and immediately drove the car to the main house, got out of the car and said he would put the luggage in the trunk; he asked her if she wanted to ride in the front or back and she said the front. Bob proceeded to open the door and help her in. By the time Jezalee arrived at Paul's office it was around 1:00 PM; Bob asked her if she wanted him to take the luggage up to Paul's office and Jezalee said she needed to speak with him and would not be long. Bob said he would be waiting in the car and not to rush. He went around to open her door, then got the luggage for her.

As Jezalee got in the elevator she was nervous and just wanted to get this over with as quickly as possible. Once she got to the 11th floor, the elevator door opened and she froze for a split second but managed to start walking down the long corridor; as she kept walking her sixteen years of marriage flashed before her eyes, she was remembering all the times she would surprise Paul at work in his Italy and Paris offices with a gourmet meal and he would take a thirty-minute break to have dinner with her. There were times that the thirty minutes ended up being an hour or so when they dimmed the lights, locked the door, and made love. Jezalee knew this time she would not get the same reception that she had grown accustomed to. As she approached the lobby area, she opened the door, rolled the luggage right outside the entrance of his private office; it appeared his secretary, was out to lunch, but the rest of his staff were busy working in their offices. Paul looked up and was quite surprised to see her; at first, he had this wonderful feeling that came over him and was hoping she was coming to say she loved him and did not want a divorce. "This reminds me of the times you brought me dinner?" Paul sweetly remarked. "Well, this is not one of those times," Jezalee sternly said. He was caught off guard! "Why are you here?" Paul asked. "I told the children we are getting a divorce," Jezalee regretfully said. "You what?" Paul asked. "You heard me!" Jezalee said with tears welting up. "We made a deal that we would tell them together; why would you go behind my back and do such a thing?" Paul want3ed to know. She looked upset and apologized to him and said she did not know what came over her; but Jezalee knew that morning she had to tell them. Paul was white as a ghost and became furious. Jezalee then informed him she thought he was still upstairs sleeping and was going up to ask him if they could tell the children before they go on vacation; but Nell said you had already left for your office. I went ahead without much thought and told the children. After I informed them, you had an affair, the children did not want you to go on vacation with them and they wanted you to go back to Paris. "Oh! So, you are speaking for them now," Paul hurtfully said. "Yes! They certainly do not feel up to seeing or talking to you right now, I do not know if you can comprehend how, they feel but it is not good," Jezalee admitted. "I am sure you told them that I have a second son also!" Paul said angrily. "No! But I did came close to telling them, but I wanted you to see the look on their faces when you tell them about Jonathan," Jezalee said with a concerned look. "Just so you are clear about the vacation, I asked them to discuss the thoughts of you coming or not and they came back to say they unanimously agreed not see or talk with you right now. After they gave me their answer, I told them I was out of line and should have waited to tell them with you after the vacation was over. I know you are very mad at me, and you have every right to be. I kept your secret in me for six months and I should have waited so you and the children could have had a great vacation," Confessed Jezalee with much regret. "You did all this on purpose, you knew they would react that way,'' Paul said as he glared at her. She looked at him with contempt and said she was taking back her apology and informed him she had canceled his flights from the vacation and booked him back to Paris. "Paul, you have known me half my life; you know I am not cable of what you are accusing me of. I have already explained and profusely apologized; I made a grave mistake and feel miserable from the results," Jezalee replied.

Jezalee let Paul know she had packed his clothes and his luggage was right outside his office door and as she was walking away from him, "I have already tried to tell you I am not with that woman and never was and never will be with her," Paul yelled out. "You were with her long enough to get her pregnant, Jezalee pointed out, that was all she needed to know," as she cried. Jezalee looked at him sternly with tears streaming down her face and let him know he was a disappointment to her. She also reminded him that he needed to tell the children he has another child. "You will break their hearts into as you did me. I hope you can be man enough to tell our children why I want a divorce,'' Jezalee trembled as she blurted out her thoughts.

"Jezalee, I am furious with you, I have every right to feel this way. I thought I was going to have a great vacation with the children. I will never accept your apology after speaking to them about the divorce without me being there," Paul said angrily! "Oh! Really, well, I decided I did not want to wait and be in the same room with you when you told them I wanted a divorce because you had a son with another woman; so, I did it my way. I am tired of talking to you and I am sick of your indiscretion and need to leave now," as Jezalee had nothing else to say. Paul abruptly said how much he loved the children; he wanted to see them today! "That's nice! But it is not going to happen. We do not always get what we want, you will see our children when they want to see you, not before. As far as loving your children; you should have thought about that when you were in bed with the devil. When you went into the arms of another woman, that said it all! It is bad enough to hurt me! but our children are hurt just as much. Having a child with another woman adds that much more humiliation for me and our children, if you do not see that you are in crazy denial," Jezalee fired back! "Another thing! You disgust me and I cannot stand the sight of you anymore," Jezalee said before she rushed out the lobby to get away from Paul.

Jezalee ran down the hall to the nearest elevator. When she walked out of the building, Bob could see she appeared upset, and he asked her if she was going to be okay. She smiled and said she had better days but would recover. He asked her if she needed to go anywhere else before he drove her back to the O'Malley residence. She said she just wanted to go back and be with everyone. As Jezalee rode across town she could barely keep herself from crying out, her face was swollen and eyes bloodshot. She did manage to think about the past again and her mind could not help but transcend time when she used to help Paul make decisions about their companies, what stocks to invest in on the market, and go over business developments together. One thing Paul always admired about Jezalee was her good head for business and respected her input. Jezalee knew she would miss being a part of that process. When they reached the O'Malley residence, she was relieved of something she should have taken care of months ago. Now, she was finally ready to go on with her life.

As soon as Jezalee walked through the front door her children ran to put their loving arms around her. "What is all this?" she smiled and said. She smiled and said. "We missed you and glad you are back," Alexander said on behalf of them. Jezalee walked over and said "Hi" to David and wanted them to know how kind and generous they had been; and she felt so embarrassed to bring out her family's dirty laundry in their most elegant and gracious home. "That is ridiculous! You are our friends, and we are honored that you feel close enough to us to share the bad with the good. Our family will always be here for you," David eloquently assured her, as he walked over and gave her a strong hug and whispered in her ear, it is all going to be okay it will get better as time goes by.

David informed everyone that Nell and Mallory were in the kitchen, and he was happy to say, it was Italian feast night in honor of the Albanese's. I hope everyone is looking forward to dinner; bring on your appetites. "The children and I love all Italian food, it smells incredible; I hope you do not mind if I go up to take nap until dinner is served, I am exhausted," Jezalee admitted. "By all-means, go rest and once the table is set, we will come for you," David said. Jezalee said she wanted to go in and say hi to Mallory first. She walked in the kitchen and was so happy to see her. Mallory looked up from stirring her special sauce and walked towards Jezalee. "Are you okay dear?" Mallory said as she knew Jezalee had been crying a lot. "I have been better but have a lot of weight lifted off my shoulders now," Jezalee said with relief. "How did Paul take it?" Mallory curiously and sincerely asked. "He was shocked, beyond belief and we had many heated and hurtful moments," Jezalee sadly remarked. "Well, you have had quite a burden to carry all by yourself and I am relieved for your sake you have gotten most of it out in the open with the children. You needed to share this pain with them and that way the four of you can heal together. "Now, you go upstairs, get under the covers and sleep until dinner is served. It should be a good three hours from now," Mallory insisted. Jezalee gave Mallory a hug and kissed her cheek and walked upstairs to get some rest.

Jezalee woke up several hours later from her nap, got up, washed her face, and changed clothes. She looked at the clock and thought dinner was probably, close to being ready so she thought she should go downstairs and join everyone. She was looking forward to being with everyone and could not wait for some homemade Italian food. As Jezalee was walking down the stairs, Alexander came up from behind, "there's our beautiful momma, may I escort you to dinner?" "Why of course my love," she said. They walked towards the dining room and noticed no one was there so they headed straight for the kitchen where they could hear people talking. Nell and Mallory gave Alexander and Jezalee a hug. Jezalee asked if she could help in any way. Mallory said we just finished, the girls are ready to set the table, and the boys can get the drinks. After the table was set and the hot and cold foods brought in, they sat down to an amazing Italian dinner that everyone raved about. Once Jezalee was seated around her family and friends she perked up and ate a little of everything the ladies had made.

Paul,

I have decided to inform the staff, the children and I would like to move to San Francisco; I am hoping they will want to move with us and would be excited to have an opportunity to live in the states; I will not persuade, them one way or the other. If it is not conducive to the entire staff, I hope you will be in agreeance that we could temporarily stay in the Paris house until we decide what we are doing with our properties.

After we return from our vacation; if the staff is on board to move here, I will be flying home to start packing the things I want for me and the children. You can have whatever you want, prior to me flying over. I will rent a house here in San Francisco while I look for the right place to live.

Let us arrange a time to meet at Marcels; after I return from vacation with the O'Malley's. We need to go over all our businesses, properties, and investments. I am hoping you would let me have the deed to the country estate; that has always been the children's favorite place. We can take care of the divorce proceedings when I return.

I want you, above all else, to have the same relationship you have always had with our children. I will help them come around to being their old selves with you. Just because we are getting a divorce does not mean I do not respect how you have been an integral part in their upbringing of our amazing children, and I want it to remain the same. You have always been the greatest father and I will always love that about you. If I could have handled the situation better without it draining the life out of me, I would have agreed to never tell the children; but I did not have it in me. I am so sorry for that! No matter where we go or what we do, no one can ever take the time away from us that we had together. I am not going to let what you did make our marriage any less than it was. We had a great friendship and love for many years. Thank you for being who you were during our lives together. Please give our children space for now and I will keep encouraging them to call and write to you. I want us to get through the divorce and remain friends for the children's sake, we owe them that.

Fondly,

Jezalee

While Paul was flying home; he tried to relax but his thoughts constantly went to Jezalee. He was tormented knowing how much he hurt the only woman he had ever loved and knowing his children were already devastated over the divorce. Paul's mind was racing at the thoughts of confessing to his children, he had another son. Maybe someday he would be able to sit down with Jezalee and tell her how sorry he was. At the present time, he knew he was at a dead end trying to tell Jezalee the whole truth; there was nothing he could do to make her believe him.

Paul reflected-back to some of his recent conversations with Jezalee, he had grandiose ideas that by coming to America and going on vacation with everyone, maybe she would have a change of heart and reconsider not getting a divorce. Now, after all that she spoke unthinkingly, he knew that was not going to be in the cards as they say.

Paul's flight landed and knew he had to concentrate on meeting with their attorney and dividing up his and Jezalee assets. When he turned the key in the door and walked into a dark and quiet house, he wanted to turn around and go to a hotel. He walked over to the entry light switch and sat his luggage at the front door. He was not sure if he could stay the night there much less every day. He picked up his mail that Helga always sat on the corner of his desk. He sat down in his chair, attempted to muddle through his mail; but he briskly got up, walked down the hallway to his children's rooms, realizing he would never see these rooms filled with love, laughter, and fun times again. Paul walked past his and Jezalee's bedroom and did not have the strength to go in it, knowing how much love had surrounded that room and where their three children were conceived. He walked further down the lengthy hallway to the entrance of Helga's part of the house. He lightly tapped on her door, and she knew it was Paul; so, she let him in. She could tell he was torn up over the divorce about to take place and knew for sure he was embarrassed that everyone knew about it. Hi Paul, "I am sure you are exhausted from your flight," Helga said. He slowly walked over to and gave her a normal strong hug as he always had, then kissed her soft cheeks. Paul explained to her that he could not spend a night in that house without his family and would be staying at the nearest hotel. She looked at him with concern and asked if he would like her to make something for him; but he said he did not have an appetite. "Is there any way I can change your mind; you must be tired from your flight?" Helga said. Paul let her know he would be back in a few days to pack up his things. He asked her if Jezalee had called her and the rest of the staff to see if they wanted to move to the states with her and the children. Helga said Jezalee did, and they agreed to move and was looking forward to living in San Francisco. He expressed how sad he was that everyone was moving to San Francisco; it would be quite a painful adjustment in his life. Paul gave her one last hug and told her how dear she was as the rest of the staff was to him. "I will miss you all and hope you enjoy living in America. Good night sweet Helga," Paul said as he walked away. "I love you like a brother, and I am beyond sad about the pending divorce," Helga said as she called out to Paul with tears in her eyes. "You are such an amazing woman and so is Astrid! I love you back; I will leave a message on the answer machine as to where I will be staying with the hotel name and number," Paul sadly said.

Paul got more luggage from their storage area in the house and made his way to the master suite with much trepidation. He managed to pack most of his miscellaneous belongings. He knew he would need to call a moving company the following day to move the rest of his clothes and some of the office furniture He called the Hotel Dupond-Smith and asked if the penthouse was available, they informed him it was currently vacant. He asked if it could be available indefinitely and they said they were happy to oblige him for as long as he needed to stay. The desk clerk said the room was ready and they would send a limousine to pick him up. Paul was relieved as-soon-as he walked through the doors of the penthouse; he knew he would stay there until he purchased a new place. It was a lovely hotel, they had everything he needed, and it had plenty of space. He knew realistically, who was he kidding, why would he buy a place with him wondering around in an empty home without anyone to share it with.

It was finally vacation day! The O'Malley and Albanese families were looking forward to a grand time together. Luggage was packed and all parties were accounted for and ready for their Western Adventure. David and Bob loaded up the van then had everyone pile in. As Bob drove them to the airport the children started singing every old-time western song they could think of. Bob said his goodbyes to everyone and hoped they had a great vacation in the wild blue yonder.

When they arrived in Denver, Colorado, they went straight to their hotel and looked through their itinerary to see what they would be doing for the day. They first went to Larimer Square, the city's oldest block. They toured the Denver Art Museum then had a late lunch at a charming little restaurant. They walked around The Square, looked at the 19th Century buildings, then wanted to go to the Molly Brown Museum, who was called the "Unsinkable Molly Brown"; she had been on the Titanic Ship with her daughter in 1912 and survived.

The second and third day in Denver, they got up early, had breakfast, went to Mass at the most beautiful Cathedral Basilica of the Immaculate Conception, which stood, 210 feet tall, built from granite and limestone materials. Adam asked Jezalee how tall is the Notre Dame Cathedral we used to go to in Paris and what was it made of? "It is 226 feet materials are Ashlar and stained glass," Jezalee answered." "What Ashlar?" Adam asked. "It is the finest stone masonry," Jezalee replied. "Where is the tallest Catholic Cathedral in the world?" Adam asked. "Right now, as I speak, the tallest in the world is in Cologne, Germany we have the Cologne Cathedral, which is 516 feet tall, the materials are stone, black marble, and stained glass. Two years ago, was the groundbreaking of a new Cathedral which will be named Basilica of Our Lady of Peace, the structure will be 518 feet tall and is in Yamoussoukro, which is the capitol of Cote d'Ivoire {Ivory Coast} and will be made of marble. It will probably take at least five plus years to be completed. Adam said he knew where Germany was but not sure what part of Africa is the Ivory Coast. "It is on the south coast of West Africa," Jezalee said. "I hope someday we can go to Cologne and the Ivory Coast to see these amazing structures," Adam commented. Jezalee said she and Paul have taken the children to Cologne and they went to Mass in that incredible Cathedral and hopefully, they will take a trip to see the one being built in the Ivory Coast.

After Mass they walked around for a while, went back to their hotel, changed into casual clothes to go whitewater rafting down the Colorado River which was about thirty minutes outside of Denver. They loved it so much they wanted to add that to a yearly thing to do. When they got back to the hotel, they went swimming and got massages. David specifically booked their reservations at this hotel because it wasn't only a five-star hotel, so was the restaurant.

The next morning, they flew into Wyoming, David rented a van at the airport; they traveled through some of the most beautiful landscapes in America; the wide-open spaces with the wildlife roaming on lands as far as the eye could see. The diversity of the terrain ranged from the Rocky Mountains to the Great Plains. The state was known for "The Equality of Women" it was the first state that allowed women to vote in 1869. While David was driving them to their destination for a week, they wanted to get in the spirit of a western sort of living so the children started singing old time western songs and their parents eventually broke into song as well.

When they saw the sign to the ranch, the children noticed it said Working Western Ranch; Erica asked what is that about? Mallory spoke up and informed the children that all of them were going to be treated as ranch hands and do what any worker does, on-a-daily-basis. "How fun; but you are aware of my delicate piano hands!" Alexander remarked. "Milking a cow might be just the right exercise for your fingers," Jessica replied.

Once they got through the long pathway to the entrance, there was an oversized cabin at the main entrance, with a multitude of medium-sized cabins uniformly scattered throughout ten acres. They passed several barns, several horse corrals, and huge areas where pigs, chickens and turkeys lived and roamed around. They could see the cows grazing in the pasture; and spotted the five hundred head of cattle in the distance.

As soon as they got to the main cabin, David drove up to the entrance to register for their individual cabins. A man directed him where he could park the van and would be near their assigned cabins. Everyone jumped out of the van, got their luggage, and went to their assigned cabins. When the children entered their home away from home, they were surprised how nice and cozy they were and thought they were cool. As for the adults, they agreed! They liked them and thought! This was not so bad for roughing it.

Quite a few of the cabins were occupied, so when mealtime came, everyone went to the main cabin where they served all their meals. Right away, everyone in their group was loving the food and knew they better eat well because their chores were next.

During the day, everyone milked a cow, fed the chickens, turkeys, and pigs. They learned how to wash a horse with a hose and sponge; then they had to rinse well to make sure all the soap was gone because once it dries the horses start itching from it. A couple of the horses did not like their face hosed down; so, they sponged that part of their body. After the horse's baths it was nice to give the horse a reward by letting him drink from the hose. They collected the eggs from the hens houses then went out to the gardens to pick the vegetables and fruits.

After they were there for the week, having great meals, working hard, sleeping well; they would venture back to the ranch again. In the evenings after supper, as they called it on the ranch; there was a hoedown in one of the barns and great country music. They learned how to line dance and dosey-doe with their partner. After kicking up their heels, there was a huge campfire area where everyone could sit around and sing and have drinks and roasted marshmallows.

After they left the ranch, they drove to Yellowstone National Park; mesmerized by the dramatic canyons, lush subalpine forests, alpine rivers, gushing geysers, including the famous Old Faithful. They saw at least 15-20 geological formations. They visited the Museums around Yellowstone and David had booked them a hotel nearest to the park he could find. They decided to go on two of the tours and had great tour guides and learned so much about the park. 96% of Yellowstone National Park is in Wyoming and the other 4% trickles into Montana, and Idaho.

Their next place of adventure was Montana known as "The Big Blue Sky." They drove to Glacier National Park. When they arrived at their hotel close to the park, David knew, how much they loved the whitewater rafting in Colorado, so, he got tickets for an overnight whitewater rafting experience; two days later they took a hiking tour. The last day they went for a bike ride after they had breakfast then took an all-day fly-fishing trip.

David decided to just get in the van and drive to see where they would end up, he wanted to be away from all the tourist spots and ended up in Big Timber, population 1,600 with hotels dating back to the 1800's. It was a charming, old-fashioned town with soda fountains; décor to match the time-period, which created a trip back in time. They voted and wanted to stay there until their vacation ended. It was a picturesque small mountain town, where the Rocky Mountains and the flat plains meet, with all its scenic beauty to soak in. They stayed at The Grand Hotel, built in 1890 and it had beautiful turn of the century decor. The restaurant had incredible food and they had fresh seafood flown in every day. Their vacation came to an end; but it was quite an adventure, and they did and saw a lot of things and were surprised at the fun they had. Their favorite place to go back was, believe it or not! Big Timber, Montana.

A week after they were back from vacation, Jezalee went to Paris alone; Mallory and David said the children would be fine with them, that way she could get more done. Jezalee had kept in contact with Helga, Joseph and Nina and they were awaiting her arrival. She was overjoyed when her entire staff was willing with much excitement about moving to America. Helga would be closer to Astrid, while she was in Chicago, this was ideal for her, they could visit one another more often. Everyone's passports were in order and up to date; so, everyone was anxious to get settled in their new places.

Joseph and Nina were thrilled to be going to America. Their three children, Mary 12, Joseph Jr. 9, and Janine who was 6, were as excited as they were. The children went to visit an aunt and uncle in London while they helped Jezalee, and Helga organize and get rid of anything they did not want to be shipped to San Francisco. They drove out to check on the countryside chateau; it was such a special place, so many great memories and more to be experienced. The fifty-five acres was well maintained by a local gardener, and he had a crew that religiously came out twice a week. The chateau had an abundance of wildflowers in every color imaginable and there were various types of magnificent trees throughout the acreage. There were several trellises that led to various gardens, and they had brought in stone benches and open-pit barbeque areas. There was every type of flower planted throughout the property and they had several gazebos where one could sit and read or just enjoy the scenery. There was a river that ran through the property; it had a walking bridge to cross over to the other side and the children loved to hang out especially the summers and during Christmas. Summer was when they loved playing games in the water or sitting by the side of the river and reading for hours. They loved romping through the fields of flowers and playing hide and seek for hours at a time. When the sun went down, the children, Jezalee and Paul would pitch tents and cook their dinner outside. Once it was dark enough to see the stars they would lie on their backs and try to count them all and they usually fell asleep doing so.

Once Jezalee arrived in Paris, it was a difficult time going through both the country and city residences. Their attorney had called to inform her that Paul had moved all his belongings out of both places, and the rest was for her and their children. She had informed their attorney that she would like to keep the chateau in Saint-Germain-en-Laye. As she walked through the Paris estate, Jezalee reflected-back to all the fun the five of them and their staff had in their beautiful homes and how difficult it had been to sort through almost twenty years of personal and cherished items the first from time Paul and Jezalee first met until the present. She had her tearful moments; but Helga and Nina were there to help her sort through both homes plus they had to decide what they wanted to have shipped also. Jezalee knew Paul had met with their attorney and had the papers all drawn up; all she had to do was sort out everything in the two homes and decide what was going to San Francisco. It took eight grueling days for all three ladies to accomplish what they needed to do but now that they were done; she would call the attorney and go in to sign the paperwork for the divorce. Before Jezalee went to sign papers at Marcel's office; she had Nina and Joseph schedule the shipping company to have everything shipped to San Francisco and Mallory had reserved ten over-sized storage units. The storage facility indicated they would keep several more of the same sized units available in case they had an over-flow of more than they anticipated. Helga, Nina, and Joseph managed to sort through all their belongings and decided what would stay for donations to their Church and what they would also have shipped.

While Jezalee had a few minutes to spare, she called Alexander to see if he wanted his grand piano shipped. During the conversation he thought about it but was not sure what to do. He had a sentimental attachment; his first note was played on that piano when he was five years old. Jezalee took the burden off his shoulders; and would ship the piano. His mom let Alexander know, if all goes well, the piano will arrive in great condition. "I am going to buy you a second grand piano when I get back so, you will have two, one for the living room and one for the family room, that will take care of that," Jezalee said. His mom asked if he had been practicing on the O'Malley's piano? He said absolutely! While you have been gone; I have happily composed to new pieces to add to my repertoire," Alexander said. "Wonderful! I can hardly wait to hear them; love you dear! I must go because the Realtor is coming up the driveway," Jezalee said.

As Jezalee walked through the Paris estate once more before the Realtor showed up, she was hoping she did not make a harsh decision selling it. She called over the intercom to Helga, she was in the back part of the large estate where they had placed all the boxes to donate to their Church. When the Realtor, Mrs. Dubois arrived she was amazed that everything had been done in such a short period of time and said she could cancel out the cleaning crew she had set up to clean the estate. Jezalee informed her she had three people that had been with their family for almost fifteen years and had already called the company they used to clean the estate.

Mrs. Dubois indicated that Paul had dropped by the office earlier in the afternoon and all she had to do was read over the contract to make sure she was in agreeance, and sign. The estate was sold forty-eight hours after it was on the market. The buyer was moving from Spain; needed something right away and their home was perfect for him and his family. Mrs. Dubois had a photographer come in while all the furniture was in the house, and she said whoever did the interior design throughout the estate was a big factor in getting it sold so quickly. The Realtor asked if it was done by a local designing company and Jezalee proudly said she had done it all. Mrs. Dubois could not say enough great things about her talent in what she had created in the entire estate. Jezalee signed the papers; the house was no longer the Albanese's family home. As Jezalee walked away, devastation set in, knowing that she would never drive through the estate and see all the beauty leading up to the entrance of that magnificent, palatial estate they had made comfortable, cozy, and called home. She and Paul had worked so hard to be able to afford such an extravagant place to live. Their babies came home from the hospital and as they grew up; they had run through every inch of the estate. Later that day, she met Helga, Joseph, and Nina at the cottage, and they had a crying fest before they drove off the property.

Once Jezalee and her staff arrived at their hotel, where they would stay until they parted for San Francisco. She placed a call in to their attorney, Marcel and went in the next day to read over all the specifics in the divorce decree and she had one question for him, why is Paul giving me the proceeds from the Paris estate, since I am getting the chateau? "I asked Paul the same question; he wanted you to have that money added to the billion-dollar settlement you will be receiving; he is a most generous man, and I am happy for you and the children," Marcel said with a grin. He asked me to inform you, if it was okay that he wanted all the stocks and bonds divided up between your children and the staffs, children. Paul also added money to each of the staffs, children's trust funds to total twenty-five million dollars each. Your children currently have fifty million and that remains as is. Paul added money to all college funds, including your children and the staffs, children. Once their education was completed, whatever money remains after they have graduated, will be transferred over to their individual trust fund accounts. The trust funds will be available on their twenty-fifth birthday; prior to that, they are not allowed to be informed they have trust funds until you and Paul decide when they will be notified. Paul mentioned maybe it would be appropriate the day they complete college; you can discuss it with him at your convenience. Marcel informed Jezalee all businesses remain the same; you both are equal partners, as you are joint owners. The properties which includes, New York, California {villa on vineyard property}, Spain {villa on vineyard property}, England, France, Italy, and Argentina; Paul stipulated for Jezalee to choose three out of the five for her enjoyment and ownership. Marcel informed her that all wineries-vineyards that had villas on the property would have joint ownership and could be used by both parties as you both see fit. The other wineries-vineyards having homes on property are for the caretakers. Jezalee was in agreeance with everything; however, she had a change of heart with the Saint-Germain-en-Laye property. She advised Marcel the property should remain as a joint ownership; please inform Paul as to my decision. Marcel knew what that chateau and property had always meant to her and was surprised at Jezalee's decision. "That is quite commendable of you to share that property with Paul," Marcel happily said. "Marcel, if it had not been for Paul's intuition, foresight or insistence, we would not have had the opportunity to buy that extraordinary piece of property. I want him to be able to enjoy it as much as I will," Jezalee remarked as her face saddened.

The Saint-Germain-en-Laye chateau was especially dear to the family during Christmas time, they always had a large tree and made special ornaments that stayed there on the property. Helga and Nina had crochet stockings for everyone; and the mantle was large enough to house 15 large stockings, which included their staff and their children. There had been twelve of them living at their Paris estate until Astrid went away to college; and other three lived on the property in the country year-round. Montrose, Monique, and their daughter Veronica who was 7, lived on the property where the Albanese's, had built a home for them. They celebrated holidays with them anytime they came out to the country unless they had other commitments with their families. Everyone celebrated at this home during part of the holiday season. There were usually a few days every year that everyone would be home in Paris so they would all get together before anyone took off to be with their relatives or friends for a Christmas. The chateau was over a hundred years old, had 28 spacious rooms, which included 17 bedrooms.

In 1973, a year after their first child, Adrienne was born, Jezalee and Paul were driving through the countryside one afternoon, on a spectacular sunny, and breezy day, they spotted a most magnificent chateau and Paul had enough nerve to drive up to the entrance and inquire about the property. With fate on their side, he knocked on the massive hand carved double doors and the lady of the house gladly came to the door. Paul wanted her to know if they ever happen to sell their chateau, he and Jezalee would be willing to bid on their lovely property. Mrs. Beauchene welcomed them to come in and chat awhile. They were shocked to say the least and was astounded once they walked through the double front doors. From that day forward, they built a great friendship with her and her husband of forty years. Paul and Jezalee had only purchased their estate in Paris five weeks prior to driving out to Saint-Germain-en-Laye. Adeline and Gaston Beauchene became life-long friends and they promised when the time was right for them, they would sell the chateau to the Albanese's; five years later they honored their promise and Paul and Jezalee were the new owners of this beautiful land and chateau. The property had been in the Beauchene' family for over a hundred years and they were ready to see new blood walk through the doors.

During the summer they spent a lot more time at the estate; they would move the whole staff and their children out there for over a month or two, in between vacations; some would come and go at their leisure. Montrose, Monique, and Veronica would join them for meals, games, movies and whatever else they had planned during the summer months. Montrose had been their full-time employee the first week they bought the estate and lived inside the massive home until he married Monique. Paul and Jezalee, gave them the choice; in living in the main house with their own wing or having a house built for them. They chose to have a home built approximately ten acres from the main house; on the other side of the bridge that went across the river. Monique would take care of everything inside of the huge chateau. Montrose took care of any structural problems on the two homes and all other structures built on the property. He would oversee the landscapers to make sure they took care of all the land.

Once the Albanese's, were in the billionaire bracket of wealth; they saw to it that their properties that had anyone living on them needed twenty-four-hour protection. The chateau in the country was vast so they wanted Montrose and his family to feel secure; so, they had hired four guards and had bullet proof structures to protect them. Paul had a 12-foot wrought iron gate and fencing built around twenty of the fifty-five acres of the land, with cameras throughout the property.

Paul had called Joseph at the hotel where they were staying and relayed a message to Helga and his wife Nina and their children; he would love to take them out to dinner and spend some time together before they departed for America. They agreed to spend four days at his penthouse. They had a great time going out to eat at some of their favorite restaurants, went to the movies, had a bowling contest, and hung out and played board games back at Paul's penthouse. A lot of sad faces as they departed; but Paul said he wanted to keep in touch with all of them and they agreed how wonderful that would be. They were so upset over the divorce and loved Paul and Jezalee equally; so, it deeply affected them.

Jezalee, her staff and their three children all boarded their flight to America; they were exhausted from closing-up the countryside property and selling the Paris home. They knew they would be staying with the O'Malley's until they found a home in San Francisco. Mallory had worked diligently making sure all the bedrooms were ready for her guests. Some of the children were bunking together so that remedied fifteen people in nine bedrooms.

David and Mallory were the quintessential hosts, and they loved helping-out. Everyone including Jezalee needed to be in a nice comfortable bed and not wake up for twelve hours. Mallory had them eat a hot meal then off they went to bed. It took days for everyone to recuperate from their flight merely because they were exhausted from all the work; they had to put in to packing up two estates in a week's time.

Jezalee was highly anticipating having a difficult time finding just what she wanted and what she was used to. Her children were thrilled to see their mom and were ecstatic they would be living near the O'Malley's; at least they hoped their mom found a place in the same area. David and Mallory had taken Jezalee all over the Bay Area to find just the right house. It only took a little over a week and she found the perfect home, an estate which had just been placed on the market and was only three blocks away from the O'Malley's; the children, of course! were overjoyed and zealous. Helga, Nina, Joseph and their three children were all staying at the O'Malley's home along with Jezalee and her children. Now, they were waiting for all their shipments to come in from Paris so they could move into their beautiful estate.

Everyone agreed that they loved the area, the people, and their new home. They seemed to like it better than the home in France. Now, all Jezalee had to do once the shipment came in was to unpack. She made sure she brought every-single thing the children had in their rooms and Jezalee and Nina made sure they did not leave anything behind. Joseph and Nina's children decided not to bring much because they wanted to shop for new things once they arrived in San Francisco. Jezalee brought everything from each of her children's rooms and they could donate whatever they did not want once they unpacked. Her children were appreciative and said they would probably keep everything.

David, Mallory and their three children welcomed all ten of Jezalee families into their spacious home until they got all their things from Paris. They also said once the shipments arrive everyone would pitch in to help. Jezalee said that was generous of them, but she had been given some names of a few companies who specifically handled overseas moves and will set up and unpack everything in the home for them. Jezalee was thrilled that the estate she purchased had a huge guesthouse with five bedrooms, which was perfect for Joseph, Nina, and their children. When they went to look at it, they were so happy to have such a beautiful house.

Jezalee's new estate, upstairs had nine over-sized bedrooms, a huge game room, exercise, sauna, and laundry rooms. All the downstairs rooms were massive in size; living, family, dining, office, den, movie theater, kitchen with huge eating area, maid's quarters, which would be converted into a second walk in pantry, three over-sized bedrooms, and another laundry room. Jezalee was disappointed that it was not set up like the house in Paris where Helga had her own wing and private entrance. Jezalee had informed Helga she was having a contractor come out and do some magic to the downstairs area for her. She wanted her to have as much room if not more in the new place than she did in Paris. Helga had told her it was perfect the way it was, but Jezalee had other ideas. After she slept on the changes she wanted, she decided to add an entire wing downstairs so Helga would have her private living quarters where her wing would have one door that came into a hallway to the main house downstairs. Jezalee wanted to utilize the three large bedrooms, each with their own bathroom if the guest preferred a downstairs bedroom. She stayed up late one night and sketched out what she wanted and called a contractor to see if her plan would work. The next morning, she showed Helga the sketches which she loved. She would also have three large bedrooms, four bathrooms, a spacious living and dining room area, a kitchen, family room, sunroom, and a private outdoor patio with French doors out to the pool. She kept telling Jezalee it was not necessary, but she said, "nonsense" I am not going to have you cramped in your private quarters. Plus, I decided I want the current three bedrooms and bathrooms downstairs when we have extra company; that way we will have a total of twelve bedrooms for the main living quarters. While they were talking Jezalee was having a flashback when she and Paul decided to find a staff to live in to help run things, they both had extremely busy careers. They knew they wanted to buy an estate where there would be land and many bedrooms to accommodate a big family. When they came upon the estate they eventually purchased, the only thing Jezalee and Paul did not like was the separate wing to the house. If they were going to have live-in people, they wanted them to feel a part of the household. On that same property was a lovely guest house with three large bedrooms and it was a nice size place. When they found Helga, they gave her the option of the guest house, or the wing and she chose the wing. It was better for her because she was the cook and when and if they had children, she would help take care of them while they were at work. They eventually found Nina and Joseph who had not started their family, yet; but they knew the guest house was a perfect place to live on the property and there would be plenty of room to raise children too. As their family increased, the Albanese's added 2 more bedrooms and a family room.

PART TWO

Chris and Cathy escape————Chris rushed out the front door; as he was running towards Cathy waiting at the roadside; the entire house was engulfed in flames, there would be no survivors from the fire. No one would see the smoke since there were no signs of life within at least five or ten miles from the shack they had lived in for over a year.

Chris grabbed the duffel bag of money and could already feel the freedom he and Cathy would experience. He was thankful the Crockets had been gone all day; he would have enough time to clear his head and plan where he and Cathy would go once, they left their miserable life.

Earlier in the day, before the Crockets arrived home; Chris pulled the duffle bag from under the floorboard and to his astonishment, there was over three hundred and thirty-five thousand dollars. He was relieved there were enough smaller denominations because being as young as he and Cathy were, people would probably have their suspicions with one hundred-dollar bills. He did not know the cost of most things out there in the world because the Crockets kept them pretty much isolated; but he knew that they had a lot of money to help them get started in a life they had never known. Once they were gone from the shack, they would have to learn about life, like they have never known before. Chris was excited for he, and Cathy; but nervous knowing everything would be foreign to them. He knew that they had never been exposed to enough to understand what it was going to be like to live a good life; but he had learned enough in his young years when he would overhear the Crockets discussing money and how much certain things had cost. Chris and Cathy were lucky there was plenty of money for them to survive a long time.

When the Crockets came home that night, they were pleased that Chris had made their favorite meal of spaghetti and meatballs. Cathy had set the table and made sure their beer and cheap bottle of red wine was next to their plate. While the four of them ate their dinner, Chris was nervously shaking inside, and Cathy felt sick to her stomach. They were trying to act like they always did around the Crockets; but that night was not like any other night. As the children sat there listening to the Crockets arguing and getting drunker by the minute; they just wanted everything to be over. Once the beer and wine bottles were empty, Chris asked if they would like some more to drink. Dodge perked up in his harsh-toned voice and said ''What do you think! The bottles are empty, aren't they?'' Chris replied, "Yes sir! And got up, walked over to the refrigerator to get a beer and a bottle of red wine out of the cupboard." Chris asked Dodge if he wanted anything else before he sat down to finish his dinner. Dodge pounded on the table with his clenched fist and told Chris if he wanted something else, he would tell him; now sit down and shut up! The slovenly dressed Kate looked over at Cathy and warned her, "the kitchen better be spotless when I get up in the morning or I will drag you through the house by your hair.'' As Kate got up from the table, she could barely walk a straight line to the bedroom. Chris and Cathy sat at the table until Dodge finished off both bottles of beer and red wine. Chris's heart was pounding so loud against his chest and was worried Dodge would hear it and yell at him. Cathy was tapping her right foot and was scared Dodge would slap her in the face like he usually did. The drunken slob finally got up from the table but tripped on the way to the bedroom; Chris hurried over to help him. Chris nudged him along the way; once he got him close to the doorway, Dodge fell forward onto the bed and passed out. Kate was already out for the night snoring. Chris and Cathy knew what they had to do now! Cathy grabbed their bag of clothes and ran out the front door. Chris started pouring the containers of gas over the Crockets bodies, throughout the rundown shack; and their stolen car; he lit the matches and ran.

Once Chris caught up with Cathy, they ran as far as their tired legs would take them. He knew it would be much harder on Cathy since she had gone through an abortion earlier that day. Dodge had gotten her pregnant and Chris was not about to let her carry that monster's baby; that is when he knew they had to escape. He was relieved he knew about pregnancies, abortions, and women having a menstrual cycle. When Chris and Cathy were over at the Crockets friend Dawson's house, he overheard him having a conversation with his girlfriend and demanded her getting an abortion because he did not want to have anything to do with her if she was pregnant. Since they were spending the night, he checked out his book collection and found a dictionary and a set of encyclopedias and looked up the two words and cringed when he found out what the words meant. Once they were taken back to the Crockets, one night Chris informed Cathy if she started bleeding in her private area, it meant she was menstruating, and it would happen every month; if she did not have it every month, meant she was more than likely pregnant.

Two days before they escaped, Cathy told Chris she was throwing up, her stomach was swelling, and she had not menstruated for 2 months; from the information he found in the books, she thought she may be pregnant. He was sick to his stomach; he immediately checked to see how much money he had; he remembered when they were in the car going to Dodge's friend's house, he saw a women's free clinic. Chris immediately informed Cathy that he needed to take her to the there and they would check her out. The clinic was at least 4 or 5 miles away. When they arrived, he made up a story that his sister had been raped; but never saw who he was because he had a mask on. He said if their father found out about this; he would disown her. The receptionist asked them to be seated and a nurse would be with her shortly. Chris demanded to be in the room and hoped that would not be a problem. The nurse called Cathy's name and Chris said he wanted to be with his sister. The nurse said that his request was unusual but would ask the doctor if he would allow it. The doctor let Chris sit by her side and he held her hand as the nurse sedated her. The doctor had the nurse explain everything, step by step as the procedure began. Chris was shocked that it went quickly, and they thanked the doctor and nurse and walked out to the receptionist desk. The lady handed Cathy pain medicine and a pamphlet with instructions in case she had any complications. When they walked out the door, Cathy felt relieved and finally free from that monster, Dodge's baby growing inside her. As they were walking back, Chris told Cathy they had to escape that night; they could not take any chances of Dodge touching her ever again.

After escaping they walked for a few hours and finally spotted a neon lit sign that said vacancy at a rundown, flea-bitten motel in Winkelman, Arizona. They slept for the first time without being sexually abused in the middle of the night or woken up by the Crockets "having loud sex." They got their first night of real rest, in between, fighting off the bugs. The next morning after they woke up, they both took their showers in the filthy, dilapidated stall, got dressed in their old-tattered clothes, and asked the hotel desk clerk how far it was to the next big city! The desk clerk said the closest city was Tucson, it was about an hour and a half away. Chris asked him if there would be a train or bus coming through town. He let him know that a bus would be stopping in fifteen minutes going to Tucson. Where do we buy tickets?'' Chris asked. "We sell them here,'' answered the desk clerk. "How much are two one-way tickets?" Chris asked him. "That will be six dollars for two tickets,'' replied the desk clerk. Chris made sure that the stubs showed from Winkelman to Tucson and three dollars each; it was all legitimate. He thanked the desk clerk and asked him where they went to wait for the bus. The desk clerk pointed to the bus stop sign right outside the motel.

Once Cathy and Chris got on the bus, they knew they were taking a ride to their new and safe life. While being on the bus, they overheard a couple discussing how excited they were to visit a big city like Los Angeles. The entire time on the bus, the couple kept talking about the various things there was to do, and see, and hoping someday to permanently move there. When the bus arrived in Tucson, Chris watched where the couple went and walked in behind them. Chris tapped the young man's shoulder and asked him if this was the line to buy a ticket to Los Angeles. The young man said yes and hoped they had a nice time in the city. Chris thanked him and knew that Cathy and he would want to be somewhere that had a lot of options; he knew for certain that a small town would not be the right thing to do. Once they bought their tickets, it was only a half an hour until they boarded the next bus. They decided to take a direct route to Los Angeles, so Chris went up to the window and purchased their one-way tickets. When they arrived in Los Angeles bus station Chris went up to the ticket counter and asked one of the employees how they would get to a nearby hotel; the gentleman pointed to one of the exit doors and said wait outside, near the curb, there will be plenty of yellow taxicabs to take you to your destination. Chris asked him if he needed to buy a ticket from him and he said the driver had a meter in his taxicab, and you pay by how far you go in the cab. The gentleman let Chris know that as soon as they get to where they wanted to go, the meter would indicate to the driver how much you pay before they are dropped off. The gentleman was beginning to realize these two young kids had probably never been in a big city or seen a taxicab. He immediately let Chris know to make sure they had small bills, of one's, and fives when the driver asked them to pay, also encouraged Chris to give the driver a fifty-cents tip as well. Chris thanked the gentleman for explaining how to get around the city; off he and Cathy went. As soon as they walked outside, they saw several taxicabs picking up people and other ones waiting for customers. They saw people running towards the taxicabs and waving them down to get a ride. Chris held onto Cathy's hand and with the other, he waved down a cab driver. The driver stopped to pick them up and asked where they were going, and Chris said they wanted to go to a really nice hotel. The cab driver said which one? Chris said to a hotel that was not far from a main library in the city. The driver nodded as he drove off; he took them to one of the nicest hotels in the heart of the city. The cab driver also let them know, the hotel he was taking them to, was in the center of the city, with easy access to wherever they wanted to go. Once they got to the hotel, Chris asked the driver how much they owed, and the fare ended up costing three dollars and Chris added a fifty-cent tip. The driver thanked them and drove off.

As soon as they arrived at the hotel, Chris asked the desk clerk if they had rooms with a safe. He said all rooms had a wall safe in the closet area. Chris then asked if they could have a room facing the city and preferred something above the 6th or 7th floor as well. He also let the desk clerk know Cathy was his sister so they would need two big beds. The desk clerk asked how long they would be staying, and he said until they find a suitable apartment. The desk clerk informed him the hotel gives a twenty-five per cent discount for persons in transition; looking for a place to live. Chris thanked him and thought that was nice of the hotel to accommodate them. The desk clerk asked for a driver's license or another form of identification to get them registered. Chris said someone stole his wallet and hoped it would not be a problem. The desk clerk said that would be fine; they would have two rooms on the 7th floor, facing the city. Chris thanked him and signed in as Chris Davidson.

They were relieved to be in the hotel, that was safe, beautiful, and friendly. The prices were a little steep; hopefully, they would be able to find an apartment within two months. Once they got settled in their room, they bought a newspaper; looked up apartments and houses for rent. Chris was smart enough to know spending money at an expensive hotel would bleed them financially and was hoping they would not have to be there for any length of time.

Cathy came out of the restroom and looked at Chris; he was pale white, as if he had seen a ghost. He asked her to join him at the table; and proceeded to show the newspaper clippings to her. Cathy started crying when Chris read the caption under the photo of the murder scene; couple murdered in vehicle on freeway; shot in the back of the head at close range. Two-year-old daughter missing. The second photo, couple murdered in vehicle on freeway, both shot in the back of the head at close range; one-year-old boy survived; however, his twin brother missing. They knew the Crockets purposely blacked out the information written about where and when the murders took place, and the names of the victims. They knew now that they did not want them to know their real names so they could go to the police or where the murders took place.

After glancing at the articles several times, Cathy, and Chris had no doubts the Crockets had murdered their parents. All along, they told them, their parents gave them up because they did not want them. Chris turned to Cathy, his eyes forming tears. The Crockets said they would kill them if they ever ran away. "I was stupid to believe anything those sick, evil, pigs said to us!'' Chris said trembling. "You have been so brave, do not feel stupid for believing those monsters, they brainwashed us, and we had no idea what the truth was," Cathy said as she looked at him with sorrowful eyes. She took his hand in hers, Chris yanked his hand away. He ran his fingers through his hair and walked over to his bed. "Just visualize how terrifying it must have been for our parents,'' Chris commented. He looked down at the money sprawled out on the bed. "What matters now is we are safe, secure, and together,'' Cathy said as she walked over to Chris. "We were brought together by circumstances; but we have survived, and we have each other,'' Cathy smiled through her tears and turned to Chris. He looked back at her, apologized for abruptly yanking his hand away, smiled and hugged her tightly. "You are right sis, let us get this money stored and hit the hay,'' Chris said. Cathy helped Chris put the one-hundred-dollar bills in the safe. While he was making a list of the other denominations he had to count, Cathy first took her luxurious shower. By the time she was done, Chris had counted the money and had placed more in the safe. While Chris took his shower, Cathy turned on the television, which they had only seen at Crockets friends' house, when he took care of them several years ago. After Chris came out of the bathroom, he got under the covers and felt the comfort of the luxurious bed which he never imagined he would be sleeping on. He asked Cathy if hers was comfortable too and she said, "It is like nothing she ever dreamed people slept on." Cathy turned off the television and they talked for a while; deciding on what they would do first thing tomorrow. They both fell asleep in the middle of a conversation and did not wake up until 10:00 the next morning.

First thing Chris and Cathy did, was go to breakfast in the hotel restaurant. They had never had pancakes or waffles, by the photo on the menu, they started salivating over them. When their breakfasts arrived, they had no idea what whipped cream, strawberries, or syrup tasted like. Their very first bite for both-of-them was a taste they had never had and kept wanting more. After they finished their breakfast, Cathy said, "I wonder if this is how people eat every day?" They both looked around the restaurant and saw quite a few people eating the same thing they had just devoured. Before the waiter approached them with the bill, they skimmed over the menu once again and said they wanted to eat there every day. They saw so many dishes that looked amazing and could not wait to eat there again.

While they were with the Crocket's, they had limited foods at their fingertips. Breakfast was always dry cereal with watered down powdered milk. Lunch and dinners were always canned vegetables, spaghetti and meatballs, smashed potatoes, rice, noodles, spam, bologna, hamburger helper, wonder bread, and other boxed foods. When they saw the menu at the hotel, it was foreign to their palette. They never had any fruit unless at Dawson's house; sometimes the Crockets would buy canned fruit cocktail.

Before they left the hotel, Chris went up to the desk clerk to ask him where they could buy clothes that were not too expensive. The man gave, them each a pamphlet that had a list of all the department stores in and around the vicinity of the hotel. The desk clerk circled a few department stores in the pamphlets that were not high end; but had nice apparel for them. They were excited to venture into their first department store, to search for brand new clothes, which they had never had.

Once they arrived at the first department store; they decided before they purchased anything, they would observe what people were wearing and buying; to get some idea as to what type of clothes and shoes to buy. They knew this would help guide them in their buying spree. Over the next five hours they went to several department stores and experienced what it was like to have something new. They told themselves, they would never have used clothes or shoes from a second-hand store, ever again. When they tried on shoes without holes in them, they were feeling overwhelmed with excitement. They had one of the shoe salesmen help them with the sizing, because the old shoes they were accustomed to, were either way too big or so tight they could barely walk in them. They thought it was very clever that they had a metal device you sat your foot on and it had numbers that would determine what size shoe a person wore. When it got time to try on clothes, they asked one of the sales ladies if she could help them decide what they looked best in. She went around and selected at least six outfits for each of them and walked them to the women's and men's dressing rooms. They could not believe how nice both salespersons had been in helping them shop. They were in their dressing rooms and could not believe they would be looking into a mirror and seeing how they looked in each item. After they both came out with their various outfits, the sales lady gave them some good advice as to what they should buy and how to make the most out of their wardrobe. This was the first surreal experience they encountered and admitted, they felt so alive and maybe this was what normal felt like. Cathy asked Chris if she could buy a purse like she saw other women carrying; he explained to Cathy she never had to ask him because half of that money was hers. She knew the purse would be a good place to keep their spending money when they went out. She purposely bought a purse with a long shoulder strap so no one could yank the purse from her body. They also purchased two large suitcases on rollers. When they arrived back at the hotel, they hung up their new clothes; dumped their old worn-out, tattered ones, their holy ill-fitted shoes along with the dirty, filthy smelling duffel bag, in the nearby dumpster outside the back of the hotel. They had also bought pajamas, which they had never seen before; they only had street clothes to sleep in. They counted their money every night and made a list of everything they bought and kept the receipts; Chris was finding out how to be older than his years and he was doing a great job of it. Cathy told him he did seem older because once he turned 14 his voice was much deeper. He was always meticulous and now it would pay off since he and Cathy had to watch where every penny went.

Now that they had a nice hotel to stay in and good food, they would check out the nearest library. Once they got there, their focus was to locate their families and to search through a newspaper for rentals. They were anxious to let their families know they were alive. They quickly found out that the physical newspapers that were over a year old, were on microfiche. The Librarian informed Chris and Cathy where they stored the microfiche and they were by year, month, then by day. Since they were not sure of their ages; they were going by what the Crockets and told them. They did not want to take any chances; so, they started back to 1945, and thought that was a good starting point. They did not think they were that old; but wanted to play it safe. Chris had added up all the days in those nineteen years and knew they had to go through approximately five thousand, seven hundred and ninety-five days of newspapers on the microfiche. They were both overwhelmed, but knew they had to find their families.

Chris had a lengthy conversation with Cathy and decided they needed to find someone that could get them fake birth certificates, and a California driver's licenses for them. He had remembered overhearing Dodge talking to Kate about getting two more fake driver's licenses for them; so, Chris knew, he and Cathy needed documents to show they were eighteen and nineteen, and with Chris having a growth spurt, just before he turned fifteen, to five feet ten inches tall, he could pass for a for a nineteen-year-old boy easily. Cathy was five feet three inches tall, which was a few inches below the average height for a girl, eighteen-years-old as well. He said they could pretend to be brother and sister, even though they did not look alike.

It took longer than they anticipated in finding someone that would make them fake documents; after almost two months they found a young man by the name of Bullet, that had taken over his dad's business. They initially asked him if he thought they could pass for eighteen and nineteen, and he assured them, they were tall enough and appeared mature; so, they should not have a problem. He knew they looked older than fourteen and fifteen, and Bullet informed them he had to make them old enough so they could rent a place to live in. Chris asked him if they could use the last name Davidson, since he used that name at the hotel; he said no problem. When Bullet was done, they could not believe how professional the documents were. Bullet indicated he had made up their birthdates since they had no idea when they were born. When they had checked in at the hotel, Chris told the desk clerk their last name was Davidson; so, he asked Bullet to use that as their last name. They were now Chris and Cathy Davidson, brother, and sister, born in Holland, Michigan, in 08-05-1945 and 11-30-1946, to George and Estelle Davidson. Bullet made two separate driver's licenses, one showing it was issued from Ventura, California; where they just moved from, the second one was showing, issued in Los Angeles. He said the one from Ventura could be used until they found a place to live in Los Angles, once they did find a place, they would need to go to the DMV and have an address change done, they would issue them new ones with their current address. Chris and Cathy could not believe they had a driver's licenses and birth certificates; they had never been behind the steering wheel of a car. They knew eventually Chris needed to learn how to drive; but that was on their list of to do things in-the-near-future. They were not burdened with that task anymore; and were grateful they finally had their identifications out of the way.

They were having a difficult time finding a place because of their ages and no jobs. They were losing patience trying to find the newspaper articles on microfiche. Several weeks after they had their identifications, they found four rentals they were interested in. The first three places ended up not being what they wanted; so, they hoped the last one would work out. When they called the number, the owner of the cottage, Jenny O'Conner, said the cottage was still available. Chris asked if they could come by in an hour and she said that would be great. Jenny, the owner, was a sweet forty-five-year-old woman, recently widowed and basically wanted someone to live on the property so she would not be by herself. The cottage had always been used as a guesthouse when relatives or friends came to visit; now she wanted to permanently rent it out.

When Chris and Cathy arrived, they rang the doorbell to the main house and Jenny answered the door. She introduced herself, then walked them through the cottage and talked a while; she had a good feeling about them. After the owner finished showing them around, she asked them what they thought of the place. They let Jenny know immediately they loved the place; it was in a great location and was something they knew they could afford. She asked them to come back to her house and she would have them fill out the rental agreement. Even though, neither Chris nor Cathy ever saw the inside of a school building, they self-taught themselves anytime they could find something to read. The Crockets were forced to teach them some because they did all the cooking and cleaning wherever they lived and had to learn to read labels. When Dawson, took care of them, he would always have a slew of books he let them keep and while they were there, he would read to them as well. When they got to her house, Jenny asked them to make themselves comfortable while she went to get a rental agreement from her office. The owner was thrilled they loved the cottage and most importantly, she felt comfortable around them. Jenny invariably trusted her instincts when meeting people for the first time and her husband had always admitted it was a great gift she had. Chris read over the agreement and wanted to know if they could pay for a full year in advance. Knowing how young Chris and Cathy were, Jenny advised them, it may be better to just pay monthly, that way they could put their money in an account and let it draw interest. He thought about it for a few minutes; then thanked her for the good advice. Chris asked if they could pay six months and would take her suggestion and open a bank account with the rest of their money. "That's a deal!" Jenny smiled and said. Before they signed the agreement, he noticed a clause that said if after one year they wanted to extend their agreement, the monthly rental amount would remain the same. "Am I reading this contract right, you will not raise the rent?" Chris asked. "Yes! it is, as long as you live here, the rent will remain the same," Jenny answered. After their signatures were on the rental agreement and dated; she handed over the keys to their cottage. They thanked her and were thrilled they would not have to live at the hotel anymore. They were so excited and could not wait to celebrate back at the hotel restaurant with a fancy meal.

After Chris and Cathy got their keys to the cottage, they told Jenny if she ever needed anything done, they would be happy to help her. They said their goodbyes and went back to their new and lovely cottage. Chris and Cathy walked back through their new place and could not believe this was where they would be living. They could not wait to get back to the hotel to start packing up their clothes. He suggested to Cathy he felt they should buy Jenny some flowers and chocolates, and she agreed. They walked a few blocks and saw a Safeway grocery store and was pleased to find out they had what they needed. They bought Jenny fresh flowers and a variety of chocolates to choose from. He remembered the color scheme Jenny had in her home; so, he put an arrangement together, in beautiful hues of pink, lavender, and yellow; then bought her a box of chocolates, as well. They hurried back to Jenny's, rang the doorbell, and presented her with the flowers when she answered the door. "What is all this?" Jenny said as she smiled. "Just a little something to say thank you for renting the cottage to us," Cathy and Chris said. "Oh! My goodness, these flowers are gorgeous, and I love chocolates, they are my sinful delight," Jenny remarked. "Enjoy the chocolates and flowers; we will see you tomorrow," Chris commented.

Cathy and Chris celebrated that evening with a steak dinner at the hotel restaurant; they hurried back to their room to start packing their belongings and got their money out of the safe. The next morning. they opened a bank account with a thousand dollars; Chris found out they had safety deposit boxes and put most of the money there. They kept ten thousand dollars to place in the floor safe at the cottage; Jenny showed them the built in safe in the floor and could change the combination so they felt the money would be safe there.

They were finally settled into their new place and could not be any happier. Now, it was time to get back to searching for their parents on the microfiche. They tried to be the first to arrive when the library opened and the last to leave. Every night when the library closed, it was just another day that they had no sign of finding anything on their parents' murders.

They loved their independent life, as it was and Jenny was an-added-bonus; they could not believe how sweet, and amazing she was. She usually invited them to go to the movies with her on Fridays or Saturdays and she introduced them to their first bag of popcorn which was added to their list of snack foods they loved. They had never been to a movie theater; so, this was an experience they were thoroughly enjoying. Jenny invited them over for dinner on Sundays and never questioned them much about their lives. They both had made sure they found out as much about Holland, Michigan and Ventura, California in case she or anyone else ever asked them about the place. If anyone asked them what schools they went to, they would say they were home schooled by their parents.

After living in the cottage for a year, Chris asked Jenny to teach him how to drive. She was happy to oblige him and said he was a courteous and cautious driver. Jenny took him to buy a car and he paid cash for a second- hand car that was two years old. Chris enjoyed driving, he took Jenny and Cathy on mini-trips and loved exploring California and its beauty. He felt free and in charge as he drove them places, he never knew that he and Cathy would ever have the life they were experiencing; it was always at their fingertips but never imagined it being there.

After living in the cottage for three years, Jenny treated them like she did her own children and they found out first-hand what it was like to be loved. She would have birthday celebrations for Chris and Cathy, with several presents to unwrap, take them to dinner and bake them beautiful cake. They always returned the favor by Chris making a delicious dinner for her and Cathy baking Jenny's favorite birthday cake. They were introduced to great celebrations and holidays; Jenny had been the one to generously invite them to her home for all of them. They loved their new-found life and being so lucky to meet and know her. When Christmas was introduced to them; they could not believe how magical and mesmerizing it was. They would go to Christmas tree lots with Jenny and their experience was overwhelming; the smell of the fresh cut trees, pine cones in baskets scattered throughout, and listening to beautiful Christmas music over speakers, while they picked out that perfect tree. They would go to department stores and choose beautiful ornaments and lights for their tree; then go back home and spend hours listening to Christmas music and decorating their tree. The first time they put up a tree, they would sit there for hours taking in the beauty of the glistening ornaments and ever sparkling multi-colored lights. Jenny brought life into them that they had never known existed and she was an honest, kind, and nurturing soul they had always been void of. She taught them how to play cards, lots of board games and how to dance and have fun at any given moment. Her three children came home for visits quite often and they were each a year a part in age and attended college in different states. They looked forward when the girls came home for a visit. They had learned to start trusting people and seeing goodness verses evil, that the later was what they had been accustomed to.

The entire time they lived in the cottage, they never had nightmares as they did when they were bound by fear being with the Crockets. Every night they went to bed, they were safe, happy and knew they were finally blessed with their new existence.

They tried to stay in good spirits knowing they would eventually get the answers they needed on the news clippings they had; but it was gnawing at their emotional state, looking day after day, month after month, and now it had been two years. They were extremely frustrated because they felt they would have found what they were looking for by now. The alternative they had was to go to the police; but they were worried that Chris could go to jail for setting fire to the house and the Crocket's; so, they decided to let that be in the past. Not knowing their true ages was requiring a strenuous effort on both-of-them. As far as they could remember, from when they were at Dawson's, they remembered him telling someone on the phone he was taking care of them for a few days, and they overheard him tell someone they were seven and eight. That is all they had to go by, but they never asked him if he knew when their birthday was.

They had learned so much from Jenny while living in her cottage and had many conversations of what it would have been like to have a mom like her. They never knew anyone could be as nice as her and hoped the rest of their life they would meet more people like her. They had met quite a few of her friends and relatives and they seemed pleasant as well. When anyone asked them where they worked, they said their parents got killed in an auto accident and left them enough money to live on without working. They said they were doing research at the library because they were contemplating writing a book on the history of the California Missions.

One day, after they had breakfast, they ran out the door hoping they had not missed their bus that took them near the library. They had just made it by a minute. Once they arrived at the library, they started their normal routine and had always hoped that would be the day they would find the clippings from their parent's murders. After looking through the news clippings for about four hours, Cathy was getting hungry and asked Chris if he was ready to have lunch and he said sure. He said he would keep looking through the microfiche while she got their food across the street at their favorite delicatessen; he would meet her outside at one of the benches.

Cathy was gone for quite some time; the delicatessen was extremely busy that day, Chris was getting hungrier by the minute and was ready to stop researching through the microfiche. He decided he would stop and join Cathy after he looked a few more minutes. Chris went to the next screen; he suddenly spotted the photo of the news clipping on Cathy's parents' murder. There it was in black and white, her parents' names, where they were from and where they had been and what their two-year-old daughter's name was who was never found......

PART THREE

The shipments arrived, everyone sorted out their lives from the boxes and crates and within two weeks, pretty much everything was in its place and looked great in the main house. Joseph, Nina, and their children loved their new home so much and they bought a few accessories; but needed to go furniture shopping for the living, dining, and bedrooms. For the last two weeks they had been living in the main house with the Albanese's until they purchased beds.

One morning after they got the children off to school Jezalee was having breakfast with the staff and said she had a great idea. "This could be dangerous." Said Joseph. She asked them to get their walking shoes on because she was taking the three of them furniture shopping on her dime. "Absolutely not! You have been overly generous all these years," Nina commented. Helga seconded the motion. "Well, I am not taking no for answer; it is my gift to the three of you for coming to America. Plus! Without you three, all these years, my life would have been turned upside down with my career and helping Paul run our businesses and raising three children," Jezalee replied. You may as well get ready to go because we four are going furniture shopping whether you want to or not!" As Jezalee smiled and said. Nina and Joseph looked at one another then at her. "Let's go, you will never let us hear the end of this if we do not agree," Joseph said with a bit of humor. They hugged one another then walked out the front door. They were would to be gone most of the day and part of the evening looking at furniture and accessories. Jezalee had left a note for Adrienne to let her know she was-in-charge of the children until she and the staff got back from furniture shopping. She had their dinners already prepared and needed to be heated up and a salad was in the refrigerator. Jezalee said she would call her later to make sure everyone had their homework done.

It had been a great and quite satisfying day for Joseph, Nina, Helga and Jezalee because they managed to find some beautiful furniture, and accessories. Most of the furniture was custom made pieces and would take a month to arrive; everything else would be delivered in about a week. The staff was beyond appreciative of what Jezalee, and Paul did for them. After they finally finished shopping, Jezalee took them out to dinner at a seafood place and they talked about their children and how well adjusted they were in school. They were thankful that Mallory had given Jezalee the names of the best custom furniture and specialty shops to check out. Joseph and Nina could hardly wait for their children to see the bedroom furniture, which would be delivered in a week.

Joseph and Nina never thought they would be living in America; but was excited over the move. They were especially happy knowing that they had learned English right along with the children while they had been tutored along with Astrid and the Albanese children. When they applied for work with the Albanese's they never thought of the positions as long term; however, they paid them well and when they started having children, the sky was the limit as far as Paul and Jezalee were concerned. They had been extraordinarily blessed with great wealth between the two of them and wanted their staff and their families set up with a retirement fund and eventually set up a trust fund for each child and would pay for their college education. They, of course! Did the same financial set up for Helga and her daughter Astrid. She left home a year ago for Chicago and loved college. Both families would receive a bonus every year due to their loyalty to Paul and Jezalee, who they considered family from day one. They started out giving their staff 30-day vacations and after a few years they increased it to 45 days, and there were numerous times all the staff would join the Albanese family on vacation in addition to their regular vacation days. They would receive a Christmas bonus in November and their yearly increase in salary, which was substantial.

Jezalee went over one day and let Joseph and Nina know that she was expanding their house from 3,000 square feet to probably 6,000. She asked them if they prefer a ranch or two-story home. She had worked on both scenarios, and they could choose what they would prefer. There was certainly enough land to build the extra 3,000 square feet or they could choose the two story. Nina let Jezalee know she did not need to go to all that expense because the house was a nice size for them. "I want you and the children to have more room;

especially as they get older," Jezalee said. "I see your point; I just did not want you to think you need to do it for us to be comfortable; because it is a beautiful home as it is," Nina replied. "You and Joseph have been with us before you had your children, Paul, and I always wanted the five of you to have everything you deserve," Jezalee commented. "That is so kind and generous," Joseph added. "You must know how much the five of us love and adore you; this is us paying it forward for you to have a home that you can have for the rest of your lives," Jezalee remarked. "I do not know if you remember the conversation Paul and I had with you several years ago when we said you could choose to live on the estate when you retire; or would buy or build you a house wherever you wanted to live," Jezalee reminded them. "We both remember the conversation and when you mentioned that to us, we thought! Who are these two and where did they come from?" Nina smiled and laughed. "You are aware most people are not like you and Paul?" Joseph responded. "Paul and I have never understood people who have money and do not let others be benefactors if they have been a big part of their lives," Jezalee replied. "With that said! Paul and I may be divorced; but we agree that you, your children, Helga, and Astrid will always be a part of our family and we will always be there for you," Jezalee said. "You know how much Joseph and I love you all and have been so blessed and fortunate to be a part of your staff and certainly feel like family," Nina happily commented her with her thoughts. "Thank you dear! We all love you too! I was just thinking! You and Joseph can look over my sketches and maybe you want the children to be a part of it also; but if you want the floor plan to be different than what I have here, make notes and I will look-over any changes with you in a few days," Jezalee said.

Jezalee had masterfully decorated her new home with extraordinary taste. She had an eye and instincts for design; preferring her home grandly scaled with beautiful and unique surroundings. She was attracted to an entrance of a home; a first impression would set the tone of what was yet to come throughout the home. Jezalee was most comfortable with mixing and matching unique, unconventional, and whimsical patterns with strong, vibrant colors, and touches of pastel accents where appropriate for her taste of balancing out a room. She loved filling her home with old, new, whimsical, and sophisticated accessories that she had purchased on her many travels over the years. Jezalee had been obsessed with old-world elegance; but she invariably added new world touches here and there to give a room full dimension. She loved mixing rather extravagant pieces with inexpensive gems she would find. Jezalee had quite a collection of works of art and objects that created a warmth which was displayed throughout her home and placed where they would make a statement. She never understood people referencing a room that was sparse as "less is more"; it is quite contradictory. "All that is "more", is the space that is not filled in a room. Jezalee loved having color surrounding her and knew how to expertly display and mix pattern on pattern. She used the finest of materials on all her sofas, chairs, drapes, bedding, and wherever else material was needed.

Have such a large estate with so many bedrooms, she was able to design the guest bedrooms in different and unique styles from the next; half of them were in colorful palettes and the others were in pastel, white or ivory. She had finally finished the interior and exterior of the entire estate and was thankful that was exactly how she visioned it would be when she purchased it.

Helga's remodeling was complete, she had 3,000 Square feet and was overwhelmed by how beautiful everything turned out. She had her own intimate paradise and could not wait to get her new furniture out of storage and start the decorating process. She had Jezalee help her decide where things looked best, and as usual, she perfected space better than anyone could.

Nina, Joseph, and their children were so happy coming to America. Their remodeling turned out more than what they hoped for. They now this amazingly gorgeous, spacious, two-story home with 6,000 square feet, six bedrooms and seven bathrooms, they were overjoyed at the expansion. They were happy that Jezalee had insisted they put in an elevator in case they chose to live there when they retired. The movers got their new furniture out of storage, and they were now finished with decorating with some help from Jezalee.

Two weeks later, Helga had invited Nina, Linda, Nell, Jezalee and Mallory over for lunch and wanted them to see her place. She finally had it completely decorated. When they took the tour, they were so impressed how the addition looked as if it had been a part of the original structure and Helga had decorated it beautifully. Helga loved her new place and was so excited for her daughter Astrid to see it when she came home for Christmas. She went with a colorful palette to accent all her winter white furniture which was sensational. After the four gals ate lunch, Helga opened the French doors that led out to the pool, patio, and the gazebo; it was such a gorgeous day, they sat outside, and Helga brought out dessert and drinks and they sat and chatted for a while. Jezalee had an oil painting of Helga and her daughter for her bedroom, and a beautiful oil painting to go in her dining room. She also had an oil painting of Astrid for her bedroom when she came home from college. Helga, of course! Loved the paintings and could hardly wait for her daughter to see them.

A week later, Nina and Joseph had Helga, the Albanese's, and O'Malley's over for dinner, then they took a tour of the house. The children insisted they see their rooms first and were decorated beautifully for the girls and handsomely for their son. Joseph Jr. said his sisters had too much foo-foo girly stuff in their room. Of course! The girls said his room looked like a dungeon with dragons everywhere; they thought how disgusting! The rest of the home was beautifully decorated with primary colors, plants filling the room in abundance and right above their gorgeous living room sofa was an oil painting, that exquisitely fit in to the rest of the décor, and it was a gift from Jezalee. She had a portrait painted of the family and it was hanging above the fireplace. She also had surprised their children with a personal oil painting of themselves, which was near and dear to them; they went wild with excitement when she presented them to the children.

All the children, including Nina and Joseph's, were acclimated to their new schools and since they knew English fluently, it made adjusting so much easier. The classmates they had met, loved their Italian and French accents; so, they did feel self-conscious. Mallory's children made sure they introduced them to all their friends so they would have a good start in knowing a few people starting out in a new school. Jezalee was thrilled that the transition had been easier than she anticipated.

Jezalee had decided to invite the O'Malley's for Thanksgiving since Mallory was planning a Christmas party. Everyone in the two households were coming. Nell, Helga, Mallory, and Jezalee cooked and baked for three days and danced and sang their way through all the prep work that needed to be done, before Thanksgiving Day. Bob and his Family were going back East and Nell, after she has early Thanksgiving with Jezalee's family, Ronan is picking her up and she will spend the rest of the day with him and his children.

Mallory wanted to have a Christmas Party mainly for Jezalee to meet more new people; she invited 500 guests and knew it was a big undertaking. Any other person would be overwhelmed by inviting so many guests but not Mallory, she was in her element. She asked Jezalee, Helga, Nell, Nina, and Linda to come over one day during the weekend to add some recipes to the party's menu. The caterer always liked adding a few of their client's special recipes for their event. They unanimously chose five appetizers, and two entrees. This was going to be the social event of the year and Mallory wanted everything perfect. She was delighted the ladies helped her with one decision she needed help on.

Mallory was so impressed how Jezalee had taken the bull by the horns and laid the foundation for her roots to grow and prosper in San Francisco. The children and Jezalee were well adjusted to their new life and did not regret leaving Paris. She knew it could not be easy going through the divorce and picking up their entire lives in one country and replanting them in another; however, things were working out better than she could have ever imagined.

With the Christmas Party just three weeks away, Mallory and Jezalee went shopping for their gowns. Mallory, of course! Knew all the shops, department stores, and dressmakers in the Bay Area. After a week of searching for just the right gowns to wear, they were getting discouraged because they could not find what they were looking for. They spotted a new shop and decided to go in and see what they had available. To their surprise! Remy was a new local dress designer and were impressed with everything she showed them. Jezalee chose an emerald-green velvet gown and Mallory's was black shantung silk. Remy also had a large selection of tea length dresses which the girls loved. They were so excited to wear the new designers amazing dresses and would get the word out about her wonderful collection of clothes.

Mallory hid her new gown because she did not want David to get a glimpse of it before the party; she wanted it to be a complete surprise. He had bought her the most exquisite necklace, bracelet, and earrings for their last Anniversary, so she had bought a black gown specifically to match her jewelry. David had designed the jewelry himself and carefully chose the finest rubies, black onyx, and white diamonds. These were Mallory's favorite gems and stones and when she tried on the shantung silk gown with the jewelry, she knew it was the perfect black dress to show off her exquisite jewelry.

. Mallory and David met in college at Columbia University at a pep rally. It was one of those fairytale courtships and they were still living their dreams together. David was from old money but wanted to prove to his family and himself that he could make it on his own. He never asked for a penny from his parents and paid his way through six years of college. He had gotten several scholarships, plus several jobs during his college days and managed to fit a full schedule of classes. He took any job he could handle, which was mainly assistant librarian, messenger boy, custodian, and waiter. He made most of his money once he was old enough to be a bartender. David's family wanted to financially pay for his education; however, he insisted that if he were to make it in the business world, he would have to be a self-made man. Even though David attended college without his parents help, they had taken the money they would have put towards his education and opened an account to give it to him later if he would ever agree to it. They ended up giving it to David and Mallory as a wedding gift. When he and Mallory received the five hundred thousand dollars, he was quite embarrassed but knew that it would be an insult to his parents if they did not accept the gift. He finally realized he needed to accept the generous gift and be gracious about it; his father had worked hard for his financial success and David knew that it meant the world to his parents that they had money to give their children. David and Mallory ended up buying their first house in the elite Pacific Heights area of San Francisco and lived there until all three of their children were of school age. They decided not to sell the house, so they had rented it out all those years.

David's sister, Davina lived in Australia and the family never saw her much. She ran a huge corporation and was very much a loner of sorts. She did not like traveling; so, if someone wanted to see her, they had to come to her part of the world. Davina was two years older, never been married and stayed pretty much to herself. She was highly educated and loved her family; but once she had gone on a trip to Australia; she knew she had found her oasis. David and Mallory tried to go over to see her every other year or so and she was a great hostess. Their parents loved going over there and they would usually stay month.

Mallory was from a poor family, but she worked hard to receive scholarships. After her first year in college her dad, Thomas got hurt on the job due to a defective machine which he tragically lost his right hand. The Manufacturing Company settled out of court, they granted him twenty million dollars; it changed the Mc Neal's lives forever. Mallory's dad was right-handed; so, he had extensive physical therapist to strengthen his left hand and was meeting with a psychologist to work through the trauma with loss of his primary hand.

Mallory and her brother Danny now had their education paid in full. They both were not forced to have odd jobs to survive through school any longer. Their dad knew they were very savvy, and he trusted them with some of the settlement money and they ended up investing in real estate and over the years they quadrupled their investment. While they were doing their part in helping increase the family wealth, their mom, Valerie, and their dad Thomas decided they wanted to open a restaurant and within the year they were so successful they started opening more and within five years they had a string of them from the East to West Coasts. They were so relieved they never had to worry about bill collectors ever again.

A week before Mallory and David's Christmas Party, Jezalee asked the O'Malley's over for a slumber party and said to include their staff. She knew how exhausted Mallory was from planning the party and it was time for her to relax and have some well-deserved family fun. The house was large enough; so, all the children were in one wing playing games and listening to the latest hit songs, while Mallory and Jezalee were in another wing of the house with complete silence. Jezalee asked the ladies if they would like to go see Father of the Bride and they unanimously said yes. Now! They just needed to ask the men if they would watch over all the children. When Jezalee asked them, they were all in; especially since they loved playing games with them. When the children found out the men were in charge-of the troops, as they called them, they were so excited because they loved having these three cool guys around.

After the ladies saw their movie, they went to Bunny's Diner and ordered six desserts. They were enjoying ladies, night out; after talking for a good two hours, they decided to have some added fun. Whenever a good-looking guy came in, they had to rank him from 1 to 10, then they had to go up to the guy that was a 10, no matter if he was with a gal or not. During that time, there were at least fifteen guys, ages probably between twenty to fifty years old. There were six that they considered a 10 or above ranking. They went up to the six men and handed them a ten-dollar bill and told them they were a ''10''with all around great looks. Even the gals that were with them thought it was a great game. Heck! Jezalee said, "who would not want the guy they are with, to be a ten. They had so much fun, and no one dissed them, so it was all good.

The girls arrived back at Jezalee's; they checked on the children and they were still having fun. When they walked in, the men and boys were dancing to the Bristol Stomp. They were in a contest to see who was, the best dancer, they had already crowned Bob the winner of the twist and it looked like he may win this one too. His son Manny passed out on one of the sofas and had not moved a muscle. They said he danced earlier and was so cute, then he went over to ask Janine and they danced together. "I hope you took photos because this is going to be one for the books! Photo albums, that is!'' Mallory commented. The girls had participated earlier, but they were having more fun watching the guys, dance.

The gals split everyone up and said it was time for bed and they had all the bedding lined up; guys on one end, girls on the other. The adults said good night to the children. Everyone was spending the night and Jezalee had already assigned a guest room for each couple.

The next morning the children were up early for breakfast. It was a free for all in the kitchen; each kid wanted something different; there was bacon sizzling in an iron skillet, pancakes were being made, one of the kids just wanted a piece of Helga's amazing lemon cheesecake; another kid wanted French fries from scratch, and the breakfast list did not end with just those dishes. Surprisingly, after the kids finished eating, they pitched in and cleaned the kitchen to where no one would ever think nine children had come in like lightning and had nine different breakfasts. It was all Alexander's idea; he told everyone that if they cleaned up the kitchen the way it was when they came in, his mom would more than likely let them have more sleep overs; there was a method to being responsible. And, they had a great time the night before and they agreed, it was not so bad cleaning up after all.

Jezalee had awakened, the children were finished in the kitchen and dressed for the day. It was around noon; she popped her head into see what the children were up to, and it was quiet; and they were just hanging out and challenging one another in different word games.

Jezalee went to the kitchen and started preparing a nice breakfast for the adults. Mallory and the rest of the ladies walked in while she was in the middle of brewing some tea and coffee. "Hi there! I hope you ladies are having a fine morning?" Jezalee said. They said they felt great. "How about yourself?" Helga said. Nina said they should do this more often. "I agree! What smells so delicious? Mallory replied. "I have Italian basil, tomato, quiche baking in the oven; they will be ready in thirty minutes." Jezalee said with a thank you to Mallory. While Jezalee was cooking up sausage and bacon, making waffles, fried potatoes and putting together fruit cups, the rest of the adults started coming into the kitchen. The ladies asked if they could help and she kindly said, "No way! I want you gals to relax and watch me slave away," Jezalee replied. As they were sitting around the kitchen table, Jezalee thanked the ladies for a great evening together and the men for stepping in and keeping the children entertained. They each said it was a wonderful evening and they would want more get togethers, like that.

Alexander popped in to see how the adults were doing, he took a couple of photos and said, "I do not get it." "What don't you get?"

Jezalee said. "This is such a great photo, and I am telling you none of our friends that have staff members working and living with them have never had a meal with their families, they do not know their first names, the staff must eat in the staff quarters, and they certainly would never sit at the same table, or have dance contests, or go to the movies together," Alexander commented. "Your friends and their parents do not know what they are missing, and they are very narrow minded. Right here! Right now, is what life is all about, sharing and caring for one another; there is not a person sitting at this table that I would not take a bullet for and none of you ever forget that. I do not say that lightly either; I know how much each person brings to the other's lives and that is the best gift you can give and receive. You are such a fine young man to notice how people around you can make a difference in our lives," David spoke from his heart. They just sat there as Alexander said bye and went upstairs. "Wow, between Alexander and you, David, I think we could have a great President and Vice President of America in-the-near-future," Bob said with sincerity. They clapped and kept eating; but once they were done, they realized what an inspirational young man Jezalee had. "Thank you! The children and I do discuss such matters and they are concerned about how we live in this society and do not comprehend how some people are shoved aside like they do not matter." Commented Jezalee.

Mallory was attending to last-minute details for the Christmas Party; David was home on vacation and was helping wrap presents to put under the trees for their guests. They wanted everyone who came to their soiree to leave with a small token of their appreciation. They had finally wrapped the last present; all five hundred were sat under the fifteen and twenty-foot trees that were throughout their palatial estate.

The days flew by and here it was just two days before the biggest social event of the year. By now, everyone had gotten their clothes for the elaborate occasion and were waiting for the last-minute things to take care of, such as manicures, pedicures, hair, and make-up done by professionals.

The caterers, florist, DJ, bakery, extra lighting crew, valets, and extra security had come to the estate few days ahead to make sure they knew where and when to go to the areas they would be working or delivering to. Mallory checked off the vendors after she them met individually.

Mallory was relaxing, having a cup of tea with Nell, when the phone rang; "Hello! "Mallory said. "Well! Hello! my darling, how are you?" David said. "Fine Honey, where did you get to?" Mallory asked. "Oh! I decided to talk to Santa to make sure I had all my shopping done for Christmas," David answered. "Well, do you?" Mallory asked with a smile on her face. "Yes! Finally, and by the way, I found that jacket Adam wanted so badly," David happily said. "Great! He will be thrilled. Honey, thanks for taking care of that," Mallory said. "Hey! What is a guy like me good for if I cannot run around and take care of a few things to please my beautiful wife!" David replied. "That is so true, my love. Will you be home soon?" Mallory remarked. "Probably in about an hour, the traffic is bumper to bumper," David said sadly. "Well! Just so you know, it is just you and me tonight," Mallory said with enthusiasm. "He perked up when he heard that! Really! Where are the children going?" David asked. "Sleepovers at their friend's houses," Mallory answered. "You know what that means, an extra romantic evening, just you and me, baby! You better be prepared because I am in a very romantic mood for you," Commented an aroused David. "I can hardly wait to get you undressed!" Mallory said with love making in her thoughts. "Well! Hold that thought, get some soft classical music playing, dim the lights and light the candles, I am going to fly home over this traffic!" David anxiously replied. "I love you honey be careful driving and I will see you in an hour," Mallory said. "Love you more, as he is humming his favorite tune in the car," David replied.

The evening proved to be filled with lust, passion, and much affection at its highest degree. They always had pure love for one another; David and Mallory never tired of one another, they knew where each other's hot spots were, and they constantly proved their love for one another. As David gently held Mallory's breasts in the cup of his oversized hands, she put her arms around his muscular body and began to stroke his back ever so lightly. She knew that every time she touched his back a certain way, he got chills of rapture. He looked down at Mallory's beautiful face glowing from the dim lights and candles lit in the bedroom. Once they embraced,

David passionately began kissing her. Their tongues clung to one another's lust filled mouths, their bodies were on fire. They both slid down under the silk sheets and made love that night for hours. After they were both euphorically satisfied, they took a little rest then rolled out of bed. They walked into their luxurious bathroom David started running warm water in the tub as Mallory poured a few drops of vanilla essential oils in. She felt it with her hands and said she wanted to make it hotter while he lit the candles around the tub. They both loved the scent of vanilla in the tub when they wanted to relax. They soaked in the tub for about a half an hour, got out, dried off and headed directly back to their romantic setting in their bedroom suite. As they faced one another at their bedroom windows, they dropped their towels to the floor and went into one another's embrace and soft and slowly kissed as David ran his fingers through Mallory's silky, blonde, soft, thick hair. She placed both her hands at the nape of his neck and gently worked her fingers through his thick chestnut mane. David took Mallory's hand in his and walked her towards the king-sized bed; they felt the heat of each other's body, as they both traveled into a sexual ecstasy state one more time. David and Mallory moved their bodies with expertise precision, knowing their bodies' reaction to one another. That night, like so many other nights in their beautiful marriage, they fell asleep in one another's arms after making love.

The next morning David and Mallory woke up early, went out on their bedroom terrace; it was warmer than usual for December; they ate breakfast outside. David said he had some great news; there is a new employee I hired months ago and thought Jezalee would be a great match. At first Mallory was not too excited because Jezalee's divorce was not final and did not think she would be interested in meeting someone so soon. "It will not be a blind date; I will nonchalantly introduce them at the Christmas Party," David said. Okay! "I will go along with that; but it pretty much will look intentional," Mallory said. "What is his name and what does he look like?" Mallory asked. Well! "His name is Jim Stark, he is around 6'2'', sandy colored hair with blue eyes; he is a very good-looking man and all the women in the office swoon over him every time he enters a room," David replied. "What does he do at the company?" Mallory asked. "He was hired as our international consultant," David answered. "Has he ever been married?" Mallory asked. "Yes, unfortunately his wife and son died in a boating accident off the Atlantic Coast," David sadly answered. "Were they alone on the boat?" Mallory asked. "Yes! I guess his wife was a sailor at heart, but the boat capsized, and they both drowned," David said. "Oh! My, that poor man! When did this happen?" Mallory asked. "About three years ago," David answered. "How tragic! Lives lost too soon!" Mallory sadly commented. "I know, it is difficult to comprehend such a loss. I feel so sad for him!" David remarked. "I know, I do too! This might be just what the doctor ordered for both Jezalee and him," Mallory said. "We will soon see!" David remarked. "I sure hope so, because I know Jezalee has been so sad for such a long time," Mallory commented. "Well, let us keep our fingers crossed and hope for the best with these two." David remarked.

The day had finally arrived; Jim would be introduced to the lady he had followed in magazines for a few years. He knew that the O'Malley Christmas Party was the ideal time to meet Jezalee. He was thankful, he had overheard David talking to his wife about wanting to introduce him to Jezalee. If they had not set that in motion, he would have managed to pick her out of the crowd and introduce himself.

Before Jim got ready for the party, he was thinking how far he had gone in his life to get to where he was at that moment in time. As a child, he never got the opportunity to read much and had always been curious about so many things. When he arrived in New York, he did not need to work because his dear friend Deanna's parents insisted on paying his rent in an upscale apartment, and by not having to pay-rent he had enough money as-long-as he was frugal. When he spotted the Manhattan Library, a few blocks away, he decided to check it out. It was overwhelming at first, but he wanted to read anything he could get his hands on. Jim became obsessed and realized how many things he enjoyed reading about. When he was not in his apartment he would constantly be at the library or at his apartment reading until he would fall asleep. He started reading books for knowledge, took notes and would study law, history, economics, etc. Even though he was doing most of his reading to learn, he also loved to escape into books of magic and crime novels. During his journey through books, he went over to the children's section and was inquisitive what types of stories they had for young children. Jim wanted the feeling of what it would be like to be a child; so, he started with the nursery rhymes, Dr. Seuss, The Velvet Rabbit, and the list continued until he pretty much read every child's book they had on the shelves. After his traveling back in time, he tried to place himself sitting on his mother's lap while she read all these extraordinary stories to him. Jim always wondered if his parents had not gotten murdered, if they would have been a great mom and dad, he was curious if they would have loved him the way he sees how his friend Deanna and Eric show love to their children. He wondered if his dad would have been athletic and maybe could have taught him how to play sports. His questions in his mind about his parents were endless and was curious what they looked like; were they madly in love, did they go to church, had they gone to college? He knew he would never know!

Here he was in San Francisco, living in a high-rise building, in an expensive penthouse, working for David at his Import-Export business, and would finally get to meet the woman of his dreams. Jim proceeded to the hidden compartment at the paneled wall and wanted to look at Jezalee on the covers of several magazines; he became interested after he read the articles on her. He was obsessed after seeing her photos, reading about her, and knowing she had just moved to San Francisco; divorced woman with three children. Nothing would prevent Jim from meeting and knowing her; he deserved someone like her. He was willing to move from his great place in New York to pursue her in San Francisco. Jim knew eventually he would get something out of all those magazine articles he read at the New York Library. The first time he went through the magazine rack at the library, grabbed about a dozen and started thumbing through them; was curious about articles in the magazines and sat there reading all of them. Some of the articles were interesting, some he did not understand; and others were boring. Since he had gotten to New York and found this whole new world of books with all the subjects anyone could read and learn; he realized how he and his dear, sweet friend Deanna were so sheltered from the world of knowledge. He loved spending every waking moment at the library; it was this haven of words that kept him coming back. He had tried so many times to forget how he and Deanna had lived as children and all they endured; here he was Jim Stark, got the career of a lifetime, would start dating one of the most stunning women in the world, and all he needed to do now was marry her.

Jezalee woke up and was in a fantastic mood; she was thrilled about the party and the people that would be attending. She had never been to such a huge party hosted by close friends and so special to her. David and Mallory were an exceptional couple, and their hosting would be a night to remember. For a moment there Jezalee was thinking back to all her Christmases in Paris, Italy, and New York. The Christmases she had in New York as a child were forever embedded in her childhood memories; the throngs of people coming from all over the world to Rockefeller Square to be mesmerized by the tree lighting ceremony. She would sit and admire the advanced skaters before she went out on the ice. She loved the pretty outfits her mom always bought her every winter season; but her favorite part of Christmas was when her parents took her to see the department store windows decorated with Christmas scenes; especially where Santa was waiting for the next child in line to sit on his lap. Jezalee would wait patiently until she was the next child to sit on the jolly man's lap to tell him everything she wanted for Christmas.

When Jezalee started college, she met Paul and was thrilled that he loved Christmas as much as she did. They loved their Manhattan and Tuscany Christmases; they spent half their Christmas holidays with each of their families. Once they moved to Paris, Jezalee parents frequently visited them. She had been away from the states for so long and was happy getting ready for the children and her to have their first Christmas in San Francisco. She finally felt at home in the Bay Area and never wanted to live anywhere else; she was happy her children had embraced life here as much as she had. Jezalee missed working at the Louvre and Notre Dame; but kept in touch with the people she worked with from both extraordinary places. When she left, Jezalee made a point to let her co-workers know they could always call her, if they needed her expertise in anything that came up.

Jezalee had been disappointed her dear friend in Paris, Marilyn De Beaux, was not able to come for Christmas; her sister was ill, and her brother-in-law needed help taking care of their four children during the holidays. So, she opted for New Year's Eve if her sister was on the mends. Marilyn had been born and raised in the states; she and Jezalee had met in Paris at an Art Gallery opening; they were instant friends and had known one another for thirteen years. Marilyn had never been married but led quite an interesting life with her tales of adventure as a renowned Archaeologist. She was world famous due to some of her findings over the years and the books she published on the history of her excavations. She had also written four children's books; Jezalee's children were so excited when they each received their copies. They loved the part in the books when they said she would remove the earth carefully and systematically from an area; in order, to find buried remains.

Jezalee quickly embraced the idea she had better stop daydreaming and get out of bed. She had a lot to do, and it was not going to get done lying in bed. While she was making herself a cup of coffee, Adrienne had come in to join her. Jezalee apprised her she was hoping the four of them could go shopping. "Why mom?" Adrienne asked. "I want to buy the O'Malley's something special for being instrumental in us getting settled," Jezalee answered. "Can we let Alexander and Jessica sleep and just you and I spend the day together?" Adrienne asked in a pleading voice. "That is a wonderful idea; I will ask Helga to see if she will be here to watch over them," Jezalee answered. Just as she was walking to her wing of the house, Helga was coming down the hallway towards her. She had just gotten back from the hair salon and did not have anything else to do. Jezalee wanted to make sure she did not have to leave the house because she did not want to interfere in her plans before the party. She looked at Helga's new hairdo and told her how exceptionally beautiful she looked. Helga was around forty-five and was a striking woman of German-Italian descent; Jezalee had seen her dressed up and her hair was always so pretty, but the new hairstyle was the best she had ever seen her wear. "Helga, your hairstyle makes your gorgeous brown eyes electrifying," Jezalee commented. As she blushed, she thanked Jezalee for the compliments. "I am leaving a note for the children to make their beds take and take a shower. They can heat up their breakfasts in the oven, and just relax until the party. Hopefully, this shopping expedition will not take too long," Jezalee said. "She took another look at Helga and said, wait a minute! You are supposed to get your hair done with us; did you decide to go to the salon instead?" Jezalee asked. "No! I wanted to practice on my hair and when they show up, they will see how I want mine style," Helga answered. "I really do not know if they can top what you managed to do but it is nice to get our hair washed and professionally done on occasion. That is a great idea to show them exactly what you want for the party. Men! Watch out! Here comes our beauty queen," Jezalee commented.

Jezalee called Nina to see if she and Joseph needed to run any errands before the party. She said Joseph was going to take care of their children while she went to pick up the hostess gift she bought for the O'Malley's; afterwards, Nina was going to relax until she met up with her and the rest of the ladies, getting their hair and nails done. Jezalee let Nina know she and Adrienne were going shopping and would be back in a couple hours.

Jezalee and Adrienne walked around town, thoroughly enjoying the Christmas carolers and Santa in the store window at Macy's and the hustle and bustle of the shoppers on the streets and in the shops. A couple of hours had gone by and no luck in finding that special gift Jezalee was looking for. She was about to give up because they were running out of time and needed to get back home and get ready for the party. As they were slowly walking down the street, suddenly Jezalee spotted a small out of the way shop and told Adrienne she wanted to check it out. Adrienne commented, "Don't you think it is a waste of our time, the shop is so dinkie?" Adrienne commented. "No! It looks like a fun place to browse around; besides, it has a great name "Curiosity Stops Here;" just the mere name intrigues me enough to go in to check it out," Jezalee remarked. Adrienne started browsing and spotted some great artwork, fine antique jewelry, one of a kind hand painted vases and exquisite China. As they looked around, Jezalee's mind was wandering into the past to the time she ventured into little, out of the way shops with her parents; those were such fond memories. The three of them always found some great little gems and some extraordinary artwork, they still have displayed throughout their home.

Suddenly, Jezalee eyes saw a magnificent hand painted peach vase with a man and woman standing, holding hands; they were surrounded by lush trees, flowers, and other intricate details over the entire vase. She realized the couple looked like David and Mallory; they had the same color of hair, and their heights were proportioned to theirs, then they spotted the two doves flying over their heads. Jezalee asked the shop owner if she could see it closer; he said he would place it on top of the mahogany table it was near. He called for his son to come to the front to help him; they placed the four-foot vase on the table and Adrienne and Jezalee got a closer look and were amazed at the beauty of the designs. Adrienne looked closer, Oh my gosh! Mom, they look like David and Mallory posed for this vase. I am so excited you found something so beautiful for them. The shop owner, Mr. Chow said, "That is wonderful! Maybe they posed in another life because the vase is close to two hundred years old. Jezalee said she would take it; the shop owner said it is a little pricey, fifteen thousand dollars; she smiled and said, it does not matter, it is for two very-special people in our lives. He looked at Jezalee, "You are a most generous friend." Mr. Chow remarked. "Thank You! Mr. Chow they are a special family to us," Jezalee remarked. She asked him if he needed cash, check or credit card. "Credit card is good," Mr. Chow answered. Thank you! Mr. Chow, and handed her card over to him. He then asked her where she wanted it delivered; she gave him the O'Malley's address and indicated she would meet Kevin there at the entrance to their home if 7:00 p.m. was good for him. Jezalee gave Mr. Chow her phone number to call if there was a change of delivery time. His son Kevin went to get the original shipping box and carefully wrapped it before placing it in the box. As Jezalee and Adrienne waited for Mr. Chow to ring up the sale, she thanked him for having such lovely and very-special items in his store and when she had time to leisurely browse; she would come back. He told her it was a pleasure meeting her and Adrienne and blessed the rest of their day.

Once Jezalee and Adrienne arrived back home, they had four hours before the hairdressers would arrive. While they were gone all morning, Mallory had called and left a message with Helga for Jezalee to call her when she got back from shopping. After Jezalee went to say hi to the children she asked Helga if she would like to join her for a cup of coffee or tea and Helga said sure! They both sat down in the kitchen and talked for a while. Jezalee got out some cookies she baked, and they had them with their coffee. She was anxious to see Helga's gown that just arrived from Bergdorf-

Goodman; Helga tried the gown on, and Jezalee said it was perfect! "Oh my! Helga, the gown is breathtaking on you," Jezalee. commented. "Why "Thank you" Dear, I really do love the dress, I had Astrid help me pick it out when she came for a weekend last month," Replied Helga. "Well! You could not have chosen a prettier gown; it is a sensational classic and will never go out of style," Jezalee said. "Did you see Nina's gown?" Helga asked. "No! What does it look like?" Jezalee curiously asked. "It is a smash hit as my mother used to say," Responded Helga. "I cannot wait to see her in it, I am sure she will be a knock-out," Jezalee said.

Jezalee called Mallory to ask if she needed the troops to come over to help-out. She told her everything was going smoothly and on schedule; in fact, she said she was going to take a nap until the hairdresser and nail lady showed up. You know, I think I am going to take a nap too; I got up so early this morning and all sudden my eyelids are heavy, and I want to look rested when we show up.

Morgan knew that the Albanese clan of ten would be the first to arrive so she let the rented doorman know, she would answer the door when they arrived then he could take over afterwards. He said he would be waiting in the wings and told her to just wave him over when it was time for him to take over the reins. Morgan had only been at the door for a few minutes, and she saw the limousine drive up. She opened the double doors, quickly ran down the stairs to greet everyone; as they piled out of the limousine, she hugged each person and said Merry Christmas. Just as they were getting out of the limousine, Kevin was in his van, delivering the vase; proceeded to get it out of the van and Jezalee approached him. Morgan walked down to meet Jezalee and was curious what was in the large, gold wrapped box. She let her know it was a special thank you gift for her parents. David and Mallory were in the house and had just finished talking to the caterer. They saw Jezalee and the rest of the clan and met them at the entry. The double doors were open, and they spotted the large box outside the door and were perplexed as to where that came from because they had not ordered anything. David and Mallory greeted everyone and asked Jezalee if she knew who dropped off the large box. "Yes, as a matter of fact! This is a gift from us to you. Where would you like Kevin and the men to temporarily set it?" Jezalee asked. Adrienne said whoever helps bring it in the house, be extremely careful because it is extremely fragile. The men made it up the stairs into David's den; he locked the door behind them. Jezalee thanked Kevin for helping them and he drove off. Mallory looked over at Jezalee, smiled and said, "What in the world! It is huge and extremely heavy!" Adrienne said, you will find out after the party is over, or whenever you are ready to open it.

Thirty minutes later Morgan waved for the doorman; he was Johnny on the spot; the doorbell was consistently chiming for the next several hours. People were pouring in like cattle; especially the first hour. Every corner in the house, and the three outside tents were filled-to-capacity. There were friends, immediate family, relatives from afar, teachers, and business associates. There were flash bulbs constantly going off; everyone wanted a photo taken next to the elaborately decorated trees throughout the estate and in the tent. The outdoor heaters did not seem to be necessary after all; the December night was a perfect temperature for an indoor-outdoor event.

David was so pleased at everything his wife had accomplished for this major event; he knew she was one of a kind. As he was looking at all the people that came, he thought of the evening he and Mallory had been to the biggest dance of their college year, rooms were packed, elbow to elbow, just like tonight. The dance certainly was not posh like their party, but the biggest difference was everyone at their party had touched their lives in some way. He looked over his shoulder and saw Jim Stark mingling with guests, he was currently talking with Morgan's history teacher. David wanted to make sure he tracked down Mallory so they could introduce Jim to Jezalee before the night was over. He spotted his wife, took her to a corner of the room and whispered he had seen Jim and it was time to find Jezalee before the night was over. Once Mallory met Jim earlier in the evening, she felt he was worth pursuing. David got Jim's attention; in the meantime, Mallory needed to find Jezalee, she hurried through the crowded rooms and found her talking with Nell. As the ladies kept talking, Mallory was getting nervous and knew she had to work fast to break up their conversation without being rude. She wanted to make sure Jim did not leave the party before he met Jezalee. Mallory made up an excuse that she wanted them to meet some of the ladies from the American Cancer Society and she pretended she was trying to find them amongst the crowd; little did they know, she knew they were in one of the tents dancing with their spouses. Mallory acted surprised when she could not find them but spotted David with Jim. She told the girls to follow her and see what David was up to. The three ladies walked towards the two men as they got closer Jezalee noticed how handsome the man was standing next to David. As Jim spotted Jezalee coming towards the two men, he was hoping she was not dating anyone. David introduced everyone and when he was finished Nell excused herself so she could round up her family. The four of them talked for about ten minutes then Mallory interrupted them and said she needed to excuse herself because she needed to oversee the food and drink situation. David put his arm around her small waist and said he wanted to grab a snack. Jim and Jezalee were alone, as anyone could be with a crowd of people surrounding them. Moment by moment it seemed as if the music was getting louder, so Jim suggested they go to a quieter area; they decided in-order-to talk they had to go in one of the tents or just be outside. As they walked out the front door, Jim walked a few steps behind her, then he extended his hand, lightly touching her lower arm just to let her know he was still following her lead. They made it outside, down the stairs to the side garden area where there were just a few people sitting; there were still chairs around the beautifully lit area due to the enormous Christmas tree that was decorated in the garden. Jim says, "Now, is this better?" "Sure! I can hear you, as they both laughed. She asked Jim how he liked working in David's company; he said it had been great and he is one heck of a boss. I also needed a big change in my life and coming out West was the best thing I could have done for myself. She asked him where he was from, and he said he was born and raised in Cape Cod and had a home there and a place in Manhattan. She said she had always wanted to go back to Cape Cod; she had remembered it well from when she was young, and her parents took her there. Jim asked her where she was originally from and she said Manhattan, then moved to Paris after she got married. Jezalee asked Jim how he liked New York? He said he loved it; but needed a change from the Cape and the Big Apple.

Over the course of the evening as they talked, she mentioned how thrilled she was to be back in the states. He said he never thought he would like San Francisco as much as he does. He found out about the position at David's company and thought maybe it would be a good fit for him and so far, it had been. He asked her how she knew David and Mallory; she told him they had met while they lived in Paris to get his division up and running. Our oldest daughters became friends while they lived there. We all became friends; my husband and I really had a lot in common with David and Mallory and we have been close, ever since. She explained how they ended up in San Francisco and said he was genuinely sorry she went through a divorce. Jezalee then asked him if he had ever been married and he said yes; I am a widower. Jezalee was embarrassed that she had asked him; but she had no idea that would be his answer. She looked at him and said how sorry she was for his loss and hoped that he was healing as well as he could. Jim expressed his appreciation and began to tell her that it was not just his wife he lost; his son died too! Jezalee eyes welted up with unexpected tears, she tried to hold them back for his sake, but they were uncontrollable. Jim looked into her beautiful emerald-green tearful eyes and said it was okay to cry. I cried for a solid year over their deaths then I knew I had to put myself together and try my best to go on with my life. He did not say how they both died, and she certainly was not going to ask him. By this time Jezalee heart was pounding as her eyes were affixed to his. He gently stood up and asked her if she would like to mingle in the crowd for a while. She said that would be great! As she got up, he took her hand in his, they walked slowly to the closest tent and went directly to the dance floor. Jim asked Jezalee to dance and for the remainder of the evening they were inseparable. David and Mallory spotted them out on the dance floor, they were pleased they had connected so well. "Well, Mr. Matchmaker, I think we have a match thanks to you, I hope you are happy now," Mallory said in the most complimentary way. "I am happy, Jim needs someone in his life probably more than Jezalee does; but if she is ready that is a win, win for them," David replied. Mallory smiled as she squeezed both her husband's strong hands. He kissed her on her sensuous red lips and said he was proud of himself and that she agreed for Jim and Jezalee to meet. They both felt they were a striking couple together and hoped there would be a date for them in the future.

At the end of a successful Christmas Party, Adrienne rushed over to her mom and asked, "Who was that hunk you were on the dance floor with?" Smilingly, but very nonchalant, Jezalee says, "Oh! He happens to work for David, he is a nice man." Adrienne rolled her eyes! "Mom, he looks like he is more than a nice man; I would call him a gorgeous hunk!" Yes! Her mom admitted he was attractive. "Really mom! Did he get your phone number?" A concerned Adrienne asked. "Yes!" I would never have given it to him if he did not work with David." Jezalee remarked. It was after 2:00 AM, all guests had left except the Albanese ten. Everyone left with a beautiful hand painted ornament, a holiday basket filled with goodies and a memory of a spectacular evening. A night filled with phenomenal food, specialty drinks, incredible desserts, great Christmas music and songs from the 50's to the current craze. Mallory thought it was only fair the children had their own tent, and it was a huge success. They had a dance contest and each person danced by themselves and one of Morgan and Adrienne's friends won first prize; she was so excited because she got a trip to Disneyland for her whole family; all expenses paid, including hotel and food. Second place was one of Adams' friends and he won one thousand dollars. Third place went to another one of Adams' friends who won five hundred dollars. All in all, the teenagers had a great time because they had a DJ specifically for the music they liked. They were served the same food the adults had, and Mallory added some of the children's favorites.

After the guests had left, excluding their children, staff, the Albanese's, and their staff; who would be staying over for a sleepover, David wanted to thank his incredible wife for putting on such an elaborate party; a lot went into the preparation, and she knocked it out of the park. Everyone he had the privilege to speak with at the party said it was the best party they had ever been invited to. He hoped everyone in that room had as much fun as everyone else seemed to have. They stood up and clapped for Mallory as she put her hands over her face. "You all are embarrassing me," Mallory quipped. She stood up and gave David a hug and said without the support of this incredible man at my side every day, I would never have been able to get it all done. Everyone clapped again and Mallory and David said, "That's enough you guys and dolls, we love you, and whomever wants to stay up all night, be our guests the bedrooms, family room and game room are ready for occupancy," Mallory added. All the children knew where their bedroom was, in the game room with all their bedding waiting for them, and there was plenty of bedrooms for the adults. They decided to stay, especially since there were leftovers from the party, and no one would have to cook in the morning.

Before they retired to their assigned rooms for the sleepover, Morgan asked if her mom and dad could open the mysterious large box that Jezalee bought as a thank you gift. David and Mallory asked whoever wants to watch them open their gift from the Albanese's, follow them into the den. They stood around as David and Mallory began to rip off the gold iridescent, paper wrapped around the gigantic box. Once they opened it, they realized they had to turn it a little on its side to begin to lift it out of the box. It took them a few minutes with the help of Adam and Alexander holding the bottom secure. They finally succeeded in getting the vase out of the box; they gasped with delight. Mallory and David were flabbergasted at such an extraordinary gift. "Wow, that is the most beautiful vase I have ever seen; but I really have not seen many." Morgan commented. They chuckled! Mallory asked David to turn on the overhead lights so they could see it better. Adrienne told them that the couple that were hand painted on the vase looked as if David and Mallory had posed for the hand painted vase. Everyone got closer to see the resemblance; they were in awe. "It is uncanny! Mr. Chow said the vase was hand painted by an Englishman and is over two hundred years old. You two must have posed for it in another lifetime," Adrienne commented. David and Mallory smiled, looked at one another; David says, "I knew you looked familiar the first time I saw you," they thought how cute! Mallory seriously then said, at first! "I thought you had it hand painted for us." This is beyond extraordinary! We will treasure it forever. "I think I want it to go in the foyer so people can see it as soon as they walk in the house. This gift is exceptional, but it is too generous!" Mallory commented. "If it was not for you and your family, I do not know how we would have gotten through some of the rough spots in the last six months; when I met you over a year ago in Paris, I knew then we would be lifelong friends, I just did not know we would be your neighbors. It has been a bittersweet time for us; but I would never have weathered through it without your support. This is a token of our appreciation; I did not realize how difficult it would have been bringing ten people over here and getting settled if not for your generous help. You all mean everything to all of us," Said Jezalee. "Since we are going to leave the vase in here tonight, I would feel more comfortable with the doors kept locked; I do not want such a lovely vase to get broken with so many guests coming and going. He looked over at Mallory to make sure it was okay with her. By all means! I will not relax until I find the perfect spot in the house, and it is secured down with earthquake proof material. You know me! As soon as I wake up tomorrow the first thing I am thinking of, is where I want to display it," Mallory said.

The O'Malley's and Jezalee talked for about half an hour after everyone else went to bed. Jim's name came up; Jezalee said he was nice, polite, and attractive. "I was quite embarrassed when he told me his wife and son died, I could barely keep it together; he said he had cried for about a year and knew he must go on with his life so he sold everything and did not want to work for a while; then once he knew that working would keep him busy, he got his resume out to different companies," Jezalee confessed. David said he had come at the right time, after Charles Dandridge getting killed by a hit and run driver. "He loves his job and San Francisco has grown on him," Jezalee remarked. Mallory perked up! "Let us get to the important part, did he get your phone number? "He did!" Jezalee replied. "Awesome! Did he tell you how his family died? Mallory asked. "No, I was not about to ask him," Jezalee answered. "The two of them were out on a boat and it capsized, and they both drowned," David sadly said. "Where was Jim?" Jezalee asked. "He was supposed to be with them but had a last-minute job needing attention," David answered. "This conversation was very much needed; but I am mentally drained and very sleepy," Jezalee stood up and gave them a hug, thanked them for introducing Jim to her! The party was such a smash hit! I don't think anyone could ever top this! Good night you two!

When David and Mallory went to bed, they were feeling rather good spirited after Jim and Jezalee had such a great time together. Mallory said, "Maybe this will help her forget about Paul. They both noticed each month she was away from Paul she spoke less and less about him. They knew Jezalee was upset over Paul's actions, but she still had strong feelings for him, that was undeniable.

The next morning, no one was at full speed, they lounged around in pajamas and did not go to Mass. "This is the first time we ever missed Mass on Sunday," Mallory said. "It is okay, but I am sure someone from the Parish will call us to see if we are all okay," David replied. "You are right, the call will come right after the last Mass of the day," Mallory commented. "How sweet is that? Checking up on you!" Jezalee said as she laughed. "We have been going there since before we got married; we are as they say, part of the furniture after all these years," Mallory remarked.

The rest of the day was filled with eating scrumptious leftovers and decadent desserts from the party and watching old movies. "You two never stop with being the great host and hostess, you two are quite a duo together," Jezalee said. "Why, thank you, that is so sweet of you to say. We love having people over and this place is big enough to accommodate a lot of people; that is why we bought it, we enjoy entertaining and people staying over," Mallory replied.

Jim had called Jezalee a few days after the party and asked her out; but she said it would have to be after the first of the year because she was busy. He said he would call her sometime after the first week of January. Jezalee wished him a Happy New Year, they cordially said their goodbyes and hung up. After Jim hung up, he was not pleased with the outcome of his call; he now had to be patient and not let this fester in his thoughts.

Christmas had come and gone; everyone was ready for the New Year to begin. Jezalees friend Marilyn had come for New Year's Eve and was able to stay a few extra days. The children always loved when she came for her visits because she always had such great stories to tell about her Archeology quests. They had a fun-filled visit with Marilyn, she was hoping they would find time to come back to Paris when school was out and stay with her for at least a week. She had so many artifacts to show them which would be a part of her next book.

It was the beginning of a new year, 1986; the O'Malley and Albanese families, had always believed in giving back so the four of them did a lot of volunteering and taught their children to be altruistic at an early age. The children knew the true meaning of lending a helping hand. They knew with the wealth their parents had, they would always donate money and would volunteer. The

Albanese children were excited to help-out at the Boys and Girls Club after school; but missed helping at their Paris family center, and the people that came through for assistance. The O'Malley children helped-out after school and most summers went to their Camp for a month or two. Both families enjoyed helping at a couple of the soup kitchens in the city, as well. They were thrilled that Jezalees children had joined them at the Club because they had been shorthanded for a long time. They were such a big help and all the boy and girls that came after school adored them as well as the O'Malley children.

Years ago, in Paris, Paul and Jezalee had bought an old building, remodeled it, and set up various rooms with new clothing, food to serve hot and cold meals and food to stock up on and take home, a library with a reading room, athletic rooms where families could play various sports, a board game room, a dance studio, a center for young mothers to feed, clothe and play with their babies-toddlers, and a room with a piano, drums, and other various musical instruments. etc. They wanted this to be a place where individuals or families could come, that were either homeless, lost jobs and/or needed a helping hand until they could re-enter society or the working force. Jezalee was successful, working tirelessly on fundraisers to keep the center up, and running. Initially, the Albanese family donated one million dollars and yearly gave five hundred thousand. It took a while to name the center; they decided on Centre Communautaire Familia de Paris. The Albanese children were in elementary school when they opened the center and Jezalee would take them there every weekend and have them help-out.

When Jezalee decided to move to America, it was with much regret she and her children would not be around to be a part of the daily activity that was going on at the center and be there first-hand to see the people walk-in without hope and knew they had a place to come to, to build their hopes and confidence up.

When the doors first opened at their center, they wanted to hire people that had lost their jobs and wanted to be gainfully employed. They had been so fortunate to find the right fit for the center and when Jezalee decided to move away; she knew she was leaving it in good hands with all the staff. Before she turned the reigns over to them, Jezalee indicated she would be back every month, and was only a phone call away.

Even though Jezalee and her children would not physically be at the center anymore; she would set up the fundraisers at first then turn them over to whomever she felt could take it over without losing their best benefactors. Once she chose the right person she would fly to Paris and have a meeting with the people that had been so loyal to her and Paul's cause.

Jim called Jezalee the second week in January and he asked her out and she accepted. They had a nice time and were going to set up a time to go out with David and Mallory at David's request. After the first date, Jezalee decided she wanted group dating. She was not sold on going on one- on-one dates; she felt uncomfortable. She let him know she preferred doing things in a group atmosphere and he said that was fine. They went to dinner, local plays, enjoyed going bowling and loved going to the movies with her children. They had a few dinner engagements with the O'Malley's and a few of Jezalee newly acquired friends. David and Jim liked golfing and they would also play some sports with the children.

The O'Malley's enjoyed Jezalee, and Jim's company; they socialized together and Jezalee felt comfortable going out with Jim with couples or in a group setting. Jezalee knew he seemed to be a nice man, that was currently enough for her; but she knew if she ever did get serious with anyone, she would want them to be of her faith because it was important to her. So far, there were two drawbacks with him, Religion and never mentioned his wife or son. Jezalee had a conversation with the O'Malley's, and they were puzzled by Jim never talking about his family also; there had been numerous occasions that he could have fit it in a conversation. Granted, they agreed, it was a painful subject; but most people than not, eventually would bring up their dearly departed.

Jim called Jezalee three weeks in advance; asked her if she and the children would like to go skiing up in Tahoe for the 4-day weekend that was coming up for them. He had checked with David earlier and he was assured his family would be up for snow, skiing, tobogganing, etc. Jezalee thought that was a great idea then called

Mallory to see if her staff would like to go because she wanted to ask hers as well. Jim called David back and they were looking forward to the up-and-coming weeks ahead; they both needed a breather from the constant traveling. Jezalee and Mallory confirmed with their staff, they were ready for some R and R themselves.

The children and adults could hardly wait for the four-day getaway; they had no idea that David and Jim had helicoptered to Incline Village, Tahoe, on the California side, to look at a few properties that a Realtor had faxed to David that were for sale. David had not been successful at renting one large enough for all of them so he decided it would be nice to have a place up in the mountains to take advantage of the summers on the Lake and winters on the ski slopes. The town was a quaint little village of 5,000 residents. There were several large cabins and some modern structures that David was interested in; until he found the perfect semi-modern structure with a cozy feeling and purchased it. The day the guys ventured up there, a rock star had put his house on the market with just what David was looking for, 9 bedroom, 11 bathrooms, with views of the majestic mountains and trees all around the property. The town itself was at 5,000 elevation and they would be at over 8,000 elevation which overlooked the entire town, and you could see the lake in the distance, through some of the giant redwood and pine trees. "This is quite a place to have up in the mountains,'' Jim commented. David was thrilled this beautiful house came on the market because he knew Mallory would be ecstatic over the purchase. He transferred the money into escrow and signed the papers and they said they could have his wife sign at their local bank, and have it notarized so the house could close escrow in a few days.

When David and Jim got back to San Francisco they called the ladies and asked them if they would be available to go out to dinner and they both said they did not have any other plans. The guys chose one of their favorite restaurants and arrived a few minutes before the ladies did. After Mallory and Jezalee got to the restaurant they spotted the guys over at their favorite table and join them. The first twenty minutes was deciding what to order then they talked about how their day went. Just before the food was served, David let Mallory and Jezalee know it was tough finding a rental this late in the season so David pulled out photos of the house he purchased but did not tell the ladies right away that they would be closing escrow on this beautiful house in a few days. David had about thirty photos and the ladies both gasped at the magnificent architecture and the interior. Both Mallory and Jezalee said who would ever rent out such a magical place? "That's the thing! They did not let us rent it out!" David answered. "Then why do you have the photos?" Mallory quizzically asked. He then reached in his briefcase and pulled out the escrow papers with both their names on them. She had to take a second look at the paperwork. "You actually bought this without consulting me?" Mallory commented. "I thought you would love it," David looked at her and quietly said. "I do love it; it's stunning! I cannot believe someone would sell this incredible house. Great find my dear!" Mallory smiled and said. "Well! It, kind of fell into my lap; a rock star owned it but has houses all over the world and he has never been able to spend much time here to really enjoy it," David happily said. "It was a fluke that we went up there today because I was going to do everything by phone and fax and decided it would be best to go in person. Can you believe it! It went on the market as I was talking to the Realtor!" David said. The rest of the evening was small talk, and they did discuss what they were planning to do once they got to Incline Village.

The Tahoe house closed escrow the next day; within three days everyone packed their skiing gear and off they went in a caravan fashion with three SUV's packed to the ceiling. Whomever had the least people in their vehicle had the most snow gear. No matter what vehicles they ended up in, they had fun listening to music and rocking out all the way up to Tahoe.

The night before the trip, Mallory had everyone over for dinner and they had spread out the photos of all the bedrooms and everyone had to choose straws as to what room they would be sleeping in. The children could hardly fall asleep, knowing they would be driving up to Tahoe and staying four days. Everyone got up extra early to have a quick breakfast and get on the road before the traffic got bad. Since everyone was going to be away from both estates, they had the security company assign two extra security guards at each home; David and Mallory had used them for years.

Once they arrived at the "Castle on the Mountain" as Alexander called it, they took a walk through the spectacular house and got all their luggage and skiing gear out of the vehicles and placed in the 6-car garage.

David informed the ladies they were off duty; he had hired a local chef to prepare breakfast, lunch, and dinner meals for everyone; he would come up at 8:00 a.m., 1:00 p.m. and 7:00 p.m.. They had boxed cold and hot cereals, canned goods in case they were snowed in, all types of juices, sodas, milk, and alcohol. David had a local meat market bring up a variety of steaks, seafood and poultry to be placed in the freezer if they ran out of food. The children were happy that David made sure there was every kind of snack food for those movie night evenings if someone was so inclined. "I hope someone brought chocolate to make Smores," Adrienne immediately inquired. "Do you really think I would forget your chocolate?" David said as he smiled. Adrienne laughed and said she would love him forever. He came over and gave her a big hug. He turned to the rest of the children and said he found out what their favorite things were and there was a bag of goodies for each of them with their name on it too.

They loved the house and especially thought it was extra special with the wrap around patios on the first floor and terraces on the upper levels; there were majestic views that were breathtaking. The triple paned glass window structures were amazing because you had a 360-degree view from anywhere in the house.

Everyone was having a great time; David assured everyone they would try to come up when time allowed. He also extended the invitation to his and Mallory's staff, Jezalee and her children and staff and of course! Jim, as well. After they had an early dinner, they sat around the marble and stone fireplace in the family room, sang songs, had hot chocolate along with a variety of different cookies. They took photos and videos up on the ski slopes, in town, at the lake and in and the surrounding area of the beautiful home.

David could not have felt better time knowing his wife, children and all the rest of the gang was having a great time. He was glad he could spend every moment with his wife and knowing she did not have to clean, make a bed, or cook. He had hired a maid service as well and they came up every day.

When Sunday rolled around, everyone wanted to attend the beautiful Saint Francis of Assisi Catholic Church in Incline Village. They had seen magnificent photos of the stained-glass windows that were behind the altar at this Church and wanted to see how effulgent they were in person.

The ladies were being so spoiled, and they said they never wanted to leave this fantasy. They did not have to cook or bake; and as soon as they got up, food was already for them on the dining room table. On Sunday, after they ate breakfast, everyone got ready to leave for Mass; with one exception, Jim did not go. David asked him if he would like to join them, and he said he would stay back and hold the fort down. This was the only one thing Jim did not do with them and Jezalee found out early on their friendship he would not go to Mass with them, so she knew not to say anything.

On their last day there, they went downhill, cross-country skiing and tobogganing. Everyone knew how to ski so there were good times had by all. They met up at the local ski resort and hung out for about an hour to have a quick lunch before they got back to the slopes once again.

By the time everyone arrived back at the house, they were completely exhausted. The ladies got out of their ski clothes and put bathing suits on; they could not get to the indoor swimming pool fast enough. The pool was heated to 90% and they were in heaven after being in the snow all day. The men were playing pool and then poker in what was considered the "men's quarters children played games while the men and women were enjoying themselves.

When everyone returned home, they quickly got back to their regular routines. When the children were back to school, they were looking forward to getting back to their after-school volunteering, hanging out with their friends, and working diligently to get the best grades in their classes.

It was May, Jezalee had gone to family therapy with the children for eight-months and they had made great progress. The sessions had helped them deal with the divorce, not take anyone's side, and actively started calling their dad and occasionally sending him notes. Paul called Jezalee several times to thank her for doing such a great job with the children. He had informed her he was waiting to tell them about Jonathan when they came for their summer vacation.

There was only two weeks left of school and the children were getting excited to see their dad, uncle, and both sets of grandparents. Paul would be surprising the children after they spent a week in Paris; they would meet up with their grandparents and Uncle Peter in Greece. Paul bought a yacht which was docked in Corfu, and they would spend a month traveling to the different ports and end in Italy.

Jim had asked Jezalee if he could come over and hang out with the children since he would not see them for two months and she said that would be nice. He played board games with them, took them to a movie and one night came over and insisted he was making dinner for all of them; including the O'Malley's since they would not see Adrienne, Alexander, and Jessica for the summer months. A few nights before the children left, Jim gave them some money to buy themselves something extra special or spend it anyway they wanted to; the children each gave him a big hug and thanked him for being so generous and thoughtful. At the end of the evening Jim kissed Jezalee for the first time and she did not resist. She felt nothing; Jezalee was used to kissing Paul and Jim certainly did not live up to what she was used to.

That evening, after Jim went home to his penthouse; all he could think of was Jezalee and their first kiss. He knew we wanted to take it slow before that first kiss; but there would be nothing stopping him now. He would wine and dine her while her children were gone.

Jezalee had settled in for the night, curled up on her bedroom sofa reading Danielle Steels' first published novel, Going Home, from 1973. She knew she had published twenty-two novels since then and had read sixteen of them. She admired her dedication to her craft and her novels were something she looked forward to reading whenever she had time. She was deep into her novel when Paul called to finalize what day the children would be coming. Jezalee let him know she did not have any special plans with the children so they could stay until a week before school. "Are you sure?" Paul asked. "I think they need to be with you more and the summer is a great opportunity for you to keep the bond you have with them," Jezalee answered. "Thank you! I appreciate that," Paul replied. They said their goodbyes; however, at opposite ends of the world, they were feeling, a void in the hearts that they had only felt since they divorced! They were pining over one another in silence.

It was time for Jezalee to let her children fly to Paris on their first vacation without her. She knew the children would have a wonderful time with Paul and both sets of grandparents and their dear Uncle Peter. Little did they know their dad had a huge yacht waiting for them in Greece. As soon as Paul had purchased the yacht, he called Jezalee to make sure she would agree to let the children sail the Mediterranean Sea and she thought it would be a fantastic and memorable experience. She reminded Paul the time they rented a yacht and took the children on their first sea adventure. While Jezalee was reminiscing, Paul knew being aboard a yacht without her for the first time was going to be difficult.

The children knew how hard this would be on their mom and they were sad she would not be with them; but they knew they would be able to call her whenever they wanted. Mallory and her children joined them so they could give them a proper send off as well. After the children were on the plane, they still waited until it took off before they left the airport. Afterwards, Jezalee asked if everyone would like pizza; Mallory and her children thought that was a great idea. Jezalee, and Mallory called their staff and asked them if they would like to join them at Jezalees for pizza and salad and they said yes. As soon as they got to the restaurant, Morgan elected herself to call everyone, and they placed their order. While they were waiting for the pizzas and salads to be done the children tried to keep the conversation going so Jezalee would not have her mind on her children up in the sky blue yonder.

By the time they arrived back at Jezalees with the food everyone was starving. David was working late so Mallory called him to say they were over at Jezalees, and she had saved him a few slices of his favorite pizza and made sure she did not forget his all-time favorite Caesar salad. After everyone hung out for a couple of hours, it was time to go to their respective homes and call it a day.

The Albanese children landed safely and were thrilled to see their dad. They were loving their dad's spacious penthouse and room service; they said they could certainly get used to the comforts of the hotel. "They will oblige us with whatever we want and will, no matter the time or day and no matter where they have to go," he smiled and said. "How fancy!" Jessica said. "They do treat me like I am Royalty; but I have not figured out why yet," Paul said. "Dad, I am sure no one gets the penthouse unless they check out your portfolio," Adrienne said. Paul looked and smiled at her; he did not know that she would know what a portfolio was and just gave he a quick wink of the eye.

The next evening after Paul and the children had gone to a movie, he took them to a very high-end restaurant and after dinner and dessert he wanted to tell them that he had a seven-year-old son. He looked across the table at his loving children and knew they were not ready; he was certain he was not ready either. He had been talking to them continually for months and thought the vacation would be the time to engage in the conversation of him having another son; but once they got there, he did not want to spoil the great time the four of them were having.

Paul nervously called Jezalee the next day while the children were taking their showers. He explained he was getting ready last night to tell them about Jonathan; but he looked at their faces filled with fun, and laughter and it was not a good time. Paul brought up the idea that last year they were given the news about their divorce just before they were going on vacation; telling them about Jonathan while they are on vacation would spoil their time with him and the rest of the family. Jezalee agreed and with Paul and was disappointed in them for thinking it would be an opportune time to tell them. "What were we thinking?" Jezalee commented. Paul comforted her and said they were married a long time; Jonathan and their divorce was all new to them and they were still trying to figure it all out. While she was carefully listening to Paul, she immediately had these feelings come over her and she could not think straight.

"Are you there Jezalee?" Paul asked. "Yes! I was wondering when you should tell the children about Jonathan. There is no right time; let us keep it in our mindset that you will need to tell them; but make it later," Jezalee replied." "I appreciate that!'' Paul replied. "I have an idea! Whenever you are ready to tell the children, I think I should be nearby; so maybe when you come to visit; you can do it then," Jezalee suggested. Paul was relieved at Jezalee's nonchalant attitude and was in complete agreeance and thanked her for the support. "Well! I hope you and the children have a grand time with your parents send my love to them," Jezalee said. "Thanks! But! Do not forget! They will be seeing your parents too," Paul reminded her. "Oh My! How could I forget them? They called me last night and are looking forward to seeing all of you," an embarrassed Jezalee said. Paul came close to saying he wished she were with them; but he kept his thoughts to himself. Paul was still on the phone with Jezalee when Jessica ran out and asked if he was talking to her mom. He said she is waiting to talk to all three of you. Alexander and Adrienne came out of their rooms within seconds after Jessica was speaking with their mom.

After Paul got off the phone, he had one thing on his mind, his dear beloved Jezalee, how much he yearned to be by her side. While the children were still on the phone with their mom, Paul stepped into the dining room, sat down at the table, and pulled out his engraved leather wallet Jezalee had bought him for Christmas a few years back, he glanced at a wedding photo of them and stared at it until he had tears in his eyes. He pulled out a family photo of the five of them and wanted to go back to that time in their lives. He could see the children from where he was sitting, and they were still on the phone with their mom. He wiped his tears away.

As the children were finished talking to their mom, Jezalee asked to speak with their dad once more before they hung up. Alexander quietly called his dad from the living room and said, "Mom wants to talk with you," Paul quickly wiped his tears then walked to the phone. "Yes! Jezalee, you need to talk with me?" Paul said. "Yes! Before I hang up, I wanted to reassure you I understand the reasons it would be best to tell the children about Jonathan, at-a-later-date; I am with you one hundred percent, in waiting until a more appropriate time," Jezalee said. "Thank you, for not being mad at me over waiting; it is going to be difficult, humiliating and I do not think they will ever respect me for what happened," Paul replied. Jezalee could hear the pain in his voice and did not know how to react; but she just encouraged him to remember what a great dad he has always been, and she would pray they will be more forgiving than angry. "From, your lips, to God's ears," Paul said. Then they said their goodbyes.

Jezalee was so thrilled to speak with her children and knew they were in for a lot of fun, excitement and adventure with Paul, Peter, their parents, and hers. She knew there was one person missing but she knew after the divorce, it was not the same and she had to deal with that emotion that came up more times than not. After she hung up, she cried herself to sleep thinking about the most wonderful man she ever knew, other than her dad. She tried not to think about Paul; but so far, it had been impossible. She would keep that to herself. She wished she had never gone to London.

The next morning, Jezalee asked her household crew and their children to join her for dinner that evening; she wanted to take everyone out to Alioto's Restaurant at Fisherman's Wharf. As soon as they had all arrived from Paris last year, this was one of the first places they would all go to, and it was one of their favorite restaurants to go as a group. After they ordered dessert, Jezalee pulled some sealed envelopes from her purse, stood up, and started handing one to each person at the table. They simultaneously looked at her and she said, "Open them up." Once they opened them up, they did not understand because they each had airline tickets for different places. She sat down and began to tell them she wanted all of them to have a great two months off for their summer vacation. Helga had a round-trip ticket to Chicago to see her daughter Astrid, then there were two more round-trip tickets to Greece. Then a one-way ticket back to San Francisco. They had not been to Greece in years and always wanted to go back to together. Joseph, Nina, and their children had round-trip tickets to Australia where they had family and friends. They were thrilled to see their family; it had been in a while. Inside the envelope was hotel vouchers at the places they would be staying while on their trips. In addition to that, she gave them each ten thousand dollars to enjoy themselves.

A week later Jezalee 's staff and children were on their vacations, and she realized how dismal it was, not seeing their children running in and out of the house to get cookies and milk from Helga and playing and swimming in the backyard and invariably wanting to dance with her. She was alone with her thoughts in their palatial estate; with the outside guards watching over her; but she could not stop reminiscing about the love of her life. With the house being empty she could not control slipping into the glorious and romantic past she always had with Paul. Jezalee had been questioning why she asked for a divorce and realized she was miserable without him at her side than ever before. She was religious and knew there was forgiveness in her heart; but when Gloria's voice resonated in her thoughts it was difficult to come to terms with Paul's indiscretion. Jezalee knew it did not stop her from constantly thinking about him.

Jim had called Jezalee to see if she wanted to go to the movies and dinner the day her staff went on their trips; but she said she would have to take a rain check because she was deep into her research on her books. He then asked her if he could make plans for them to go to Napa and visit some of the Wineries the following weekend and she said that sounded great, but she only had Sunday available. Jim told her he was hoping they would have the entire weekend to themselves. Jezalee indicated she had a dear friend from college coming in on Friday from Chicago and would be staying two days with her. Jim was annoyed but did not want to let on that he was. She said her friend Natalie would be leaving her house early Sunday morning, at 7:00 a.m. and taking her to the San Francisco Airport. Jim said he would pick her up by 8: 00 AM if that was okay with her. After Jezalee hung up the phone, she was so relieved her friend Natalie was coming; but grateful that she had an excuse to not go away with Jim. Ever since she told him the children would be gone to Paul's the entire summer, he took it for granted they would be making plans for the two of them. She did not like the fact that he assumed she had nothing better to do but be with him. Jezalee and Jim had done a lot of things together as a couple and with family and friends; but, by no means had she ever given him the impression she was in love with him and would never consider going away with him. She was beginning to feel he felt differently about her than she did about him. She liked having a male companion, but she did not want to be tied down with anyone at this time in her life. Jezalee had indicated after their first date, she preferred to see Jim in a group setting. The more she thought about their friendship; maybe she should have kept it platonic and never gotten intimate with him. Granted, he was very handsome, intelligent, and fun to be around but maybe she had been giving him the wrong signal by having sex with him that one time. She knew she had a lot to think about; having sex with Jim once and it did not go well; there was no passion. Jezalee had only been intimate with Paul and she could certainly feel the difference between the two men. Paul was a passionate man with sincere emotions; whereas; Jim was clearly a person without the emotions that should go hand in hand with sex. She could tell Jim did not know how to touch a woman's body; or maybe it was just hers. She had never had anyone to compare Paul to and thought all men would be the same in bed. Jezalee did not want to ever have sex with Jim again and if he ever insisted, that would be the end of their friendship.

Jezalee could not have asked for better weather when Natalie arrived; they sat out on the patio overlooking the lush grounds on the estate. They had not seen one another since Natalie's husband William's funeral three years prior. They had a lot of catching up to do and planned to go into Berkeley on Saturday to meet up with another one of their college friends, Alan, who was a professor at UC Berkeley for ten years. Jezalee had such a great time with her Alumni friends and did not want the night to end; the three of them decided they would not let so much time come between their next visits; especially since Jezalee now lived in the states. Alan had just gotten back from being on a year-long Sabbatical at the University of Barcelona. He had arrived back from Spain and his wife Elaine, and two children, Daniel and Bridget had flown to Colorado to visit his parents for a week. He was going to join them later at his in-law's home in Washington State. 'He first had to take care of things at the college before the semester started.

While the three alumni were having a great time discussing their college experiences and some of their professors, they liked and disliked; Jim was pacing back and forth in his penthouse. He was upset that he did not get his way about the weekend plans he wanted to have with Jezalee in Napa Valley. Jim wanted to see Jezalee as much as possible while her children were with their father; he had not been as successful as he had planned to be. He walked into his library, sat down at his lavish mahogany hand carved desk, and opened-up the drawer where he had placed the diamond engagement ring. He stared at the royal blue velvet box for the longest time, then reached in the deep drawer and pulled it out. When he opened-up the box and looked at the ring, all he could think of was proposing to Jezalee. He held the 4-carat diamond ring in his hand then had a flashback of his childhood; he was heavily perspiring and at that moment threw the ring across the room. He was shaking, became dizzy and disoriented but managed to walk over, bent down, and retrieve the ring that had landed in the corner of the room on the hardwood floor. He began pacing as he looked at the ring in the palm of his hand; hoping he had not damaged it in any way. After he stopped pacing, he walked over to his desk, sat down, and looked at the ring one more time before placing it back into the box. He left the room, still shaken up about his flashback as a child; still having the ring in his possession instead of being where it belonged, on Jezalee's finger; he was vacillating when he wanted to pop the question. He was going to bring the ring with him on their trip to Napa but the more he thought about it, he knew she would think it was too soon and he did not know what he would do if she said no to his proposal. He decided that next Valentine's Day would be more romantic setting and give him more time to get closer to her and the children. He knew that he had eight months and had to make the best of it. He was not going to let Jezalee get away.

Just thinking about wanting to marry Jezalee and knowing he had to wait, had put Jim in a state of panic; he remembered as a child and a teenager, he would hyperventilate, pace, sweat and be in a state of mind that made him very anxious and wanted to scream but could not because he would have a muzzle gag on his face. He got up from his desk and knew he had to get out of the penthouse, he grabbed his car keys and went for a drive. Once he got behind the wheel of the car, he kept having the same childhood flashback over and over. He was driving at a high speed, the city lights blinding him, and he was sweating profusely. Suddenly he saw lights flashing in his rear-view mirror then a siren went off; he realized the police officer was flashing for him to pull over. As he pulled over and turned off his engine, the police officer came near his car, he then rolled the window down. The officer asked to see his driver's license and vehicle registration, he handed them over to the officer, he was shaking and still sweating. The officer noticed Jim's condition; he proceeded to inform him he was going twenty-five miles over the speed limit. He asked him to step out of the vehicle; Jim did as the officer requested; he then asked him if he had consumed any alcohol, or any drug substances and he politely told him no. The officer shined the flashlight on Jim's face then asked him if he was okay. "I was driving then suddenly I felt sick, I got chills and could not stop sweating," Jim said. He asked Jim to try and walk a straight line and he managed to do so, even though he was still not feeling well. "I am going to give you a warning this time; but make sure the next time you start feeling sick, carefully pull over at a safe spot and rest until you feel better," the officer informed him. The officer noticed Jim had a built-in car phone and suggested he use it if he needs assistance in getting home. Jim nodded his head and thanked the police officer and said he would rest in the car until he felt he could safely drive back home and if he got worse, he would call a friend to come pick him up. As the officer drove off, Jim sat back in his car, locked the door, and rolled up the window and sat there for ten minutes until he could calm himself down. He closed his eyes, laid his head back on the headrest and knew he needed to get back to his place and figure out when he was going to ask Jezalee to marry him and was hoping to not keep having the flashbacks of his childhood.

Jezalee and her Harvard friends had a wonderful visit; but it was getting late, and Alan had an early appointment with the Chancellor at the university and needed to get a good night sleep. They said their goodbyes and planned to meet up again after he and his family got acclimated back to their old routine.

By the time Jezalee and Natalie got back to her estate, they were tired but decided to have a cup of tea before they went off to bed. Natalie and Jezalee had been thrilled to be able to spend an evening with Alan after not seeing him since Natalie's husband William's funeral. The three of them called one another from time to time and wrote letters to keep abreast of one another's lives; but being able to see one another in person was like being back in college. Alan and Natalie, with their families, had visited Jezalee and her family several times in Paris and Jezalee and her family had come to Berkeley and Chicago to see them as well. Jezalee knew when

Natalie's flight back to Chicago was, so she had called for an early pick up with a limousine service to take her to the San Francisco Airport. Natalie thanked Jezalee for arranging for her transportation to the airport. They both promised that the next time they got together it would be with their kids as well.

Jezalee's divorce had a jarring effect on Natalie and when Jezalee had called her, she just listened, took it all in, and knew that her friend would be okay because she knew how strong she was. She asked Jezalee how it was going with Jim, and she said she likes him as a friend and that is all it will ever be. I cannot consider a true relationship with another man until I stop thinking about Paul. Natalie said she had met a nice man and they started dating two weeks ago. The ladies agreed that dating someone other than being with their husbands had been quite traumatic. Jezalee kind of laughed; old Natalie she thought she would know when the right guy comes along when she gets weak in the knees. Natalie knew the love and respect both Jezalee and Paul had for one another, and she was not the type of woman to marry on the rebound. Jezalee admitted if she had not met Jim at the O'Malley's Christmas party; she would probably still not be dating anyone. She said she just did not have the type of personality to try and meet men and was not interested in getting married any time soon. Natalie had the same type of marriage Jezalee had, and her husband William's death was beyond comprehension; it was a huge void in her and her children's lives.

The next morning at 6:00AM Jezalee made sure Natalie was awake; she had already taken her shower, was dressed, and followed in right behind Jezalee to the kitchen. Jezalee had made her famous ricotta and lemon, extra thin pancakes, along with homemade whipped cream and fresh berries. When Natalie walked in, she could smell the maple syrup that Jezalee had heated up and the coffee brewing. They sat and enjoyed breakfast for the next hour before her ride was scheduled to pick her up. They both pulled out small calendars that they kept in their purses and were trying to decide when they could get together again. Natalie was, of course, sad that Jezalee was divorced but extremely overjoyed that she lived back in the states after all the years living abroad.

"I hope you and the children can come to my Christmas Party on Saturday, December 20th," Jezalee said. Natalie said they would be there with Christmas bells on. "Please do not make a reservation at a hotel because I have more than enough bedrooms." Jezalee said. "That will be wonderful!" Natalie replied.

It was time to go, the limousine arrived, and Natalie hugged Jezalee, and they said their goodbyes. Natalie promised to call her in a few days to see how she was doing. Jezalee told her after her trip to Napa with Jim, she would be staying close to the house because she wanted to take full advantage of the children on vacation, so she could devote all her time to her books. As Natalie threw her a kiss and waved goodbye from the car, Jezalee returned the gesture, with au revoir, dear friend. The limousine drove away and Jezalee knew that Jim would be there any minute for their trip to the beautiful wine country in Napa Valley.

Jim arrived at 8:00 a.m. sharp and Jezalee knew he would be on time, as always. She heard his car drive up; but she was going to wait until he rang the doorbell; she did not want him to think she was anxious by watching for him. He got out of the car, walked up to the doorway, and knocked on the door. They said their good mornings and Jezalee offered to make some coffee to take on the road; but he declined and said they would stop on the way to Napa. The first thing Jim asked her, if they could drive to her Winery-Vineyard and Jezalee said she preferred to go to the others if that was okay with him. "I have heard a lot of great things about how beautiful the property is; and the wine is superb. I do not understand why you would not want to show it to me," a disgruntled Jim commented. Jezalee felt Jim was pinning her into a corner; she refused to let him get away with it. "Jim, Paul and I own that Winery together and I prefer you not visiting it for that one reason only," a very adamant Jezalee said. Jim was quiet for a few seconds then said he understood.

As they were driving out the front gate of the estate, Jim asked her if she would like to hear some music and she said sure. He turned on some classical music; told Jezalee to feel free to change the station if she wanted to hear another genre of music. She said the music was perfect for their trip and they both engaged in small talk, which got a little heated at times. He asked her how her evening was with her college friends, and she talked about Natalie and Alan and how close they had been at Harvard, and they were going to try to see each other more often since Alan was back in the states. Jim could not help but ask her if Alan was married and in the back of her mind; she thought it was a strange question to ask. She told him he was happily married, had two children and is a Professor at the University of Berkeley who had been on a year Sabbatical in Spain. Jezalee got a little sarcastic and said, oh! You probably want to know about my friend Natalie, she is a widow and has been for three years with two children. He could sense that Jezalee was irritated and tried to change the subject; but before he could she asked him why he did not ask her if Natalie was married. He thought quickly and said he was just getting ready to. "I beat you to it," Jezalee laughed it off and said. He felt a little squeamish then changed the subject. He asked her if she would send his regards to her children when she spoke to them. Jezalee said she had certainly pass that along to them.

Jezalee decided to change the music to a pop station and at least now she felt she could keep busy singing words to some of the songs so she would not have to talk so much with him. The trip took a little over an hour and a half because there was a huge festival in the Napa Valley that weekend; so, the traffic was a little heavier than usual.

Once they arrived in Napa, they parked the car downtown; walked around and were trying to decide what Wineries and Vineyards to visit. Jim asks where her Vineyards were in Europe and Jezalee said she and Paul owned them together and they were in France, Italy, Argentina, Spain, and Napa.

After Jezalee and Jim vacillated on what places they wanted to tour; she suggested they choose two that were over a century old and one more that was less than thirty years old. As they stopped at a quaint little restaurant, had a cup of coffee and a piece of pie, they looked over the list of Wineries and Vineyards, which was hundreds, they finally had their three choices; Sattui Winery, in St. Helena, Sterling Vineyards, and Chateau Montelena Winery, both in Calistoga. Jim purchased a map of the Wine Country. They made it back to the car and off they went on their wine tasting excursion.

Jezalee appeared to be having a pleasant time at the two Wineries and the one Vineyard and had sampled some great hors devours and gourmet cheeses with exquisite wines. Even though Jezalee did not drink alcohol, she learned over the years by aroma she could appreciate the delicacy of a superb wine to offer to family and friends that really enjoyed it. Jim would tease her, knowing she and Paul owned Vineyard-Wineries and she did not drink wine; other than to cook amazing sauces, roasting, sautéing, and baking with them. She let Jim know that wine was not just for the almighty drinking; it enriched so many recipes whether an entrée, an appetizer, or desserts. By the end of the tours, Jezalee ended up purchasing five dozen bottles of their finest wines from each Winery and Vineyard and Jim had gotten two dozen at each one. They were both proud of the selections they chose to add to their wine collection.

Jim had suggested they go to one of the restaurants in the Napa Valley before they departed for home. Jezalee spoke up and said she heard rave reviews about Sally Schmidt's French Laundry from friends. "That sounds perfect! Great reviews are good enough for me," Jim said. The restaurant was on the way back towards Napa in a small town called, Yountville; with a population of two thousand, very pristine, quiet, and picturesque.

When they arrived at the well-known, restaurant they were famished and the first thing Jim noticed, it was not in English; he asked her if there was anything great on the menu. Jezalee looked over at Jim and smiled and started reading the French menu in English to him. After they decided what they wanted she ordered their meals in French and when they started being served the appetizers, entrée, and dessert, they both agreed this was above and beyond; a five-star restaurant.

By the time Jezalee and Jim left the restaurant it was around seven o'clock; while driving back to San Francisco, he was thinking of asking Jezalee if he could spend the night. He knew things between them had been slow moving because he always slipped up and interrogated her about her friends and especially putting down Paul whenever he got the chance; he just could not help himself.

Jezalee looked over at Jim and asked where he had been for the last half hour? She caught him off guard; he said he was just thinking about what a great day they had together. Jezalee agreed, it was a lovely day and Napa was a special place. Jim said they would have to come back when they could stay longer. They listened to some music for the rest of the trip. About thirty minutes before arriving in San Francisco, Jim asked if he could spend the night with her. Jezalee hesitated for a minute to get her thoughts in order; she told Jim she was too busy to have company. Jim was staring straight at the road and wanted a better explanation. "I do not understand why you are so busy that we cannot spend more time together. I love you Jezalee and want to spend every waking hour with you. There! I said it!" As Jim blurted it out. Jezalee perked up but did not want to deal with the way the conversation was going. She paused for a moment, put her thinking cap on and told him she was trying to get a lot accomplished while her children were away on vacation. Jim tried to interrupt her; but she would not have it Jezalee had such a wonderful day and evening and did not want it to end the way it appeared it was going to. Jim, you really need to stop questioning me after I have given you an answer to something. The night I met you, was a happy night for me; when we were introduced; I thought to myself, here is a very tall, handsome, intelligent, and funny man. We danced, laughed, and basically started to get to know one another that night. He kept listening as he drove and did not know where she was going with her conversation; but he knew he had better let her say what she wanted to say. Jim, we have had just a few dates together and the rest have been with other couples or groups. I would not consider us exclusive by any means. It has been a difficult transition for me; and I am still not clear what I want. I married the man of my dreams, and we had an incredible life until he cheated on me. I wanted to make sure I was not dating you on the rebound from my husband and that is still a work in progress. My children and I have had some great times with you; but you need to understand that does not mean I want to treat our going out and doing things as if we will ever get married. You have already made me feel that you are leaning in the direction of having a closer relationship with me than I care to indulge in. I know you want more than I can give you right now and I do not feel upset that I said no to you. I feel sometimes you put me in a tough situation because the children and I like you; but that does not always mean I am supposed to fall in love with every man my children get along with. Jim did not say a word because he got the sense she was not finished. "Sure, we had sex once, that does not qualify us as being a couple and I am not sure if that was good for either one of us. I am not close to dating anyone on a regular basis, much less have sex and all the emotions that may come from that. Will I ever love again and want a man to put a ring on my finger and be married; that is not even on the table at this time in my life. If you are ready for a commitment maybe you need to find another woman who is looking to fall in love and want all the things you want. I am not that woman, and I will not keep seeing you if you insist every time; I give you a reason for not seeing you as a threat to your ego and our friendship. You have mentioned the word relationship several times in the six months I have known you; there is no relationship! We have a friendship, and I cannot give you more than that." As Jezalee adamantly concluded. Jim did not say a word.

They finally arrived at Jezalee's estate; he was getting ready to open his car door and she said she wanted to finish her thoughts while she was in the car. He removed his hand from the car door handle and sat quietly while Jezalee continued.

"I will give you a better explanation why I am not being available for anyone; I have been behind on my research for both my books, and I have precious time while the children are away. I wanted my staff and their children to also have an incredible vacation by giving them two months off while my children are not here. I sometimes like having complete solitude surrounding me while I am working on a project; but I also like it when there is utter chaos. This is one of those times when I need as much time to myself and everyone else understands, and you should too. I agreed to go on a day trip to Napa Valley with you and it was nice; but it was still not enough for you. Nothing is ever enough for you, and it places tremendous pressure on me; you are like an uncle to my children, and it is meant the world to the four of us. If you cannot understand what I am saying to you, what is the use of seeing me and my family? Right now! All I need is a friend and if you need to wine and dine a woman to become Mrs. Stark, you are wasting precious time with me. I cannot be the person you want me to be," Jezalee finalized how she felt.

Jim had listened tentatively and was furious at what she was saying but he knew he had to keep himself composed and not say or do anything irrational. He knew to make things better he had to magically come up with something to say. "Jezalee, I am so sorry and apologize for any frustrations and ill will that I have caused you. It boils down to the mere honest fact that I fell in love with you early on, after we had a couple of dates, and everything felt so right. I presumed that we were worthy of looking toward a future together as husband and wife. I am a single man, no children and just want what every man eventually wants out of life, a woman to come home to and love her the way she deserves to be loved and have children or be the best stepdad, a child could have," Jim said.

"I realize now I have gone about it all the wrong way and I am deeply embarrassed over my actions and wish I could make them up to you," Jim commented. As he poured his heart out Jezalee was attentive to everything he said and knew she had to handle her response very carefully.

"Jim, thank you for being so honest with me and know that I have been honest with you from the very beginning of us meeting one another; and what I mean by that is, I was honestly interested in getting to know you, and wanted you to have a friendship with me and my children. I felt so comfortable around you, and you have always been so good with my children. Whenever we danced, had moments to ourselves, I must be honest, I wanted to kiss you, hold your hand while strolling down a street, and it also felt natural to have sexual urges over you. A woman would be crazy and stone cold if she would not want to be with you. I have feelings and I do care you; but, in love I am not. Do I think things will change; they could over time, but I do not have a crystal ball or able to predict my future with anyone," Jezalee replied.

"I have more at stake than you do; I am a divorcee with three children to raise and I cannot think of marrying anyone, anytime soon. If I should ever marry, that person must understand that my children do have a hands-on father who will always be in my life due to having three children with him. If-and-when I should ever marry, I cannot have a man that will question me as to why I need to see my ex-husband. There are times I will be with Paul on special occasions ad significant events that come up in our lives. Whomever I marry must respect my ex-husband; Paul would have to know, if I ever should marry, he will, need to show respect, tolerance and know that my new husband would be a big part of our children's, lives as well. So, I am hoping you can maybe see things a little differently from my perspective. After what I have explained to you, hopefully you can understand my concerns, so I am going to let you make the decision if you want to still be mine and the children's friend or not," Jezalee told him. Jim had calmed down a little and knew he wanted to keep seeing her. He asked Jezalee if it was okay if they continued their conversation in her house. He let her know he would not stay any longer than to finish the conversation they had started in the car. She agreed and he was happy with that.

They got out of the car, she went to unlock the front door, while he got her wine cases out of the trunk of his car. After he made his way through the house and to the wine cellar to set the cases of wine down, Jezalee was in the kitchen making a fresh pot of coffee and a kettle of water on in case they wanted hot tea instead. She called out to let Jim know she was in the kitchen; he made his way there after he washed his hands. Jezalee asked him if he wanted coffee or tea and he said coffee. After they got their cups of coffee, they walked into the family room and sat across from one another. She looked him in the eye and asked him to proceed with his thoughts. Now that they were in her home, a much better atmosphere than a car, he was still nervous but would try to explain where he was coming from. Jim took a few sips of coffee but was nervous; but started to talk to Jezalee. "Ever since I met you, I also wanted to get to know you more and that included your wonderful children as well. When I arrived in San Francisco, I was not sure what to expect from making the drastic move across the country. David had been such a great man to meet, to know and to work with; he had never met a man as terrific and down to earth as he was. Not only have we become great colleagues; we have a growing friendship with much respect for one another. He is the reason I decided to stay here and have this great life. Once I got into a routine, I could not see myself living anywhere else. I suppose I came here at the right time; David said that all his employees were invited to their Christmas Party and as reluctant as I was at first to socialize; with David's insistence, I showed up that night. That was some party! They had it all planned that the two of them should be introduced to one another. It was a night I will never forget and be forever grateful to David for suggesting that we meet. I cannot say I was not nervous, because I was as soon as I saw you; you took my breath away. I want you to know it took every ounce of courage to ask for your telephone number that evening. I do not know whatever possessed me to ask you to dance because I had never danced in my life," Jim said. As Jezalee was listening to Jim, she was surprised at some of the things he was saying. She kept thinking about his wife and son and was certainly not going to ever question him again or mention the tragic accident; but things did not seem to add up as he was talking. He did not say why he came here and the part about never dancing seemed strange. It was odd to her that being married that a couple would not have danced at their wedding, and he was in a business that people continually socialized. Jim glanced at her and asked her if she had been listening to him and she spoke up and said she had heard every word. Jim then said when he first called her for a date, he was not sure he had done the right thing. "Why do you say that?" Jezalee asked. He said he was not sure if he had the time because of his demanding work schedule; but David convinced me I needed to at least try and see what happens. So, that was the beginning! I never regretted calling you for that first date and you are so right! I jumped in head-first and every time I was around you and your children; I was getting more attached and feeling a sense of belonging and being a part of your lives. I realize now, after everything you explained to me, I was too demanding and out of control with our relationship. You and your children have been so hospitable and loving to me and that meant so much that I kept feeling closer and closer as we got together. I felt a part of something special knowing and being around you and your children. I do want to keep seeing you because you mean so much to me; however, I only want to go out with you, do things with you and your kids, if you think you will want me around. I will not put pressure on you anymore; but want to have good times like we did. I have always enjoyed your company and want to be around you when it is good for you. I do not want to damage what we already have. I have put it out there that I am in love with you; but at the same time, I do not want that to scare you away. I now know you do not have those same feelings and maybe never will; but right now, is what counts and I think we can have great times together, we can have sex if we choose to do so or not, we can travel, go dancing, to the Opera, the Ballet, whatever we choose to enjoy as a couple of friends enjoying one anthers company. I promise from this moment forward I will be more sensitive to your situation. You are the best thing that has ever happened to me and if you want us to just be friends, I am in. She said, okay! We can be friends but no sex. If that is the way you want it, I am fine with that, for now! She laughed and said, go right now! Thanks for a great day. You are more than welcome.

That night was the first time Jezalee did not feel like Jim would be pressuring her anymore about a closer relationship; she was much more relaxed and enjoyed being with him. As for Jim, he knew he had said all the right things and having sex with her would help his cause sooner than later. He bought that diamond ring for a reason, and it was just waiting to be worn.

Once Jim arrived home, he brought up the cases of wine and set them in the wine cellar. After he placed the wine where he wanted it; he went into his library, opened the drawer where the engagement ring was kept and set it down on his desk. He kept telling himself that Jezalee was going to be his wife and he had to figure out how to orchestrate ways that it would happen

That night Jim did not sleep well and kept reminding himself that he wanted one thing in his life to be the way he imagined it to be. He had Jezalee continually on his mind and he knew patience on his part had to come into play or she would stop seeing him.

Jezalee woke up the next morning in great spirits; most of the trip to wine country with Jim had been semi-fun; she was relieved they both aired out their feelings and they could go forward and see what happens with their friendship. With everyone on vacation, she was still having a tough time dealing with Paul constantly popping up in her mind. She needed her thoughts to be focused on the work she needed to get done on her books. There would not be another ideal time like this, with no interruptions. Jezalee had showered, got dressed, then headed for the kitchen to make a casserole after she had her breakfast. Now that she had her meals planned out for lunch and dinner, she had gathered her notes and pages of her books and made her way out to the patio near the pool. It was an extraordinary day outside and she was going to take full advantage of the beautiful weather. As Jezalee got settled outside, she drank her fresh cup of coffee with one of Helga's sweet rolls. She had a smile on her face as she thought of that beautiful lady and her lovely daughter Astrid becoming a part of their family so many years ago. She missed Helga as much as she missed her children. Helga had left her a sweet note saying she had made six dozen sweet rolls to have on hand while she was on vacation; she had even wrapped them individually and placed them in the freezer. Jezalee was as close to Joseph and Nina and their three great children, as she was with Helga and Astrid. She dearly missed them all; but knew everyone worked so hard and never took a long enough vacation. had already gotten postcards from everyone, including the children. Jezalee placed them on their kitchen bulletin board and glanced at them every time she walked by them. Oh! How she loved the people in her life; she had been so fortunate.

Jezalee called Centre Communautaire Familia de Paris and spoke to her staff to see how things were going for the week. She called them every Friday to get updates to see what the traffic flow of people coming into the center was and especially wanted to make sure that the list of benefactors stayed the same or more added. Jezalee still made the calls to possible benefactors then followed up with sending a brochure with her and Pauls' insight to the center they started, and they could browse through the brochure and see photos of what the center looked like. After she sent them out, she would call Rene at the center to let her know she would follow up with the possible benefactors and set up an appointment for Rene too give them a personal tour.

The following week was pretty much the same ritual every day for Jezalee; doing more research on her book, calling a few friends, calling her publisher, and staying at home and doing some side novel reading. She had the phone numbers of the hotels where her staff was staying so, she would check in with them to make sure they were having a great time. Jezalee missed them so much; but knew that they needed to have time off and just have fun.

Jim never slept very well; there was no difference from one night to the next. He kept having the same nightmares and once-in-a-while he would dream about attending school and having best friends to hang out with. He felt he had worked hard for the life he currently had and wanted to keep it that way. Jim realized there were so many ways a person's life could go; but he also knew you got out of life what you put into it.

Last week with Jezalee was the perfect example of how good life can be; he knew she needed time and he was willing to stay around long enough to eventually get her to love him. Jim had loved living in San Francisco and was pleased that he had David, not only as his boss, but a great friend as well. He had learned over the past few years, with persistence, you can accomplish anything you set your mind to. He knew he had come a long way; and no one was going to keep him from getting what he wanted. The days flew by, and Jim had not heard from Jezalee; however, he was going to wait a few more days. When he went into work the next day, he asked David if he had seen Jezalee and he could honestly say she had not been over at his house. The only thing David knew, was Jezalee working fastidiously on the books. "I love that about her! Jezalee is determined on her interests," Jim said. "She is highly intelligent and goes after what she wants," David remarked. "Truer words were never said," Jim said as he smiled. They went on working the rest of the day trying to decide when they would need to take another trip to Spain and Portugal, to meet up with some new clients.

Jezalee called the children to see what they had done so far on their vacation, and she was so happy they were having such a great time. The three children missed their mom; but thought it was so sweet that she let them spend extra time with their dad. She spoke briefly with Paul and hoped the rest of their time together was as great as it has been. Paul thanked her for being so generous with the time the four of them could have together.

Jezalee managed to get quite a bit done on her books and got ready to go over to the O'Malley's for dinner one evening. She took some of the sweet cinnamon rolls out of the freezer to take over to David and Mallory's for them and their staff to enjoy for breakfast.

When David got home that night, Jezalee was already a fixture in the kitchen helping Mallory with dinner. He said, Wow! It smells like delicious Chinese food." Jezalee looked at them as they gave each other a sweet kiss. While they were having dinner, David mentioned to Jezalee that Jim had asked if he or Mallory had seen her. I told him as far as I knew you were busy with your books and neither me nor Mallory had not seen or heard from you. She began to tell them about their trip to Napa and a lot of the conversations they had. Mallory and David agreed it was a conversation that had to be said.

Jezalee and Jim got together with David and Mallory a few times before her children came home from vacation. She had a pool party at her house; invited staff, Alan's family, people she worked with on charities, and the O'Malley's. Mallory and David saw a difference in Jim and Jezalee noticed it as well; but she was reluctant to trust him anymore. She thought back to their trip to Napa, their lengthy conversation and felt it had helped Jim understand they had a friendship and that is all she wanted. Jezalee had no idea what was really going on in Jim's mind but would eventually find out.

Before the children came home, Jezalee was invited to Alan and his family's farm in Napa. She stayed two relaxing weeks and enjoyed every minute with Alan, his wife Elaine, and their two children, Donald, and Bridget. Jezalee got up early every morning, gathered eggs from the hen house, fed the pigs and went riding with Elaine, before the rest of her family woke up. Jezalee was glad she had some quality time with Elaine, it had been too long since they had seen each other. She asked her when she comes into the city, they should meet for lunch. Elaine said anytime was good for her after they open-up their home in Berkeley in a couple of weeks. Jezalee said she would pencil her in for three and give her a call and they can set a day and time. She said she could come to Berkeley for lunch if that was better for her. Once they were done riding the most beautiful horses Jezalee had ever seen, Elaine started making a good old-fashioned country breakfast for everyone.

When Jezalee left their farm, she was so refreshed from being there, having great company and delicious country meals, it was difficult leaving such a comforting, country environment. As she drove the countryside, she decided to stop at Paul and her Winery-Vineyard and visit the staff for a few hours. She informed the staff she was staying at the Villa on the property and called the O'Malley's to see if they would join her for a couple of days. They came up and had a great time. Jezalee introduced them to some of her local friends, staff, and the caretaker at the villa. Before the O'Malley's and Jezalee were getting to go home; David suggested leaving her car there and drive back with them. She had two other cars at home and decided to leave the car there permanently.

When Jezalee arrived home, she knew she had to get ready for the troops running up and down the stairs, filling up the house with the lovely sounds of their voices, Alexander playing a beautiful piece on the piano, checking their homework once school was back in session, asking what's for breakfast, lunch, and dinner. The most she thought about, above all else, was wrapping her arms around them and give them a strong hug and kiss. She had a few days before her children would be home so all she did was her yoga, did some swimming, read a book, and just relaxed.

It was time for Jezalee to pick up her children at the airport; she was in happy tears. The children had a great time and knew that Paul and the rest of the family had enjoyed the children immensely. Now, it was time to catch up on everything and have a little time with them before school started in a week.

Created with Sketch.

Life was going full speed ahead; Jezalee's staff arrived a day after her children got home; everyone was getting back to their routines and school had been in session for about a week.

Several months had gone by and Halloween was upon them. Jezalee and Joseph worked all day, up until dinner most days. The entire estate, including Joseph and Nina's house, the Albanese house; and the interiors and exteriors was unquestionably decorated as if you were walking into the houses of Dracula, Frankenstein, with mummies, and ghosts. Jezalee had sketched out how she wanted her house and the lavish grounds to look, Joseph and Nina stayed with the same theme, the spookier the better. Eventually they had called the troops in after school and they pitched in, Jezalee and Joseph said this was going to be their Halloween gift to the whole family. She and Joseph worked for two weeks, and all their efforts ended up Spooktacular. Each day when the children came home from school;

they could not believe all the progress they had made in a day towards what would eventually be a Halloween extraordinaire. Jezalee and Joseph definitely, outdone themselves, from all the past years they had decorated. They were thankful they had kept years of decorations and each year was more impressive than the next. They were proud of the end results; it was exciting to see their efforts had paid off. The children invited their classmates, friends, and neighbors; it was going to be a spooky extravaganza. Jim had called her and said he wanted to help; but she let him know that this was a project that she and Joseph do every year and did not want to ruffle any feathers, so to speak. She thanked Jim for offering his services and hoped he dropped by on Halloween for their spooky event. He assured her he would be there in full costume.

The children were excited because everyone RSVP'd and were attending the spooky event. The entire neighborhood, plus people coming into their area for trick or treating were lined up taking photos and videos of the amazing Halloween decorations; in what they called Halloween Spooksville. Jezalee and Joseph were exhausted; but knew it was well worth their efforts. Even the guards were dressed up in costumes. Nina and Helga, with the help of the children, had made up special games and Jezalee hired fortune tellers, clowns, people on stilts and sword throwers. It was quite a spectacular event; and everyone was dressed in funny, unique, scary, elaborate and off the wall costumes. Once Halloween was over, everyone had the same effect people experienced when Christmas was over the next day, Halloween withdrawals were evident. Jezalee let it be known she and Joseph may have put up all the decorations; but they were not about to be the ones taking them down. Joseph assembled the children and managed to get everything down in a few days. They had huge storage units across town and Joseph rented a 26-foot truck to drive the six truck loads filled to the brim. Bob came over to help load up and brought the O'Malley children and of course! Jezalee children helped as well.

It was Thanksgiving week; Jezalee and her children were invited to Alan and Elaine's family farm for the celebration; along with Alan and Elaine's parents, siblings, and a few of their close friends that lived nearby. They knew at least thirty people, if not more, were coming so Jezalee and Elaine planned their menus and were excited to celebrate with some amazing recipes they were making. The Albanese's arrived Wednesday morning and Jezalee and Elaine sat down and went over their menu once again. Jezalee spoke, with her two weeks before and they decided what the two of them were going to cook and bake. Jezalee had made a variety of pies, cakes, other desserts, and including her families favorite dressing they always made. She had fulfilled her duties as Elaine had also. Now, she was ready to help in the kitchen with whatever needed to be chopped, diced, boiled, roasted, or simmered.

They had a great three days with lots of great leftovers. They went to the movies, joined a group of neighbors for some outdoor games and everyone took turns riding the four horses they had. Jezalee's children had so much fun on the farm and got along great with Donald, who was 12, and Bridget was 14. They invited them over to their house regularly after spending time with them.

Jim had been invited to Florida for Thanksgiving with his friend Deanna and her family. The O'Malley's flew to Connecticut to be with their parents and other relatives, as did Helga, Joseph, Nina, and their children went to relatives as well.

It was three weeks until Christmas, Alan and his family and Natalie and her children were able to come to her Christmas soiree. Paul was bringing his girlfriend and her sister a few days before the party, and Jezalee and Paul's parents were coming. She knew this was going to be an extra special Christmas because Jezalee had not seen Paul's parents since the divorce. It would be a reunion of sorts, and everyone was looking forward to all the fun.

Joseph and Bob made sure they ordered the largest tent possible so Jezalee could do her magic with Christmas in its full glory. She worked days in the tent to get everything perfect but knew the most important thing would be the children lining up to see Santa. Jezalee had life-sized mechanical dancing elves circling around the 20-foot elaborately decorated Christmas tree. Santa sitting on his king-like throne, with Santa helpers keeping the children busy while they were in line to see the jolly old man. Helga and Jezalee were constantly cooking and baking around the clock, and they could not have been happier.

The O'Malley family came over several nights prior to the party, to spend the night. Each of the children had bought presents for one another and exchanged gifts upstairs around the tree they had decorated. Jezalee had the room sound proofed so they could have music as loud as they wanted it. She had a guest bedroom just for Mallory and David; she informed them no one else can sleep in that bedroom; it would always be reserved for them. "Where is our reserved for David and Mallory plague to place on the door?" David asked with a grin on his face. "That is a stupendous thought! Thanks for the idea! Next time you spend the night your plaque will be up," Jezalee answered.

A week before the party, Adrienne called Morgan to see if she wanted to the spend the night because her family was decorating their family room Christmas tree. That night, Morgan helped with decorating while the five of them a sat by the roaring fireplace blazing, popcorn overflowing in bowls, and piping hot cocoa filling the brim in their favorite Christmas mugs, with whipped cream dripping down the side of the mugs. They had decided to make a few extra ornaments for the tree and were covered from head to toe with glue, glitter, and cranberry stains, they had a lot of fun and ended up with 20 handcrafted ornaments that would be added with the other homemade creations they had made over the years. These special adornments always dressed up the family room Christmas tree where they opened their presents. The family and Morgan decorated the family tree they next morning after they had breakfast.

A couple of days later Paul, his girlfriend, Sophia, and her sister Leila, was driven up the winding driveway to Jezalees opulent estate. He knew that she had been busy with her extraordinary decorating talents. There were life size mannequins dressed in old fashioned clothes from the 19th century, artificial snow flurries with Mr. and Mrs. Snowman close to the entrance welcoming you with their mechanized movements saying Merry Christmas. The life size mannequins in the horse drawn carriage were singing Christmas Carols. The exterior was like a holiday scene from a Norman Rockwell painting. The style was a colorful exaggerated realism meets Andy Warhol's eclectic pop art.

Jezalee's friends, Natalie and her children, and Alan, Elaine's and their children arrived the evening before the party and Jezalee took all her house guests out for dinner, then they came back and hung out in the family room while Alexander played Christmas music on the piano. They sang along while he played; Jezalee brought desserts and drinks for everyone.

Everyone seemed to have had an amazing time at Jezalee's Christmas Spectacular; especially Paul whenever he could get a quick glance through a crowded room of guests. The love of his life; is all he cared about. He could not keep his eyes off her, she looked sensational. He tried to make her jealous by bringing Sophia; but he knew she could read right through that. After he showed up at Jezalee's home with Sophia and Leila, he had realized he made a huge error in judgment. Jim would catch Paul eyeing his ex-wife and when he noticed it; he would quickly go up to Jezalee and comment on the great turn out she had. He kept trying to cling to her all night and she finally asked Jim to try and meet some other people because he was smothering her. When Jezalee was in conversation other guests, she would look through the crowd to find Paul; to see if he had Sophia at his side. When her and Paul made eye contact; they both kind of smiled and would nod at one another or wave.

It had been a sensational Christmas Spectacular; everyone had a grand time; and as far as the tent, it was the biggest hit for the children. She had approximately 125 guests, which included the children from the Boys and Girls Club with their families; going from the house to the tent and Jezalee was so thrilled they accepted her invitation. Jezalee not only had Santa and his helpers; she hired a group that stayed in the tent singing Christmas Carols. She also could not resist have girls from a local Ballet Theater dressed up like sugar plum fairies that danced throughout the evening for the guests; and had the boys in gingerbread costumes giving out cookies. There was an assortment of fruits and candy on sticks that you could dip in the giant chocolate fountain and various types of hot and cold drinks. There were gifts for all the children that attended and gift bags for all the other guests.

Christmas was over for another year, Jezalee was thrilled to spend some time with her mom, dad, and Paul's parents. Paul was sad about leaving and it was not just about missing the children; he was always thinking about Jezalee, and he knew he would never love another woman but her.

Paul was back in Tuscany and exhausted from all the traveling he had been doing; before and after his trip to spend Christmas with his children, Paul had been in London, New York, and Rome on business. Paul tried not to think so much about Jezalee; but she was always on his mind. He knew that he and Sophia had some fun times together; but it was not the same and knew it never would be. When Sophia met Jezalee she thought she was one of the most beautiful women she had ever seen. She noticed when Paul was around Jezalee and their children his spirit, smile and eyes lit up like a Christmas tree. Sophia adored his beautiful and well-mannered children and wanted to get to know them better. She respected Jezalee and knew what a wonderful person she was and had been a great wife and incredible mother. She was a woman that had it all and one night of Paul's life had shattered their family. Sophia was glad when Paul had told her the whole story; but Jezalee should have listened to the whole story. Paul told her it was a closed subject as far as Jezalee was concerned; the damage had presented itself and she had moved on with her life and appeared happy.

After Paul left, Jezalee was feeling an overwhelming void but had to keep it hidden. She knew she would be going to the Governor's Charity Ball on New Year's Eve; but all she could think of was Paul and the New Year's Eves they had together. That day while the children were out with friend's, Jezalee decided to relax in the family room and look at old photo albums. She sat there all day looking at the happy moments she and Paul shared together when they first met at college, their wedding, the births of each child, school photos and special photos of each anniversary. She was thankful that Helga was gone for the day with Nina because she did not want anyone to see her crying. By the time she felt the need to put the rest of the photos away for another alone moment; she could feel that her face and eyes were swollen from crying so much. After placing the albums back in their place, she headed upstairs, got in bed, and took a nap.

On the other side of the globe, Paul was at his penthouse in Paris. He had not been the same since he left San Francisco and needed to be alone. Sophia wanted to celebrate New Year's Eve; but he declined saying he was going to be with his parents; he lied and wanted to be alone and not see or talk with anyone. Paul knew he had made a mistake in coming to Jezalee's Christmas party because it took every ounce of strength not to sweep her off her feet and tell her how much he loved her. He felt down and out of sorts ever since he said goodbye to his family, and it was getting more difficult each time he saw them.

Jim was relieved Paul was finally gone after the holidays. He was worried about Jezalee falling back in love with him, which he kept thinking that must be why she was sometimes aloof about their relationship. He knew that their relationship had grown since their trip to Napa and was proud of himself because he did take a step back and let her lead in their dating, which she preferred going out with other couples, as she insisted on. Little did he know, Jezalee never fell out of love with Paul.

David, Mallory, Jim and Jezalee were going to the Governor's New Year's Eve Charity Ball at the Capitol in Sacramento. The ladies had purchased their gowns months ago and were excited to socialize with some friends they had not seen in a while. The event was to raise money for underprivileged children and their families. Jezalee, Mallory, and Elaine had worked diligently helping to make this event a great success by having earlier fundraisers, to present the money at that evenings Ball. They had raised more money than any other group that evening, plus their personal money they donated.

As much as Jezalee thought about Paul, she did not want Paul to ever know how much she was still pining over her lost love. She did have fun with Jim; but she could not pinpoint what her intuition was warning her about him; other than the fact he never brought up his deceased wife or son. The O'Malley's and Jezalee had noticed Jim was distant for the last few months and he would say he was fine. She knew if his demeanor stayed the same or got worse, she would prefer not having her children or herself being around him any longer. After being married to Paul, it was difficult dealing with someone like Jim who appeared to be obsessed over her.

It was New Year's Eve and Jezalee and Mallory let the children have some friends over at Jezalee's since Helga, Joseph and Nina were staying home. Jim was looking forward to double dating, so to speak, as the four went to the Capitol. When they arrived, the first thing Jezalee admired was the Neoclassical structure of the Capitol building; she had studied the architecture of all the Capitol buildings in America when she was in college and knew the history of all of them. She had remembered that this Capitol had been completed between 1861 and 1874.

The night proved to be special; the cuisine was perfectly delicious, they raised a lot of money, the music was fantastic and seeing friends they had not seen in a while and meeting some new people they had looked forward to being introduced to. Jezalee was so thrilled to see Alan and Elaine at the Ball. When Jezalee and her children spent Thanksgiving with them, they decided to make sure they were seated together at the event; especially since they had done so much work towards the Ball. Jim had met Alan and Elaine at Jezalee's Christmas Party and really enjoyed speaking with them and at least it was two more people he would be able to talk to. Jim asked Jezalee to dance but said she did not want to; she wanted to socialize with friends and people she had not seen in a while. The Governor and his wife managed visiting each table and strike up conversations with people. Jim had a moment when he just sat back; and everything seemed surreal; never in his wildest imagination he would be at any Governor's Ball. Jezalee was talking with Elaine and was in deep conversation; Jim began to sweat and excused himself from the table and told Jezalee he had to use the men's room. When he managed to find the men's room, he went and stood in front of a mirror and kept staring at himself; men were coming and going and they really did not pay attention to him, so he just stood there glaring back at himself and had to splash cold water on his face because he felt flushed. He went into a sitting area of the men's room and sat for about ten minutes, until he could get his bearings. Jim got up, looked in the mirror once again, before he left to go back to the table, where Jezalee was currently talking with Mallory, and Elaine. While Jezalee was talking, she looked up as Jim approached the table and kindly asked Jim if he was feeling okay and he said his stomach was a little queasy; but was feeling somewhat better. Mallory asked him if he wanted to leave because she certainly did not want him getting sicker. He told her he was feeling better than he had and he wanted to stay.

Later, on the way home in the limousine, Jim was quieter than usual and the three of them thought because he felt sick, he wanted to rest. By the time they dropped Jim off he had a few conversations with each of them; but needed a good night's sleep, and hopefully he would feel better tomorrow. He said his good nights and rushed out of the limousine. After he was dropped off, David did mention to the girls that Jim had been acting a little different at work lately. "In what way dear?" Mallory asked concerned. "Well, he has been much quieter, staying to himself, not going to lunch with us and constantly talking to himself," David answered. "Can you hear the conversations he has?" Jezalee quizzically asked. "No, it's in a low voice," David answered. "I wonder what is going on, because he usually talks to you about whatever is on his mind," Mallory replied. When they arrived at Jezalee's the children were sound asleep; so, she said let us not disturb them. "You and the staff come over for brunch tomorrow; whatever time is good for you," Mallory said that would be nice, is noon a good time? "Perfect," Jezalee happily replied. They said their goodnights and off Jezalee went to her bedroom.

When Jim arrived home, he rushed to the living room. He laid down on one of the sofas and just stared up at the ceiling. He knew he had not been himself for months and it always boiled down to his remembering so many things from his childhood; he could not let go of the feelings he kept having. He was tormented by his thoughts and was doing the best he could to try and forget his past, knowing it may interfere with his plans to marry Jezalee.

Jim fell asleep that night on the sofa, woke up the next morning still in his tuxedo. He immediately got up; took off his clothes and headed straight for a hot shower. Jim decided not to call Jezalee; if anyone called him, he would not answer the phone. He was happy he had purchased the penthouse in the building because even if someone wanted to come up to see him, there was no way up to his place without the doorman calling him. He decided to call down to his doorman, Gary and inform him if someone dropped by or called the front desk, to let them know he would be gone for a few days; he let him know he would be working and did not want to be disturbed under any circumstances.

Jim felt relieved that he would not have any disturbances for a few days. He knew he was getting close to asking Jezalee to marry him and he wanted to take the time now, while he had a few days off from work, to plan everything. He had decided months ago that Valentine's Day had to be the perfect time to propose to her. Jim knew he had been right in waiting; because they had gotten closer, and he wanted everything to be romantic. He checked out an extraordinary restaurant that would oblige him and close on Valentine's, evening and be open only for the two of them. He was paying a hefty sum to have the place to themselves. He had offered the owner four times what he usually makes in an evening on Valentine's Day. Jim was ordering her favorite flowers from the best florist in town, buying her favorite chocolates from Germany; he had already purchased a gorgeous diamond necklace that she had admired in the window one day while they were taking a stroll downtown. He was feeling much better today because he had great thoughts for his future.

Jim was going to stay home for a few days and not leave the building; so, he had ordered meals from several of his favorite restaurants and had them delivered before he left for the Ball the night before. He purposely did not want to be around anyone because he had been having nightmares that perpetuated irritability the following day. These nightmares were coming more frequently, and he could not get a good night's sleep. He always had the same horrific dreams, day after day, and night after night. He was drenched when he woke up from the nightmares and had to change his clothes and sheets.

Jim called Deanna and Eric to see how they were doing and wanted to see what they did for New Year's Eve. He adored Deanna and really enjoyed her husband, Eric. When he went for Thanksgiving; he could see how happy they were and what great parents they were. When Deanna answered the phone, she always talked like she had a smile on her face, and it immediately got Jim in a good mood. He wanted to get her opinion if she thought proposing to Jennifer {that is the name he used instead of Jezalee when he spoke with Deanna} on Valentine's Day would be a great idea. She was excited for him and hoped he had a big wedding. He asked her to be his best woman, in place of a best man. Deanna said she would be honored for the privilege of standing next to him when Jennifer walked up the aisle. He began to tell her what he had planned, she was quite impressed. "You will be the first person I call after she accepts my proposal." Jim joyfully said. Deanna was so happy to hear he was doing so well and wanted to get married. When he went for Thanksgiving, he had brought photos of her and the children with him and she told him then, how beautiful Jennifer was and such great looking children. He informed her; he had changed his name to Jim Stark. He never wanted to see or hear the name Chris ever again. Deanna completely understood, and thought it was a fantastic choice; anyway, she thought he looked more like a Jim and congratulated him on the great choice.

Jim knew how miserable he had been the last month or so at work and respected David for not saying anything to him. He knew in a few days he would be back at work and would hopefully go into the office more clear-headed and able to concentrate more on his job. He had thought about telling David about proposing to Jezalee; but he did not want to jinx it by letting anyone other than his dear Deanna know what he had planned. She mattered more to him than anyone and no one could ever come close to second; she knew him better than anyone else and he respected her thoughts on the matter of the heart.

While Jim was figuring out the things he wanted to do for the next few days, Jezalee was across town just waking up and needed to get busy in the kitchen with Helga. It was brunch day and she wanted to have the food ready by the time the children came down to eat. Before Jezalee had gone to bed last night, she wrote a note to Helga and placed it by the coffee pot so she would know that the O'Malley clan would be joining the rest of them for brunch. When David and Mallory arrived, they asked if Jim was coming over. Jezalee said she did not want to invite him since he seemed under the weather, and lately he had been too clingy towards her; she could only take so much of him. "We understand he has put too much pressure on you; just stand your ground and do what is best for you.

About a week later Jezalee invited the O'Malley's, and Jim over for Italian food night; they arrived around 6:00 PM, had dinner then played different Trivia games. The next night all of them went to a movie and afterwards headed to Bunny's Diner for late night dessert.

Jim felt things were working out beautifully with Jezalee and was counting the days he would be popping the question. Even though the O'Malley's were a part of the last two nights get togethers, he knew he was winning over Jezalee's heart. She could see that Jim had been in a better mood and he seemed so much more relaxed, and Jezalee and the children enjoyed his company. She made sure she kept things on a friendship basis and no intimacy was involved.

Several weeks had gone by and Jim had given it serious thought and decided not to propose to Jezalee on Valentine's Day. He had a feeling she or her children would figure out he may be proposing since it is the most romantic day of the year. Everything was purchased, wrapped and ready to give to her. He knew this was the right time because they had been doing a lot as a family and having more special platonic evenings together for quite some time.

One night, a week before Valentine's Day, he called Jezalee just before she tucked the children in bed and asked her if they could go for dessert; he said he wanted to talk. In the back of her mind, she thought maybe this was it! He wanted to finally talk about the deaths of his wife and son. She quickly said sure! He said he would pick her up in about twenty minutes; she knocked on Helga's door and said Jim was picking her up to go for dessert and would she mind watching the children. "Of course not! take your time," said Helga. Ever since they had security around the clock; they felt safer, and it was a little easier to go somewhere in a moment's notice; than it was before. They had always had the electronic gates which would be difficult to climb over the wrought iron fencing with it being twelve feet high. Now, with their four security guards around the clock, on the estate grounds no one could get in through the gates. They had cameras surrounding the entire estate. If anyone came within a foot of the gates, a silent alarm alerted the guards from the main office and on the property. At the entrance of the estate, Jezalee had two bullet-proof structures, with a guard at each station inside, and the same at the exit of the property. Paul had insisted ever since it was public knowledge that he and Jezalee were billionaires. Helga said she would be awake, so no problem. Jezalee changed from her pajamas into a nice dress and combed her hair and applied lipstick and was ready to go whenever he arrived. She had kissed the children goodnight, let them know she would be with Jim, and said Helga would be downstairs, if they needed anything. Jezalee waited outside for Jim, he was getting used to having to stop at the entry gate and showing his driver's license to a guard on duty. She saw him coming up the driveway, waved then walked down the steps and got in the car. As they approached the exit, Jezalee informed the guard what time she would approximately be returning, and he made note of it. After they passed through the gates, Jim leaned over and kissed her left cheek. She asked him why he called her so late? He said he wanted her to spend time with the children and he knew this was their bedtime.

Jezalee asked him where he was taking her; and he said to a little French restaurant he found out several months ago. When they arrived at the restaurant, the valet opened her car door and helped her out of the Porsche. Jim came around to her side and reached for her hand as they went into the restaurant. When she walked in, there was no one else around and candles lit everywhere. She asked if there was a phone available because she needed to call home, they pointed her in the direction where the public phones were, and she dialed Helga and told her where she was and she would be home soon. When she returned, Jim told her she could have called from his car phone. She looked over at Jim and asked him what was going on? Well! Let us have a seat and order maybe an appetizer before dessert. Jezalee felt this would not be the place he would discuss his wife and sons, death. She thought was acting strange, lighting candles, no one else is in the restaurant. Jezalee irritatingly let him know she was not hungry; but a dessert would be fine. Jim motioned for the maitre'd to come over to bring the dessert list. They looked it over and both decided on cheesecake. "This is a very elegant restaurant, and we are not dressed appropriately; what is so urgent that you got me out of the house on the spur of the moment? I would rather like to have a little notice, especially since I have children and had to ask Helga to watch them last minute; I normally do not do that to her," Jezalee asked nicely. Jim apologized and said he just got the nerve up to see her tonight; just as he said that the maitre'd came with their dessert, he placed it nearest to Jezalee as he said Bon Appetit. Jim looked at her, reached over for both her hands and as he did, soft music started playing in the background. He then said, "Let me give you the first bite, he picked up his fork, took a portion of the cheesecake from the top and as he came towards her mouth, she saw something sparkling and it was not the fork. As she peered at the diamond ring he said, "Will you marry me?" Jezalee was shocked! She sat back in the paisley printed tapestry chair and let Jim know it was preposterous! "I am not in love with you; and we had a conversation some time ago. My feelings are the same; I said it then, and will say it again, look elsewhere for a wife if you are so desperate to get married. I do not relish having this conversation again. I was very honest with you; I was willing to remain friends and that was it," Jezalee said with a stern look in her eyes. He looked at her and appeared sad and was speechless. She asked him to take her home immediately because it was getting late, and she had a lot to do tomorrow. They did not eat any of the cheesecake, got up and left. The valet drove the car to the front entrance and helped Jezalee into the car. After they both got in the car, they did not say a word as Jim drove her home. Once he got her home, he said goodnight, she said nothing. Jezalee walked up the stairs, opened the front door and closed it behind her.

Jezalee noticed a light on in the kitchen, so she headed in that direction; there Helga was baking cookies for the children. She went over to Helga and apologized for keeping her up. "Dear, you can always count on me, it does not matter what it is time, are you okay?" Helga asked. "Not really!" Jezalee said with frustration. "What happened? "Jim had a restaurant close early, had candles lit everywhere, soft music playing, and he asked me to marry him," Jezalee answered in a disgruntled manor. "Well! What did you say?" Helga said curiously. "Of course not!" Jezalee vehemently answered. "You do not want to marry him?" Helga asked. "Absolutely not! I do not want to marry him or anyone else right now, as I told him and to be honest; I told him I may never want to get remarried," Jezalee answered. "Jezalee, the only reason you do not want to, is because you still love Paul," as Helga perked up to say. She smiled then gave Helga a hug and said, "I have never stopped loving Paul and probably never will. This confession stops here because I do not want anyone knowing how I still feel about Paul," Jezalee was adamant. "You know me! I would never tell anyone. It is only your decision as to how you feel about someone. I love you Jezalee and I want you to be happy," Helga lovingly says. "Thank you! Now! Go to bed and once again, I appreciate you watching the children," Jezalee said as she hugs Helga. "You are always welcome, goodnight boss!" Helga smiles and says goodnight. "You had better stop calling me that; or I am going to demote you!" Jezalee laughingly replied. Helga kissed her on the cheek then hugged her goodnight.

Jim could hardly make it home after being turned down. Once he arrived at his penthouse, he went directly to his wine cellar, removed a few bottles of wine, and threw them as hard as he could up against the wall. The wine splattered all over the walls as the glass shattered everywhere. He felt like he did as a child; but he was able to vent his frustration out. He was trying to calm himself down but was having a difficult time. Jim looked at the room, pieces of shards everywhere, he turned away and walked out and closed the door behind him. Jim went to his library and looked over at the gifts he had chosen so carefully for Jezalee. He had taken the presents to a specialty shop to have them wrapped in paper of her favorite colors. As he glanced over at the boxes with the diamond necklace in one and her favorite German chocolates in the other; he realized the two envelopes would need to be returned. In one were tickets to go to Belgium, which Jezalee had mentioned she had wanted to go to the famous spa in Spa Belgium; when she had vacationed there the spa had been closed due to renovations. She had always wanted to go back there to go to the famous spa, it was the world's first spa which opened in the 16th Century in Spa, Belgium. He had purchased an open-ended date to come anytime they could fly there. He walked over to the round table where the gifts were sitting on the table where he set the diamond ring down; with one whoosh, knocked everything to the hardwood floor. He had called the florist first thing in the morning and cancel the flowers for Valentine's Day.

Jim left the room and walked down the hall to his bedroom. He got undressed and got in bed. He was trying to calm down; he wanted to call Deanna; but it was three hours later and did not want to wake her. He really felt it was the right time to propose to Jezalee because they had been having so much fun together, he could see she was enjoying having him around more, and he got along immensely with her three children. They had known one another for fourteen months, and he thought that was enough time to know if she was in love with him or not. Jim was confused; he thought the two of them could be compared to David and Mallory. He knew he had to decide if he needed to end the friendship and meet someone else or keep trying. He finally calmed down enough and fell asleep.

Jim woke up at 4:00 AM shaking and sweating from a nightmare. He jumped out of bed to take a shower and did not realize how early it was until he glanced at his clock. Jim was relieved he had fallen asleep after calming down a little. He knew it was a little early but certainly could not go back to bed. He decided he would apologize to Jezalee and tell her how much he loves her, and she was worth waiting for.

Jezalee woke up early the next morning, called Mallory to tell her what happened with Jim last night. David was listening on the extension. "Dear, what is going on so early in the morning? Mallory asked. "Well! I thought you would enjoy hearing this. Jim proposed marriage." Jezalee answered. "No kidding! Well! What was your answer?" David curiously asked. "The only thing that was logical, a big no, I have old him numerous times I do not love him and never will!" Jezalee answered with disgust. "What was his reaction?" Mallory asked. "Well! Let me put it this way, we never said one word before he dropped me off at home," Jezalee answered with relief. Mallory and David were happy she said no because they knew she was not ready for marriage; they also knew deep down she was still in love with Paul but would not admit it.

David arrived early at the office; he had a morning appointment with one of his corporate attorney's and needed to go over some paperwork before he came in. While he was looking over some paperwork that came across his desk, he saw Charles Dandridge's name; he slumped down in his chair and felt saddened that he was no longer with him, he had been so close to him over the years and losing a colleague was devastating. He still had a difficult time knowing Charles had gotten killed by a hit and run driver; they never found the person, and there were no witnesses around at the time. He knew no one could ever replace him but he knew how lucky he was to find Jim when he did. Jim was able to step right in and take over Charles's work, which was a relief for David and the company. David was still slumped over while he was staring at his colleague's name; he was a man he had admired since he was a young college student and worked for Charles part-time when he was a professor. When Charles retired, he went to work for David, and he was like a second dad to him.

When Jim arrived at work, he went directly into David's office. He asked him if he had a few minutes and David motioned for him to sit down. Jim began to tell him about the proposal and how terrible he felt after Jezalees answer. David let Jim know that Jezalee had called his house early that morning. He looked forlorn at David, he knew he had blown it and was hoping after a few days he could call her and apologize. David asked him to back off for a while because Jezalee informed he and Mallory that she was not in love with him. David tried to explain that when someone has been married a long while like Jezalee and Paul had; it takes some huge adjustment to try and fit in as a single person with children to raise. Jezalee will no longer want your friendship if you keep pressuring her about marriage. I would leave that subject closed; you are lucky at this point if she wants to continue a friendship. He wanted Jim to know how difficult things must be; with what he went through, losing his wife and son. Jim got up out of the chair and thanked him for his time and insight. David found it to be the perfect opportunity for him to bring up the death of his wife and son; but, as usual, there was no comment.

Jim decided to store the necklace and other gifts in the same drawer that housed the engagement ring. He had to stay optimistic and was going to save the gifts he had planned to give Jezalee for another time. He had also bought a gift and candy for her children and returned everything after he got off work the next day. When Jim got home that night he felt so alone and was upset with himself. He kept racking his brain, "Why did I do it?'' I should have waited for her to say she is in love with me. He wanted to call Deanna but did not want to disappoint her and especially not bother her with his dilemma.

Jim did not call Jezalee for several days; when he did, he profusely apologized, he felt so embarrassed. She tried to explain to him that she was just caught off guard and marriage was so far off her radar. She reminded him once again that friendship is all she could have with him. They never spoke of him proposing to her after the apology. There was a coldness between them for several weeks or so; but things went back to normal, at least for Jezalee.

Jezalee nor Jim ever mentioned the proposal to the children. they Jim came over whenever Jezalee and the children were not busy. Everyone got along and the kids really enjoyed Jim because he was up for whatever they wanted to do.

Created with Sketch.

Alexander was now twelve, a seventh grader, popular in school; and President of his class, the girls were continuously flirting with him. He was five feet, eight inches tall, with light chocolate brown eyes and thick jet-black hair with a great style that complimented his chiseled bone structure; a mirror image of his father when he was that age. He loved sports and had an athletic body; but made-a-decision that year to spend more time with his piano lessons. As it was, he was ahead of all the other students at the Piano Academy and started composing more of his own music. The Piano Academy was quite impressed with his advancement, and he was thrilled to find out he would be performing in the local youth symphony orchestra. Jezalee and Paul had started their children with piano lessons when they were each five years old; however, the girls never were enthusiastic about learning; but were encouraged to keep up their lessons and learn piano enough to be able to play well. Alexander excelled from the beginning, he came home one day and said he wanted a grand piano to practice on and an upright piano for his room. Once Alexander began his piano lessons, he was a serious student; practiced every day for several hours and began composing his own pieces. When the children at the Boys and Girls Club found out Alexander could play piano, that was the first thing they asked him to do. He immediately found his niche at the club and the children would gather around and listen to him if he kept playing.

Jessica was now fourteen, a freshman and completely enthralled in reading books and her school studies. She was a voracious reader and constantly had her nose deep in her schoolbooks or the latest novel. Jessica was gorgeous but played down her lovely Italian, looks. She liked a no fuss look with her thick, beautiful natural, blonde, almost white hair. Everyone teased her after seeing her siblings with their jet black, hair; they would say she must have been adopted; she explained there were Italians with blonde hair and her grandmother Elene was a natural blonde. Jessica usually did not wear any lipstick; she liked the all-natural look, she had the same light chocolate brown eyes, like her brother and dad. She was also 5 feet 7 inches tall. Jessica had set her standards high for herself and never backed down from anything. She had several boy admirers; but she was an extremely focused young girl. She had a passion for loose dresses so she could wear a stylish belt and would adorn her wrists with bangles. She kind of had a bohemian-playful look.

Adrienne was now fifteen, a sophomore, very studious, very social, and had wanted to be a psychologist at an early age. She also loved world history and fashion. She took after her mother more than the other two siblings and her style was very sophisticated with a feminine twist. She did not like wearing very many accessories; she was more of a minimalist when it came to adding accents to her attire. Being five feet, ten inches tall, Adrienne knew she could basically wear most any style with her height. The only drawback with her height so far was some boys were intimidated by it; so, there were not that many guys chasing after her. She was okay with that because she was very mature and her main goal was to be focused on the bigger picture, her future. She hung out with a group of teens along with Morgan and that was enough for her. The boys may not have swooned over her; because they were shorter than her, it was not her looks, she had strikingly beautiful features, with emerald, green eyes, long black lashes, and raven hair that looked like shining satin.

Jezalee had been working diligently on her books and going rather well. Mallory and she were busy helping at different charities and would also give their time to the Salvation Army, the Boys and Girls Club while their children were in school during the day, and food banks.

Jezalee had been busy with her children, summer was approaching; they had a few days left of school and looking forward to seeing their dad and the rest of their family in Italy. The children had done extremely well in school and were anxious to let their dad see their grade. Jezalee was busy overseeing how the children's school projects were going, and she managed to work on her books as well.

Since the children were going on vacation, Jezalee had a brainstorm one morning, she called Mallory to ask her if she would like to go away for a girl's week or at least a weekend in New York. She was actually on the same wavelength and was about to call her. They both laughed and said let us book our flight. David and Jim were going to be gone to Japan for business meetings all next week and thought that would be a great time to get away. Mallory suggested going for the week, since David would be away. Jezalee said her Manhattan penthouse was available since the new tenants would not be moving in for a month. Mallory booked their flights for the following Sunday and managed to get tickets to two Broadway plays. "I hope you do not mind, while we are in New York I need to meet with my publisher and give her the updates on my books," Jezalee said. "Of course not!" Mallory said. Jezalee asked Mallory if she would call her in-laws to see if they could meet them for dinner while they were in the city. Patrick and Kathleen were looking forward to seeing the gals and got tickets to see a musical after they went to an early dinner.

When the children came home from their last day of school Jezalee said they were going to have dinner with the O'Malley's. The children decided to pack before they changed clothes, they were so excited to have a summer with their dad and his family and maybe get to see their mom's parents too. The children were so excited to see their dad and were already packed and ready to go. "Let us get going, I can hardly wait for some of Mallory and Nell's cooking," Alexander said. Mallory explained to the children since their dad would be on a business trip for a week in Japan and she and Jezalee would be going to New York for a week for some girl fun; she surprised her children and signed them up for a one month, summer camp; they said they were over the moon happy because they would be able to help the camp directors with the kids.

David and Jim left for the airport for Japan several hours before Joseph drove the children and the ladies to the airport. The children were excited to be in Italy again, Jezalee and Mallory could hardly wait to get to board their plane to the Big Apple an hour later. The O'Malley children would be driven by Bob to their campgrounds around noon the same day.

Mallory loved Jezalee's place and was so delighted they had decided to come to New York when they did. The two-story penthouse; totaled seven thousand square feet with an outdoor terrace. There were huge trees for shade and privacy, potted flowers to beautify the surroundings, full-sized shrubs to fill in empty spaces, and a full set of patio furniture, a barbecue pit, outdoor heaters for winter and mist sprays for those humid summers. The gals sat out on the terrace while they were planning what they wanted to do for the next week, besides going to two plays, and a musical. Afterwards, Jezalee gave Mallory a tour of the penthouse and had her choose one of the bedrooms so she could get settled in. That night they decided to order-in and had Chinese food delivered. "Your Penthouse is magnificent! Did you ever live here with Paul?" Mallory asked. "No, we bought it as an investment and thought when we retired, we would move here part-time." Jezalee answered. "I did not realize the elevator went up to your second floor as well, I thought it just went to your garage." Mallory surprisingly said. "That was one of the reasons we bought in this building; other places just had stairs to the second and third floors," Jezalee said. "Even if I sell it, it is a great feature for anyone if they prefer not to use the stairs," Jezalee remarked.

The ladies stayed busy every day while in New York; they went loved the two Broadway plays and the musical. They spent time in Little Italy, Chinatown, walked through parts of Central Park, went to Tavern on the Green, bought some clothes in a few of their favorite shops and decided on their last day there, they would revisit the Statue of Liberty, they both had not been back to see her in years. They both had called a few friends and had gone out to two luncheons and three dinners before returning home.

After Jezalee and Mallory returned home from their New York jaunt, Jezalee went right back to her books writing and stayed a recluse for a few weeks before surfacing again. The children were having a great time with their dad and the rest of their family in Italy. Mallory's children asked if they could extend their time at the campgrounds because they were doing a lot of extra activities with some of the children they worked with at the Boys and Girls Club at home; Mallory spoke to the head director, and he stated how much all the children loved having them and begged for them to stay longer if it was okay with her. She said most definitely!

Summer was flying by, and the O'Malley children loved summer camp and were so glad they decided to stay for eight weeks. When David got back from Japan, Mallory and he felt like newlyweds not having the children around; they missed them something terribly but knew they were having a grand time.

Days had past and Jezalee kept busy; met up with a few friends for lunches and dinners that she had not seen in ages. Mallory and David came over quite often for dinner and Jezalee to their place. They admitted it was getting harder each year when the children extended their vacations but that was them growing up and showing their independence. Helga and Nell got together and planned joint barbecues for both families including the staff as well. Jim had been invited to a few of the gatherings; however, Jezalee would not attend if he would be there. Jim called her several times to ask her to take a drive along the coast; but she declined each time. She did not want to be in a car with him for hours; so, she would always make up an excuse and he knew he had to go along with it, or she would not see him anymore. He was getting tired of her attitude, and he would try to think of how he was going to address the situation. Jim knew Jezalee had been distant since he had proposed to her and was racking his brain how he was going to get closer to her. He knew he would never stop trying to get closer to her; it was just a matter of time.

Joseph and Nina's children came home first from visiting relatives so Jezalee asked them if they would like to go to Disneyland before the rest of the gang returned and they welcomed the idea. Helga was not going since Astrid and her daughter's boyfriend Nicholas was coming for a visit. Jezalee completely understood and asked the O'Malley's if they wanted to join them and called Bob, Linda, and

Nell if they were interested; they were excited about going. Linda knew their son Manny would be thrilled about going. David made the flight reservations while Mallory packed their bags. Joseph Jr. was jumping for joy, and Janine could not wait to buy a T-shirt in a gift shop and go to the Haunted House, and Mary just wanted to go on as many rides as she could. Manny was a little younger and Joseph Jr said he would be happy to go on some rides with him; he always wanted a younger brother and when he moved to America, he was so excited to find that Bob and Linda had a son. They got together a lot on each other's property and David even had a new tree house built on their property for them to hang out in.

The Disneyland trip was a great success, everyone got to do what they enjoyed the most; so, everyone was satisfied. Jim had heard about the going to Disneyland trip and was mad Jezalee had not invited him.

After the Disneyland trip, Jezalee poured her heart and time into more research on all the Cathedrals, Museums, famous buildings, and other structures in the world. There was only one week before school started back and Paul was wrapping up his and the children's vacation. He had checked in with Jezalee a couple times a week and she was so happy they were all having a grand time.

The O'Malley children arrived home a week before Jezalees children; but once they were all home and settled, they had a big barbecue at the O'Malley's. They each shared vacation experiences and were all looking forward to the new school year. Manny was the biggest surprise of all because he normally was a quiet child around a group but not then, he had a lot to tell everyone about the rides and seeing Mickey Mouse and Goofy, who were his favorite characters.

Created with Sketch.

The children seemed relaxed after their vacations and looked forward to catching up with their friends. Jezalee got busy with some of her fundraising charities and still had more research to do on her books. She was happy Jim was working more hours than usual and that took pressure off her to see him more than she wanted to. She was realizing more than ever, Jim needed to date other women because there was no future for them. She understood why she wanted him around because she wanted the children to think she had moved on from Paul. Who was she kidding? Jezalee wanted to make Paul jealous as well. She now had to think about the children and how much they liked Jim. Jezalee was thankful they never once mentioned they wanted her to marry Jim; so, she knew they probably liked him as a friend. She would eventually be forced to tell Jim they could not be a part of his life anymore; due to his obsession over her.

Time was not stopping for anyone; after school resumed, the children were busy with their studies, Adrienne spent a lot of time reading all the books she could find on Psychology, she was tutoring a student that was having a tough time in some of her classes; so, she volunteered to be her study buddy. Jessica joined a local Book Club and met once a month to review the books with the other club members; she was the youngest member, and everyone was amazed with her insight in the books they read. As for Alexander, he had become someone to reckon with by the pieces he had learned at the Piano Academy and was researching every piece by Mozart, Beethoven, Chopin, Liszt, Brahms, Rachmaninoff, Debussy, and Shubert. He was composing more of his own work and the family was astounded at his accomplishments. Alexander's current goal was to attend Juilliard School of Music or San Francisco Conservatory, possibly research information on a school in Vienna.

Jezalee bought a yacht she intended to leave docked in Lake Tahoe and they had been enjoying the Tahoe area every chance they got. While in the area they always stayed at "Castle on the Mountain." When she and the children could not go, she let the O'Malley's, their staff and hers use the yacht anytime they wanted.

Jim never joined anyone going on the yacht; he said he was afraid of water since he was a child. They thought that was odd since he had a boat that his wife and son were on when they drowned. He had even told David that he was responsible for their death because he could not go sailing that day with them. They were not about to question his reasons and, certainly knew they would never have an answer to that.

Jezalee and Jim seldom went out, especially after his proposal. She did not want him to get the wrong impression. Jezalee was incredibly relieved that he had not put any pressure on her because she was not going to have sex with him. She thought he may not want to get intimate with her to make her jealous or want him more, which she had no interest. Jezalee was still in a quandary as to other times she was around Jim, he seemed to be in another world, she could not figure out what that world was. When they attended several events, separately, Jezalee could see he was distant at times, and she could see his mind would wander and be talking to himself. She asked him on several occasions what was he thinking about, and he would perk up and say everything; other times he would fire back a smart remark. She was not the only one that continually noticed his mood swings and they appeared to be more often, than not. David said he had these mood swings at work as well; but he was still working diligently and without any problems. He told Mallory and Jezalee that Jim was highly intelligent and knowledge on a myriad, subjects. There were times he could not figure out Jim either; but he was not going to question it because he was such an asset to his company.

The O'Malley and Albanese families went up to Incline Village-Tahoe for Thanksgiving. Mallory and David's parents came from back East as well as Mallory's brother Danny with his family. David had the entire meal catered and the ladies said it was the first time any of them had not cooked or baked for Thanksgiving and was able to enjoy the day without walking into the kitchen to.

Jim had gone to visit Deanna and her family and had extended his Thanksgiving and stayed for a full week. Jim loved visiting with Deanna and was crazy about her children and thought her husband was terrific. He wanted to be happy like they were, but he did not have the skills to manage it.

Jezalee was happy that Paul had invited her and their children to his villa in Pisa, for Christmas and his parents and hers would be joining them. His brother Peter would not be able to come due to all the festivities at his Church; however, they surprised him and were sitting in the front row pews celebrating Midnight Mass on Christmas Eve with him. Before they went to Mass that night, they decided to go door to door and sing carols to anyone that would listen to them. They were elated at how many families came outside to hear them sing and offered them hot cocoa, mouth-watering Italian desserts. This was a Christmas that Jezalee would never forget, she expressed her feelings about how great it was; but Paul silently had the same thoughts and kept them to himself.

Alexander brought several copies of the December Issue of Beautiful Estates, he was so proud to show off his moms, spectacular entry into the magazine showing their 1986 interior and exterior Christmas décor. He gave one to Paul and to both sets of grandparents and they said they would treasure the issue.

Once everyone got settled in Paul's villa in Pisa, he surprised them with a family trip to the country estate in Saint-Germaine-en-Laye. They were so excited to be able to share at least some time there during the holidays. He had called ahead to Montrose and Monique and asked them to get the Christmas decorations out and do their magic. He made sure to invite them for the Christmas festivities. Montrose was thrilled to hear from Paul and made sure everything would be done before they arrived. He also said they would be available to join them and thanked Paul for always including he and his family when they came out to the estate.

Montrose and Monique got the estate ready for the Albanese's and their parents to celebrate four days of Christmas in their favorite place; kit looked exceptionally magnificent. Montrose surprised them with cutting down a beautiful tree that took center stage when one opened the front double doors. He had strung lights up the lengthy driveway to the entrance. Monique had all their decorations throughout the house and in the rooms, they knew they would be there for four days. Montrose had left several dozens of their most delicate and unique ornaments to add to the tree to bring more spirit to their stay. Having Montrose, Monique, and Veronica able to share two days with them was an added gift for everyone; they were an exceptional couple with the sweetest daughter.

Jim was irritated that Jezalee went to Italy for Christmas; but he was not about to let her know how he felt. He informed her he was going to be spending Christmas in New York and had invited Deanna and her family to spend the holidays there with him. Jim lied to Deanna and told her he was going to Italy for Christmas because he did not want her feeling sorry for him, knowing how much he wanted to marry Jezalee. Jim, on the other hand, had booked a flight to New York as soon as Jezalee told him she and the children would be spending Christmas in Italy. He had the great idea to go back to where everything began to get better for him; the Midtown Manhattan Library that he loved so much. He came into that Library basically knowing nothing and after years of going there, his whole life changed. He found out he was not dumb, even though he never went to school. He knew he had a thirst for books but was deprived as a child. This Library opened-up his life beyond his expectations. He was also fortunate when he was able to live rent free in a lovey and spacious apartment, all due to Deanna's mom and dad. While he was there, he ate breakfast in his suite at the Plaza Hotel; then off to the library he would go. He would stay there most days until it closed and if he got hungry, he would get a hot dog from one of the outside vendors to curb his appetite or wait until he got back to his suite. He was having a great time in New York by himself; it was like de ja vu from years of being there. Jim decided not to return until January 4th because he wanted to hang out in the library as-long-as he could; before getting back to San Francisco. There were Librarians and domestic staff that remembered him for all the hours, months, and years he spent there, getting his education on everything he could. While Jezalee was at Paul's villa, she had pain in her heart and regretted the divorce.

She could see that Paul appeared happy, she needed to see it first-hand, that way she knew unfortunately things worked out they were meant to be. Jezalee came close to asking Paul about his son; but she felt it was off-limits, so she changed her mind. He still had not been able to break the news to their children; she did not care if they ever knew at this point. On the last day she and the children were at Paul's, she came to the realization that Villa would never be her home; it was a place to visit.

When Jezalee got back with the children from their lovely Christmas with the family, she got out her journal; which was growing cobwebs since her last entry; and wanted that Christmas entered as one of the best she ever had. They were invited to spend New Year's Eve at Paul's as well; but she wanted to beat the crowds at the airlines and be home sooner. The O'Malley's were not coming back until New Year's Day; so, Jezalee had planned an intimate party with her staff as well as David and Mallory's since they were around. They had a great time bringing the New Year in together.

While Jim was in New York he had decided to buy a few gifts for Jezalee, her children and staff. He also bought for all the O'Malley's and their staff as well. He had bought Christmas gifts in San Francisco for Deanna and her family and had them sent the first week in December so they would get them in time to place under the tree.

On Jim's flight back to San Francisco, he was thinking back to the times he and Deanna never knew that holidays existed; they were isolated from knowing there was a holiday of any kind; they were never out and about in public during July 4th, Halloween, Thanksgiving, or a Christmas. They were amazed once they got out in the unknown what they had been missing their entire childhood. It was similar, to how it was when someone goes to prison, never seeing what is out there and they got out ten or twenty years later and there would be so many changes and things they had never seen.

Every holiday Deana and Jim would talk about Jenny O'Conner and what joy and surprises she gave to their lives. She brought so much unexpected happiness their way and blessed them every day they lived in her cottage. They stayed in touch with her until she died in 1975 from hitting her head from a fall while shopping in a grocery store. They had known and loved Jenny for over ten years. They would go see her a couple of times a year and she would fly out to see them. She was the first person that they loved, and she did in return. they had finally sat down with her and told her the truth after they had been living on her property for a year. Jenny, of course was devastated what these two children had endured and said she would take their secret to her grave and that she did. When they went to her funeral it was difficult on them, as if she was their mother. She had been a woman of substance who had been a pillar of the community, had encouraged and inspired people that needed guidance in life. Jim and Deanna had always looked up to her for the kindness and love she exuded. There was close to three-hundred people attending her funeral; everyone one of them was a person she had helped in some way or the other. Jim felt when Jenny was laid to rest, his heart went with her. She left an indelible mark on both Jim and Deanna's life and their sadness never lessened; especially with Jim he never met his family.

When Jim landed in San Francisco he called Jezalee to see if he could come over and maybe take her, Helga, and the children out for dinner to celebrate another new year ahead for all of them. She thought that was so sweet and she asked the powers to be, and everyone said yes. He was at their house within an hour and brought everyone's presents and set them under the tree. Jezalee said, "What is all this?" Jim answered, "Just a Christmas present for each of my five, favorite people. They went to get Helga to see if she was ready to go out to dinner and she had just changed clothes. They gathered around the tree, and he had Alexander hand out everyone's presents. They let Jezalee open hers first and she told him he should not have been so generous. She thanked him on his exquisite taste in the earrings, gloves, and scarf. Helga was next; when she opened the present saw that it was a beautiful red coat, she immediately tried it on, and it fit her perfectly. Helga walked over to Jim, gave him a strong hug, and thanked him for the gorgeous coat. The children all opened theirs at the same time and were overjoyed getting ski outfits and lift tickets. They ran over and gave him a big hug as well. Alexander got up, went to the tree, brought the last present over to Jim. He was shocked because they had never mentioned exchanging presents. He started opening the huge box and started to choke up when he realized it was the first edition dated in 1768 of the first published Encyclopedia Britannica and the next set was dated 1968, it was the two-hundred-year anniversary edition and the current one published in 1986. He was stunned! "How did you ever find the first publication of these? And the two hundred anniversaries set? You all are amazing. I will treasure these always." Jim said he would cherish them forever. Jezalee adds! and these should fill up a whole shelf, in your, library. He laughed. "Now, I think we have all worked up an appetite so let me take you all out for dinner," Jim kindly offered. "Whose, deciding where we are going? Helga asked. The children decided they wanted to go to Pier 39 and pick a restaurant there. That is what they did and had a great evening with great seafood and good conversation. After dinner, they wanted chocolates of some sort; so, they headed for Ghirardelli's, and each got their favorites.

Jim dropped them off at home and took his special gift to his place. When he arrived home, he had set the box down in the library and wept. He had never gotten anything so special and was so elated for these gorgeous encyclopedias. It was quite a treasure he received.

The next morning, while Jezalee was gazing out her bedroom window she was-euphorically reflecting-back to her life with Paul. More times than not, Jezalee would become nostalgic over the life they had together. Why did things happen the way they did? Sometimes she wished she had just accepted what he did and had them see a marriage counselor; she kept thinking that was one of the reasons she waited six months before she revealed to Paul that she knew about Gloria and his illegitimate son. In the back of her mind, she knew more than likely if they had kept this all a secret it would eventually come out. Even though she loved her life in the states and her new friends she had acquired, she was still void of that special bond she had with Paul. She knew she had grown a lot since the divorce but sometimes she wondered if it was all worth it. Jezalee cared for Jim, they had a lot of fun together, but she knew she would never fall in love with him. Paul was her first love and the father of her children; divorce had never entered her sphere of thoughts all the years they had been married. She never discussed her feelings about Paul with the children because she did not want them to get the wrong impression that they may get back together. She was having wonderful reflections on a life she once had with the love of her life; however, he made a major moral mistake, and it changed the course of their lives forever. Jezalee heard the phone ring, and she had the answer machine pick it up; she could hear Jim's voice but decided she just could not talk to him after thinking about Paul. She would make her excuses later.

It was tough for all the children to leave the holidays in the past and get back into the school spirit as they say. Jezalee was working tirelessly on her books, Mallory was redecorating her and David's master suite and wanted to find a new place for the exquisite vase they had gotten from the Albanese's. They loved where they had placed it; however, Mallory was never one to keep things in the same place more than a year or so; it was the Libra in her. She called Jezalee and asked her to come over and help her decide where she should place the vase and get some ideas for her bedroom. When

Jezalee arrived, she had just baked lasagna she thought they could have for lunch, Mallory could smell the delicious aroma as soon as Nell answered the front door. Jezalee sat the hot dish in the kitchen while the girls decided what to do with the huge vase. Jezalee suggested placing it in the living room next to the grand piano, with the gorgeous chandelier overhead would shine down on the vase. Bob wheeled it into the living room to let the girls see how they liked it there. "Oh! My goodness! This! is the perfect place, by the piano," Mallory said.

The girls had Nell and Linda join them for the fantastic lasagna and Mallory always had a dessert nearby. They had lemon cheesecake or carrot cake to choose from and the four of them opted to have coffee with their desserts. They each could not decide between such scrumptious desserts; so, they had a small slice of each. They discussed what they were going to try and accomplish for 1988 that did not happen in 1987.

As spring was to a close, the weather was still exceptional and Jezalee had been busy doing more research on her book and doing a lot of charity work with Mallory. The children had been focusing all their energy into their studies, getting ready for the last six weeks of school.

Paul was busy as usual with work and seeing Jonathan on his monthly visits. Jezalee parents were getting things lined up for their trip to Europe and scheduling in time to see their grandchildren. Jim and David had been extremely busy and had done a lot of traveling to South America, the Asian countries, and Europe. Jim knew the children were going to spend the entire summer vacation with their father and it was his time with Jezalee. He would show her how much greater he can be as a boyfriend and hopefully future husband. He knew he had to win her over in the next couple of months while her children were away. He was going to wine and dine her and make her forget that ex-husband of hers.

Created with Sketch.

It was finally a week away until school was out, Jim knew that Jezalee had informed Paul he could have the children all summer. He was hoping he could see her more often and try to start a romance with her and possibly go on some great weekend getaways. Jezalee was in her room listening to music while she thumbed through Architectural Digest; just as she was about to get to the interior designing part of the magazine, Jim called. Jezalee almost did not answer but she had not talked to Jim for a couple weeks; so, she answered the phone. They chatted for a few minutes, and he said he just wanted to call to say he was thinking of her and wanted to let her know he was hoping while the children were gone during the summer; they could plan a few weekend getaways; Jezalee said she was not sure she wanted to go anywhere because she was going to be busy while her children were on vacation. When they hung up, he threw the telephone across the room. He told himself! She is not going to get away with treating me this way.

Jezalee had been extremely busy with the Centre Communautaire Familia de Paris and was getting ready to expand the building because they had such an influx of people that needed help. Paul went over to the center to check out how he wanted to proceed in making more space and decided to buy the building next door and was meeting with the city planning committee and an architect to see how they could connect the two together. When Paul called Jezalee about his suggestion, she thought it was a brilliant idea and it would certainly give them the opportunity to have more people come to the center for clothes, food, recreation, music, dance, and reading.

Jim had called Jezalee to let her know he was getting ready to go to Spain on business and when he got back, he would love to take her out of town for three or four days, maybe to Santa Barbara or Carmel to relax. She let him know it was out of the question because she may need to go to Paris to oversee a building she and Paul were renovating. Jim bluntly asked her, why couldn't Paul have someone else go in her place, since he is so rich? Jezalee, slammed the phone down and was furious at what had just come out of Jim's mouth. He kept pushing the wrong buttons and she knew he needed to back off; she was not about to go anywhere with him.

School was officially over, when the children got home, they were excited to hand over their report cards with all A's. Jezalee was so proud of them and was anxious for Paul to arrive later that evening to see what the children had accomplished in school. Paul was spending a couple of days with them prior to their leaving for Paris and Italy. The children were overly excited to see their dad, both sets of grandparents and their uncle Peter; however, they had no idea their dad would be coming two days before they left on vacation, and they would be traveling with him.

While the children were changing out of their uniforms, Paul called and asked Jezalee if it was okay to let the children know about Jonathan when he arrived, and she gave him the go-ahead. He said he had an emergency meeting in New York and thought he may as well fly to San Francisco since he had purchased a private jet and was hoping it would be okay for the children to fly to Paris with him instead of on the commercial jet. He let her know that he had not canceled their commercial airline tickets just in case she was against them going on his jet. She was shocked but told him since you bought the jet, maybe you can help transport ill patients from one hospital to the next when you are not using it for business or pleasure. "A great idea; I will certainly give it some thought; Jezalee, you always know the right thing to do," Paul replied. "She asked who was flying the plane?" "Well! It certainly will not be me!" Paul quickly affirmed that thought and they both laughed. He said he had hired four ex-fighter pilots and they work exclusively for him; plus, he had hired a couple of stewards to oversee whoever is on board.

She asked Paul what time he had be in San Francisco, and he said his plane would land at 4:00 PM. Jezalee invited him to dinner and to plan on staying with them until he and the children left for Paris. He said that was kind of her; but he had reserved a room at the Fairmont Hotel. She said it would be nice if he could stay with them for the next two days since they are flying out together. "I do not want to be in the way; it is probably best I keep my hotel accommodations," Paul said. Jezalee said she could have Joseph pick him up; he said his secretary had made a reservation with a limousine service and not to bother Joseph. "Okay, but at least come for dinner, the children will be thrilled," Jezalee replied. "Now! You know I cannot pass up your or Helga's cooking," Paul commented. "Well! You chose a good night to come because we are having an all-out Italian meal with tiramisu for dessert," Jezalee remarked. "Perfect timing on my part," Paul said. "Yes, it is!" Jezalee agreed. "Paul, why don't you come straight from the airport; you will have more time with the children," Jezalee asked. "Okay! I will go along with that, see you around 5:00," Paul answered. Jezalee was smiling at the other end of the phone and said, sounds good! It will be a nice surprise for the children and great for Paul.

After the children changed clothes, they came directly into the kitchen for their after-school snacks. They were discussing all the things they wanted to do after their dad picked them up in Paris. They started writing down all the things they wanted to do with him and their grandparents; they were hoping their uncle Peter would be able to take some time off away from his Priestly duties. Jezalee walked in after she got off the phone from Paul and asked the children what they were up to, and they showed her their list of things they wanted to do on their vacation. "Very impressive," she said. "Mom, can you join us for part of the vacation?" Alexander asked. "That is sweet of you to ask; I would love to do that; however, this is your father's time with you," Jezalee answered. "Just thought I would ask," Alexander relied. "Dear, I appreciate your honest efforts; however, things are different now. I hope in-the-near future we will be able for the five of us to do something together," Jezalee commented.

Jezalee took Helga aside to let her know that Paul would be coming for dinner and would arrive around 5:00. Helga was so excited to see him, hoping the children would have a wonderful summer with him. She knew Jezalee would be lonely but wanted the children to keep their bond strong with their dad.

Paul's driver had picked him up from the airport and drove him to Jezalee's home. Paul, being outgoing, struck up a conversation with the driver and asked him his name and how long he had been working for the limousine service. The boy said his name was Gregory Stanton and started the limousine service as soon as he was 16; while going to college full time. Paul asked him what college and what he was majoring in. He said he was a medical student at Stanford by day and a limousine driver by night. "Good for you, keep the studies up and get those good grades," Paul was impressed and said. Paul knew he needed to get in the house; but he wished he had more time to talk with the young man. He asked Gregory if he could wait until he finished visiting with his children and said he would pay him triple for his trouble. Gregory said he could wait for him because he could turn over calls to another driver. Paul said to just leave his luggage in the trunk; and he would see him in a couple of hours. Paul gave him some extra money and said he should go get a good meal and he did not need to be back for at least two hours. He said he was paying him from the time he picked him up at the airport to the time he would drop him off at the hotel he would be staying. Gregory said that was fine because he could study for his exam in the car while he waited for Paul.

Paul walked up to the double doors, rang the doorbell, and tried to hide as best he could behind a large plant that was at the front landing. Alexander yelled out he was the closest to the door and ran to answer it; at first, he did not see his dad, then Paul kind of moved away from the plant, then Alexander saw him. He grabbed his dad; Paul almost fell into the plant and they both started laughing. Alexander took his dad's hand after he hugged and kissed him and said he could not believe what a great surprise it was him showing up unexpectedly. By this time, Jezalee was at the door and asked them, what in the world takes so long for you two to come in the house? "Is it okay that dad is here?" Alexander nervously asked. "Dear, I invited your dad and wanted it to be a surprise for all of you," as Jezalee smiled at Paul. They made their way into the living room where the girls were. Jezalee said she would check with Helga to see what time they would have dinner. Helga was in the kitchen and said the food would be ready in thirty minutes and Jezalee relayed the message to Paul and the children.

Paul asked the children if he could speak with them in the living room while they were waiting for dinner and they said sure! Jezalee said she would leave the four of them and go help, Helga. The children had his undivided attention and he let them know how much he had hurt their mom; it was so painful to think what he put her through, and it was something he would have to live with the rest of his life. Secondly, hurting the three of them was agonizing for him as well, and could not imagine what pain they had been in. Thirdly, this was the part that he was afraid to confess; he looked at the children, tears streaming down his face, and said, "I have a second son!" They looked at one another in bewilderment and then Jessica ran towards him, was out of control, and started pounding on his chest with her clenched fists and yelling out how much he hated him. Adrienne and Alexander quickly got up, ran towards her, and pulled her away from their dad. Paul sat down in the nearest chair while Alexander and Adrienne grabbed a hold of Jessica, who at this point was hysterically crying and fighting them off like a wild animal.

Jezalee heard yelling and ran to the living room; she saw Paul and Jessica both crying. Adrienne and Alexander ran over to their mom and told her what Jessica had done. Paul looked up at Jezalee and said he should leave. "No! What happened!" Jezalee asked. "Mom, Dad was apologizing for hurting all of us; then told us he has another son, that is when Jessica ran to him and started beating on his chest like some wild animal; he just stood there and let her do it," Adrienne spoke up. Jezalee could see both Paul and Jessica had been crying and wanted to get to the bottom of her attacking her dad. She asked everyone to sit down, and she had something to add to this situation. She peered towards Jessica and said she was not going to tolerate violence in her home. She explicitly told Jessica, it did not matter what her dad told her, she was never to hit anyone in this household, or any other place for that matter. She explained to her daughter she had never seen signs of violence from anyone in their household while she and Paul were married and never wanted to see it now. "I never had a reason to have a reaction like this; not only are you two divorced but he has a kid and I hate you, Paul," Jessica yelled out. Jezalee rushed over to her and said she had crossed and there would be consequences you will have. I can certainly understand your feelings because it has been difficult for me as his wife. "Jessica, you are going to have severe repercussions for this outburst of beating on your father, yelling at him, and fighting off your brother and sister. I do not ever want you to show this type of anger in this house again or you will be going off to a boarding school," Jezalee unequivocally stated. "Another thing! Do not think I would not do it; they are extremely rigid and if you cannot abide by my rules, you will be gone from this house," sternly said her mother. Jessica was still shaking and sobbing but felt hate for her father. Jezalee ordered her to go to her room and she was not to come out until she had decided what she was going to do.

Paul walked out of the room and Alexander went after him and said, "wait up dad! He gave him a hug and said how much he missed and loved him." Paul was taken aback for his son's sincerity and hugged him tight then kissed him on the cheek. They stopped in the hall and Alexander asked him if he would come to his bedroom and he said sure. They both entered his room and went over to his sitting area and sat down. Alexander wanted to talk first; dad, I can imagine that was so hard for you to tell us you have another son. "This was something that should never have happened, and it has destroyed our family forever. It is difficult to live with this at times; but I need to forge ahead and believe that someday I can forgive myself," Paul looked directly at him like man to man and said. Dad, I forgive you and I am old enough to know that things happen in life when we least expect it and need to deal with it head-on. I look at it this way, I now have a brother and it is not a bad thing to me. The worst part of this is you and mom not being together. We are missing out on so much not having you around and I know that mom misses and loves you too! Mom and us, can have fun with Jim or anyone; but mom is not in love with Jim, and he is our friend and that is it! He nor any other man will never take your place, as a husband, a dad or best friend. I know she regrets divorcing you; she lives with that every day. She is suffering from being humiliated by the only man she has ever loved, and her heart is weak from not having your love. Mom thinks she has us fooled but we know she is still madly in love with you. Paul was looking and hearing his son for the first time as a boy who was way beyond his years. He thanked his son for his undeserving words to him and said they both better get back to the girls.

Jezalee asked Adrienne to get Jessica so they could sit and talk over a few things. As Jessica and Adrienne entered the living room, Jezalee had Paul and Alexander join them; they were sitting on two sofas facing one another and Jezalee was sitting in a chair; she looked at Paul and said Jessica has something to say to you. Before Jessica spoke, her dad said, "Listen, it is my fault this all happened, and Jessica was not prepared for what I had to say," Paul remarked. "Paul, no one deserves to be beaten and I will never excuse Jessica for what she did to you. You have caused us to change our lives and not be a whole family anymore; but I will never tolerate violence in this home," Jezalee sternly commented. "Jessica, I think there is no reason for you to talk tonight; I have decided what your punishment will be and there are no changes to my ruling. Your vacation is out, tomorrow you will say your goodbyes to everyone and will be going away to a place called Therapy Camp for a month; if all goes well there, you will have the privilege of meeting up with your brother and sister to have time with your dad for the rest of the summer. If that camp does not help you, I will be sending you to a boarding school and you will not be joining your brother and sister, and you will be writing an apology letter to your dad," Jezalee said. "What kind of camp?" Jessica quietly asked. "One that mainly helps young teens that have pain and need to be able to talk about it with Clinical Psychologists in that field," Jezalee answered. Her mother said, after a month, she would pick her up from Camp she had better have a good attitude and if you do, you'll be able to meet up with everyone for the rest of your vacation. If I hear that you have acted up around your father and grandparents, off to boarding school you go. You will not be able to call any of your friends until one week prior to school is back in session." Jezalee said. Jessica started crying again and Jezalee told her to go to her room where her dinner will be served. No one had ever seen Jezalee react like this before, and they knew that she meant business. Paul felt so guilty over what happened and after Jessica went to her room; he asked Jezalee and the children if he could say something before, she left. They stayed in the living room, and he said he felt terrible how Jessica felt about him, and it was all his doing, and he did not know if Jezalee should go to the extent that she was with her punishment. She surprisingly looked at him and said, "you are not the head of the house here and I am the one that makes the rules and decisions," Jezalee explained. Adrienne and Alexander glanced at one another and knew for the first time in their lives as being the children of Jezalee that they both better listen and not say a word. "You are absolutely right, I was way out of line; I am not your husband anymore, this is your house, your rules and I need to realize things are different now," Paul said shamefully. "Paul, I should not have said it that way and I am truly sorry, I hope you can forgive me," Jezalee profoundly said. "There is nothing to forgive," Paul quickly answered.

The children were still sitting on the sofa as quiet as church mice when Helga announced that dinner was ready. Jezalee asked Helga to have dinner with them but before they sat down to eat, she asked her if she would not mind taking Jessica's meal to her. They waited for Helga to return and the five of them sat down to dinner. Alexander and Adrienne kept glancing back and forth at their parents while they were eating and realized how much they missed seeing both at the table having meals together.

While Jessica was in her room it gave her time to think of how she reacted; now she felt embarrassed and had asked Helga after they were done with dinner if her mom would come up to her room. She said she would relay the message to her. Dinner time was pleasant, but Jezalee did not want anyone to notice how happy she was that Paul stayed for dinner; not realizing Paul was having the same thoughts that it was nice of Jezalee to invite him to share a meal. He would give her a smile or two when their eyes met, and it was difficult knowing he would be leaving after dinner was over.

The five of them enjoyed their meal and there was a lot of small talk. Paul wanted to know how Astrid was doing in college and Helga was proud to say she was a straight A student every semester. He remembered when Helga and Astrid came to be a part of their household, Astrid was the cutest, happiest, and tiniest five-year-old he had ever seen. She would get lost in their rambling estate and would yell out she was lost. He and Jezalee were just as proud of her as her mom was. The children had a nice conversation with their dad and let him know they were excited to be able to spend so much time with him during their summer vacation. Paul thanked Jezalee for letting the children come for the summer and his parents and brother were just as thrilled. She said that was the least she could do knowing how much time she had with them.

The phone rang, no one was finished with their meal; Jezalee said whomever it was, can call back later or leave a message. Twenty minutes later Paul was sitting in the family room having dessert with everyone and the phone rang again and Jezalee did not want to talk.

Alexander went up to his bedroom to get the latest song he composed to show his dad and Jessica opened her door and whispered to her brother to have their mom come up to see her. When Alexander went downstairs, he told his mom that Jessica wanted to talk with her. Jezalee went upstairs to see what she had to say. She knocked on her door and her daughter said to come in. "What do you want?" Jezalee asked. "To apologize for hitting dad; I do not know where that anger came from; but he struck a nerve I never knew I had," Jessica answered. "I understand! That is why I am sending you a way to deal with whatever is bottled up inside you; hopefully, you will find answers as to why you went after your dad in a violent frenzy," Jezalee sadly commented. She looked at Jessica and said, "If you think I am going to back off from my ruling because you are apologizing, you are sadly mistaken. You need to learn an early lesson in life; when you do wrong things, you have to pay the piper," Jezalee said as she walked away from her daughter, towards the door, and would see her tomorrow for breakfast. Jezalee shut the door behind her; as she headed downstairs with tears in her eyes; she felt miserable what she was doing but violence was not in her vocabulary and her daughter was going to learn from professionals she will never get far in life if she is pounding on people with her fists when she does not like what they say or do.

The phone rang once again, Jezalee got up from the dining room table, excused herself so she could answer it. Jim was calling and asked her, where had she been, because he had called about an hour earlier? "That is true; but you also called twenty minutes ago. I have nothing to say to you and hung up," she was still mad at him for always trying to interfere in her business with Paul and was not about to talk to him while Paul was there.

After dinner, Paul excused himself, got up from the dining table and said his goodbyes to the family. He thanked them for the incredible meal and needed to get some work done before he went to bed. Alexander interjected and asked his dad if he would stay with them until they left for Paris. He let him know he already had a suite at a hotel nearby. Alexander looked at his mom and asked her to convince his dad to stay; Adrienne seconded the motion and Helga smiled and laughed as she said she would third the motion. "You know you are out-numbered; and we have plenty of guest rooms; so, it looks as if you had better stay," Jezalee sweetly said as she smiled and raised her eyebrows. "Well! Since I am outnumbered and want to stay in the good graces of my family, I had better cancel my reservation. I also need to tell the limousine driver he can go," Paul quickly said. "You mean to tell us he has been out there all this time?" Alexander says. "Yes! I was going to ask him in; but he was studying for an exam, and I thought I was going back to the hotel," Paul answered. "Have the young man come in for a home cooked meal and dessert," Jezalee said. Paul went to get Gregory; he could see he was studying away and taking notes. Paul tapped on the window; Gregory rolled it down so he could talk to him. Paul asked him to come in to meet his family and if he had gone to get dinner. He replied he kept studying instead. Paul said there is some incredible Italian food and dessert calling out your name, so you may as well come in and eat. He let him know he would not be going to the hotel after all, he was spending a couple of days there. Gregory got out of the limousine, reached in his pocket to hand over the money Paul had given to him to buy his dinner. "Please! You keep that money, buy your lunch tomorrow," Paul said. "Thank you," but I cannot take money I have not earned and placed it in Pauls' hand. He could see by Gregory's actions; he was a fine young man. He looked at the boy and said, "Okay! But you must come in so you can have a good meal; you need the nourishment to study better," Paul has insisted. Gregory got Paul's luggage out of the trunk and carried up the steps to the front door. Alexander greeted them and asked Gregory, please come in and join us. Helga heated a plate of food she had made; the family introduced themselves and sat down near him while he ate. Adrienne asked him questions about Stanford because that was the only college she ever wanted to go to. Her mom finally asked everyone to leave the poor boy alone so he can finish his meal. He said it was okay; but she insisted. After Gregory finished the meal, he raved about the food and told Helga she needed to open a restaurant and he would eat there every day. Helga thanked him and said she would bring the dessert in. "You mean, you are going to spoil me more?" Gregory said. "We aim to please! Hope you like Tiramisu," Helga replied. "I have never heard of this dessert; but it looks fantastic," Gregory commented. "Wow! Can you adopt me as he smiled? Seriously! I have never had this dessert before; and it is in a league of its own," Gregory said with his mouth still salivating from the Tiramisu. "This is my all-time favorite dessert that Jezalee makes, I could eat it for breakfast, lunch, and dinner," Paul remarked. "Thank you dear," Jezalee said to Paul. "Do you live at home Gregory," Jezalee asked. "Yes! With my mom, dad and three sisters," Gregory answered. Adrienne asked him if his mom liked to cook and bake, and he quickly said he was not sure she knew where the kitchen was. "You are quite a comedian," Alexander remarked. "Seriously! My mom never cooks, my dad does; and it is a hit and miss with him," Gregory smilingly said. "You are welcome back here anytime for some great cooking and baking," Jezalee promptly replied. "His eyes lit up, I may just take you up on that great offer; a person never knows who they are going to meet; and have the best cuisine a person could experience. I hit the Jackpot tonight," Gregory sweetly said. Jezalee asked him if he was going straight home and he said yes; so, she packed up all the leftovers and the rest of the dessert to share with his family. He stayed for about an hour or so talking with the family then noticed how late it was getting and excused himself since he needed to study some more for his exam. They asked for his home phone number and Jezalee gave him hers; Paul did likewise and said to call him. There was just something special about this young man and they wanted to see what he did with his life. Paul handed him his money and said he hoped to see him again soon. "You have paid me too much money," Gregory said. Paul insisted and told him to be on his way so he could get his studies done. They said their goodbyes him as he left, arm in arm with the leftovers. They were impressed with him and wanted to keep in touch with him. When he got home to tell his family about them, his parents, Richard, and Joan had heard of Paul due to some business transactions and said he was one of the youngest billionaires in the world. "You mean, I was having a homemade meal as I sat around the dining room table with billionaires?" Gregory asked. "Yes! Indeed, you did! I will give you the latest magazine written up about Paul's accomplishments that began when he was a teenager; it is quite an extraordinary story," his mom laughed and said. "I know Jezalee through some charities she helped fund; we sat next to one another at several luncheons," remarked his mom. "Paul lives in Paris and Italy, and he thinks he and Jezalee are divorced,'' Gregory said. "That is correct, I remember her saying her children's father lives in Europe," remarked his mom. "They took my name and number because they want to keep in touch; and asked me to come over anytime," Gregory commented. "That was certainly nice of them," remarked his dad. "They have a beautiful daughter named Adrienne," Gregory bashfully said. "Now I am getting the big picture!" His dad grinned and said. Gregory blushed but did not say a word.

After Gregory left, Helga visited with the family for a while; Paul excused himself because he was tired and needed sleep. Alexander said he would take him to a bedroom across the hall from him. He said that sounds good, so he led the way. Paul got settled in one of the guest bedrooms and while he was in the middle of reviewing some business documents, he could not stop thinking of Jessica's reaction when he mentioned Jonathan, he did not know how he would ever repair the damage to his family. If only Jezalee would listen to what really happened.

Paul was still hurt about Jessica's reaction about his son Jonathan; he knew how difficult it must be with the divorce and all, especially since he had always been so close to his three children. Paul loved Jonathan but knew he would never have the kind of relationship he originally had with his other children. The time he spent with Jonathan, he saw a sweet and very well-adjusted boy, no thanks to his mother. The boy called him Uncle Paul; he could see him once a month; there were many times he came close to divulging who he really was. Gloria had not married so Jonathan only had him as a male role model. He wrote to his son every week and called him quite often. Gloria had been dating a single man for about six months, a nice man, had a good job but she said she was never going to get married unless Paul himself was interested. She knew there was not many men as wealthy as him, so she was not looking to find a man and get married; Gloria knew she had a great thing going with Paul. Gloria would always answer the phone when he called to talk with Jonathan, she made him sick to her stomach. He had bought a beautiful place for them so Gloria could raise Jonathan in a lovely environment. Paul also made it clear if she expected money from him every month, he made a stipulation in their written agreement that Jonathan be raised a Catholic, go to the best schools and live the way his other three children lived. She did not want to live outside of London; so, he bought a magnificent two-story apartment that was five thousand square feet, in an upscale area in the city and they loved it. He paid for all their expenses; she stopped working and did basically nothing. Gloria knew she was a horrible, conniving person the way Jonathan came into this world; but she had been poor all her life, and the only way she knew she may be able to have money was to do what she did to Paul. Jonathan loved Paul so much and said he was sad his dad died before he was born; but he considered him more a dad than an uncle. Paul said that was so sweet of him and he made sure that Jonathan knew he would always be just a phone call away no matter what. In the back of Paul's mind, he had thought if only he had been able to tell Jezalee the truth about the rape; Gloria goes to prison, he gets custody of Jonathan and he and Jezalee adopt him. Then, he would wake up his mind to reality and know he was dreaming pure fantasy.

Jonathan was now nine, growing by leaps and bounds and looking more like Paul and Alexander when they were his age. He was an excellent student, loved to play piano and saxophone, dance, and was quite a card shark when he and Paul played card games. Gloria was not a good mother to Jonathan; she never gave him much attention and refused to let him have friends over. After his homework was done, he had read a lot and listen to music in his room while he danced. He had been in such a great mood as soon as he knew Paul was coming for his monthly visit. When Paul came into town; Jonathan enjoyed going to concerts, plays, sports games, board games, and just hung out at Paul's London Penthouse. Jonathan would always ask Paul if he could live with him. Paul asked Jonathan why he did not want to live with his mom. Jonathan cried and said she never did anything with him like other mothers did with their sons and she would not let him have friends over. Paul really did not know what to say but he knew he had to respond. Well! Jonathan, there may be times that your mom is under pressure or stressed out over things that you do not know about. Paul did tell him he wished he could live closer and see him every week; but his business only brings him to London once a month. Jonathan asked if he could come to Paris and hang out with him during the summer. Paul said that is a great idea; I will talk to your mom to see if you could come to stay for a month. Jonathan's eyes lit up and gave Paul a big hug and said he loved him. "I love you too and don't you ever forget it," Paul said with tears in his eyes. He tried to talk Gloria into letting Jonathan come to Paris for a month during the summer; but she told him that was never going to happen. He was livid and knew that he needed to seek an attorney and try to get Jonathan away from her. Right now, all he could think of was Jessica's reaction and he felt like a heel. He knew after this summer when the children went home, he was hiring a team of attorneys to win custody of his son.

Paul had finished his work, took a shower, and got his pajamas on; just as he was turning down the covers to slip in between the sheets Jezalee knocked on his door and he said come in; he was surprised it was her and she wanted to thank him for staying with them until they flew to Paris. She asked him if it would be okay to let Alexander and Adrienne know about his big purchase, and he was all for it.

As Paul walked behind Jezalee to go to Adrienne and Alexander's rooms, he was thinking how radiant she had looked all night and she was even prettier in her floral satin robe. Oh! How he missed having her in his life. They knocked on Adrienne's door and asked her to come with them to Alexander's room and then knocked on his door; they entered after he said come in. Jezalee said your dad has something to say to you two. "Another surprise!" Alexander commented. "Yes!" Replied Paul. "Oh dad, you are not getting married to Sophia, are you?" Alexander asked as he frowned. "Absolutely not! Why would you even think that?" Paul asked. "Because you already came up with one humdinger and I was just thinking that would be the next thing," Alexander answered, feeling embarrassed he said it. "No! I purchased a private jet; so, I will not need to fly commercial anymore," Paul commented. Alexander stood on top of his bed and kept jumping up and down with excitement; Adrienne screamed as loud as she could and joined her brother and they both held hands and kept jumping. "Please do not break the bed or your limbs because we do not want you two to end up in the emergency room," Paul said. Jezalee seconded the motion and said keep all that excitement once you are on the plane. They could not believe their dad had a jet and they were going to be the only passengers. "You two get yourselves to bed now because morning comes early," Paul insisted. After they jumped off the bed, Paul and Jezalee walked over to the children and kissed them. As they were walking out of Alexander's bedroom, he asked if he could sleep with his dad to cuddle up in bed. "Of course, son! We have not done that in a long time, "Paul happily said. "If you are going to sleep with dad, mom, can I sleep with you?" Adrienne asked. "I knew that was coming; come on sweetheart, we know how to cuddle too!" Jezalee said as she walked over to Adrienne and took her hand in hers. They let out a girlish giggle and walked down to Jezalee's bedroom. Paul and his son looked at one another and smiled and said, ''girls will be girls," and went off to bed.

After Jezalee had hung up on Jim for the second time that day he left his penthouse, got in his Porsche, took a drive down to the beach, got out of his car and ran along the shore. He was gone for at least an hour then decided to go back home. Once he got home, he took off his sand filled shoes, started pacing the floor barefooted and threw the phone across the room and knocked down a lamp that shattered over the furniture and all over the floor. He walked away from the mess and could care less about what he had done. He walked out of there then went into his bedroom, looked at himself in the mirror, picked up a vase off the dresser and threw it at his mirror image and watched the glass fall from the frame and all over the top of the dresser and onto the floor. By this time, he was ready to get his gun and drive over to Jezalee's house and aim it at her. He walked down to the library to get the gun, suddenly he realized as he was taking it out of the secret compartment, if he showed up at her house to shoot someone, she would never marry him. He started sweating profusely and closed the compartment and walked to his bedroom to lay down. Jim started getting flustered and his whole body was trembling, he was too weak to get up and eventually fell asleep. Jim woke up around 4:00 AM from a dreadful nightmare and ran to the bathroom to throw up. He jumped in the shower, dried off and went back to bed for a couple more hours.

The next morning Jezalee woke Jessica up and told her she had forty-five minutes before one of the camp employees would be picking her up. She showered, had a quick breakfast; and said her goodbyes to the family. As she got in the Therapy Camp van her mom and dad turned to one another and both had tears in their eyes. "I am so sorry Jezalee," Paul regretfully said. "Paul, it is going to be okay," Jezalee remarked. They sadly walked back into the house, as the van drove away.

Paul was downstairs talking to Helga and Nell while they prepared breakfast for everyone. The O'Malley's were invited for breakfast as well as all their staff! Jezalee was out on the patio setting up the table, chairs, and place settings. Adrienne and Morgan were getting the drinks. The men took the food from the kitchen and set it on the table. Everyone sat down for their breakfast. "Aren't we going to wait for Jessica to join us?" Morgan asked. "Jessica is not here! She is going to a camp to become nicer." Alexander spoke up.

"Alexander, I think I will handle this if you do not mind!" Jezalee said. "I am so sorry mom." Alexander said feeling so bad afterwards. "That is okay! Everyone, you may as well know, Paul let the children know he has another son named Jonathan; Jessica started beating on her dad then went after Alexander and Adrienne who tried to hold her back from continually beating on her dad; she started fighting them off. I sent her to a camp that specializes in teen behavior, and she will be there for a month and if they feel she needs to stay longer, I will make sure she does," Jezalee said sadly. Everyone was very silent; and Paul knew Jezalee had to explain the situation and he was okay with it. Alexander started telling jokes to liven up the breakfast meal and everything went smoothly after that. After everyone was finished eating, the O'Malley's had a previous engagement to meet one of David's old college buddies and they were going to spend the day with him and his family. Nell stayed long enough to help Helga and Adrienne clean up and get the dishes in the two dishwashers.

Paul, Alexander, and Adrienne played ping pong outside while Jezalee watched them. It was a lovely day to sit back and enjoy watching her family having fun. She started thinking about her dear Jessica and how disappointed she was with the rage she had shown her father and her siblings. She was hoping and praying that the camp was all it said it was because Jessica needed to be accountable for her actions and needed to not show violence towards anyone, ever again.

Created with Sketch.

The phone rang, it was Paul's parents; Helga went out to get Paul. As soon as she spotted him, she said "Paul, it is your parents." He picked up the phone and his mom and dad were crying. He calmed them down and asked them what was wrong. They began to inform him that Jonathan, Gloria, and her boyfriend had been in a tragic automobile accident. Gloria and her boyfriend were killed instantly. They proceeded to let Paul know that Jonathan was alive and had a fifty percent chance of survival. Paul's thoughts were racing, he turned white as a ghost and fell back into the nearest kitchen chair. Helga saw him, was concerned, ran out to tell the rest of the family to come quickly to the kitchen. Alexander looked over at his dad and could see he was cadaverous and looked like something bad had happened. "What happened dad?" Alexander frantically asked. Paul could not talk. Alexander grabbed the phone from his dad then asked who was there and he heard his grandparent's voices. They began to tell him about the devastating car accident, and he now knew that Jonathan, was in a hospital in Rome and was fighting for his life. After Alexander hung up the phone he was concerned about his dad. He told his mom about the tragic accident, and she went over to Paul. Helga got him a cold glass of water and he took a few sips then handed the glass back to her. Jezalee looked at Paul and he could not talk; he started crying so Jezalee tried to comfort him. Adrienne had gotten a phone call; so, she had no idea what was going on; she walked in seeing her dad crying and Jezalee next to him. Alexander motioned for Adrienne to come over where he was; and he began to tell her what happened. She ran over to her dad and told him how sorry she was that Jonathan was in the hospital.

Paul was still crying so Jezalee took him by the hand into the living room and sat him down next to her. The children and Helga walked in, they sat down across from Jezalee and Paul. "Alexander, please start from the beginning," Jezalee asked. "Well! There was an automobile accident and Gloria, and her boyfriend were instantly killed; they were on a dirt road and a small commercial truck hit them head on. Jonathan was in the back seat, and he survived; however, he is in critical condition with a fifty percent chance of surviving," Alexander regretfully said. By this time, Jezalee, Helga and Adrienne were sobbing. Paul was desperately holding himself together as best he could; he tried to stop crying; his eyes were red and swollen. Jezalee asked Helga if she would take the children to her place so she could speak alone with Paul for a few minutes. "Of course, dear!" Helga replied. Alexander and Adrienne followed Helga to her wing of the house and told them they just needed to give their mom and dad some time alone. The children made themselves at home and they asked Helga to sit with them. They were crying off and on for a boy they never met but knew he was their father's son, and how difficult it must be for their dad.

Jezalee was still sitting next to Paul when she asked him if she could help in any way. She offered to call his pilots to see if they could get clearance to leave sooner. He thanked her and said he would call them as soon as he cleared his mind. "Whatever you want, we will do, we are here for you, and I want to say I am so sorry about Jonathan. Paul, if you do not mind; I have one request!" Jezalee sadly said. "What is it Jezalee?" Looking at her with desolate eyes and said. "Could the children go to the hospital with you?" Jezalee asked. Paul looked adoringly at Jezalee and thought as he looked at her; this was so typical of this amazing woman he had married so many years ago. "I would love for them to meet Jonathan, even under these-tragic-conditions," Paul suddenly gave her a smile and said. "Thank you! I believe it is important for them to be with you at a time like this. We will say a special prayer that Jonathan is strong and resilient; and he will prove to the doctors, he is a fighter," Jezalee got up, kissed the top of his head; and said she would leave him alone with his thoughts.

Jezalee went to Helga's wing and could see that all three of them had been crying. Helga asked her to sit down for a while; so; she sat across from the three of them. She explained to the children that everything stays as planned with the exception that they will go to the hospital to be by their father's side; he is going to need to draw strength from the two of you and be on your best behavior please help him get through this.

While Jezalee was talking to the children in Helga's living room, Paul made his way up to the guest bedroom. He went directly to one of the cozy oversized chairs for a while and thought back to his innocent son for whom he never told him he was his father; here would be another regret he had in life. He stayed upstairs for the rest of the day. The children got up to be with their dad and they could not find him; so, they ran back to their mom and wanted to know if she knew where he was. "He is probably up in his bedroom; but why don't we just let him be by himself for now, since he has a lot of things to sort out," Jezalee recommended. The children agreed, so they each went to their respective bedrooms and stayed in there all day. They were hoping their dad would come to see them; but he did not. The longer Paul set in the bedroom chair, all he thought about was Jezalee and how he was wishing she would walk in, and they both lay down on the bed, side by side, he needed the comfort of her next to him.

Jezalee asked Helga to go up and ask Paul if he was hungry; he told Helga he did not have an appetite; but thanked her for checking on him. Jezalee and the children left Paul alone and they knew he would come out once he felt like seeing everyone. During the morning, Paul managed to call the hospital to get an update on Jonathan; but he found out quickly they would not release any information unless he was a relative. He explained who he was; but they said until they had proof; they would not be able to provide any information on Jonathan. He called the hospital where his son was born, and he told them of his dilemma; they immediately asked him to get a paternity test done; the London Hospital encouraged him to go to the nearest hospital immediately and request the test and fax it to them and they would send it over to the hospital in Rome. In the meantime, the nurse said she would call over to the hospital in Rome to inform them that Paul was going for the test; and she would let them know she was typing up her statement as a witness that the mother of Jonathan informed her who the. father was and would quickly have it notarized and faxed to the Rome Hospital. Jonathan's mother told her Paul was the father; but did not want his name on his birth certificate. Paul told the nurse that the hospital indicated to him, since Jonathan's mother died and he did not have proof he was the father, they could do whatever surgery or procedure on his son without permission, since it was a life-or-death situation. He thanked the head nurse and said he was calling a local hospital immediately to see when he can get the test. Paul called the 411 information, operator and asked for the phone number of a hospital in the San Francisco area. He called the nearest one and they indicated for the fastest results on a paternity test would be at the Stanford Hospital. He called them and they could do it as soon as he could get there. Paul went looking for Jezalee; he found her reading out on her terrace in her bedroom. He explained what he would be doing and asked if she would go with him to Stanford Hospital and she said, "Let us go right now." Jezalee went in to tell the children she had an errand to go on with their dad and would be back in a few hours. As soon as they arrived at the hospital, they asked the information desk clerk where Paul needed to go for his paternity testing. The lady at the desk said they have been expecting him and directed Paul to the area he needed to go to. Before Paul went to get tested, he asked Jezalee to find out who she needed to speak with to donate five hundred thousand dollars to the hospital. Jezalee spoken with the

Hospital Administrator and filled out the donation form, which just needed Paul's signature. The Administrator thanked them for their generosity and told Jezalee the cafeteria was open and once Paul was done with his testing, to go there and they would bring the results to him. Jezalee and Paul went to the cafeteria and had a bite to eat while they waited for the results. They were there for three hours and once he had the results, they let him use their phone to call the London Hospital. He spoke with the nurse, and she told him as soon as she receives the test results from Stanford Hospital by fax, she had an affidavit ready to go with the results and will have it notarized with her as the witness to what Gloria admitted to after she had Jonathan. By late afternoon, California time, everything had been taken care of and he informed the hospital in Rome that he was flying in from California and would be immediately coming from the airport to the hospital.

The Rome Hospital looked over the documents, called Paul and went over Jonathan's medical issues. The doctor indicated his son had 4 broken ribs, two broken legs, air built-up in both lungs that caused them to collapse; that brought on serious breathing problems for him; also, there was air in the chest, pushing against his heart and other parts of his body, which would have caused a serious problem if they had not treated him as soon as they did, a tension pneumothorax would have killed him. The doctor explained that Jonathan had severe trauma to the brain and needs to be in a medically induce coma to protect the brain from swelling any further. Being in a coma will work by minimizing the energy expenditure of brain cells and by minimizing or preventing the brain to swell any further. There is not a lot of room for the brain to swell because it will be pushed up against his skull. The doctor thanked Paul for getting the paternity test results to them in a timely manner, he explained to Paul it was imperative they perform a medically induced coma because it could save Jonathan's life. We believe that is the only way we can possibly save him, and there, is no guarantees with that. Paul was holding back his tears and said, yes! Doctor, I have complete trust in what you are telling me, and I want you to do whatever you can do to save my son's life. Jezalee was near Paul and was anxious and afraid all at the same time, to know about Jonathan's condition. After Paul hung up the phone, he sat down near Jezalee and told her all the injuries Jonathan had. She was devastated that a little boy would have to go through such devastating trauma.

The hospital called back two hours later, the doctor indicated they had done the procedure and would monitor Jonathan for the next 24 hours. Paul informed the doctor his flight information and what time he would arrive at the hospital. He indicated he would like to get clearance for his parents to go see his son prior to him arriving and that there would be a Priest coming as well, and he explained Peter is Jonathan's uncle. He called his parents and his brother; they said they would be over to see Jonathan immediately.

Paul had already alerted his crew to be ready to fly him and two of his children to Rome. Mark, one of the pilots called back immediately to inform him they had just gotten clearance for take-off time. Paul asked Jezalee if the children could be ready in a half an hour to leave for the airport. She said absolutely! Under the circumstances, you need to get there as soon as possible. I am going upstairs to help children get ready. He followed in behind her and packed his personal belongings and was done in ten minutes. He went in the direction of the children's rooms and with Jezalee help they were ready to leave. They had pretty much packed everything in advance and were more excited that they got to go on a private jet. One of the pilots called for a driver to pick them up in thirty minutes. The children and Paul waited in the living room for their driver.

"I know this is a long flight; but it will not be long until you see Jonathan, and you will help him through this," Jezalee said as she looked over at Paul and said. Paul gave Jezalee a hug and thanked her for everything. She said her goodbyes to them then pulled Adrienne aside and asked her to oversee Alexander and she assured her mom she would. She asked that she made sure her dad gets plenty of sleep so he can have strength to visit Jonathan. Adrienne said she would watch over her dad; she knew his stress level would be high once he saw Jonathan in the flesh. I am sure he is hooked up to monitors, tubes and whatever else they had to do for him. Jezalee kissed the children goodbye then made her way over to Paul and said she would pray for his son's life to be saved. He kissed the top of her head; just as she hugged him, the car arrived. Jezalee stood waving at them as they drove away. She was sobbing as she walked into the house. Jezalee ran upstairs to her bedroom and threw herself on her freshly made bed. She laid there, was half asleep when the phone rang; it was Paul, they were getting ready to take off and he wanted to call her and thank her for being so gracious about everything. "Paul, I care what happens to Jonathan; Gloria should never have kept him from knowing you as his dad,'' Jezalee was trying to comfort him at a critical time in his sons life. "Under the circumstances, I thank you for helping so much," Paul replied with a heavy heart. "Paul, there is no need to thank me!" Jezalee said with much love. They felt a black cloud over them knowing that Jonathan was fighting for his life. Paul was having regrets knowing his son was thousands of miles away in a sterile hospital, hooked up to machines, nurses and doctors watching over him, praying they would be able to save the life of a 9-year-old boy who does not know his father is a live and, on his way, to be at his bedside.

Paul and the children landed at 2:00 a.m. Rome time and 11:00 a.m. California time: they went straight to the hospital where his parents, Elene and Antonio were waiting for the children and him to arrive. Paul's brother Fr. Peter arrived about a half an hour later and they met with the medical team that was overseeing Jonathan's condition. Dr. Giovannetti, Paul and his brother went into Jonathan's sterile, bright lit room; as soon as Paul saw all the machines hooked up to him, he broke down. "We need to pray for Jonathan and hope he is strong enough to heal," Peter said to Paul. Paul stood close to Jonathan's bedside as he held his right hand, then asked Peter to begin with his prayer. The doctor and Peter walked out after the prayer and Paul slid a chair over to Jonathan's bed and was hoping for a miracle for his dear, sweet, innocent son. When the doctor came out of Jonathan's room, he informed Alexander and Adrienne they could go in to be with their brother and dad. They slowly walked in and saw their sad father hunched over in the chair and praying for his son to live. The children walked closer to their dad and Adrienne placed her hands on the back of his shoulders; Paul began to cry. The two children had streams of tears covering their cheeks and Alexander came closer to his dad and gave him a hug. The doctor came in and asked if the children could go to the waiting area and they proceeded to walk in single file......Once the children were in the waiting area, they ran over to their grandparents and gave them a hug, then their uncle Peter had come from the hospital

Chapel and went over to his niece and nephew; by this time, the tears were burning their faces and Peter knew they needed consoling. He went over to his parents and said he would be back in a few minutes but wanted to take the children to the Chapel. They proceeded to follow their uncle; as they walked in the Chapel, they genuflected next to a pew then slid next to one another, knelt, and prayed for Jonathan to live. After the children finished praying their Uncle Peter came over and sat in the pew in front of them. He wanted to talk about Jonathan's condition; he assured them that he had the best specialists trying to keep him alive; but the prognosis was not good, and he wanted to prepare them before they faced their dad again. He spoke to them for a good fifteen minutes; they thanked their uncle for making them feel much better and they would just keep praying and wait it out with their dad. Peter let them know that they should do whatever the doctor wants them to do, and Paul may or may not want them present if Jonathan gets worse. They said they understood and walked out of the Chapel feeling better than when they went in.

Adrienne and Alexander went over and sat with their grandparents for the next five hours. Peter went in to see how Paul was doing, he was holding back the tears as he held his son's lifeless hand. Peter pulled up a chair and sat next to his grieving brother. He asked if he could speak to him and Paul said, "Of course!" Peter talked with him for a good half hour and by that time the doctor came in to ask them to step out to the hallway. They both got up at the same time and walked out behind the doctor. Dr. Giovannetti basically informed them that they had run extensive tests and would have the results back the following day after 3:00 ; he requested they try to get some rest, come back tomorrow. The doctor assured Paul, he would call him if the test results came back sooner or if anything changed, good or bad then he said his goodbyes; he had already spoken to the rest of the family, and they were waiting for Paul and Peter. It was now 8:00 a.m. Rome time and 5:00 p.m. California time.

Antonio and Elene had gotten hotel rooms a block away from the hospital for everyone, as they walked out of the hospital there was silence until they reached the hotel. Everyone was drained of possibilities of what Jonathan would go through if he lived and they were praying whatever would be best for him is what God would want for him. The grandparents had reserved the penthouse suite that had four large bedrooms. When they got up to their suite, they sat in the living area and talked for a while; Paul left the room and said he had to make a call. He did not tell them he would be calling Jezalee; he felt she was the one person he wanted to talk with in private. Jezalee had fallen asleep after she spoke to Paul and the children. She jumped out of bed, straightened up the bedspread and pillows, took a shower, got dressed and fixed her hair; she then called the O'Malley house and left a message on the machine about Paul's son.

Jezalee was on pins and needles worrying how Jonathan was; she lit a candle and prayed off and on; she was wondering how Paul and the children were doing. She was reading in her bedroom, the phone rang; when she heard Paul's voice; she panicked for a second because she was worried about what he was about to say. Paul was glad Jezalee was home; he automatically started crying. "Paul, how is your son?" Jezalee asked quite concerned. "Jonathan is in a medically induced coma which will hopefully help the swelling on his brain to go down; if it does not, it is not good," Paul sadly said. Jezalee asked Paul when would, he know if the coma was helping. He explained to her that they took a myriad of tests that will give them more answers; they will have the test results around 3:00 PM tomorrow unless there is good or bad news prior to the tests coming back. "Paul, would you like me to fly over, because I will," Jezalee said sympathetically. "You would do that for me? Paul said, surprisingly. "Of course!" Jezalee said with sincerity. "I think that is so selfless and loving of you," Paul said with love in his heart. "We have known and loved one another more than half our lives; the divorce does not mean I do not care about what you go through; you are the father of our children and you have been an exemplary father," Jezalee reminded him. Paul thought it would be great for her to be there since the children have been pretty upset after seeing Jonathan hooked up to so many machines. "As soon as we hang up, I will call for the jet and see, what is the earliest time they can get into the San Francisco Airport; they are currently at LAX airport. "I will be waiting for your call and hope it can happen because I really want to be there," Jezalee comment. As soon as Paul hung up, he called his pilots; they were able to get clearance to fly out of San Francisco to Rome at 12 p.m. Paul was happy knowing one, that Jezalee asked to come and the second, the plane was ready to take off soon. He called Jezalee back and she was packed and ready to go. "Dear, you have not changed a bit! You have invariably been the most positive person I know and one step ahead of everyone," Paul laughed and kindly said. "I try to stay positive, whenever possible," Jezalee remarked. Paul ordered a driver to pick her up at 10:00 a.m. After she got off the phone with Paul, she called Mallory to let her4 know she was leaving for Rome to be with Paul and the children. David got on the extension phone in his den and they both said to give Paul their condolences and they will go to Church tonight to light candles and pray for Jonathan's recovery. She thanked Mallory and David; said she knew how they feel about what Paul did to her and the children, and she felt the same way; but Jonathan was innocent in all that happened. "It does not matter the circumstances of Jonathan's birth; all children are a gift from God; and he is fighting for his life right now and he needs all the prayers he can get," David and Mallory said. "Thank you, dear friends!" Jezalee sweetly said. "You are welcome and have a safe trip to Rome," David and Mallory replied. Just as she was saying her goodbyes to David and Mallory, she asked them if one of them could let Jim know she is going to Rome. Of course! David said he would take care of that. As Jezalee hung up, Gregory had arrived. The doorbell rang and she hurried out the front door. Jezalee had let her staff know she was going to Rome to be with Paul and their children; she was not sure when she would be back; but would call them after she knew more about Jonathan's condition. They had given their condolences and were all praying for Paul's son.

Once Jezalee got settled in on the jet, the male steward, Roger asked if she wanted something to eat or drink and she replied, maybe later. The second steward Harry came up to her and introduced himself and said he would be taking over for Roger halfway through the flight. She sat back, buckled herself in and they took off for Rome; the plane took off at around 12:00 p.m. Jezalee knew it would take thirteen hours in the air and would try to take a nap the last few hours they were flying. After being up in the air for at least an hour she looked around the elaborate jet and realized what Paul had accomplished in his life thus far and was so proud of him. Jezalee could not help but go into her memory bank and think of when they met and all the hard work it took to get to where they were in their lives today. She was wishing she could forgive Paul for his indiscretion; but she thought back to when she found out how she felt; that day changed her life. Jezalee knew that Paul felt guilty about what he did, and he wanted to talk more; but she could not bring herself to listen to anything else he had to say. Here she was on his private jet, going to Rome to be by his side because his illegitimate son was fighting for his life. Jezalee could not explain why she was determined to be by his side; but thought maybe it was to show the children, even though they were divorced she wanted to support Paul in a time of need. Jezalee also knew, the distance she created away from him, did not dissipate the feelings and love that were still there, like the day they became husband and wife.

Jezalee prayed for Jonathan's life, and he would have a full recovery; she knew that with Gloria's death, Paul would be raising his son and she was not sure how that was going to affect their three children. She knew that all of this was hopefully in-the-near-future; and from that moment on they would figure everything out. The co-pilot Michael came back and sat with her for about a half an hour; she found out he had gone to Harvard as a Pre-Med student then decided he wanted to be a pilot and loves what he does. He and his family live in Incline Village Tahoe and moved there in 1980 and loved the small town, atmosphere. She talked about how much they had been up to Incline lately because their friends have a vacation home there. He said whenever they get a chance to come up his way, he and his family would love to have them over for dinner. Jezalee said that sounds great and we will probably be up there for Labor Day weekend; but do not hold me to it. No worries! We are there all year round so whenever you can get up our way, give us a call. That is sweet of you Michael; I will, for sure. During her flight she had a chance to speak with the pilot in command, Richard, and the stewards. The other two pilots on board were there in case there was an emergency. All four pilots switched off every other flight and were on call whenever Paul needed them. He employed these four men and two stewards. This was the perfect job for them because Paul paid them more than a commercial pilot would receive and they would be there whenever Paul or anyone else in the family needed them. Jezalee felt safe on board with these six capable men to get her to her destination; she decided to sleep for at least 6 hours. When she woke up Harry said if she wanted to freshen up and take a shower, he had set out linens and toiletries for her. He let her know they were forty-five minutes away from Rome. She took a quick shower, got fresh clothes on, did her makeup and she was ready before the plane landed

Jezalee said her goodbyes to the crew; her driver was waiting to take her directly to the hotel. She arrived the hotel at 10:00 a.m. As soon as the penthouse doors opened the children were grabbing their mom to give her a sandwich hug and kisses; this whole time Paul was in the background and was wishing he could do the same; but he knew when to back off under the circumstances. She asked Paul where she should put her luggage and Alexander came over and took it to her room. Jezalee spoke with Paul for a few minutes to find out if there was any changes in Jonathan's condition and was sad to hear there was no improvement. Jezalee went toe her room and unpacked her clothes and toiletries. Adrienne came in and thanked her mom for joining them and she felt much better with her mom coming over.

Paul interrupted the girls and asked them to look at the menu from the hotel restaurant to choose something for lunch; thirty minutes later Paul's parents joined them and decided to stay until they went to the hospital. Once they were finished, Jezalee called Mallory before the family left to go see Jonathan. While everyone sat in the waiting area Paul checked in at the nurses station to make sure it was okay to go in to see his son. They said that Dr. Giovannetti got the results and was getting ready to call him. The nurse said she would have him paged and meet in Jonathan's room. When Paul walked in to check on his son, he looked so small in the over-sized private room. He pulled up a chair to sit as close to Jonathan as he could. Paul was praying over his bed when the doctor walked in; he stood up to greet him and was hoping his prayers were answered with great news. The doctor had the test results and with much regret, unfortunately, it was not good news. Dr. Giovannetti, being the compassionate doctor he was, with an exemplary bedside manner; he placed his arms around Paul and said he had prayed for a miracle that Jonathan would have made it through the medically induced coma. He assured Paul he and his team of doctors did everything humanly possible to save his son. Paul broke down crying and said how difficult it was going to be to walk into the waiting room to tell his family; Paul said with much trepidation, he did not think he could get through it. Dr. Giovannetti said he understood and would certainly inform his family. The two of them left Jonathan's room and walked down the long hallway to the waiting room where his family had been waiting patiently; hoping the doctor had great news about Jonathan. As the doctor approached the family, who were seated close together, he cordially said good afternoon everyone. Dr. Giovannetti looked at the Albanese family, he could see it on their saddened faces, they intuitively knew, it was not the news they were wanting to hear. Paul sat down next to Jezalee, and the doctor began explaining the news was not good, the test results showed no improvement and Jonathan's brain had not relaxed for the swelling to go down and was pressing against his skull. Paul did ask me, what would have happened if they had not performed a medically induced coma? He would have died within a few hours. The family was stunned at the outcome and were trying not to break down in front of Paul; but it was out of their control, their emotions took over. Paul asked, if he could go in alone to see his son again. "Of course! The doctor walked with Paul into the room, with the overhead fluorescent lights shining down on Jonathan's lifeless body. Dr. Giovannetti turned to Paul to let him know this was always the most difficult part of his profession when a child would not make it. "Doctor, I know you have done everything possible by bringing in specialists from the states and here in Italy; it's just that, he then started choking up, Jonathan did not know I was his dad," Paul sadly said with much remorse. Dr. Giovannetti put his arms around him to console him and said how sorry for this boy not to know who his dad was. The doctor asked if he would like the rest of the family in the room when Fr. Peter comes in. Paul said yes as he had tears streaming down his face. The doctor went to the waiting room and asked the family to join Paul as he says goodbye to his son. Before they had arrived at the room, the doctor had his medical team disconnect the machines from Jonathan, unplug them and roll them out of the room. As each family member walked over to Paul, they stood beside him as he held both his sons small hands in his and said a silent prayer as his tears fell on Jonathan's bed cover. The children came closer and had their arms on their dad's shoulders. On the other side of the hospital bed was Jezalee, Elene and Antonio who were sobbing at the thought of a nine-year old dying right before their eyes Fr. Peter was standing next to Paul and the children. Dr. Giovannetti said he would leave them alone, as it was time for Fr. Peter to give the last rites to Jonathan. Paul turned to the doctor and asked him to please stay; he nodded his head yes at Paul and stood with the rest of the family. Fr. Peter took his hand and placed it at Jonathan's forehead and gave him his last right rites.

Jezalee asked Adrienne to take hold of her one of her dad's hands that were holding Jonathan's and asked everyone else to take the hand of the person next to them, as they gathered round the hospital bed. As tears fell from Fr. Peter's cheeks, who was profoundly saddened to begin his prayer for the nephew he had only seen a few times. Adrienne could not control her emotions and had to run to the women's room, to throw up. Jezalee waited for the prayer to be finished and ran to make sure Adrienne was okay. She saw that she had thrown up in the sink and grabbed some paper towels to clean her up first then cleaned out the sink. After Jezalee cleaned everything up, Adrienne was crying and said she felt so sad that she never wanted to meet Jonathan until it was too late to feel different about him being her stepbrother. They walked out of the women's room; went back into the room where Jonathan was still lying in the bed. As the doctor was leaving, he said they could spend as much time as they needed to say goodbye. After they left the hospital, Paul knew he would never see Jonathan again other than at the vigil and his funeral, then they would say their goodbyes at his gravesite. The rest of the evening no one talked; they each kept to themselves. Paul's parents had gone back to their room at the hotel while Peter had gone back with Paul and was in solitude in the living room because everyone else went to their bedrooms. After Peter left, Paul went to his bedroom and called all of Gloria's relatives, which was just a handful of people. They were mad at Paul because they did not get to say their goodbyes to Jonathan. He informed them Jonathan was only allowed to have immediate family with him. He had been told they came to the hospital and tried to gain entrance into Jonathan's room but there were doctors and nurses overseeing him around the clock. They were told only Paul, his family, and their Priest could see Jonathan until he was out of his coma. The hospital explained to Gloria's family they had every right to call Paul to get updates; but they could not release any medical information; they never did call him.

Paul decided to come into the kitchen area and get a cold glass of water and saw his brother sitting there reading from the bible. "I thought you left?" Paul said. "I did, I went to check on mom and dad and told them I would be here for a while," Peter answered. Paul asked if he could sit awhile with his brother and Peter replied, "Of course!" Paul sat beside him and asked the normal question every parent seemed to ask when a child died; why do some children die so young? "None of us ever have the answer we want to hear because why should an innocent child die so early in their life. We do know, when a person dies, they meet the heavenly father and that is the ultimate, goal for all of us. Many times, people will say it is because certain innocent young children are chosen to do God's work and it is the unknown; we are not sure of," Peter answered. Paul let Peter know he had asked Gloria numerous times if he could have Jonathan and he would have given her any amount of money to have full custody of him and of course she was always adamant that he would only be considered his uncle. Many times, when he brought the subject up; the answer was always no. Peter asked Paul why he did not he get an attorney and take her to court. Paul explained that he had threatened to take her to court to tell the truth how Jonathan was conceived; but she had the bouncer and bartender persuaded be her witnesses that I came on to her. Those two weasels were ready to perjure themselves for her. I could not take the chance in this going public and affecting our businesses and my family. She had been setting up this plot for a long time. "I understand now, the situation she placed him in," Peter sadly remarked. Paul let his brother now that demonic woman only let him see Jonathan once a month. Jonathan had continuously asked Paul if I would convince her to let me raise him. Peter asked why Jonathan wanted to be with him instead of his mother? He told me on several occasions that his mother never did anything with him, and he was always sent to his room when she had anyone over. She never went to school functions like the rest of the parents. When he saw me, he was hungry for attention, and we had great fun together. He was a wonderful boy and had so much potential; he loved music, drawing, sports, and was an avid reader and did exceptional in school. He basically came home, did homework; and lived a solitary life as a kid. I do not know how he had such a great attitude about life; but he did. "It sounds like he was a lot like you in that you were always a happy kid and did not let anything phase you," Peter commented. "Well, we had a great upbringing and maybe if we had a parent like Gloria; we would not be who we are today," Paul said. "That is not necessarily so because many children have horrible family lives and end up being extraordinary people with great accomplishments," Peter answered. "That is true! Jezalee and I would see it all the time when we volunteered together at some of the homeless centers and when we visited children and their families living in ghetto areas. When we opened our family center in Paris, we saw it first-hand. In fact, it amazed us that some of the parents who were drug addicts had the sweetest children that still did well in school and seemed happy even though they were forced to take care of themselves and many times their parents as well," Paul replied.

Peter left to get back to his parish; he bid farewell to everyone before he left. Jezalee had stayed in her room so she could call her staff. The three of them said they were booking a flight as soon as possible. She told them to hold off until she made one more phone call and she would get back to them. Jezalee called Mallory and David to let them know that Jonathan had died. David said he and Mallory were booking a flight immediately and coming to the funeral. Jezalee knew they had guests and important ones at that. She asked if their guests had already left? David said he made reservations at the Fairmont Hotel while they were gone; he knew that family and friends were important to them and understood the importance of them being at Jonathan's funeral. "I will let Paul know you two are coming and my staff will be at there as well," Jezalee said. Nell was close by while the O'Malley's were talking on the phone and Mallory let her know that they were coming to Paul's son Jonathan's vigil and funeral; she immediately said she wanted to pay her respects as well and she would call Bob and Linda. Mallory thanked her and asked David to keep Jezalee on the line a little longer. Linda told Nell they would both be coming and would call a friend to take care of Manny while they were gone. Mallory got back on the phone to say that their staff were coming too. David said that makes eight of us will be flying. Jezalee let Mallory know, they would meet them at the Rome airport. "Let me call you two back when I have answers on the flight schedule of Paul's jet," Jezalee said. She rushed in to ask Paul if there was a way, they could get the O'Malley's, and the staffs from both houses here in time to be at the vigil and the funeral. He was shocked they wanted to come. "Jezalee, did you insist they come?" Paul asked. "No! I just mentioned that Jonathan passed-away and they are dropping everything to get here," Jezalee answered. Paul said he would charter another jet asap. He asked how many would be coming and she said eight. Within twenty minutes he had a schedule for them on a private jet. Jezalee called the O'Malley's, and Helga back with their flight time and a limousine would pick them up in two hours. All staff members were coming from both households, plus Ronan, Gregory, and his family. They would arrive in Rome at 10:00 a.m.; Paul scheduled a driver to pick them up and bring them to the hotel. Paul called Franco and Rosa to have the villa ready for his guest that were coming from California; thy would be traveling with them on his private jet the following day to Pisa.

It was late so Paul asked Jezalee and the children what they wanted for dinner. They said they did not feel like eating and he was not hungry either. After the children went to sleep, Jezalee asked Paul if they needed to buy an outfit for Jonathan to wear and he said that was a great idea. She offered to go with him in the morning to pick something out. He thanked Jezalee for being there with him to help him through his grief. She replied by saying she knew if things were in reverse, he would do the same for her. They both knew one another so well and this was a testament to how they were when they were married.

Jezalee got up before anyone else and had ordered room service to send up a pot of coffee and some sweet rolls. They also brought up the Rome and London newspapers she had requested. Paul got a call from the airport that everyone would be arriving at the hotel in a half an hour. Jezalee opened-up the newspaper from London and began to read a few articles. When she got to the obituaries; she glanced down at the names like she always did in any newspaper she read. She spotted Jonathan's name and began reading; to her disdain Paul's name was never mentioned in either the Rome or London obituaries. She was so upset, she quickly got up, walked to Paul's bedroom door, and knocked rather loudly. He said, "Come in." Jezalee had the obituaries in her hand and proceeded to hand them over to him. As he read the obituary you could see by the expression on his face he was seething. He jumped up out of bed and told Jezalee thank you for finding this. He showered, shaved, and got ready for the day. By the time Paul came out showered and dressed, everyone had arrived. They were all sitting in the living room area talking to Jezalee. When he walked into the room, everyone stood, walked towards Paul, and gave him hugs and condolences. He thanked each, and every one of them for coming at such a solemn time. "Please do not think I am rude; but I have something that is vitally important that I am forced to take care of immediately," Paul let them know. Jezalee explained his brief absence and asked everyone what they would like for breakfast because she would have room service bring it up. In the meantime, we have sweet rolls and coffee; Helga and Nell, you need to go to their in-house baker and give him your recipes because they pale in comparison to both yours. They laughed! Jezalee took everyone's order and within thirty minutes they were sitting at the dining room table having breakfast. The children were still sleeping, and they didn't want to disturb them until were finished.

Before the breakfasts had arrived, Paul called both newspapers and had them retract what the obituaries said, after that, he called Gloria's relatives to inform them he was disgusted at how they handled Jonathan's death and obituary. He explained he had both newspapers retracted to say he was his father. He informed them there was a change of plans and he gave them the times at both the vigil and the funeral. He decided Jonathan would be buried in the plots he had already attained in Pisa for his entire family, near where they lived. As Jezalee was hearing his conversations, she realized that is one thing they had not discussed during the divorce proceedings. She decided this was not the time nor place to discuss what they should do. After Paul completed all his calls to Gloria's family and friends, the funeral home, and burial arrangements for his son's last days on earth; he asked Jezalee if they could talk for a few minutes before they woke the children up. She could not imagine what was on his mind; but she said she was all ears. He began talking about the burial plot he had for the entire family. He apologized for letting that slip through the cracks during the divorce settlement. Paul wanted to know what her feelings were on the subject. Jezalee looked forlorn and was caught off guard and asked him if they could discuss this another time under the circumstances. He looked at her and felt awkward he brought it up. "Why! Of course! I do not know what I was thinking," Paul said. Jezalee smiled and said there is only one thing all of us should be thinking about right now; your innocent dear boy Jonathan and make his nine years count while he lived. "Thank you Jezalee," Paul walked over to kiss the top of her head. Jezalee said their breakfast had just arrived and said let us join our family and we will wake the children after we finish. Gregory and his sisters were going to wait and eat breakfast with the Albanese children. Adrienne was so pleased to see Gregory, and the children all sat down to have breakfast together.

Paul called his crew to informed them, he had another son, who just died from an auto accident. They would be flying his son's body from Rome to Pisa. Everyone hung out at the penthouse while Antonio and Paul went to the morgue and instructed the driver of the hearse to follow them to the airport because his son would be boarding his jet for Italy. Paul wanted to make sure the casket was on the plane prior to the rest of the family coming to the airport. Once they arrived back at the hotel everyone was ready for their flight to Pisa. He had the two limousine drivers waiting downstairs to take them to the airport. Paul had made sure Jonathan's casket was in a place that no one could see it. After, everyone was seated on the plane before take-off, Paul stood up to thank everyone; he was so touched by them wanting to come to his son's vigil and funeral, it meant more than they will ever know. "That is what friends are for," David replied. "Jezalee informed me you had very important international guests staying with you, I feel bad you had to uproot them," Paul commented. "No worries my friend, they completely understood," David replied. Paul thanked them once again and the plane took off. While the plane was in the air, he talked to each person that had come a long way to pay respects to his son. When the plane landed Paul had everyone depart the plane; then had the pilots take the casket to the hearse awaiting to take Jonathan to the Church where they would have a vigil. Paul informed everyone that they would be staying at his villa, that was not far from where his parents lived, and they would be there if they needed to get in touch with any of them. He let them know that Franco and Rosa had set up all the bedrooms and Rosa would cook anything they desired while they were there.

The next day was filled with anticipation of Jonathan's vigil, funeral, and burial; they knew they had to be ready to get through the vigil which would be difficult. The vigil and funeral were held at the Piazza dei Miracoli aka Square of Miracle Church where five generations of the Albanese family had attended. Paul asked his papa if he would say something from his heart on the day of the funeral, after his brother Peter did the Homily. Antonio said he would be honored because he knew he wanted to pay respect to the grandson he never knew. Paul informed his family he would feel more relaxed at the vigil and would say a few words about Jonathan.

When the attendees entered the Church for Jonathan's vigil, they were able to view him in his copper and bronze, brushed silver blue open casket. He looked so peaceful, lying there in his favorite color, blue. Jezalee and Paul had him dressed in the perfect dark blue suit, light blue dress shirt, and Mickey Mouse tie, his favorite Disney character. Jonathan was a nine-year-old who loved dressing up; his friends at school called him "swank" because he was always stylish. Paul knew he would have loved the ensemble they chose for him. Each family member came up one by one to place a photo of themselves so he would never be lonely. An altar boy carefully closed and sealed the casket. The immediate family singly laid a white rose on the casket and walked away to the first row and sat down. Elene turned her head to several pews behind them; she saw her and Antonio's brothers, sisters, nieces, nephews, cousins, and friends. The remainder of the pews were filled with Jezalee, and the O'Malley's staffs, Paul's two-hundred employees from around the globe, and the Stanton family, which Gregory was instrumental in making the arrangements for them coming to pay their respects. When Paul first saw them outside the Church, he thanked them for coming. Six friends of Gloria's were sitting in the last row and Paul did not want to see or talk to them; but felt it was only right that they invited them for Jonathan, since he did interact occasionally with them. Gloria's funeral had been two days prior and that is one place Paul could not think of going to after all she put his son through, must less, what she did to him in-order-to conceive a baby.

During the vigil, those in attendance offered prayers to the family, and observed the scripture through readings and reflections. One of the senior Albanese's neighbors sang, and Elene read poetry, while the Eulogy was said by Paul during the vigil, he wanted the attendees to know how much Jonathan meant to him and all the things his son loved about life. He was filled with curiosity and had so many attributes and was well on his way to accomplishing what he set out to do. He may have only been on this earth for nine years;

however, he fulfilled many things he wanted and loved to do. Paul went on to say many great things about his son and you could tell from his eulogy he was extremely proud of Jonathan. It was a tragedy his life was taken away from him; just as he was getting started in life. It was a night to reflect on the times Paul had with Jonathan and what kind of boy he was. David and Mallory would look over at Jezalee then Paul and thought how brave Jezalee was to be at Paul's side. Mallory said she was one brave and classy lady, David agreed and said it was such a shame how this tragedy got worse by a little boy only nine years old dying. I am glad he was close to Paul. After the vigil, Paul said his goodbyes to all the attendees. Jezalee and the children were so proud of him standing up at the altar and knowing how difficult it must have been to see his son, lying in his casket as he spoke of their wonderful relationship.

The time flew by as Fr. Peter officiated the funeral the following day. Paul had decided early on that he would not be able to stand up in front of everyone that day; so, his papa was going to read what Paul was feeling about Jonathan.

It was time to enter the Church; when opening the doors to the rows and rows of pews, it was overwhelming peering up to the altar knowing Paul's nine-year-old son was housed in the small casket. Paul walked arm in arm with his parents on either side of him as they entered the Church; it felt like the longest walk in his life. Behind them was Jezalee arm in arm with their children. Beyond that point was pews filled with the rest of the attendees.

Paul's immediate family held one white rose for purity, they walked up, and each laid a rose on top of Jonathan's closed casket. Gloria's funeral had been two days earlier and that is one place Paul could not think of going to after all she put his son through, must less, what she did to him in-order-to conceive a baby. Time flew by as Fr. Peter officiated the funeral, Jonathan's grandfather, Antonio went up to the altar, looked out to family and friends; then looking directly at his saddened son, expressed to him what a tragedy it was to stand before them, knowing his grandson was no longer a life. He let them know that everyone in their family had always prayed and wished they could have had the opportunity meeting Jonathan. Not knowing or seeing Jonathan had been the most difficult thing for his family could face, other than his early death. They missed out on his very short-lived life. He thanked his son for always sharing great stories and treasured photos of Jonathan whenever he got to see and do things with him. He told two of the priceless stories and everyone laughed and knew that Paul and Jonathan had a great bond. He looked out to their family and friends that were present and thanked them for coming to pay respects to a little boy that none of them had the privilege of meeting and knowing. Antonio went on to let them know that Paul had finally gotten the okay to have Jonathan meet and visit them; but the unfortunate tragic accident prevented it from happening. Before I step down from the altar, I want everyone here to know it was a travesty that Jonathan was forbidden to know Paul was his father and before he died, my son was going to do whatever it took to obtain custody of that dear, innocent boy. May my deceased grandson Jonathan rest in peace and hopefully knows who his father is, and the rest of his family are. As Antonio stepped down, he had tears in his eyes then slowly walked over to his son and kissed him. By the time he was finished speaking there was not a dry eye in the church.

When the funeral was over, Paul, Antonio, Alexander, and Fr. Peter carried the casket out to the hearse, they gently placed Jonathan in the vehicle. All the limousines were lined up to take the family and friends to Jonathan's resting place. In advance, Paul had called each of Gloria's friends and family members, and expressed under the circumstances only wanted family, friends, and employees only at the cemetery to say goodbye to his son. Once the funeral was over, they were more enlightened at the situation that Gloria had placed everyone in and they now realized how unfair she had been not to let Jonathan know Paul was his dad; they fell prey to her ways and were feeling terrible at how they had succumbed to being just like her. As they walked out of the Cathedral, they wanted to go up to Paul but decided, they were lucky to be invited to the funeral after not including Paul in the obituary and trying to take over everything after Jonathan died. As the procession followed the lead from the police through the streets of Pisa; Paul, Peter, their parents, Jezalee and their two children were in the first limousine behind the hearse. The second limousine had Jezalee parents and the O'Malley's and the third one her and the Albanese and O'Malley staff; Gregory and his family in the one that followed. all the rest followed behind in a single line. When they arrived at the Camposanto Cemetery, where it had just started drizzling, by the time they walked about 100 feet towards the mausoleum it was pouring rain. Once inside the vestibule mausoleum, the casket had already been carried in and placed in the crypt. After Paul's brother said a prayer, the crypt was sealed. After the ceremonial ritual was completed, everyone paid their last condolences to Paul and his family; they drove away from the Cemetery.

The Albanese family was having everyone over after leaving the church and cemetery. On the way back to Paul's parent's home, everyone was silent, exhausted, and sad. The children just looked at each other and were devastated over the whole process of dying and being buried. By the time they arrived at Antonio and Elene's they were ready to be alone; but the Albanese's, had food, beverages, and desserts catered by their best friend Alberto, who had the best catering business Pisa. They knew they had to thank everyone for coming to Jonathan's vigil and funeral. There would be over a hundred plus people and Paul knew Jonathan would have liked them celebrating his life, even if it was short on earth.

When the limousines stopped at the senior Albanese's home, the children could not get out fast enough. Adrienne ran up to the limousine Gregory was stepping out of and was so happy he and his family were able to attend the funeral. Paul had given the children a heads up that they could hang out in his old bedroom until all the guests left. Adrienne and Alexander asked their dad if it was okay if the Stanton children hung out with them and he said sure. Paul and the boys brought food back for the six of them.

Alberto had everything set up everything in the ball room; it was a room they used for huge gatherings and had added it after the boys became teenagers, because they had so many friends over all the time. Jezalee was talking to some of Paul's aunts and uncles and excused herself to go check on the children. Just as Jezalee was about to open the door, Paul was leaving. "Looks like you beat me to it," Jezalee commented. Alexander said he and Adrienne wanted to stay away from the crowd of people and their dad had gotten them some food. Jezalee said she came back to make sure they were alright, and it sounds like, your dad has made sure you're well taken care of and doing fine. Jezalee thanked Paul and said she had better get back to her conversation with a few of his relatives. After everyone had stayed for a few hours and paid their condolences; they left, but the O'Malley's and both staffs stayed a little longer to have some quiet time to speak with the Albanese's. Paul made sure he had limousines ready to take them to their hotel and their flight was scheduled for the next morning.

Later in the evening Antonio answered the telephone and it was his son Peter; he had some incredible news and could not wait to tell the family. He knew it was a sad day; but he was hoping and praying this would lift their spirits. After Antonio asked him a second time, "what did you say?'' Everyone gathered around, and he put Peter on speaker. He prompted Peter to say it once again so the whole family could hear him. The Pope had appointed me as a Cardinal; everyone started dancing, clapping, and yelling out "Bravo." Peter said he was sorry to call at such a time, but he knew it would be in the local paper tomorrow morning and he wanted to give them the news before they saw they got it second hand. "I thought you had to be a Bishop first," Paul said. "That is how it usually is unless the Pope hand picks someone personally," Peter answered. "Wow! What an honor; you must be a good Priest as he laughed after he said it." Said Paul. Paul asked him where he was right now, and Peter said he had just walked out of the Pope's office. Peter knew that today would always be a bittersweet memory with the burying of Jonathan and him being appointed a Cardinal personally by the Pope. Elene asked her son when they would have his ordination and he said he would let them know as soon as the Pope gives the go ahead. After they got off the phone, they were still jumping for joy and knew that it was a special honor for the Pope to choose Peter.

The rest of the evening was spent listening to some Alexander playing some pieces he had composed. While he kept everyone entertained, his grandma was baking him his favorite cake. He told everyone not to disturb his grandma when she is baking because he wanted the cake to turn out perfect for consumption. They laughed! An hour later the cake was done, and Alexander said he was done also! He raced away from the grand piano and sliced a huge piece of the double fudge chocolate cake before it had en cooled down. Elene asked everyone if they wanted a piece of cake and they said they would have a piece tomorrow. "More for me," Alexander commented. "No one wants any now; but I am sure they will want to help you eat it tomorrow," Jezalee remarked. "Darn," Alexander smiled and says. It was getting late; so, the children went off to bed. Paul asked to speak with Jezalee; so, they went into the living room and sat across from one another. Paul asked her if she had been okay with everything, and she said she did not know what that meant. He said he felt awkward under the circumstances; she told him not to worry because she wanted to be there for him and to pay her respects to his son. Jezalee insisted everything was copasetic or she would not have come. He said he just wanted to get things out in the open and to never place her in a compromising situation. She assured him she was good and to never worry about such things.

Jezalee wanted to let him know what a lovely funeral it was and giving great homage to Jonathan was truly meaningful and wished she had gotten the opportunity of meeting his son. When she said his son, it hit him like a ton of bricks; the idea he had a son from another woman was devastating to him; but he had to keep up a good front for Jonathan's sake. Jezalee asked Paul when the jet would be ready to take her home and he said in two days; she said that would give her a little time to visit more with their parents and she was looking forward to just hanging out with them. Paul said he had called his crew and they had their flight schedule for her return home. They went in to kiss the children goodnight then went in separate directions, he went to his room, and she went into the kitchen to say goodnight to his parents and let them know she would be leaving in two days. Elene and Antonio loved Jezalee so much and always prayed that the two would get back together someday. That night, a grieving Paul was ready to go to sleep and all he could think of was his ex-wife; he had such strong feelings for her and wanted to tell her; but he knew when she filed for divorce that was the end. Jezalee spoke with her ex-in-laws for an hour then walked down, which seemed a never-ending hallway to her room. When she passed Paul's room; she wanted to bust open the door and slide in bed next to his muscular, familiar body. She missed the warmth of his hands and body touching hers. Oh! How she missed his presence; with sexiness oozing out his pores. As she walked farther down the hall, she stopped at the bedroom where her parents were and lightly tapped on the bedroom door hoping her parents were still awake. Her mom called out to come in and she went over to give them a goodnight kiss. They spoke for a few minutes then Jezalee quietly closed their door and went to her room. Once she opened the door, looked around; immediately noticed everything was just as it was the last time she and Paul slept in that room. It was the first room and they slept in after getting married. She could not shake the thoughts or feelings of Paul; it was overtaking her, especially being with him at her home, then coming to be by side while they waited the outcome of Jonathan's multiple injuries. She managed to get undressed, take a shower and got in bed. Everything in the room was still the same; family photos on one wall of the Albanese's, a magnificent oil painting of Pisa, that Peter had given his parents as a gift. In the middle of the room was one large arched window and in front of it sat two beautiful periwinkle blue velvet vintage Italian Louis XV style armchairs that she and Paul loved sitting in, while they had the fireplace ablaze on a cold night or reading one of their favorite novels on a beautiful spring or summer evening. She kept glancing at Paul in the photos; tears came and suddenly she felt this tremendous loss that overwhelmed her. Jezalee got up out of bed and went to the bathroom to throw cold water on her face to hopefully feel a little more-calm-and-relaxed. She had not been in that bedroom since she and Paul brought the O'Malley's to meet his parents. Such memories she felt! If only these walls could talk.

Jezalee was trying to go to sleep, but her mind kept racing towards Paul, Jessica, and Jonathan. Not being married to Paul anymore had been a constant fact that she made a grave error and did not know if she could ever forgive herself for divorcing him. As for Jessica, she felt such a void with her not being around; but she knew that she had to stand strong, and her daughter had to know right from wrong. Then, there was Jonathan the mere fact that a little boy died that belonged to Paul and was not hers. She was hoping once she got on the plane and landed in San Francisco, she would be able to get back to her routine and have her thoughts and feelings not constantly being entwined with Paul.

Paul tossed and turned for the first hour in bed, he got up and took a shower, hoping that would help him relax his body. Of course! He was sad that his dear sweet Jonathan was laid to rest and was overwrought with grief; but his thought cycle always ended up with his radiant, intelligent, creative, and demure Jezalee. He did not want her to leave; he wanted her in his arms and never let her go. After things settled down in a few days or so, he decided he needed to see a therapist hoping that talking to someone would help him get over her; he knew he had not done so well on his own.

Jezalee kept waking up during the night and wee morning. Trying to go to sleep was bad enough; but once she finally picked up a book and started reading, she fell asleep with the light on. Unfortunately, the book did not help with keeping her asleep. Now her mind was racing, not only of Paul but Jessica, as well. She had a dream about Jessica meeting Jonathan, and they were fighting over Paul; Alexander and Adrienne each grabbed one of them and said they would shake some sense into them, they kept shaking them like they were rag dolls, then she woke woke-up.

Jezalee could not go back to sleep after that, so she got up to take a shower, got dressed, changed out the sheets, made the bed and went to the kitchen. Who was there? Paul, of all people. When Jezalee walked towards the kitchen, she spotted Paul and was just about to turn around and he said, "good morning," so she had no choice but to stay there. He asked her if she would like a cup of coffee and she said yes; so, he poured her a cup and sat down next to her. They both felt uncomfortable and was hoping the other one would start a conversation; but they did not. Jezalee decided to get up, said thank you for the coffee and walked out of the room. Paul sat there, numb, and embarrassed, he felt awkward he could not startup a conversation with the only woman he loved.

An hour later pretty much everyone was up, and Elene was cooking breakfast for everyone. Paul sat and talked with his mom while she was preparing the food and asked him what was wrong. He, of course, said "nothing mama." She sat down next to him, took his hands, and said, you have never been a good liar, so tell me what is going on in that head of yours. Okay mama, it is Jezalee, I cannot sleep, and I constantly have her in my thoughts. "I figured as much, your papa and I have had several conversations about the two of you, and a few with her parents as well, we always come up with the same conclusion, it is going to work out the way it is supposed to. We four believe in our hearts, you two will get back together somehow, someway; have a little faith. Now that you are, jet setting here and there for business, invite her to join you since she is part owner in the businesses," Elene said. "Mama! You are a genius! Why didn't I think of that?" Paul asked with enthusiasm. "Because you have a mama that will," Elene answered.

The next two days flew by and time for Jezalee to board the jet; Paul, their children, and his parents came to the airport to give her a send-off. Though she came for one reason, a child's funeral, she was leaving with wonderful thoughts for everyone's future. Maybe with Gloria gone, Paul could put everything behind him, except for keeping all the fond memories he had of the times he spent with Jonathan. He had nothing holding him back to start a new life.

As Jezalee was boarding the plane, she turned around to wave to everyone and was wishing she were staying. She knew that this was going to be a rougher flight back; mentally that is! She knew she had to keep busy, so she would read a while, write a few notes to some of her friends, and knew the crew was always available to talk with. Jezalee thought it was nice his entire crew came to the vigil and funeral to pay their respects. Paul had informed the crew about Jonathan and understood the circumstances which was not for public knowledge at that time. Jezalee was not looking forward to the flight but knew it was much better than flying commercial.

When Jezalee arrived home, she was mentally exhausted but knew she better perk up and get her mind in a better place because she would soon be picking up Jessica. She walked into the kitchen and Helga was baking bread. Jezalee rushed over to her and gave her a big hug and kiss on the cheek and asked her how she knew she would be home now. She smiled and said Paul had called her to let her know when she would arrive home. Jezalee asked her if he had mentioned anything else. "As a matter of fact, he asked me to take good care of you and not leave you alone," Helga said. "What does he think I am going to do?" Jezalee asked. "He just said he knew you were going through a lot with Jessica away, the funeral and the children being gone for the summer," Helga answered. "He is right! I do feel lost for many reasons," Jezalee admitted. Helga looked at Jezalee from across the table, took her hand and gently squeezed it and told her maybe she should have stayed a little longer with the

Albanese's. Jezalee thought for a minute and said maybe she should have. Helga asked if she had spoken to Jessica, and she said no; the parents are not allowed to have any communication. Jezalee broke down crying and let Helga know that it was difficult to be near Paul especially with Jonathan's tragic death; I saw the pain he was in and at times I felt as if his son was mine because I felt the same pain. How Jonathan came into this world was no longer an issue; he was Paul's flesh and blood and that is all that mattered. A few times I had my mind wandering and would fantasize that Jonathan would have a full recovery, I would love him like he was my son and Paul's, and we would live happily ever after with our four children. Then! I would wake up to the fact we are not together anymore; and I came back to the reality of things. "Dear, you still love Paul, and I do not know if you have forgiven him; but I do know you wished you had never jumped in to getting the divorce so soon. When Paul arrived back at the Paris house without you and the children, he would never be the same; he could not even spend one night in that house without you and the children. I tried to get him to stay but he packed a few things as quickly as he could and went to a hotel. Not going on that vacation with everyone, broke Paul in half. When I saw him, the next day moving the rest of his belongings out, he looked lost, sad, and could barely speak with me without breaking down," Helga stood up and went over to Jezalee and said. "When he came here with Sophia and Leila, I never saw him once look at Sophia as if he loved her in the Biblical way. I have lived around you and your family all these years and I can pick up on what is real and what is not. Trust me! When I say he does not love her, it is true! As, for you and Jim, you have never admitted loving him; but he obviously is in love with you and wants to marry you. I do not think you will ever be in love with anyone else unless you can get Paul off your mind. I hate seeing you this way; do you want to stop seeing Jim and try to date other men or maybe no one for a while?" Helga asked. "I am not interested in Jim, even as a friend anymore; he has proven from time to time he is obsessed with me, and it is not healthy. I am not going to put myself through being around someone like that ever again. I am not going to date anyone until my feelings are not all about still loving Paul. I have been wrapped up with Jim because he gets along so well with all three of the children; but I should not be seeing him on how he treats them. Sure! I was drawn to him because he is quite handsome, charismatic, and friendly; but he has many cons, one being he is not Catholic, he is too obsessed with me, he speaks badly of Paul every chance he gets, he has mood swings that seem to be getting worse as time goes on. He seems to lie about things from his past and it bothers me and the O'Malley's that he does not mention his family that died a tragic death. There are times when he could have fit them in with our conversations; but he never has, it is as if they never existed. He asks me questions about when Paul and I met and were married but never anything about when he met and married his wife. I also feel uncomfortable when he questions my feelings for Paul; I finally told him Paul is off limits and he will always be around because of our children. When I have the time and energy; I will find out more about him; but I currently have too many other things that are more pressing. I know there is something missing, but I cannot decipher what it is. You know how I am with my curiosity and once that happens, I need to dig until I get answers," Jezalee remarked. "Jezalee, you are an intelligent woman and are doing the right thing because you do not love him and never have; just be cautious in your Sherlock Holmes attempt to finding anything on him," Helga said. Jezalee smiled at Helga and thanked her for listening because it helped her clear her head. "I love you so much Helga; you are the sister I never had, and you mean everything to me. We have always been so close and able to talk about whatever is on our minds. There is no one else I feel more comfortable with when it comes to matters of the heart, than you!" Jezalee said lovingly. Before she said goodnight to Helga, Jezalee wanted to thank her for graciously coming to the funeral. Helga took Jezalee's hand and said she could not imagine being there for her and Paul.

When Jezalee woke up the next day she called Paul and the children to see how they were doing. Everything was quiet around the Albanese household; but Paul said he wanted to keep busy and had some fun things planned to do with the children. Paul handed the phone to Alexander and Adrienne, and they said they were trying to be in good spirits for their dad but were missing their sister. They asked Jezalee how much longer Jessica was going to be at that camp and their mom said she had to be there for a month; so, it is going to be awhile. Their mom informed them that she would be spending a few days at home with her before she joined them in Italy. Jezalee asked if they could put their dad back on the phone and they handed the receiver to Paul. Jezalee let Paul know that it may be a good idea for Jessica to be home with her for at least a couple of days after her camp experience and he agreed. Paul thought it was a good call because the two of them needed to square things up. Paul said when time gets closer to her coming home; he will have his jet ready for take-off. She thanked Paul for purchasing the private jet and hopefully Jessica would not be as nervous on his plane as she was on commercial flights. "You know, I forgot about how she reacted every time we flew somewhere; I have a great idea, I will fly with her," Paul said. "Chivalry is not dead! That is so enduring of you; she will love that! Her every own escort. Jezalee reminded Paul that he should be the one to let Jessica know that Jonathan passed-away. Paul thought for a moment and suggested that she ask her therapist at the camp how to approach the subject. Jezalee agreed and would call her right away to get her thoughts on the matter. "While I have you on the phone, I was curious why Sophia was not at the hospital or funeral," Jezalee commented. Paul was taken aback that Jezalee would ask such a question. He finally spoke up and said he did not feel it was necessary since they were just friends. "I did not mean to pry," Jezalee remarked. "That is quite alright!" Paul said. While they were still on the phone, his parents asked to speak to Jezalee; they wanted to reassure her that they would help keep the kids minds off the death and funeral of Jonathan. She thanked them and told them how much she loved them.

The children were missing their mom and did not like the fact when Sophia came over to see Paul, she acted as if she was her replacement. They expressed their aggravations to their dad, and he said he would have a talk with her. He had not let his children know he was getting ready to break up with her; so, this was the ideal time to meet with Sophia and tell her it was over. Paul called Sophia and asked her to meet him for a drink near her Boutique; she agreed to a time and place. While he was waiting in the restaurant-bar, Paul was not looking forward to having the conversation but knew it was long overdue. They had fun together but all he ever did was think of Jezalee; so, it was unfair to Sophia knowing there would never be a future for them. As he finished with his thoughts; in walked Sophia, smiling as usual. She sat down and asked how his day had been. "I need to have a serious talk with you! and I have not looked forward to this one bit," Paul said. She looked bewildered and really did not know what to say. She had a puzzled look on her face and said to just begin whatever is on your mind. Paul began to tell her he had never stopped loving Jezalee, and it was not fair to either of them to keep seeing one another. Sophia glared at him as her eyes welted up with tears and was without words. Sophia was certainly caught off guard but decided she needed to say something. She looked him straight in the eyes and said she thought they would eventually get married. He told her he had never spoken of marriage, and she assumed wrong. He explained he had tried, after the divorce, not to have feelings for Jezalee; it had not happened. He told Sophia when they met, he thought he would get over his marriage but never did. Sophia's face turned red, and she looked as if she was going to throw something at him. Paul said he did not understand her reaction and it is not as if they shopped for rings. She was furious at him and said that no couple spends as much time as they have and not end up together. "Are you kidding me! That is the craziest thing you could say," Paul sarcastically said. He continued telling her that she was out of line because a lot of people want companionship; but it does not mean they will get married. "Sophia, I do not understand why it is so difficult for you to comprehend the fact that I could never marry you; knowing how I still love Jezalee. My wife divorced me, I never wanted that to happen. I cannot be anymore, precise in thought or expression about how I feel," an aggregative Paul said. "You led me on, and you know it!" Sophia said. "We had sex one time, that does not constitute a walk down the aisle, by any means, and I certainly never led you on. Another thing! My children had a complaint about you, and it was disturbing to me," Paul bluntly said. "Go on, what did they have to say?" Sophia asked as she rolled her eyes. "Well! They got the impression you were trying to take their mother's place; I believe them,'' Paul said rather quick minded. He stood up and said he was sorry; but she needed to move on. He hoped she would find a man that would love her, as he loves Jezalee. "You deserve happiness with the right person; you are a wonderful lady, there is someone special out there; I wish love and happiness comes your way," Paul said. As Paul walked away, Sophia saw her future leave.

Jezalee made a call to Centre Communautaire Familia de Paris and spoke with Renee to give her great news. They purchased the building next door; Paul was able to obtain a permit to renovate and begin construction. The architecture's design will connect the buildings from the ground floor. They will renovate each floor of the new building while they break through the first-floor side walls and connect them with a walk-thru structure of glass and stone. Jezalee let Renee know that she and Paul had been tied up with some other business transactions. Paul will be there next week, and the construction crew will begin the same day. Jezalee was pleased the benefactors came for a tour of the center and was impressed with what the center had accomplished so far, and they had signed contracts to invest and would be willing to donate yearly. The benefactors agreed the Albanese's had built an amazing place and were interested in seeing the expansion into the building next door. She thanked Renee for doing such an outstanding job and let her know that an employee that had been with her for ten years would be coming in to help her out. She said Monique and her husband take care of their country chateau and she would be able to come in whenever Renee needed her. Jezalee gave Renee, Monique's home number and asked her to call and introduce herself.

A few days later Jim called Jezalee, to apologize. She asked him if she could call him back in ten minutes and they will talk. After they hung up, Jezalee sat down and briefly wrote down what she wanted to say to him. She knew one thing for sure! She was not going to say she did not want to see him anymore quite yet. Jezalee wanted to take some time to think of how and when she might be able to dig into his past. She called Jim back and asked him if he could come over for lunch out by the pool. Jim came over an hour later and Jezalee had everything already set up for them, to enjoy the summer weather, and have a delightful meal together. She had some classical music by Puccini and Vivaldi playing while they ate and had conversation. He finally brought up the death of Jonathan and how sorry he was for Paul's loss. "I guess Paul is getting paid back for what he did to you and your children," Jim said rather sarcastically. Jezalee just sat there stunned thinking, why anyone would ever make a comment like that. She looked at Jim and asked him to please go and was not sure she ever wanted to see him again. I have had enough of your off the wall remarks and I explicitly said my children's father is off limits for you to ever comment about. From where I am sitting, you will never come close to being the man Paul is; just go! As Jim walked away, he turned back to her and said, "I would never have cheated on you! Then made his way through the house, slammed the door behind him as he left. Jezalee went to Helga's to talk. Helga invited her in and could immediately see something was wrong. She motioned for her to sit down and tell her what was on her mind. Jezalee broke down and told her what Jim had said and she could hardly believe anyone could say such an awful thing; especially since he had been warned to never talk against Paul. Helga asked her how she felt now that he was gone? "I feel very relieved and upset," Jezalee answered. "Dear, I think the big issue here is the fact Jim is a very jealous man. Think about it for a minute! Here is a man in love with you; he is great with your children, and it appears he is monogamous," Helga reminded her. Jezalee looked at Helga and was surprised because it was if she wanted to remind her of Jim's good qualities. "I am surprised you are defending him?" Jezalee commented. "That certainly was not my intention, and I am sorry you took it that way," let me add something to that; he knows that Paul cheated on you and had an illegitimate child and I think he loves you enough that he hates the fact someone would hurt you in that way after so many years of marriage," Helga replied. "I see your point; but I still think he should have kept it to himself; I have a hard enough, time knowing what happened to my marriage," Jezalee with regret. "Well, hon! I know how difficult this has been on you and it breaks my heart to see you go through any pain at all; you are one of the most wonderful people anyone could ever meet and know. I love you and I am sorry if I spoke out of line," Helga said sadly. Jezalee went over and sat next to Helga and gave her a big hug and let her know she needed to hear what she had to say, and she was not out of line and has always respected her thoughts. "I usually tell Jim immediately if I feel he is out of line and give him the chance to explain himself; but this time I just could not see it in my heart to give him a chance to say another word," Jezalee confessed. "I think you are right about him! If you still want to delve into his past life just apologize to him; but keep your distance as much as possible. If you decide not to pursue spying on him; then do not apologize and say good riddance now, you do not owe him anything. If you want to find out about his past; then apologize however you see fit. You will know when the time is right," Helga advised her.

When Jim arrived home, he went to his library, opened-up his secret compartment where he had a loaded gun; pulled it out and walked over to his sofa and sat there glaring down at it. He reminded himself of the times he had pulled the gun out and almost shot himself in the head. He did not remember what stopped him then and he was not sure if this would be another one of those times. He laid down on the sofa, still holding the gun in his hand, closed his eyes and thought about who he was as a child, who he had become and where would he be going in the future. He was thinking about Deanna and how happy she had been all these years. He was so confused and wanted to be good; but he did not know how to be. Deanna had been right all along; he should have gotten help; but he was too embarrassed about his past. Jim knew he should have kept his mouth shut about Paul; but he could not help himself at that moment. He knew that may have been the end of Jezalee forever. He was perplexed; this was a pivotal moment and did not feel he had any other choice; but to end his life. He started sobbing uncontrollably and his hand was shaking; the phone startled him, he dropped the gun to the floor. The answer machine went on, he heard Jezalee's voice saying she wanted to speak with him and to call her when he got this message. He wiped the tears from his face, stared down at the gun on the floor and knew he had come closer to pulling the trigger than the times before. He laid there for a good hour and did not know what to do; he was not sure he was in the right mind to call Jezalee back; but, on the other hand maybe he needed this opportunity because he could at least hear her out. He got up to go to the kitchen and poured himself a glass of ice water and sat for a few minutes contemplating what he should do. He was getting ready to call Deanna and ended up calling Jezalee. Jezalee said she did not want to talk over the phone and was it okay if she came over, Jim was surprised! He thought fast and said, sure, come on over. After they hung up, he quickly went to the bathroom to see how he looked from crying and his eyes were swollen; immediately splashed his face with cold water hopefully to look somewhat back to normal by the time Jezalee arrived. He changed into some fresh clothes and combed his hair back in place. As he looked, into the mirror and said, "Miss Jezalee you just saved my life, and you don't even know it." It is just a matter of time, and you will be mine.

Jim called the doorman to let Jezalee up whenever she arrived. He was waiting at the door, and he took her hand as she walked in. He knew he wanted to be the wounded bird so to speak, so he let her take the lead to see where she would go from there. He asked her where she would like to sit, and she said in the living room if that is okay. He said sure! He offered her something to drink and she was not thirsty. He sat across from her and the first thing he said was he was happy she had called. She said she wanted to be honest with him and said she was shocked at what he said about Paul; especially since she had a serious conversation with him explicitly saying he was off limits. That was Jim's cue to now speak. "Dear Jezalee! I know I was so out of line, and I knew better; I am just so torn up at what you went through; and it is all because of his indiscretion. I hope you can forgive my thoughtless behavior; but I look at you and cannot imagine why anyone would ever stray. You are the most gorgeous, sweet, intelligent, enduring, generous, and kind woman a man could ever want to meet and love," Jim said enduringly. Jezalee looked at him for a minute and tried to take in all that he had said. Before she spoke, she got up and went to sit next to him. Jezalee took his right hand and placed it in the palms of both her hands and said she understands. She apologized and said she reacted too quickly, and someone reminded her of who you are. Jim was puzzled and asked who might that be? She smiled as she said it was Helga. Jim perked up and said he owed that sweet lady a kiss, flowers and maybe chocolates to go along with a thank you. Jezalee said that's such a lovely thought. Jim was serious! "What kind of chocolates and flowers does Helga like? "She loves Belgium chocolates and green calla lilies are her all-time favorite flower," Jezalee answered. "Let us go shopping right now," Jim demanded. "You want to do that this very minute?" Jezalee asked. Yes! I do. Let me get my car keys and tell me what florist we need to go to get these so-called green calla lilies and let us go buy some chocolates," the good-humored Jim said. Within an hour they had managed to find calla lilies and the chocolates. He bought a beautiful vase to put the flowers in and had the candy gift wrapped. While they were driving back to Jezalee's, she called Helga from his car phone to make sure she stayed home until she got there. Helga said she would be home; in fact; she was in the kitchen making sauerbraten for their dinner. "That sounds so wonderful; we haven't had that in ages, and you know how much I love it; see you in fifteen minutes," anxiously said Jezalee.

Helga was quite surprised when Jezalee walked in with Jim beside her. He made his way across the kitchen to hand her the flowers, the vase, and the chocolates. She looked up at him and said, "What is all this for?" "It is for you for saying nice things about me; that means a lot to me. Thank you from my heart to yours," Jim answered with a smile on his face. "Wow! What a kind and sweet gesture; but I don't know if I deserve all this," Helga replied. "Yes! You do, and more. Here is a fresh package of seeds to grow your own calla lilies." Jim said as he handed them to her. "You have thought about everything haven't you!" Helga said. "I tried my best!" Jim replied. "You have certainly succeeded," Jezalee warmly commented. Helga let them know dinner would be in thirty minutes; and hoped that Jim would be joining them. He said he would never pass up her or Jezalee's cooking.

Dinner was a big hit; Jim had never had sauerbraten and added that to his list of new favorites. The three sat around after dinner and talked for a while then Helga wanted to take some leftovers over to Nina and the family. Jim did not want to press his luck by staying too long so he said he had some paperwork he absolutely had to get done before going into work the next day. Jezalee walked him to the door, they hugged one another as they said their goodbyes and he hugged her goodbye. As he drove home, his suicidal thoughts had gone away, and he felt things were working out just how he wanted them to.

Created with Sketch.

The next two weeks while Paul and his parents were keeping the children busy, Jezalee was contemplating her first conversation with Jessica. She knew that Jessica was mad when she was forced to go to the Therapy Camp.

Jezalee was tired but could not fall asleep right away because her thoughts were racing through her mind over how Jessica would react when she told her about Jonathan's accident and death. She knew as soon as she woke up the next day, she would call the Camp and ask to speak to the therapist that was working with her daughter.

Jezalee slept in late and before she went downstairs to have her first cup of coffee, she called the Therapy Camp. She was able to speak with Jessica's therapist and wanted her clinical opinion on how she should handle telling her daughter about the death of her stepbrother. The therapist, Mrs. Roberts felt she did the right thing by having Jessica come to their Camp but did not want her to feel she made a mistake in keeping her there; even though there was a death in the family. Mrs. Roberts decided that it would be best for the two of them to tell her together. They both decided Jezalee would go to the Camp on Jessica's last two days being with them. She admitted to the therapist she was quite nervous over the whole thing. Mrs. Roberts encouraged her to be at peace with how she handled the situation and that Jessica had done exceptionally well. She promised Jezalee that she had been working with Jessica to help her re-enter into her family life. She also explained to her, due to privacy rules, they would have Jezalee come to a private entrance on the side of the building. Jezalee asked why and she basically informed her that they wanted to keep her identity private in case someone walking through the halls would by chance know who she was.

The next few days were filled with angst to see Jessica; Jezalee was just trying to relax enough to work on some research for her books. She called Paul and the children several times and they were either off on an adventure or visiting friends and family; so, she knew they were keeping active and busy.

Jezalee finally got to speak with Paul and the children a day before her trip to the Camp. She wanted to make sure when Jessica calls them to not let her know Paul would be flying back with her; she wanted it to be a nice surprise for her. She had dinner with Jim that night at his place but left early because he had a late-night flight to Japan on business and she needed to get packed for her two-day trip to the camp.

Jezalee was nervous as she sipped her coffee and had breakfast with Helga before she left for camp. Her driver arrived half an hour later and she was looking forward to seeing her daughter but nervous about how she was going to react towards what she had to tell her. She had time to reflect all the past years of her beautiful daughter growing up and had been so shocked at how she treated her dad.

Jezalee knew one thing, that Paul's indiscretion had devastated the children as much as it did to her.

Jessica's therapist, Mrs. Roberts sat down with her the day before she knew Jezalee would be arriving; she asked her how she felt about going home. Jessica said she was hoping she could spend a week with her mom before going to Italy. She was anxious to see her dad and her siblings; but she had really disappointed her mom and wanted to have some time to mend their relationship. She added, my mom is a very smart lady and I respect and love her in every way possible and regret acting out like a crazed animal. The month Jessica was at Therapy Camp she explained in her sessions how painful it was to watch two most incredible, loving, and devoted parents that she loved dearly, end up in divorce. She thought that was devastating enough; but, when her dad disclosed, he had a son by another woman, she had never felt anger and hurt before, and she did not know how to handle it. At the end of the session her therapist let her know that her mom was coming for her the last two days at the Camp. Jessica's eyes lit up and thrilled at the thought of seeing her mom, she could hardly wait to apologize to her. While she had been at Camp; she found a love for art and had painted a special painting that expressed her feelings. She brought the painting into her session and wanted to show it to her therapist; she was astounded when Jessica removed the cloth from the canvas. She expressed how amazed she was at her talent; especially since she indicated she had never shown an interest in drawing, much less painting. That night Jessica went to bed a happy and could hardly wait to see her mom.

As the driver pulled up to the private entrance, Jezalee thanked him as he carried her one-piece luggage and placed it at the side entrance. She rang the bell; a lady approached the door from the other side and pressed the intercom to ask who was there. Jezalee politely said who she was and what therapist was waiting for her arrival. The lady opened the door and asked for Jezalee to show her driver's license; then she handed it back to her and said thank you. Her assistant called for Mrs. Roberts, and she came immediately and walked Jezalee to her room to get settled. Jezalee unpacked her bag and by the time she was done it was lunch time. The therapist sat down with her for about fifteen minutes and went over how they would handle telling Jessica about the passing of Jonathan; she then walked her to a large room that looked like any living room in America, including a cozy fireplace for the winter months. Jessica was the only one in the room and when she saw her mom she jumped up and ran over to her. They both had tears and hugged one another like they had not seen one another in years. Since it was lunchtime, the therapist took them to a small room where they were served lunch and could talk together. Mrs. Roberts wanted them to be alone during this time and she was going to meet up with them afterwards. As they ate their meal, they talked about how much they loved San Francisco and how wonderful it was to have the O'Malley's as their friends. Jessica said how much she missed Alexander and Adrienne and could not wait to be with them and her dad. After lunch was over the therapist met back up with the girls and took them to a private room to have a session. Jessica asked the therapist if she could get the gift she had made for the family and she said sure. When she got back to the room, she sat the wrapped painting against a wall, then sat down. As the session started the therapist let Jessica tell her mom about her therapy sessions while she stayed there and how they helped her. Jezalee listened intently while her daughter talked; she was not expecting her to say the things she did. While Jessica kept talking, Jezalee was thankful she had been referred to this Therapy Camp; and saw a tremendous difference in a short period of time. Jessica had finished expressing herself and apologizing when the therapist told her there was something that they needed to tell her. She looked puzzled and turned to her mom and asked her if she was still mad at her. Jezalee reached over on the opposite end of the sofa and gave her daughter a hug and said how happy she was for the two of them to have space and time to think things out. The therapist spoke up and said your mom has something important tell you and please hear her out before any comments are expressed. Jezalee moved closer to her daughter and started with Jonathan being in a car accident. She began to tell her all the details from beginning to end and she was hoping and praying that Jessica understood why she did not take her from the Camp and join them. She let her know that her dad and siblings asked for Jezalee to bring her home. Jessica spoke up, "Mom, you always know the right thing to do; I do not know how you do it; but you have great instincts. You made the right decision, the state of mind I was in, I would not have been able to handle it. She began to cry and say how sad for dad; I cannot wait to see him and tell him how sorry I am for being out of line and regrets that his son died," sadly, Jessica said. Mrs. Roberts looked and listened to them and knew it was time for Jessica to give her gift to her mom. She picked up the painting, handed it to her mom and said she hoped she and the family would like it. As Jezalee opened the gift, she was astonished who the subject was in the painting, it was a large oil painting of Paul, Jezalee, Alexander, Adrienne, Jessica, and Jonathan. Jezalee asked her what artist did the painting and how would they know what Jonathan looked like? She was absolutely, astonished! "Mom, look at the signature in the lower right-hand corner," Jessica said. She looked at the signature closely and saw that it was Jessica's. Jezalee surprisingly blurted out JLA, which were Jessica's initials for Jessica Lynn Albanese! "I never knew you were interested in painting, and this looks like a professional artist did this and number two, how did you know what Jonathan looked like?" He mom asked. She began to tell her that she snuck into her dad's bedroom while he was taking a shower the night before she left for Camp and looked in his wallet when she found a photo of Jonathan. She painted him into the picture by memory of the photo. After the reveal of the painting, the therapist looked at both Jessica and Jezalee and said she was so pleased at how much Jessica had grown since she came to their Camp. Mrs. Roberts was impressed with the immediate interest Jezalee took in taking control of the serious altercation that occurred at their home; not letting it go any farther than it did. Unfortunately, a lot of times people let situations go way beyond where they should, and it takes months and sometimes years to heal. After this session today I have concluded that I am going to dismiss Jessica a day early because she has shown exemplary motivation in giving deep concerns and thoughts why she reacted to what her father disclosed to the children. Hopefully, she will walk away from here with the tools we have given her to know how to respond to any situation that may come up. One especially important tool we try to teach people when they come to our Camp, is to think before reacting. It is vital to understand there is always going to be things that we do not like and maybe giving us a feeling of rage within us; when something erupts it must be put out slowly and then we let our thought process take over. When we do this, we are enabling ourselves to react in a way that is not damaging to others or ourselves. At that point, it is time to discuss one's feelings and hopefully the other person/persons involved will be a good listener to that person's concerns.

Jezalee and Jessica went to their rooms and packed their bags. When Jezalee was done she asked one of the orderlies if she could speak with Mrs. Roberts before they left. He took her to the therapist's office and asked if she could speak with her for a moment and she said of course, have a seat! Jezalee sat down and began to run something by her and was hoping she would be opened to starting a foundation for the Therapy Camp. Mrs. Roberts said, "What do you have in mind?" I was thinking I would initially start the foundation off with my donation of $ 200,000. a year for five years; after the five years, I will re-access the amount to pay yearly. This money would be held in escrow for families that need help but cannot afford the cost of the Camp. The therapist was startled that Jezalee would be so generous thinking about helping people that needed their services; but by no means could ever afford to come to their Camp. Jezalee said she will meet with her attorney and get the paperwork in motion. She let the therapist know that she would have fundraisers during the year to help raise more money. Jezalee informed she would have her attorney call her direct and get any information he needs to complete the process. The therapist made one request; I hope you would consider making the foundation name after Jessica due to her being the reason this will be started. Jezalee stood up to shake Mrs. Roberts hand and said that is a great idea and I will discuss it with my daughter, to make sure she would want her name attached to the donations. Thank you for all the help and I know my girl is going home with essential tools to help her now and in the future and I will be referring others here that need help. It has been a pleasure to meet and speak with you; likewise said Mrs. Roberts.

Jessica was waiting for her mom in the private lobby area and as soon as Jezalee sat down she called for a driver, and he was there within twenty minutes. As they rode home, they talked about everything from school, fashion, movies, and makeup. It was over an hour drive which seemed quicker with the two of them together.

Once they were dropped off, the first thing they did was hang out in Jessica's bedroom and her mom helped her unpack. The second thing, she mentioned to her mom was how quiet it was in their house. Jezalee said, "Try being here by yourself?" I know Helga is usually here, but she is in her own wing so it is so quiet you could hear a feather drop. Talk, about Helga, let us go see where she is.

The girls went downstairs to make their way to Helga's entrance and knocked on the door. There was no answer; so, they called her from the kitchen phone; it rang at least five times. Jezalee could not imagine where she was so Jessica checked the garage, and her car was still there. Just as she came back from the garage, Jezalee tried calling one more time and finally on the third ring Helga answered. Jezalee asked if she was okay, and she said she had been in her sauna. Helga asked her where she was, and she said we are right outside your door. I will be right there! Helga opened the door and hugged them and asked them to come in. Helga prepared tea and had a fresh berry pie made knowing that it was one of Jessica's favorites. The three of them got caught up and decided to go out for dinner.

Once the gals arrived home; the first thing Jessica did was run to the phone to call her siblings and her dad. Paul answered the phone and was thrilled to hear from Jessica. She said how anxious she was to see them; but wanted to spend a few more days with her mom and he said whenever she was ready, he would call his crew to get the jet ready; she also expressed her sadness that Jonathan died and was sorry she had not been there for him. Paul let her know things were not the same without her being there and everyone was happily anticipating her to arrival.

For the next few days, Jezalee and Jessica just wanted to stay home to relax and enjoy one another's company, watch a movie or two and catch up with any family news. Jessica waited every night for her mom to go to bed before she pulled out her sketchbook and was preparing to paint a portrait of her. The first night she had gotten home, she waited for her mom to go to bed before she called Helga to ask her if she could use one of her bedrooms to set up her easel to paint a portrait of her mom. Helga was so excited for Jessica to begin because when she saw the portrait of the family, including Jonathan she was overwhelmed at her new-found talent. Jessica stayed up to the wee hours every night to try and finish the portrait. She realized she needed more time; so, she asked her mom if it was okay if she stayed a few extra days and Jezalee was surprised but thrilled Jessica wanted to spend more time with her. Jessica knew with the extra days she would have plenty of time to finish her mom's portrait.

The extra few days Jessica stayed proved to be busy in the morning and afternoon, shopping for school accessories to wear with her uniform. She liked to buy sweaters and socks to match, and she wanted all new shoes, underwear, purses, and toiletries. They went shopping every day and managed to take in a movie on the last day of their shopping spree. She was all set for school and did not have to worry about shopping when she and her siblings returned from their vacation.

After Jezalee kissed Jessica each night, her daughter would wait about a half an hour then tiptoe down the hallway, then slowly walk down the stairs to Helga's living quarters. The last two nights while Jessica was finishing up the portrait of her mom, Helga would keep her company and they talked and laughed about funny things that had happened over the years to each of them. Helga loved Jessica and her siblings as if they were her own children and knew she and Astrid had been blessed that her mom started working for them all those years ago. While Jessica was doing the finishing touches on the portrait, Helga brought out a berry pie fresh out of the oven and two tall glasses of ice-cold milk and celebrated the completion of the painting. Jessica had gone through the family photo albums and found a few photos with her mom wearing a beautiful pastel yellow dress; it was her dad's favorite dress on her mom, and it was one that her mom loved as well. Helga stood in front of the masterful work Jessica had done and was in awe of her talent. She asked Jessica whatever possessed you to draw and paint because you never showed an interest in this form of art? "Well! Everyone had many choices at Camp, and we had to choose some form of creativity to express how we felt; for some odd reason I ventured over to a sketch pad and pencil; it became evident from the beginning I was a natural at looking at something and able to make it come to life. I was excited when I had completed my first drawing and got praise for my efforts," Jessica remarked. "Hon, it appears from just the two paintings you have done, you have a calling as an artist and I think you may want to continue in that path; you are extraordinary and have had a well-hidden talent you never knew you had," Helga commented. "Thank you! Helga, the funny thing is, once I picked up the sketch pad at camp, I had this unexplained drive within me to paint every day; I will look at something and want to start sketching it immediately," Jessica said.

Jessica was getting ready to go upstairs to get some sleep; but she asked Helga when would be the best time to give her mom the portrait? Helga thought for a minute and said, "why don't you give it to her as you leave or have it sitting in the hallway across from her bedroom. The first thing she sees when she opens her door," "Helga, you are a genius! I love the hallway idea; that is exactly what I am going to do; I hope she will like it," Jessica remarked. "Stop that crazy talk! You know you are great so stop selling yourself short, you have a gift and own up to it little miss," Helga said. They hugged and said their goodnights.

That night after Jessica quietly sat the portrait up against the wall in the hallway, all she could think of when she got in bed was how fortunate she had been to be born into the family that she loved so much and everyone that was a part of their family circle.

Around 8:00 o'clock in the morning Jezalee woke up, took her shower, and got ready for another beautiful day with her daughter. As she opened her bedroom door; she could not help but see the portrait standing upright against the wall and was shocked! She quickly picked it up and walked into her bedroom, sat down in a chair, and was examining the details and realized the portrait had her in the yellow dress that was Paul's favorite on her. The resemblance was uncanny and when she looked down at the artist's signature she gasped as she saw her daughter's name; tears were falling down her face, she immediately went into the bathroom and splashed water on her face and dried it off. She hurried out of her room and quietly opened Jessica's bedroom door; Jessica was a light sleeper and woke up as soon as her mom walked towards her. Jezalee sat on the edge of the bed nearest to her daughter and said she found her incredible portrait. "When did you have time to do the portrait?" Jezalee asked. "I confess I have been at Helga's after you went to bed, and she let me use one of her extra bedrooms to paint in," Jessica answered. Jezalee put her arms out to hug and kiss her daughter and thanked her for such an amazing gift she will cherish it forever.

Since there was not much to do around the house, Jezalee asked her daughter and Helga if they would like to do anything special and Helga had a suggestion. Since we now have an artist amongst us, why don't we visit the de Young and Legion of Honor Museums in town today? Jessica lit up like a baseball field and asked her mom if she would mind going. Jezalee thought it was a fantastic idea thought her daughter would certainly gain inspiration from the most famous artists in the world. Jezalee called Nina to see if she would go since the children were away. Nina said she would love to go; and came over to have breakfast with the gals before they were leaving.

Jessica called her dad before they left for the day and told him anytime, he is ready to get the engines running on his jet, she was ready for her vacation. He said he had already alerted the crew and they were all on standby and could leave in two days and she was getting so excited to experience the private jet.

Jessica got dressed as quickly as she could while Jezalee, Helga and Nina waited. In the meantime, Jezalee had Nina call Joseph back to ask him if he had anything pressing around the estate that needed more than dropping the gals off at the Museums. Joseph said there was not anything urgent and what he was doing could wait for another day. An hour later everyone piled into the SUV and off they went. While Joseph was driving, "How insensitive of me! Joseph, please join us for the day; we would love your company if you were interested," Jezalee asked. "Thanks for inviting me; but while you lovely ladies are going through the Museum's I will be going to a couple of hardware stores to pick up some things that are needed," Joseph answered. "Joseph, all that can wait, please join us, really want you to join us for the day and besides, it is Jessica's last full day at home," Jezalee said. "Come on Uncle Joseph, I would love for you to join us!" Jessica said in her pleading voice. "Since you said it that way, how can I resist?" Answered Joseph. All four ladies started clapping and were all happy he was going with them for the day. By the time they finished their museum tours, they were famished and could not wait to have dinner at Zuni's French Cafe; it was Jessica's all time, favorite place so that is where they went. While waiting to be served they discussed some of their favorite artists and what a delightful day it had been. Joseph asked Jessica if she had been inspired by visiting the Museums and she emphatically said she was ready to take on her next subject; they looked at her and Helga said, "Who are you and where have you been all your life?"

"Didn't you find out in school that you could draw?" Nina asked. "No! I really did not; but we had projects, but nothing interesting to most of as she giggled; anyway, the art class was limited to really the history of art and before that I was much younger," Jessica answered.

Dinner finally arrived and they enjoyed their selections on the menu and decided not to have dessert there because Jessica wanted to go home to have some more of Helga's famous three berry pie topped off with vanilla bean ice cream. As they were traveling across town, Joseph started singing an old Irish tune he remembered from his childhood and oddly enough, they knew the song and started singing with him. It had been such great weather with four of Jessica's favorite persons in all her world and could not think of a better way to end her last day with them.

Jezalee helped Jessica pack for her trip, and she decided not to take too much with her because she wanted to buy a few things while she was on vacation. That night Jessica asked her mom if she could sleep with her, and she welcomed the idea. Once the two went to bed, they ended up talking until they fell asleep. The next morning, they both got up early, had breakfast with Helga, Nina, and Joseph then Jessica said her goodbyes to the ladies and Joseph took Jessica to the airport. The gals wanted to ride along; however, Jessica preferred saying her goodbyes to them at the house. Of course! There were water works and Jessica looked at them, smiled and said, "snap out of it, your make-up is running." They looked at one another and she was right, they had raccoon eyes from their mascara running. Jessica yelled out as Joseph was driving off, "buy waterproof mascara sweet ladies." They laughed.

Jessica could not believe she was going to be traveling on her dad's private jet; it was all so exciting. Roger, the steward met her at the gate and helped her up the steps to the jet. As she was walking down the aisle to choose a seat, out jumped her dad and she loudly screamed. Oh! my goodness dad! You scared the meanness out of me. He laughed and gave her a big kiss. After being up in the air for over an hour, Jessica could not believe how much more comfortable it was riding in a private jet compared to even first class on a commercial plane. Time went quickly for her because she was more relaxed, Jessica could get up and move around more and most importantly she and her dad had some great conversations; it was a more relaxed atmosphere. Before she had boarded the jet, she had Roger take her painting and put it somewhere to hide it. She had been so surprised to see her dad she had forgotten about the painting. The next time Roger came by she asked him to get the item she had him store for her. When Roger came by with the painting, her dad was reading some documents he needed to sign, and she asked him if he had a minute. Paul looked up and said sure! What's up sweetie! This is for you; she took the wrapping from around the canvas and set it near him. He was speechless! I thought you said you made something for me; I did! And this is it. He was stunned! Have you secretly been taking art lessons, and no one told me! No dad! While I was at Therapy Camp, they had each person choose some type of creative outlet to help with their therapy and I really cannot answer why I chose to draw but once I started, I was shocked that it came so easy for me. I realized right away I loved it and painted every day after that. "Dad, I think I got my talent from you!" Jessica replied. "Hon, I have never painted a portrait in my life," Paul said. "Dad! You have a multi-million-dollar business designing for athletes and the Olympics," Jessica replied. Paul expressed to her that his designs did not come near to the talent she has on a canvas. "Well! I still think I got my talent from you, so there!" Jessica remarked. "This is some great work my dear! Wait a minute! I was so shocked at the painting I did not realize you had Jonathan in the portrait. That looks just like him; you have never seen him," Paul quizzically said. "Actually! I have a confession, I went through your wallet and wanted to see what he looked like, unbeknownst to me, the next thing I knew I was at Camp and painting. Who would have thought!" Jessica answered. "Well! It is quite a story and a beautiful one at that," Paul commented. "You should see the portrait I painted of mom, I have her wearing your favorite dress on her," Jessica said. He smiled! you mean the pastel yellow one?" Paul hoped. "Of course!" Jessica smiled and said yea. "Well! She is the most stunning and elegant woman on earth, and I am sure the portrait is amazing, I cannot wait to see it," Paul remarked. She loves it! Jessica said. Paul kept looking at the family portrait she painted and still could not believe how Jessica made everyone look as they are. "Maybe I got my drawing gene from both you and Uncle Peter; you both are such great artists," Jessica commented. "Thank you dear! It is always something my brother and I loved doing," Paul remarked.

When Jessica arrived in Tuscany at the Pisa International Airport, she looked out the windows and saw her entire family waving small Italian flags and yelling out her name. As she departed from the jet, she ran down the steps into the arms of her siblings and cried. As they were hugging, her siblings and both sets of grandparents all surrounded her in one huge group hug. Jessica was finally on the start of her vacation and could not wait to do some fun things with everyone.

The next few weeks Jezalee wanted to be home bound and had a great idea to add an art studio for Jessica; she saw her talent first-hand and wanted to give her a place where she would have a spacious room with great lighting to paint. She called her construction buddies, and they came over and suggested she build out at the end of the hallway upstairs, past the bedrooms and they could get it done before Jessica got back from vacation.

The very next day, the construction crew had all the materials delivered, and the manpower to start building the added two rooms. It was going to be a two-story building; with the entrance being on the second floor and Jessica would have stairs leading down to the first floor for a place to house all her finished paintings, and extra art supplies. The first floor would be sealed off completely and the only access would be from the stairs leading down to the room from the second floor. Jezalee was so impressed what the foreman had suggested; and she loved the idea of a two story for Jessica's her art studio.

While David and Mallory took off for a week in Santa Barbara, to visit some friends; Jezalee invited Bob, Linda, and Manny over a day of swimming, lunch, playing frisbee and other backyard games. She asked them if they would like to stay for dinner because she had made homemade pizza with all the trimmings and Manny pleaded with his parents; so, they easily gave in. Jezalee also had a Caesar and Antipasto salad already made.

She had such a delightful time with the three of them and Manny loved Jezalee so much. He was one of the sweetest children she had ever been around and adored him to pieces. After their somewhat late dinner, Manny fell asleep on one of the chaise lounges outside. Jezalee brought out a blanket and pillow so he could rest better. While he slept, Jezalee invited Bob and Linda to enjoy the pool as-long-as they wanted to; she would watch over Manny if he woke up. Once Manny woke-up he wanted to go in the pool and asked Jezalee to come in as well. The three adults played for another hour with him until he got tired. After they got out of the pool, Jezalee asked them if they wanted to take the leftovers because she had too much food that she had to eat before it went bad. Manny walked over to Jezalee, hugged her, and said thank you Auntie Jazzier. She kissed him on the cheek and thanked the three of them for spending such a beautiful day with her.

Jezalee had called Alan and Elaine the day before and they were coming to spend two days with her. She got up early, made a variety of appetizers to have on hand, had steaks ready to broil, a chicken roasted in wine from her and Paul's Winery in Napa, and added fresh herbs; she had a pork loin cooked and had made mashed potatoes, wild rice, and egg noodles. She had plenty of fresh vegetables to add to whichever entree they preferred for lunch and dinner. She swam a few laps, did her Yoga, then got ready about an hour before they arrived.

Created with Sketch.

When children got back from vacation, Jezalee had taken Alexander and Adrienne school shopping while Jessica stayed home and made calls to her friends to see what they had done for the summer. They went to about ten stores and by that time, all three were pretty much over shopping so they stopped at Bunny's Diner and had a late lunch.

Later that evening Jezalee pulled a gift out of a closet and handed the huge package to Jessica; when she opened it, she was so happy her mom had bought her different sizes of easels, canvases and every type of oil painting and watercolor supplies she would need for an exceptionally long time. She asked her to go to the end of the upstairs hallway, past all the other rooms and notice a wing had been added. Everyone came upstairs with her; she could see that there was an extra door where there used to be a solid wall with a painting. There was a customized door with a plaque that read, Jessica's Art Studio; she opened the door to a gigantic room that was an artist's dream to paint in. It had a skylight and windows that had perfect natural lighting coming through. By this time, the whole family was gathered in the 1500 square foot room. Gees! "This is bigger than any of our bedrooms," Alexander said. "This is the space a true artist needs to not only paint but to have different spaces to house the artwork," Jezalee replied. "Wow! Mom, it is incredible, you really did this all for me?" A shocked Jessica said "Yes! Dear," Jezalee answered. Alexander piped up again and wanted to know if he became a mechanic would his mom add on another garage to the house. "Of course! I would," Jezalee answered. Jessica noticed a stairwell was over at one side of the large room and asked what that was. Jezalee said she had a two-story art studio built so she could keep extra supplies, her finished artwork, or however she wanted to make use of it. They went down to the first level and Jessica burst into happy tears. She thought it was all amazing and could do so much with both rooms. There were several windows on the bottom level as well with plantation shudders.

When school started, Jessica would get her homework done and spend most of her waking time in her studio. If no one could not find her, they knew more than likely she was in her studio working away at her next painting. They were astounded that she had this hidden talent, and it was amazing to all of them.

Jezalee got busy with some of her fundraising charities and still had more research to do on her book. Jezalee had been avoiding Jim as much as possible. They would see one another at social events and over at David and Mallory's when they had small dinner parties. She was coming-to-the- conclusion that Jim would believe if Jezalee wanted to go out for a casual lunch or dinner, he would take it as if she was falling in love with him. She was believed he did not know the difference between a friendship and love.

Jezalee called Gregory's mom, Joan and introduced herself; she said Gregory had given out their home number because she wanted to invite their family over for dinner one night. Jezalee also wanted her to know how impressed she was with Gregory and what a fine young man he was with such adult manners. Joan expressed her thank you for her kind words about her son. She let Jezalee know they had met at a charity event and sat next to one another; however never knew one another's last names. "What a small world! Who would have thought from my ex-husband being picked up at the airport, Gregory being his driver, inviting him in to have dinner; would lead to us socially meeting one another!" Jezalee commented. "Our son had a great time that evening and could hardly wait to get home to tell us how kind you and Paul were to him; he certainly shared some of that incredible dinner and dessert with us," Joan remarked. Jezalee then asked if the following Friday was open for them to come over for dinner and Joan checked her calendar and they were free for that evening. The ladies chatted a little longer after they got the dinner date and time out of the way and looked forward to seeing everyone for a nice evening. She wanted to know if there were any specific foods that they did not like and did anyone have any allergies to any type of food. Joan said they liked everything and no allergies, so make whatever you fancy for that evening.

When Adrienne found out the Stanton's were coming for dinner; she admitted to her mom she had a crush on Gregory; Jezalee liked the sounds of that. Friday could not come fast enough; and she had her mom help her choose a cute outfit.

Alexander had a crush on a girl named Stella in school and they hung out at lunch; she had come over to study with him when they had exams. Her parents were actors and were gone on location a lot. Her grandmother lived with them; so, she was well taken care of when her parents went on location for a movie or a play, they were in. Alexander would go over to her house as well; her grandma always had homemade peanut brittle and brownies readily to devour. He had dinners over there, and she was a great cook just like Helga and his mom; anytime he was invited he said yes.

Friday was upon them and an hour before the Stanton's were to arrive; Adrienne was doing the finishing touches to her hair and was having butterflies in her stomach. She briefly thought back to when she met Gregory and told herself instinctively, that was the guy she was going to marry; she was so glad she did not tell anyone her thoughts, not even her best friend, Morgan did not know yet. After the Stanton's arrived it turned out to be such a great evening and Adrienne tried not to be so obvious of her crushing on Gregory. She did feel good when he was talking with her and later in the evening before they called it a night, Gregory did pull Jezalee aside and asked her if he was out of line if he asked Adrienne to go to the movies one Friday night. Jezalee was trying not to look overjoyed and calmly said there is one condition, she and her other two children would be their chaperon's. He smiled and said that is funny you would say that because I just asked my parents if I could ask Adrienne out and they said they would be chaperoning. Jezalee laughed and said, "maybe we can all go but not sit with you two." Since Gregory got the go ahead, he walked over to Adrienne and said, "I hope you do not mind but I asked your mom if it was okay to ask you out to the movies; she said as long as there is a chaperon." Butterflies were swarming in Adrienne's stomach, as she said yes. "I guess us going to the movies will be a family affair because my parents are coming along to join your family," Gregory informed Adrienne. "Oh! My gosh! I will be glad when I am seventeen," as Adrienne laughed out loud. "It is all good, I am sixteen as well and do not mind the chaperoning because it just means our parents care," Gregory replied. "I thought you were older than me because you are in college," Adrienne commented. "I advanced two grades and graduated high school just before I turned fifteen," Gregory replied. "Were you mentally ready for college being a younger than most students?" Adrienne curiously asked. "I was pretty much ready, no one knew in my classes at Stanford that I was younger than them," Gregory replied.

Gregory, 16-year-old, dark brown hair, and eyes, square-jawed face, light-olive-toned skin, broad shouldered, movie star handsome, and 6'3" tall. No matter where he went, heads turned. Ever since he was five years old, he wanted to be a doctor and constantly would ask his three sisters to either be a nurse or a patient so he could practice being a doctor.

With Paul having his private jet, he was able to come over a lot more and Jim was certainly one person that did not fare well with his coming and going; especially since Jim knew he had to be tight lipped and not show any bad attitude because Jezalee would pick up on it. Jezalee had a plan, once the kids flew to Italy on their next vacation, she would spend all the time it took to know more about Jim; she was hopefully going to get to the bottom of why Jim appeared to have changed so drastically and been so obsessed with wanting to marry her. She certainly was not in love with him and had told him many times. Jezalee was more curious about Jim at this point and had continually seen changes in him, as David had been noticing at work and when they travel on business trips. He indicated that Jim manages to always be prepared with the workload he keeps up with and is great with business meetings conferences. David also saw a change in his personality when he was at work; but it did not affect is work. Both David, other office employees and Jezalee had picked up on his constant mood swings and slight outbursts. David and Jezalee had confronted him, but he insists he is fine.

Jezalee had invited Paul, his and her parents, Alan, and Natalie's families for Thanksgiving to celebrate with their children. While Paul was there, even though Alexander told his dad that Jezalee would never marry Jim because she was still in love with him, he asked her if she was serious about Jim and she said they were just friends and that was all they will ever be, he made no comment to that. Jezalee loved the fact Paul could come more often and the two of them could show that even through people divorcing they can be friends. Little did she or their dad know the children could see right through both of their parents and hoped in-the-near-future they would both stop, being stubborn and admit they still want to be married. There were many times that Jezalee felt like sneaking into the guest bedroom and being with him and visa, versa. Mallory called Jezalee to see how things were going with Paul being there and she was honest with her and confessed it was getting more difficult being around him, wishing she had never asked for a divorce. Continually thinking about him and would be impossible for her to move on to meet anyone else.

Whenever Paul came over; he was delighted to see Gregory and his family; he had grown so fond of this boy and was as sweet as he was smart. He was so relieved when Jezalee informed him Adrienne and he were dating. Jezalee had decided early on when they had the Stanton's over, Jim would not be a guest, only for the reason it was

Paul who had introduced the Gregory to them and wanted to keep it that way.

Gregory usually did not take the summers off; however, Paul had invited him to join his children on their summer trip to an African Safari and sightseeing on the Coast of Italy. He was thrilled over the invite and his parents thought he needed a break from all the studying he did. His parents loved the Albanese family; especially their beautiful Adrienne as they called her.

Created with Sketch.

Jim decided to spend Christmas with Deanna and her family; she had called sometime before Thanksgiving and pleaded with him to come for Christmas, and he finally took her up on her gracious invitation. He knew he would have such a great time with Deanna and her family. He could not wait to go Christmas shopping with her and just enjoy the Christmas spirit.

Jezalee, Paul, their children and both sets of grandparents had an amazing Christmas and New Year's Eve at Paul's villa in Pisa for the second year in a row. Jezalee knew she had to be careful when she was in a room with Paul; she did not want the children to get excited thinking their parents would get back together. It was a volatile situation because deep down Jezalee knew she regretted filing for divorce; but she did it and felt there was no going back. She was certainly relieved when Paul broke up with Sophia; she had been so hurt when she saw Paul with another woman; but she knew when they came to San Francisco in 86 to celebrate Christmas she had to pretend to be happy for him.

Paul was floating on air that Jezalee agreed to come for Christmas and New Year's Eve; but it had its drawbacks because he could hardly contain his composer when he was in a room with her. There were so many times he wanted to be alone with Jezalee and express how much he had missed her being his wife and him being her husband; he loved so much her. Paul had many sleepless nights over the last several years and with her not at his side had been devastating. His thoughts continuously went back to the fond memories of when they met, fell in love, got engaged, got married and had their three beautiful and healthy children. He never did take any of his happiness for granted but when it was taken away from him; he knew all he had were cherished memories of a prodigious life. Paul knew he had to maintain a stoical appearance anytime he was around Jezalee, and it was becoming almost impossible anytime she was in his presence.

While Paul and Jezalee went Christmas shopping one afternoon with their children to buy presents for the family; back at the villa the parents were trying to think of ways to get their children back together. "I do not think we should cook up any scheme because it may backfire on us, then they will be upset with us," Antonio said. "If they are supposed to be together, they will make their way back when it is the right time," Carolyn agreed. Elene had felt like that before; but she now felt they needed a push in the right direction. Mark believed they should have worked on getting them back together sooner than later; now he felt they needed to let them figure it out themselves. It was three to one so they were just going to sit back and wait; may they rise above their stubbornness and realize what they have always had and will get through anything, the love they still have for one another.

After everyone got settled in Paul's villa, they decided to fly to their chateau in Saint-Germaine-en-Laye and have four days of the Christmas spirit there. When they arrived, Montrose, Monique, and their daughter, Veronica had left a note expressing how sorry they were for missing them; however, they were driving into Paris to be with their family and friends for Christmas. The chateau looked gorgeous! Montrose and Monique had done an amazing job decorating the exterior and interior with their family antique ornaments. They had cut down a magnificent tree and decorated it beautifully. Jezalee and Paul were sorry their paths did not cross that Christmas because they enjoyed seeing them during the holidays; they were happy they were able to spend the time with their families. Montrose had left a few dozen of the Albanese's special ornaments; so, they could finish decorating the tree. Jezalee loved Monique's touch of Christmas throughout the chateau and was in awe of her creative talents. After four days, it was difficult for the family to leave; but they knew Christmas was waiting for them back at Paul's villa.

What a Christmas it had been! All the adults, plus Alexander, had made their way into the kitchen and cooked one of their specialties, and Adrienne and Jessica were embarrassed they did not know how to cook. Everyone agreed since the girls did not cook, they had to clean the kitchen and they thought that was fair until they walked in and saw every pot, iron skillet, saucepan, steamer, ceramic, and glass baking dishes had been used; not including. all the dishes and glasses for ten people. They both thought they may consider learning how to cook after all. They were still cleaning up the kitchen, after Alexander had been at the piano a good hour playing Christmas pieces while the family would sing along. At least they could hear the music and they said it made the work go by quicker.

Going to pick out a Christmas tree was quite an ordeal, only because some wanted a Charlie Brown tree, some wanted a massive full tree and others wanted a tall tree with space in between the branches. So, the decisions were made; they bought one of each and place them throughout the Villa. They bought all new ornaments for the two biggest trees and the children wanted to make a few skimpy ones for their Charlie Brown tree. Now that everyone was satisfied with their choices of trees, it was time to enjoy their fruits of their labor.

Christmas had been surprisingly special with being at Paul's villa, then at their chateau in Saint-Germain-en-Laye. It had been the ultimate Christmas for the family. They were also happy that Peter was able to manage two days of celebration with the family and he was so pleased they would be at Midnight Mass when he would be doing the liturgy. Paul was appreciative that Jezalee had wants them to remain as joint owners of the chateau; it meant a lot to him. He and Jezalee agreed they would never take another man or woman there; however, in the future, if they were serious over someone as a potential spouse, they would discuss it then.

While everyone was having such a great time; the men gave the gals a Women's Only Spa Day; as the guys put it! a ''girly'' day. The men went bowling, played pool, poker and Alexander performed some of his new pieces he had composed while at his dads.

New Year's Eve was a little more difficult for Paul and Jezalee; but they did give one another a hug when midnight came around. Of course! Everyone was hoping there would be a romantic kiss but that was not going to happen. All in all, Paul and Jezalee were both restrained from showing too much affection; they did not want the other to know how much they missed and loved the other. Their children and parents were just waiting for one sign of how much they used to love one another; but they both kept their distance but showed kindness and caring for one another.

On New Year's Day they went into town, walked around, and ran in to friends and neighbors that had the same idea. The children were walking behind the rest of the family; Alexander commented to his sisters, he just wanted their parents to hold hands, kiss and get back together, Adrienne and Jessica agreed. Once everyone stopped for a Gelato at their favorite shop, the children sat over in the corner of the room and decided to talk to their parents individually when they got back home. Adrienne decided she and Jessica would get their mom alone and Alexander would talk to their dad. The three of them went over what the other would say to each parent and they were excited to get back to the villa and get things going between the two of them.

Once back at the villa, Alexander asked if he could speak to his dad privately, without seeming suspicious. Jezalee went into her guest bedroom to freshen up and change clothes; the girls followed in behind and asked if they could speak to her. She asked them to have a seat on the sofa and would be right out after she changed. Jezalee walked over and sat down with her girls and knew something was up. Girls! "You look like you have something on your mind," Jezalee said. "Mom, over the last six months when we have been around dad, he always says, how much he misses and loves his beautiful Jezalee," Adrienne spoke up. Jezalee was caught off guard, so she sat there for a moment; she then looked at her girls and said, "If your dad said those flattering things about me, it was sweet of him, I feel the same way about him. "Really!" Jessica spouted out. Jezalee gets closer to her daughters on the sofa and tells them she will always love and miss their dad too; however, we are divorced and that does not change a lot of our feelings for one another, we just cannot be husband and wife anymore. "I want you children to know it took a lot of us going to therapy for me to regain trust, respect and caring for your father again. I am in a good place now and I know he feels the same way. It is important when a marriage dissolves that the couple do everything they can to come together for the sake of their children. You three children are our whole world and your father, and I have worked through the initial trauma that caused me to want a divorce. We want you to be happy and we are devoted parents first and foremost and dear friends that love one another,' Jezalee did not speak the truth.

While Jezalee was still having a conversation in her room with the girls, Alexander struck up a conversation saying how much it meant for the whole family to be together in his dad's home. His dad agreed and said he wished they were staying longer. Alexander got right to the issue of him and his mom. Dad! "Do you still love and miss mom? Alexander asked. "I will always love your mom. Son, why would you bring this up?'' Paul answered. "Well! Sometimes mom brings up how much she misses and loves you. I asked her what had attracted her to you, and she said you stood out from every guy because you have always been an amazing man; she realized how intelligent, ambitious, and loving you were and still are. She said, "he takes my breath away." Alexander said he was floored when his mom said hat. "Wow! That will certainly feed my ego for a while,'' Paul responded. He motioned for Alexander to sit down so they could talk some more. Paul knew he had to be careful what he said to Alexander because he did not want him to know he was still in love with Jezalee. "Son, if she said those words of praise about me, I know she had her best intentions to share that with you. Be aware that we have been in love and will always have feelings for one another. Your mom and I had a beautiful and loving marriage, then a divorce happened; it was a devastating time and harsh words were said by both of us. We have finally gotten past all that and are in a place of respect, caring for one another, and you and the girls are our top priority. I think the turning point in our newfound relationship was when she stood by my side when Jonathan was in a coma. She was so concerned over the tragic accident that happened to an innocent child. I knew at that moment we had past-over all the discernment for one another. Your mom proved to me she had forgiven me in her own way that made me feel whole again. I do not know if you are aware of this; but your incredible mother took my hand while we were in Jonathan's hospital room and said, once, your son wakes up, I will help raise him or whatever you want me to do for the two of you. Paul was crying at this point and said, that is the kind of woman your mom is and has always been," Paul said with much sadness. Dad, "I am so sorry about Jonathan, as soon as you said you had another son, I was happy, I told you that as soon as I found out," Alexander remarked. Paul smiled at his son and told him he remembered the day he expressed how he felt about the situation. Paul said he felt such a stronger connection towards him from that moment on. "You are the best man I have ever known and am glad to call you, my father. I also want to say that if Jonathan was supposed to be on this Earth for a short time, he was most fortunate to hang out with you, because you are the best," Alexander said with tenderness. They ended their conversation with a strong hug and both with tear filled eyes.

Antonio was calling everyone throughout the villa and the only ones responding were Elene, Carolyn, and Mark. The four gathered at the entryway and wondered where the rest of the gang was. Antonio realized there was an intercom system; so, he pushed the bottom and wanted to know where everyone had gotten to. Paul heard him and said he and Alexander would be right down. Antonio asked if the girls were with them and he said no, and we have no idea where they are. He once again, called through the intercom and Jessica asked her grandpa to hold on and they'd be right there in a minute.

Now that Antonio had the attention of all family members, he said he would like to take everyone out to dinner on his dime. "Don't you want to cook grandpa?" Alexander asked. "Nope! I am taking you out to the ultimate dining experience and you will never find another fine restaurant as we have here is Pisa," Antonio answered. Adrienne asked if they needed to dress up. "Why of course! Go get your ball gowns on," Antonio replied. "No one wants to get dressed up in ball gowns; that is for Prom Night," a concerned Jessica response. "You got it dear child! I was only kidding; but wearing a dress is more appropriate than Levies," Antonio said. "I made reservations for 8:00 o'clock, is that good for everyone?" Antonio asked. They agreed that would be ideal. Paul asked if he could speak with Jezalee for a minute or two and she said of course! They both excused themselves and Paul said they would join them in a few minutes; everyone walked towards the main room of the Villa and waited for them to return and were crossing their fingers that there would be a reconciliation.

Paul motioned Jezalee to follow him into his library and have a seat; he sat across from her. She was hoping he wanted to get back together but that was not the case. I do not know if you experienced what I did a few minutes ago; he began to reiterate the conversation Alexander had with him. Jezalee laughed! Seriously! The girls had the same conversation with me. Paul looked at Jezalee with happiness filling his face and he said it sounds as if they had their little speeches contrived. So, it seems as Jezalee smiled back. "They had good intentions; I give them credit for that," Paul commented. "I wholeheartedly agree," laughed Jezalee. Well! "Between the two of us, I am sure we got that squared away," responded Paul." "I think that was a good opportunity for both of us to let them know we will always be their parents and have their best interests at heart, right?" Jezalee said. "They know we care and love each other; but in a different way, right?" Paul remarked. "Yes Paul," Jezalee responded. "Let's catch-up with the rest of the family and see what my dad is planning next," said Paul. They walked out of the library and before Paul got too far, Jezalee said she needs to go to the ladies, room and will be down in a minute. As Jezalee walked away, Paul had hoped that she would have stopped him and told him everything that Alexander said was true and she wanted to be his wife again. After Jezalee left for her room, he went back to his library, went to his desk, and pulled out his favorite photo of the two of them kissing, tears streamed down his face. Paul rushed into his private bathroom in the library to splash cold water on his face; then padded it lightly with a soft cloth. Jezalee could not walk fast enough to her room; she locked the door for some privacy and laid down on the bed and cried. All Jezalee wanted from their conversation was Paul saying he wanted to be her husband again. She called downstairs on the intercom and informed everyone she was taking a nap before dinner and did not want to be disturbed. She said she would be down around 7:00 p.m. it was now 2:30 p.m.

Paul walked out of his library and caught up with the rest of the family; with the exception, of Jezalee. He looked around and Antonio said, "Jezalee is napping and will be down at 7:00. He did not want to show any emotion; but he knew she was probably upset that they even had the talk about what the children did. He was going to have to realize there would be times like this one because the children love them both and were hoping they would get back together. He was not himself for the rest of the day until they went to the restaurant. Everyone went up to their rooms and freshened up before they departed for what was going to be a dining experience as Antonio had said. Jezalee was the first one downstairs and Paul, was right behind her. They sat in the same room but did not really talk until the children came down. Once the grandparents were ready, they left for the restaurant. The experience at Antonio's favorite restaurant was one outstanding gastronomic delight; he had every right to boast because everything lived up to their epicurean expectations. Everyone sitting at their table had been to so many countries and had dined at some of the most famous restaurants in the world; but they came to the same conclusion that Antonio was so right about the cuisine; it was unbeatable. They were there until 11:00 PM and the owner gave them several desserts to polish off for the next day. When, they arrived back at the villa, they were not only tired but stuffed to the gills as Mark said. They were all sitting around the magnificently decorated, lit tree in the massive living room which was filled with rich antique wood pieces, over-sized white custom sofas and chairs, quite a collection of oil paintings on the 24-foot walls, with floor plants from 6 to 15 foot in height scattered throughout the impressive room. The fireplace was Paul's favorite part of the room, he had it custom built to his specifications where he had it framed in a rich wood then the inlay was of a rough white stone that brought the entire room together. The fireplace was blazing with wood logs just added to heat up the room. Grandma Carolyn asked Alexander if he would play some beautiful, traditional Christmas songs and before she got out her full sentence, he was already at the piano and ready to dance those pianist fingers across the ivory keys. He also played a few of the pieces he composed, and they were raving over his talent; he always blushed. It was getting late; Jezalee was the first to retire to bed after she said goodnight to everyone. Tomorrow they would be flying back to San Francisco, and everyone really did not want to leave; it had been that kind of Christmas and New Year's Eve for all of them.

Paul informed Jezalee he would drive them to the airport at 11:00 a.m. and asked her what time they wanted breakfast. She turned to the children, and they said, "not before 9:00 a.m. dad." I will see everyone at 9:00 a.m. sharp. After the children and Jezalee left the room, Antonio asked Paul, "What in the world is going on?' "What do you mean pops?" responded Paul. "You know very well what I mean," Antonio gruffly answered. "Pops, I really cannot talk about it now, another time, okay?" "Okay my son," sadly Antonio responded. After Paul exited the room, the grandparents sat around talking a bit longer then finally went off to bed.

The next morning everyone was fairly, quiet during breakfast and the anticipation of leaving was not easy an anyone. Everyone went to the airport to see Jezalee and the children off. The private jet was ready for take-off; so, everyone got their hugs, kisses, and their goodbyes in, before they stepped aboard.

Several hours after dinner on the flight; Jezalee retired to the back and laid down to go to sleep. The children had never seen their mother so quiet and to herself. Adrienne went back to make sure her mom was comfortable; and she was already asleep. She went back to her siblings and said she was worried about their mom; but she did not want to bring up their dad's name in case it was something else that was bothering her. Jessica suggested that the three of them not worry so much about their mom and concentrate on enjoying the flight instead. An hour later, the children went to sleep as well; they had a busy and fun filled Christmas and New Year's Eve and knew; school was in a couple of days and needed to get acclimated back into their daily schedules.

The O'Malley's were back home from their East Coast Christmas with their families. Jim had not left Florida yet; he told Deanna and Eric he was going to have a hard time leaving after having the best Christmas imaginable. Jezalee and the children arrived home from their flight. When Jezalee and the children walked through the front door, they could smell one of their favorite aromas, they darted straight for the kitchen. Helga was in the kitchen baking her famous miniature chicken pot pies, for lunch. "When will those babies be done?" Alexander asked. "Well good afternoon to you too!" Helga said as she walked towards Alexander and kissed him. The others walked over to Helga and gave her a big hug, kissed her, and said how great it was to be home with her. Helga said she had missed them so much and hoped they had an exceptionally great Christmas and New Year's Eve. Jezalee asked Helga how her Christmas was in Chicago with Astrid and Nicholas and Helga said she had a marvelous time and met Nicholas's parents. After they got all of that out of the way, Jezalee asked the children to take their luggage upstairs and get ready for lunch. While Helga was preparing a salad to go along with the pot pies, Jezalee sat the kitchen table and got the drinks ready.

After everyone left Paul's; he was having a meltdown, just like he experienced the year Jezalee moved to San Francisco with children and their staff. It was getting more difficult seeing Jezalee and not being her husband anymore. He wanted to have a talk with her; but he could not get up enough nerve after what she went through. Paul talked with his parents and they both agreed that he needed to ride out the storm and hope for the best. They asked him to try going to talk to a professional and see if he/she can guide him in the right direction. Paul expressed his worries over Jim; he felt he was going to get a call from the children one day saying their mom was engaged to Jim. "Son, I know he is a very charismatic, handsome and intelligent man, but you are all those attributes and more. Remember, most of all, Jezalee has loved you for twenty years. We feel there will be a day that you two will be back together again; have patience and see what transpires in this next year. The more often you see her and the children together, the odds of getting closer are much higher. When you two are in a room we feel the electricity between both of you," Elene spoke. Paul still questioned it all. "Stop over thinking it; it is going to happen," Antonio said.

Jezalee was trying to come out of the clouds from an extraordinary Christmas she had with her family; but realized having been around Paul for two weeks was as if they were still married with restraints. Every night she was there, in the same home, with the man she fell in love with all those years ago; made her feel guilty for divorcing him for so many reasons.

After lunch, Jezalee apprised Helga she would be in her room the rest of the day and the answer machine could pick up any calls. Helga asked her if she was okay, Jezalee said she was not sure and needed to journal about it. Before she went to her room, she walked over to see how Joseph and the family were doing.

Jezalee sees Joseph working out in the garden, "Hi my dear Joseph, how are you doing?" "Dear, it is so great to see you back and I am on top of the world," as Joseph says with his infectious smile. "Thanks, it is great to be back," Jezalee said. As they were talking, Nina was coming out of their home and ran over to Jezalee and hugged her and welcomed her home. "Just the lady I want to see!" Jezalee said. "What's up dear?" Nina asked. "I am going to hibernate in my bedroom all day and you do not need to do anything else for the rest of the day or for that matter, the next few days, take a few days off and enjoy being with Joseph and the children," Jezalee answered. "Thanks! That's so sweet of you!" Nina remarked. The children heard Jezalee's voice and ran out to give her a hug as they always did.

Jezalee walked back home, grabbed a hot cup of coffee, and went to her room, took her shoes off, curled up in one of her favorite overstuffed chairs and got comfortable. She opened the drawer from a table next to the chair and pulled out her journal and pen, sat for a few minutes deciding what she would enter as her first thought. While she was thinking! She looked at the chair across from her and could visualize Paul sitting there, looking at her with his loving eyes, as he always did, when they settled into their bedroom. Jezalee knew when she was closing-up their Paris home, she walked into their bedroom and knew she had to take both chairs; she could not give Paul's away; and she felt sad he did not want to take it. She had to have a reminder of him; they sat in their two matching chairs almost every night before bed, if for just a few minutes out of their day to unwind from the children and all their businesses, before they went to sleep or made love.

Jezalee knew the first entry in her journal had to be the love she will always carry for Paul. She knew that in her heart, she knew that with her last breath on this earth, she would whisper, I love you, Paul. Her second entry was about her entire Christmas experience in Italy. Paul's villa was exactly what they would have chosen if they were still together.

Jim had returned from Florida; got back in the work routine and was only back a week when David had him fly to Japan, to take care of a huge problem with some of the products that had been imported to the United States.

Created with Sketch.

Jim called Jezalee once he got back from his business trip in Japan, she let him know she was extremely busy with her books but in a few weeks, she was going to have a potluck luncheon-dinner and he was invited; she would give him more detail of the time and day the following week. He was not too happy; but he knew from the past with her that he was going to need to back off until she was ready. He was not going to let her go that easy and would play it out her way for a while. He would make his move one way or another; his second choice would not be as pleasant.

The following week Jezalee gave Jim a call after dinner hour and said she had been so busy but wanted to know how his time with Deanna and her family was during the holidays. He was pleased to hear from Jezalee and told her about the fun he had sharing Christmas with the. Jim told her he even hung out in one of their bakeries and Eric taught him how to bake a loaf of bread and a pie. "What a great idea teaching you to bake; this means the next time you come over for dinner, you and Alexander can take can bake a couple of pies for dessert," Jezalee remarked. Jim said he would love to bake them any kind of pie they like, and he would probably be best suited to be Alexander's assistant since that kid of yours can cook and bake amazing things. "That he can!" Jezalee responded.

It was now February, Jezalee and Adrienne sent out invitations for their potluck luncheon and evening dinner. They invited the O'Malley's, all their staff, the Stanton's, some of the children's friends from school, the Boys and Girls Club, Jim, several of Jezalee's friends, Alan, his family, and people she worked side by side at charity events. It was a colossal potluck event; everyone brought something. Tables were set up in a huge tent; they had board games and a band so they could have dancing for the teens and adults if they chose to join in. Jezalee wanted a gigantic crowd around, so she did not have to deal with Jim being so needy over her. She knew he would keep busy talking business when he got the chance. Outside the tent, on the lush lawn, they had egg tosses, hula hoop contests, three legged races and a dunking booth. There was a little bit of everything for everyone and they seemed to have a noteworthy time. The festivities did not end until a little after 11:00 p.m.; almost everyone had left, except Jim, he was still hanging around. Jezalee went up to him and thanked him for coming and apologized they did not get to talk more at the party. He asked her out to dinner, and she accepted on one condition, he invited David and Mallory.

A couple of months had passed by; everyone was busy with school, volunteering, hanging out with friends and just going through their daily routines. Jezalee had a few luncheon and dinner events from time to time; but she had not invited Jim over that much and when she did it was with other adults joining. Jezalee purposely kept her friendship at a distance with Jim; she and David was detecting continual mood swings and his far away trances whenever she saw him socially.

Adrienne and Gregory saw a lot of one another when time permitted in between his job and full-time school. Paul and Jezalee could not have been more pleased with the two of them dating and he was hoping if all went well, Gregory would be going on vacation with he and his children in June.

It was spring break everyone was singing at the top of their lungs to the music that was blasting in their suv's. It was only thirty more minutes, and they would be in Incline Village. When everyone arrived at the "Castle on the Mountain, the first thing they noticed, once they entered the great room, was a beautiful deep red Steinway grand piano. Alexander spotted the gorgeous piano and asked Mallory if it was okay if he tried it out. "My! My! Who do you think the piano is for?" Mallory replied. "Well! I guess anyone that wants to play," Alexander commented. "I think you are the only one we want to hear play; I bought this piano because everywhere you go, a piano should be waiting for you to demonstrate your extraordinary talent. You are going to be famous someday and we can all say with pride, we knew you when and I am sure that day is just around the corner." David said proudly. "Wow! I am engulfed with emotions over your generosity; and! By the way! This is the most awesome piano ever! Which happens to be my favorite color too!" An excited

Alexander responded. "Could you possibly play a few pieces after we get back?" David asked. "It would be my pleasure!" Alexander answered. Alexander turned to his mom and asked her if she knew about this. "No! I am as surprised as you are and it is quite magnificent, to say the least," Jezalee said. Everyone was thrilled they would now have the own personal pianist; Alexander played for hours when the time was right. They would gather around the grand piano and sing songs while he played. David knew the piano would be a great added touch to this beautiful place. Once-in-a-while most everyone went into town together and met the local people that lived year-round in the small, picturesque town. David bought a karaoke machine, and they had more fun entertaining themselves with that then going to the Casinos. They managed to get tickets to see a few performers whenever they went up to Lake Tahoe, which added to the fun they had seeing and hearing some of their favorite performers.

After everyone got back to San Francisco; they went back to their homes and relaxed knowing that work and school was waiting for them. Jezalee had a much better and relaxed time since Jim did not go on the Tahoe trip. She decided after the children go with their dad on the African Safari she was going to try to socialize more and just maybe she would meet someone to help take her mind off Paul. She thought! It would be fun to meet a Mr. Brady, a widower or divorced and has three children; they could be the Brady Bunch. Jezalee knew her children would love to see Paul and her back together; but she also knows they would love a scenario like the Brady Bunch and have more siblings. She loved watching the reruns with the children on family night it certainly captured the nation's interest.

It was Easter, Paul was in town staying with Jezalee and the children, the Stanton's joined the Albanese's and O'Malley's at Mass. After Mass, everyone helped at Church with the Easter egg hunt for the children under 12. Once they were done with that, they went out for Brunch. The O'Malley's were having David's employees and their families over for an early Easter dinner and the Albanese's, were going over to the Stanton's right after the Brunch. Joan and Jezalee had gotten together and made elaborate baskets for all the children; Gregory said he was embarrassed to get an Easter basket at his age and his mom informed him that he and his sisters would be getting one until they got married. Alexander spoke up and he looked at his mom and asked her does that apply to him as well. Of course! it does! "Don't you remember Adrienne asked the same question last year?" Jezalee responded and smiled.

The gals had hidden plastic Easter eggs with candies and money; they went outside and sat around the pool area while the teenagers hunted for the eggs. The winner with the most eggs was Gregory's sister, Reese, the most money was twenty dollars in one egg and Jessica found that one. After the Easter egg hunt Richard and Joan wanted to know all about the Safari coming up. Paul had mentioned it was a place he had always wanted to go with his family but never got around to it. He thought the age the children were now, was a better time to take them and they agreed. Before the trip was mentioned Paul had taken Richard and Joan aside and asked if their three daughters, Rebecca 15, Reese 14, Eve 13, could come because he would love for them to experience the trip with their brother and the rest of the group. With much reservation, Joan and Richard said as-long-as the girls want to go, they would agree. When they asked the girls, they said yes! They wanted to go; it would be amazing and so it was determined Paul would be taking seven teenagers on the Safari. Paul handed the children, Jezalee, and the Stanton's their itineraries where he would be, with the children, at-all-times.

As all these festivities went on from morning until night, there was Jezalee and Paul once again in the throes of a family getting together. They both did the best they could to show respect to one another and attentive to their children; but, made sure they kept a safe distance without the children thinking there was anything between them. They did not want the children thinking they were getting back together. After dinner was over the children went off in the great room they had set up for the children and the adults went into the living room and discussed world news, things that were trending and the music they seemed to love. It was getting close to time for Paul to fly back to Paris and he asked Gregory if he would not mind taking him. Gregory said this ride to the airport is on the house. No way! "I want to pay you what anybody else would charge me," Paul said. Paul said his goodbyes to everyone and thanked them for having him be a part of what turned out to be a wonderful

Easter. Adrienne walked outside with Paul and Gregory, gave both-of-them a kiss on the cheek and said their goodbyes.

Jim had been out of the country on business and decided to change his flight from Spain to Florida to spend Easter with Deanna and her family. They were so happy he was coming to share this time with them. He arrived on Thursday and asked Deanna and Eric if he could buy a few things for the children's Easter. Eric had the day off from his bakeries and the three of them went shopping while the children were in school. Deanna could see how wonderful Jim was and how much he loved his job. The children had warmed up to Jim; especially during the Christmas holidays and asked if they could call him Uncle Jimmy and that meant everything to him. He did not get back to San Francisco until the next Monday after Easter.

Jim called Jezalee to ask her if they could go out for dinner the following Friday and she said Thursday would be better. When Thursday rolled around, Jim picked up Jezalee around 7:00 o'clock and went to their favorite Mexican Food Eatery. They got caught up in what had been going on in their lives over the past month and she was so happy he was able to take a detour to go see Deanna and her family. Out of three and a half years that she had known Jim, she had never seen his face light up the way it did when he spoke about his best friend and her family. Jezalee liked seeing that side of him and wished Deanna and her family lived nearer to San Francisco; she felt it would be beneficial for Jim. He asked Jezalee if she could spend the night; she was shocked knowing she expressed to him countless times she was only interested in a friendship! "Jim, I thought you understood that we are friends, me spending the night suggests otherwise," Jezalee responded. Jim was thrown off by her comment and just said he would try to remember that in the future. She mentioned that on Friday, Alexander has a recital and Jessica was showing some of her oil paintings in an art gallery in Berkeley, and said he was more than welcome to attend both events and he said that would be wonderful; she gave him advance notice that Paul would be attending. After he heard the name Paul, he recanted the invite and said he would prefer going to an event when Paul could not make it. Jezalee just took what he said with a grain of salt and said maybe another time then; they changed the subject.

That night when Jim arrived home, he was convulsing with hatred for Paul; it was bad enough that Jezalee had invited the O'Malley family, their staff, some of the children's classmates and her staff and a few other friends to the two events. He wanted Alexander's recital and Jessica's art showing to be just Jezalee, Adrienne and him.

Jezalee was relieved that the two events were on different nights; Alexander's was on Friday from 7:30 p.m. until 9:30 p.m. and Jessica's Art Gallery opening was the following night on Saturday 5:00 p.m. until 7:00 p.m. When Jezalee called everyone to see if they could come, the majority was going to be able to attend both events. Paul was flying in on Thursday and would be able to stay until Sunday. The children were thrilled he would be able to have some extra time with them while he came to the two events.

Everyone looked amazing; but when Alexander stepped out of the limousine wearing his smashing, black velvet tuxedo with diamond studs and cuff links, he looked like a movie star with his striking good looks. Alexander was blinded by the flashing of the cameras. "He smiled, and told his dedicated fans, that is enough, I am not famous yet," Alexander said as he smiled. He could not believe his family and friends insisted on taking so many pictures of him! Alexander out-performed even himself; it paid off because he was honored with the most prestigious and coveted award of the evening for his two masterful performances; Fantasy Impromptu by Chopin and Hungarian Rhapsody No. by Franz Liszt.

Evening at the Gallery opening of Jessica's work made her somewhat nervous; but she tried to hold her composure. A couple weeks prior to the Art exhibit she had taken some sheer material, had a dress and slip made by Remi, their new-found local dress designer; when she got it home, she delicately painted pastel flowers throughout the dress and her parents loved her vision trying something so daring and quite beautiful. The gallery owner, Mrs. Goodall walked over to the Albanese's and commented on Jessica's extraordinary dress and said she looked very diaphanous and asked her who the designer was. She bashfully said she had the dress made then painted the flowers on it. Jessica looked ethereal that night; her hair was longer, cascading passed here shoulders and the overhead lights shined down on her ever-so-golden, massive head of hair.

The evening proved to be a success for Jessica; two of her oil paintings each sold for $1,200. from one buyer. The recipient commissioned her to paint a third painting and she was shocked. The Gallery owner asked him what he wanted the subject to be; he liked his artwork in threes so wanted it to be similar but in red tones, to compliment the two he had purchased. Another four sold to different buyers and the Gallery owner approached Jezalee and Paul and informed them that Jessica's going to have a great career in the art world. They thanked her for believing in Jessica and was thrilled she gave their daughter a jump-start in her Gallery showings. The owner let them know about the commissioned piece and the client would like it within three months or sooner. They were thrilled for Jessica, and she could not wait to get started on the third piece. Later that evening before the Gallery closed, the gentleman that purchased the two pieces came over to the Albanese family with the Gallery owner, she introduced Mr. Avery. When he met the family, he was shocked Jessica was a teenager and was even more impressed with her talent at such a youthful age.

Jezalee invited everyone back to their home to celebrate both special events from the last two evenings. They asked Alexander to play a few pieces and wanted to browse through Jessica's art studio. Paul and Jezalee took a moment out of the evening to pat themselves on the back and complimented each other on raising three incredible children; two that were exceptional in the arts, and the other heading towards a career in Psychology or Psychiatry.

It was the last week of the school year and Jezalee's children were revved up for their African Safari. Adrienne was especially excited because before her vacation began, she was graduating with honors, would be giving the commencement speech and her boyfriend Gregory and his sisters were joining them for their Safari. Jessica was excited to take lots of photos and be inspired to paint African life. As for Alexander, he just wanted to be able to hang out with his dad and Gregory and have some man time with them. After the Safari they would be heading their way to Pisa where Paul would be taking the children and his and Jezalee's parents on a tour of Italy for a month and maybe onto Paris.

Morgan and Adrienne had one last Teen Session with over a hundred students participating, they had started it in the tenth grade and had been quite successful. They had many people from the community come to their Teen Sessions and inspire the students to participate in some local after school activities. They discouraged teen sex, smoking, drugs, and drinking. people came to talk with the students about their regrettable experiences with those three subjects and how it affected their lives with a deleterious effect. These teens had happily turned their lives around.

Paul's plane landed and he told the crew he would have seven teenagers on the next flight and the crew just laughed and said, "Good Luck Sir." They said their goodbyes. Gregory picked him up at the airport and they were so happy to see one another; Paul was his favorite guy next to his dad and grandpa's. Paul loved Gregory like his own children; and he was keeping his fingers crossed that he and Adrienne would go the distance in their relationship. He was certainly marriage material and hoped someday that he and Jezalee would be walking Adrienne up the aisle to Gregory. He knew he was getting way ahead of their future's; but he could not help himself. It also brought back memories of the day he met Jezalee when they were in college. The guys had a nice chat on the way to Jezalee's; but what was really on Paul's mind was seeing his ex-wife. As Gregory pulled up to the front of the house, Adrienne saw them from the entryway and opened the front door. She went up and hugged her dad then gave Gregory a kiss on the cheek.

It was two days before graduation day; Paul and Gregory had arrived on time. Morgan and Adrienne decided they wanted an old-fashioned backyard barbecue for their combined graduation party and that's what Joseph and Jezalee put together. Paul and Gregory arrived; Adrienne led them to the backyard where the barbecuing had begun. David and Mallory and all their gang were there, as well as the Stanton's. Helga, Astrid, Nina and Jezalee had worked tirelessly all afternoon making all the food to go with Joseph's delicious grilled meats. They had set up a table for the fourteen children and one for fourteen adults. This was the first time Nell was having her beau Ronan over, and he was a great addition to their group. It was such a beautiful day, and everyone had brought their swimsuits and pretty much had all gone swimming at one time or another before the night ended.

Paul kept glancing over at Jezalee in her bathing suit and was getting aroused every time he looked her way. She looked the same as she did when they were in their twenties. He wanted to go talk with her; but he tried to avoid her most of the evening. Mallory kept noticing Jezalee staring at Paul every chance she got and wished she would just give in and have a talk with him.

As Paul always knew there was one person missing; it had been a year since Jonathan died and he had prayed that Jezalee would consider them getting back together. He was not going to bring it up to her; he felt she should be the pursuer, since she asked for the divorce. She could see that he never brought another woman to her house. Maybe one day he would get up enough nerve to say something to her.

After everyone got filled up on food; the parents wanted to give the girls their graduation gifts. While David and Paul walked over to the garage and drove each car out with the gargantuan red ribbons on the roofs. Everyone followed in behind Mallory and Jezalee as they walked the girls, hand in hand, through the house to the entryway, with blindfolds on. Alexander opened the front door; two cars were at the front cobble-stoned circular entrance. They had them take their blindfolds off and their dads handed them keys to their car. Both girls, of course! Started crying happy tears with much excitement. The parents felt they had earned their cars by being on the honor roll for four years, and they were two of the four students that had not missed a day of school in four years, they started a Teen Session together and met once a week to discuss any topic that other students were concerned about. They had proved to be great roll-models throughout the community to try to make a difference. After they sat in their new cars, they screamed out as they drove them into the garages; now it was time to get back to their party.

Mallory and Jezalee brought out the two celebration cakes; the top of Morgan's showed her in a cap and gown next to a mini version of her car, and of course! Adrienne's cake had her in a cap and gown as well next to a mini version of her car. Alexander and Adam brought out the dishes, silverware, and ice cream; everyone ate their dessert then participated in games afterwards.

After the party, Jessica asked her sister if she had memorized her commencement speech and she said she had. Alexander asked her if she was nervous about giving the speech in front of so many people. "I will find out tomorrow," Adrienne answered. After she said her speech aloud; they praised her words of wisdom and knew she would ace it at the ceremony. They wanted to get out the photo albums of their sister and they sat in the family room, and it became quite a nostalgic evening, with tears and laughter. Gregory stayed for a couple of hours to see Adrienne's photo albums as a baby and all the years that followed; afterwards, he went home to start packing for the anticipated Safari.

The next day went by quickly at school; Paul went into his office and did not get finished until close to dinner time. The grandparents arrived at noon and Jezalee got them settled in their guest rooms downstairs. Astrid arrived shortly after and was making her rounds visiting everyone before the graduation ceremony. The Stanton's arrived around 5:30 p.m.; Jezalee got them settled in a guest bedroom upstairs. Everyone was looking forward to Adrienne and Morgan graduating the next day. By 7:00 p.m. everyone was accounted for, including their staff and their children. After dinner, everyone headed for the family room and watched Stakeout and Three Men and a Baby. Afterwards, they went to their bedrooms for the night.

****May take out the paragraph below****

Later that evening the family, the staff with their children went to tuck Adrienne in goodnight. Paul lightly knocked on the door while the rest of them stayed quietly next to him in the hallway. She said come in, and everyone came in one by one. Adrienne looked perplexed and did not know why everyone was in her room at bedtime. Jezalee wanted her to know that each person had a gift they wanted to give to her in private. Alexander had written the melody and lyrics to a song he would play before they went on their trip,

Jessica had made a painting showing her walking onto the Stanford Campus and it had the date she would begin her college journey, Paul and Jezalee handed her a medium-sized jeweled box with a $5,000. check to buy new clothes for college, and beneath that, was an exquisite set of her first diamond earrings and bracelet. Adrienne, of course was overjoyed. Then unbeknownst to her, over in the corner of her room was a gift that had been hidden behind her antique screen. There was a huge, beautifully wrapped box from the entire staff and their children, who had all pitched in money to get her season tickets for four at The American Ballet Theater and the San Francisco Ballet Company in San Francisco for 1990. They also bought her two elegant evening tea-length dresses to wear to a couple of the performances and two pairs of satin heels and evening bags to match. They also purchased season tickets to the San Francisco Opera House and had a tea-length evening dress designed and made by Jezalee's designer, Dani and a second one made by their local designer, Remy. They bought her a pair of jeweled heels and purse to match those two, tea-length dresses. Adrienne could not stop crying she was utterly beyond overawed at her parents and their extended family, the staffs more than generous gifts. After she had opened all her surprise gifts, she told everyone she was the luckiest girl in the world to have such incredible people in her life and never took them for granted. They gave her a hug and told her to get her beauty sleep for her big day tomorrow.

It was graduation day; the auditorium was filled-to-capacity; when Adrienne walked towards the podium; a huge cheer roared throughout the walls from the graduating seniors and their families. Once she began her speech, you could hear a pin drop; every person in the 4,000-capacity auditorium was glued to every sincere and apathetic word she said. After Adrienne's speech was over, the entire auditorium stood and applauded for a few minutes. Her parents, siblings, their staff, O'Malley's, and the Stanton's were all in tears of joy over her tasteful, inspiring, and enriched speech. They were all so proud of a young girl that had determination and the forthwith of yearning to come to America and attend school.

Since Morgan and Adrienne graduated that day, it was their decision where they wanted to have their celebration dinner; they chose, Bunny's Diner. This was not a fancy place, by any means; but it was a hang out when they were at their happiest and sometimes saddest moments. There was twenty-eight people that afternoon and they had the best time together. Hearing funny jokes, great stories and lots of love going around the table as they ate their favorite foods that afternoon.

That night, after graduation was behind them, everyone went back to their prospective homes except for the Stanton's; they were spending the night at Jezalee's since their children were leaving on vacation with the Albanese's the next morning.

The next morning everyone had their bags packed and prematurely sat at the front door. When Jezalee came down, she went out to get the newspaper and laughed when she saw the bags already in position to leave the premises. She heard Helga in the kitchen who had just started a pot of coffee and had put the tea kettle on. Jezalee and Helga started making a brunch style breakfast; so, there was everything to choose from. Richard and Joan came down first then Paul was a few minutes behind them. When he walked-in he looked towards Jezalee, "This is sure a familiar scene," Paul commented. "It is a lot of your favorite breakfast foods boss,'' Helga said. "You know those are firing words dear,''' Paul said. Jezalee could tell the Stanton's looked puzzled. "That is a joke amongst us; when Helga calls one of us her boss, we tell her we will fire her, believe me, she is considered part of our family, just as her daughter Astrid, and the rest of our staff and their children are. None of them are going anywhere, we would never let that happen. They are the brother, sisters I never had and an added family for Paul as well,' Jezalee responded. "Oh! Now we understand; we were worried for you Helga," Joan commented. "Mrs. Stanton, no worries, me and the rest of the staff, have them wrapped around our little fingers and we are keeping it that way," Helga smiles as she responds. They laughed and loved her sense of humor. Paul winks at Helga and gives her a thumbs up.

The adults were having their coffee and chatted a while, before breakfast was served; the children joined them just before Helga and Jezalee set the dining room table. As they were all seated, Jezalee thanked Paul for chaperoning seven teenagers. Paul said he was delighted to, and it would get more interesting when they land in

Italy; he was adding his and Jezalee's parents for their tour through Italy. Richard and Joan thanked them for inviting their four children and said how brave he was. Joan complimented both Helga and Jezalee; she had never learned how to cook very well and raved about their culinary skills. Jezalee and Helga, both thanked her. After everyone finished, they had about a half an hour before they needed to leave for the airport. There was one last thing; Helga and Jezalee had made an assortment of meals for everyone, including a few desserts and they made sure that there was enough room in the refrigerator aboard the jet. The children and Paul were all smiles knowing they would have some homemade food to take with them. "I hope there is Tiramisu," Gregory spoke up. "Yes, dear, there is," Jezalee answered. The children cleared all the dishes, said their goodbyes and off they went with Paul. The last look Paul had was when he turned his head toward Jezalee and said goodbye. She glanced at Paul from a distance, wanting to kiss him, but turned away to close the door as they drove off. The Stanton's excused themselves to go up and get their luggage. Jezalee had already informed them she would have Joseph take them to Joan's sister and brother-in-law's house, they were going on a cruise together. Richard needed to make a business call; Jezalee directed him into her study. While he was busy with calls Jezalee and Joan discussed what charities, they were both working on next; they collaborated on a few scenarios that might help draw more people. The Stanton's left about an hour later and on their way to having a wonderful cruise for two weeks.

The rest of Jezalee's day was spent relaxing and hoping that Paul and the children would have the greatest of times in Africa and all the other places they would travel be traveling to. She told Helga she was going to do her best not to be sad. Helga asked her why she did not go with them? "You know you wanted to go with them.'' "Stop that!" Jezalee perked up to say. "Stop what?" Helga asked. "You know my mind and it is scary at times," Jezalee answered. "When there is a next time just bite the bullet and go; take your chances and have fun," Helga insisted. "We will see about that," Jezalee said as she walked on up to her bedroom.

Created with Sketch.

Jezalee's bedroom was her sanctuary; she loved the view from the top floor which overlooked her boundless grounds with their heavenly green and posh trees, sculpted shrubs, a multitude of colorful flowers planted throughout the gardens, beautiful unique stone benches, Italian statues, and an ornate water fountain with marble and stone seating. This was where she enjoyed working on her books, while her lingering eyes could wander out to her magnificent property. It was always more relaxing, and she seemed to get more accomplished viewing the outdoors from her bedroom terrace. Jezalee pretty much had done all the research, now she needed to implement the remainder of the information into the right places in-her-books. She had all the photos for her books and hopefully with great success they would lay out with just the right amount of space between them. She had been working on this project for over three years, and she was finally getting close to sending it into her publisher in New York. Jezalee had contacted a dear friend and he would be working on the cover.

Jezalee had been reviewing all her work on her two books and photos for hours and wanted to take a break. She decided to call Mallory to see if she and David would like to go out to dinner with her and Jim. Mallory thought getting out of the house for a few hours was a great idea and she looked forward to the evening. Jezalee said she'd call Jim at work and the men can tell them what time would be good. Jezalee called Jim to see if he was available for a double date with the O'Malley's; he of course said yes. She let him know that Mallory was calling David also, to see where the two of them would like to go. Jim said he would discuss the evening with David. "Do not hang up yet! I have a question to ask you," Jezalee quickly said. "Go ahead," Jim responded. "I was hoping I could spend the night if you want some company," Jezalee said. "I would love for you to spend the night; but I thought we were just friends," Jim sweetly responded. Jezalee could hear the perkiness in his voice when she asked to spend the night and knew she had to be careful what she said. "I have a change of heart and want to see where our relationship may go; if you are up for the challenge; little did he know the real reason," Jezalee replied. "I am all, for giving us a shot at getting closer," Jim said enthusiastically.

The O'Malley's, Jim and Jezalee had a delightful dinner, did some catching up on a few conversations they had not finished from the last time they had gotten together. Mallory asked Jezalee how her books were coming along. She was relieved to be done other than putting everything in its rightful, place. "How many pages in your books? "David asked. "As of yesterday, 500 pages in the one book, and 650 in the other," Jezalee answered. "Will that be 2 volumes?" Jim asked. "No, actually they will be two completely different books and stand on their own merit. When I first started, I thought I would be able to put everything in one book but the more research I did, I realized that one book would be way too big if I wanted to cover both Historical subjects together," Jezalee answered. "I am so excited for you because I know how much art history means to you and I want to buy the first copy," Mallory commented. Jezalee promised that anyone of her family and friends would, get free copies of both books if they wanted them.

After they were done with dinner, Jezalee had informed David and Mallory that she had already packed her bag to spend a night at Jim's and if for any reason they needed to get in touch with her she would be there until tomorrow night. They said their goodnights to Jim and Jezalee and were surprised the change of heart that Jezalee had, knowing of Jim's mood swings and how much he had been irritating her. Mallory asked Jezalee to give her a call tomorrow because she wanted her opinion on a few of the charities they were working on; Jezalee said she would call her in the morning after breakfast.

After Jezalee and Jim settled into his penthouse, they lit candles throughout the living room and bedroom, turned out all the lights, slightly opened the blinds to see the magnificent view which had a romantic setting with the city lights as their backdrop, but tonight she was not thinking of views, she could only think of the next day when he went to work. As they slowed dance Jezalee was feeling very guilty about her reason for being there. She knew she probably would not find anything; but she wanted to put everything to rest and the only way she could do that was sneak around his place to get answers. She had always thought in the back of her mind, that there was more to him than he let on; especially in the last year he was unpredictable with his mood swings and his sense of what is right or wrong. She did not want any loose ends; even, as a friend, she wanted answers at this point. She knew he was going to want to have sex and that was farthest subject from her mind and body. Jezalee knew she had to get through the night; so, he would not suspect why she was there. Since he seemed to always shut all of them out about things in his past, she had to see if there was something, he had left in his place that may tie in with something she felt was missing from him.

That night she knew they would unfortunately have sex, which was not easy for either one of them. He would have sex to think this would make her fall in love with him. Marriage, marriage, marriage; that was the only thing on his mind; that is what he was gravitating towards. She, on the other hand, would have sex thinking it pleased him and he would tell her more about his past. As she laid next to him, Jezalee could only remember the first experience with him which was unfavorable to say the least. Here she was in bed with him again! She was thinking! How did her life, get to this! She was getting paid back because the only reason she ever had sex with him was to forget about Paul. Now, Jezalee had her mind on one thing; finding out who the real Jim Stark was. The one time she had sex with Jim her mind drifted to Paul and their love making, that had always been a thing of beauty and purity; with Jim, she felt as if she was a cardboard cut-out. Pretending she was satisfied; made her guilt worsen. She undoubtedly knew spending the night with him, he would want to have sex. One big drawback! He was not Paul. While she is thinking of all this, Jim was pressing his lips to hers, he looked down at her and could see the flickering candlelight on her face. He could see how gorgeous she was and how much she wanted him; little did he know how wrong he was about Jezalee wanting him. She thought to herself, I had sex with Jim without thinking I wanted to be with Paul; that was another reason she knew she was not in love with him and certainly would never accept anyone's proposal until she was completely over her ex-husband. Jezalee remembered the night they had sex; first she thought she was the problem; but it was also the way he touched her, like a moveable mannequin. She at one point, had cared for him, as a dear friend because he was fun to be around, intelligent, was great with children and was very personable. That changed over time, and he had become a thorn in her side, irritating and appeared needy to the point of being obsessed over her.

So, she thought to herself! Why am I here? Well! Jezalee was a person filled with curiosity and certain things just did not add up over the last few years. She hoped there would be answers in the confines of his penthouse; but Jezalee knew it may be a waste of her time and effort.

Jezalee cringed at the thought of being in bed with Jim for a second time; but there she was that night having unemotional sex with him and she felt sick to her stomach. She just wanted the sex over with, when would he be done? Jezalee could not believe she had those thoughts coming from her. What had happened to her extraordinary life to end up in bed with someone she did not love and getting ready to spy on him for curiosity, sake. Since this was the second time; she had sex with him, nothing was different, just a different night. He moved mechanically with no emotions, with the exception, of his moaning.

Jezalee tossed and turned all night, she knew she was there to spy on Jim; but getting nervous over the entire prospect that he would come home and catch her in the act. Next thing she knew, Jim's annoying alarm was going off and she was exhausted from no sleep.

Jezalee managed to roll out of bed to prepare their breakfast; while they were having their coffee Jim mentioned that Mona, his housekeeper would be coming a few days earlier to clean his place. Jezalee was filled with anguish and fear and tried not to react to the worst information she could have been told. She purposely chose that morning knowing that it was not Mona's cleaning day. Jezalee knew she'd have to deal with it as quickly as she could.

After breakfast Jezalee told Jim she was going to relax a while before going shopping for what was needed to make the dinner at his place that night. Jim had wished he could join her for a little R and R, but had crucial deadlines, and they emphatically must be done before he left the office that evening. She gave him a hug and a quick kiss on the cheek and told him to be on his way. Jezalee knew she had no intention of going grocery shopping to buy food. She had one thing on her mind; and needed to start searching every crevice of his place. As he got on the elevator he yelled out, "I cannot wait to see you tonight, have a wonderful day," "You too, Jim," Jezalee replied.

After Jim finally left, Jezalee knew that Mona coming to clean was placing extra stress on her already taxing situation. She now knew there was limited time to explore her inquisitive nature. Jezalee knew she had about four or five hours before the housekeeper Mona would arrive; this did not give her much time to search for something, which she had no idea what she was even looking for.

Jezalee knew that no matter if she found something or not, she was never going to see Jim again. He was too negative; and did not add anything to her life. She knew he probably had a lot to offer someone other than her. Jezalee knew after her search was over, no matter what; she would meet with Jim in a few days and tell him she wanted him to find a woman that wanted to get married; preferably one that did not have an ex-husband, since he was so jealous. He had put too much pressure on her, and she never understood why he did not give up on her long before now; especially since she said she did not love him.

Jim's penthouse was large and Jezalee was worried she would not have enough time knowing Mona would be coming to clean. Starting the search was more than she bargained for, she had to be extra careful because he was meticulous. Whatever she pulled a part, had to go back exactly how she found had it. Jezalee was overwhelmed at the task at hand, looking under mattresses, box springs, closets, behind mirrors, artwork, inside pillowcases, and under rugs. She had brought some tools to work with hoping it would make things somewhat easier. Jezalee began the nerve-wracking task of removing entire drawers in case Jim had taped something underneath or behind them. He had very tall armoires in each bedroom, where she had to a climb up on a chair to reach the top cabinets and ended up finding nothing. Any furniture too close to a wall, had to be moved out from the wall very carefully. Unfortunately, there was no sign of anything in the guest bedrooms. Since Jezalee had not thought about bringing a polaroid camera to take a photo of the placement before and after moving furniture and accessories; she had to sit down, quickly drew a diagram of each room to make sure everything went back to its original place after she was done searching each item. She decided the cellar would be the last place she would tackle, hoping it would be the easiest room. The bathrooms were the next on her list and she found nothing; she lifted the toilet water tank and checked behind it also. Jezalee was struggling to pull back the wall-to-wall carpeting; but she did have a specific tool for it; so, it helped tremendously. She searched in the kitchen; Jezalee was thankful Jim, did not have a lot of dishes, pots, or pans. He had slide out drawers that could not be removed so she had to get down on her back and look under each one that was under the countertops. She checked under the tables, chairs, sofas, and ottomans to no avail. Jezalee nervously kept looking at the time hoping that Mona did not show up earlier than usual. After the kitchen, she decided to check out Jim's master suite; he had an enormous closet filled with at least fifty suits, matching dress shirts, ties, handkerchiefs, belts, and over seventy-five pairs of dress, and casual shoes. After she rummaged through every pocket or opening in all business attire and found nothing, Jezalee started on his more casual slacks, sweaters, Levi's, Polo, and T-shirts; but there was nothing there, she then noticed tucked in the very back corner there was more clothes that she never saw him wear; they looked rather old and not his style. The clothes were isolated from the rest of his expensive designer clothes. At this point, she was about to give up because she had checked every inch of every seam of clothing, and nothing showed up. Jezalee spotted an old, rather worn lumber jacket; she went directly to the pockets, they were empty, then she noticed there were some inside pockets near the chest area. Bingo! She pulled out a photo of three people; it was Jim, an exceptionally pretty woman, and a young boy, they looked like such a happy family. Jezalee realized that it was probably him with his wife, and son. She thought maybe he needed to keep the photo hidden because he was still in such pain. Finding this one photo gave her the encouragement to keep digging further. Her next task was the grand piano, the antique grandfather's clock, looking behind more mirrors, oil paintings, and prints. Jezalee decided to get the wine cellar over with; she looked in every nook and cranny, to turn up nothing. Last place to tackle was Jim's library, she opened the double doors, looked at the bookshelves, and knew it would be a daunting task at the very least. She sat down on his masculine leather sofa and looked around the massive room and had just realized something could be hidden behind his electrical outlets. Jezalee would check them out after she finished in the library. Knowing time was of the essence, she was aware concentration was needed to work expeditiously. Jezalee was trying to figure out, in her mind, where would she hide something, she did not want anyone to find. She realized she had not gone through the dishwasher, freezer, refrigerator, all the closed cabinets, garbage cans, and containers. She quickly made it back to the kitchen and got that out of the way, then dashed back to the library. Jezalee felt her endeavors were getting more complicated, and were completely, unequivocally, mentally, and physically exhausting. It was time to keep searching for Jim's past; she knew this was not an easy venture. He had wall to wall, floor to ceiling bookshelves. He had vases, sculptures, artifacts, and many other mementos from all over the world on various shelves, and most of them breakable. Jezalee got up and threw caution to the wind; she had no other choice. She was frantic just thinking about putting everything back in its place. Efforts began and she was already profusely perspiring due to her nerves taking over. Jezalee took shelf by shelf, inch by inch, with precaution of a burglar; but much slower. As she was going through this painstaking process, she suddenly thought, what happens if Mona comes in while she is in the library, she had this frightening feeling she was going to be caught and wouldn't know how to react or what to do. As Jezalee kept going through each book and everything else on the shelves, she had to have a plan if Mona showed up early; she would say she was looking for a book to read to relax. God knows that's close to the truth; Jezalee knew she needed, to relax after all this. She was beginning to think going through his books was an endless effort with no results. Jezalee had started from the bottom, she thought how stupid of me! No one in their right mind would hide something in close reach; so, she got the rolling ladder and began her search from the top. Jezalee had been searching the top shelves for about thirty minutes; suddenly to her dismay, she pulled out a leather-bound book to find out it was just a shell of a book, she nervously looked around the room then towards the hallway; she froze, then knew she had to hurry and get down from the ladder and push it back where he had kept it. She looked up at the empty space where she had gotten the fake book and ran over to get the ladder. Jezalee got up to the shelf and moved the books around; so, it did not show an empty space. As she rushed down the ladder; she heard a noise and pushed the ladder back to its original spot. She grabbed a book from the bottom shelf, sprinted to the sofa in time to put the fake book behind the suede pillow that was at the end of the sofa. Jezalee caught her breath and yelled, is that you Mona? Hello! She did not respond, she yelled out again, she did not get up because the suede pillow was bulging out and was very noticeable. Next thing she knew, it was Jim just the person she did not want to see or expect. She tried not to act too surprised or weird, she felt her face flushed. Jezalee said very calmly, "what a nice surprise." Jim bent over to give her a kiss on her lips; even at that frightening moment, she realized he was not a passionate kisser. Jezalee was so afraid he was going to hear her heart racing. After he stepped back from kissing her, he quizzically asked what was she doing? She calmly said she was rather tired after her bubble bath and decided to grab a book and relax for a while. He looked at the book she was holding in her hands and said, "Out of all the great books I have, you chose a fishing book to read from cover to cover?" She looked at the book in her clammy hands, "there are a lot of things you do not know about me Mr. Funny guy, I did not select this book to read its entirety, it was more from curiosity," Jezalee replied. "I promise not to quiz you on the various types of fish in the sea," as Jim laughingly commented. She managed to smile back at him and did not say another word about the book. Jezalee was praying he did not come home to have an afternoon delight; she certainly was not in the mood for sex and was not ever going to be in bed with him again. All she wanted was Jim to go back to work. Panic was setting in and Jezalee knew she could not get up off the sofa and take a chance he would see what she found. Jezalee was also hoping that once she did get up, there would not be an imprint of the hard-shell book from her weight pressing into the pillow. Jim sat down next to her, and she squirmed a little; fear took over that he would notice something was wrong. Jezalee gently grabbed his arm and said she felt a little light-headed; just as he was to put his arm around her, Mona arrived. Jim approached Mona and asked her if she would clean the kitchen first. "Mr. Jim, as she always called him, of course! Jezalee, knew that Mona had impeccable timing today; now there would not be a possibility that Jim would try and get romantic with her, she silently thanked God for this little miracle. After Jim finished speaking with Mona he headed back into the library where Jezalee had remained sitting on the sofa; afraid to get up while he was still there. She asked him to sit awhile and wanted to know if he had managed to finish the three deadlines earlier than expected. "No! But I decided to take a break, in hopes, by chance, to see my favorite lady here before you went grocery shopping for our dinner. I thought we could go out for lunch," Jim said. "That is so sweet of you; but I promised Mallory we would go to lunch because we need to go over several charity events that are coming up soon. I also have a few things I need to do at my house before I see you tonight," Jezalee immediately spoke up. "Instead of you making dinner for us tonight, why don't I take you out to one of our favorite night spots?" Jim said. "That is a great idea and to be honest with you, I had decided right after you left this morning, to surprise you with a night out and wanted to go home and get a sexier dress," Jezalee replied. "Well! There you go, great minds think alike. Would it be okay if I came to lunch with you and Mallory?" Jim asked. "Jim, I hate for you to think I am brushing you off, but Mallory and I have got a lot of work ahead of us and our luncheon is not a social one; we are on a time crunch because a lot of the people that were helping with our charities backed out and to make things worse, we have several people that were going to give big donations also backed out and will be giving to our charities. Now we must go to plan B, and it is not easy trying to find more help within our community, plus trying to find people to donate at the last minute. I just want to get this disastrous development taken care of so the two of us can spend more time together while the children are gone," Jezalee answered. Jim leaned over and pecked her on the forehead and said from what you are telling me, you both have a lot on your plate, no pun intended as he smiled. You are on fire today with your quick wit," Jezalee commented. Jim said he had better get back to the trenches, so he will be done before their date tonight. One more thing! Do not be too glamorous! I do not want any men hitting on my gorgeous lady. "I will take note of that; but you have nothing to worry about," Jezalee remarked. "Why is that?" Jim asked. "Because I will have my superman to protect me against the men clamoring after me," Jezalee said as they both chuckled and said their goodbyes. Jim could not get out of the penthouse fast enough for Jezalee's sanity.

Jezalee knew she had a big undertaking and needed to keep searching through the bookshelves; but how could she, with Mona there? She knew she had enough room in the bag she brought, and Mona would not suspect a thing. Jezalee returned the fish book; she could still see a little space on the top shelf where she had taken the fake book and rolled the ladder once again to the space to try and fill it in better. She heard Mona coming down the hallway and flew off the ladder as quickly as she could. She grabbed the fake book and made sure to see if it had left an imprint in the sofa and it had. She worked diligently to smooth the leather back and to fluff up the suede pillow; then, she had to race over and maneuver the ladder back to its original spot. Last thing she had to do was gather up her clothes and oversized bag from the master suite. Once that fake book was in her bag; she would get out of there. Jezalee got herself together to say goodbye to Mona; she wanted to apologize for not cleaning up the kitchen. Mona gave her a smile and said this is cleaner than Mr. Jim ever leaves it and they both laughed.

Jezalee knew she had to call Mallory sooner than later after lying to Jim about them needing to meet for a business lunch. She stopped at the front desk and asked Gary, the doorman if she could use the outside phone line to make a call, he handed it to her, immediately dialing Mallory and as soon as her phone rang Jezalee was panicking in case she did not answer. She thought, why didn't I think of this luncheon with Mallory last night when the four of them were at dinner. Jezalee guessed, she truly did not think she would find anything worth worrying about. As that thought ran through her mind, Mallory answered the phone. "I need to see you as fast as you can pick me up at Jim's," Jezalee hastily said.? "Are you okay Jezalee? A perplexed Mallory asked her. "Yes! However, I am not sure about something else; we need to quickly meet for lunch," a determined and distraught Jezalee answered. "Okay! I am leaving now," a curious Mallory replied. "Wait! I told Jim we have this lunch date already planned to go over some major problems with the charities we organize," as Jezalee explained. Thanks for filling me in because Jim just arrived at our front door. Close call my dear!" Mallory commented. "Wow! You are telling me! Jezalee responded. By this time, she was a nervous wreck because Jim never mentioned he was going over to David's. He explicitly said he had to get back to the office. Why was Jim making an unexpected visit to the O'Malley's? Did he think Jezalee was lying about going to lunch with Mallory? Mallory went in to see David and Jim as they sauntered into his den and said hi to Jim; he gave her a hug and said, "I thought you would be gone by now for your luncheon with Jezalee." I would have been there to pick her up by now; but I am running much later than I expected. Jim asked her where they were going to lunch, and she said they had not made up their mind yet. "I did not know you were going out for lunch," David said. Jim was seated going over some papers, this gave Mallory enough time to look at her husband and roll her eyes, he knew what that gesture meant. "Oh! I completely forgot you told me last night and it slipped my mind," David said. Mallory smiled and winked at him and mouthed the words "thank you." She walked over to David and gave him a kiss and said her goodbyes to the guys. Ten minutes later she was at the front door of the apartment building and saw Jezalee run towards her car. Jezalee slid into the car and divulged, "I had to get to you before Jim did. She now had Mallory's attention. "Tell me what in the world is going on; you are acting strange," a baffled Mallory said. "I know! I took something from Jim's place," Jezalee answered. "Why would you do that?" Mallory quizzically asked. "You will know when we get to the restaurant," Jezalee answered. Mallory chose Bunny's diner; after she parked the car, she asked her why are you bringing in your oversized bag? You will know soon enough! Jezalee pulled out the fake book, took out the contents; there were 2 birth certificates folded up, a miniature copy of her divorce papers, pictures of 2 babies, news clippings of the death of a husband and wife, adoption papers for a boy named Roland Anderson-Martin, the photo she found in his closet in the old lumber jacket.

The ladies started reading all the paperwork Jezalee had taken and knew Jim must have something to do with these clippings and photos, or why would he have them hidden. They looked closer at the photo of the two babies and deciphered they were twin boys in matching outfits; they could tell this appeared to be their one-year-old photo and it had the names of Robert and Roland 1 year old and birthday was 12-1-50. They looked over the adoption papers and it had Roland Anderson's name; parents Lucas and Mary Anderson as his biological parents deceased on December 24th, 1950, adopted by Janie and Stewart Martin. His surname changed to Anderson-Martin. There were only adoption papers on the one child; they thought they must have given up the one and kept the other? That would be awful! They thought it was odd the twins had the same birth month, day, and year as Jim. "What does this all mean?" An inquisitive Mallory asked. "It appears if he is one of the twins, that he may have been adopted out to a family with the last name Stark," Jezalee answered. "Does any of this make sense to you?" Mallory asked. 'I am not sure but why would they give the baby a different first name?" Jezalee questioned it. "I do not know; but why does he have a copy of your divorce papers and how did he get them?" Mallory asked.

It was a lengthy luncheon, and they were devastated as they read the newspaper clipping on how the Anderson's were murdered. As they read it, they indicated the one son must have been in the backseat with the killers, the husband was in the driver's seat and the wife in the front passenger seat holding baby Roland in her lap. "How gruesome! What happened to Robert Anderson, could that possibly be Jim Stark?" Jezalee asked. "Thank God Roland was as young as he was, at least he would not have a memory of the killings," Mallory commented. "The doctors said the baby would not have lived another day if the couple had not found the car," Jezalee said. "I still cannot believe baby Roland survived with his mother hunched over his body. Just think! According to the newspaper, that couple was not going to go for a bicycle ride that day until they heard there was a forecast for rain the rest of the week. That couple saved baby' Roland's life!" Mallory remarked. "Just envision when the couple was innocently riding their bikes, they saw a car, they got closer and saw blood splattered inside the car with two people with their heads blown off, it is like watching a horror movie come to life," Jezalee commented.

They sat at the diner for several hours and Jezalee finally remembered shed come to David's office just before the divorce was final and wanted to go over a few things with him. She knew David had her best interest in the matter and wanted him to read through a few things. She had made a copy of her original which had not been signed; but asked David to keep it until she gave him a signed original from her attorney. She had asked her attorney to draw up four originals, that way David would have one and he said he would keep it at home in their vault. In the meantime, he had his secretary make a file for the copy Jezalee had given him. She asked Mallory to give David a call, he was working in his den at home. Mallory asked him if Jim was there. David let her know he had left about a half an hour ago. "Good! Because Jezalee was a busy lady today at Jim's and found some interesting news clippings, photos, adoption papers and Jezalee divorce papers," Mallory said. He asked them to come to their house immediately. The ladies paid their bill and got all the items together and drove to the O'Malley estate.

When they arrived at the O'Malley residence, they could not get in the house fast enough, they could hardly wait for David to make sense of all that Jezalee had found. David asked the gals to pull up a chair, hand him whatever Jezalee found at Jim's, and he started thumbing through everything. He glanced at it and said they needed to spread everything out on the larger dining room table.

After David spread all the items out on the table, he began to review everything in its entirety. When he was finished, he sat down at the table with the girls and was stunned at Jezalee's findings. "Jezalee, why in the world does Jim have your divorce documents? "David quizzically asks." "He had to have gotten this from your office," Jezalee answered. "How is that possible? I have the divorce documents in our vault here at home," Replied David. "Don't you remember the day I came into your office with a copy? I had not signed the original yet and wanted you to read over everything before I signed," Jezalee said. "Oh my! I do remember that! I had Barbara make a file so if you had any more questions; I would have it to refer to. My secretary did make a file and it was placed in a separate cabinet that is always kept locked; that key is left in a hidden place, and I do not know how Jim ever got privy to that key. This is not good! The only reason someone would want to see your divorce documents is to find out what your settlement was; they would certainly know from that what you are worth. Did you ever discuss your wealth with Jim?" David asked with concern. "Absolutely not!" An angered Jezalee responded. "Well! He now knows you're a billionaire," David commented. "I do not understand why he would be interested in how much I am worth because he appears to be well off in his own right," Jezalee replied. "He does make a substantially large income working for me and he informed me he sold his properties back East. Let's face it! With all your properties, expansive, and lucrative businesses, all your other investments and the huge lump sum Paul gave to you in the settlement, he would never see this kind of money in his lifetime," a concerned David said. The more David looked over the photos, read the adoption papers and poured over the news clippings, he came-to-the-conclusion, Jim may be a fraud of sorts and was not sure how everything was inked together; but he was going to find out. "Ladies, I will make copies of all of this, and you two need to get these back to their proper place before Jim sees them gone," David said. He gathered the items, made copies, and placed them in a file folder. He came back to the dining room and explained to the girls what his thoughts were, and they agreed bringing in a private investigator would be the right thing to do. He said he had made a copy for his investigator, and he would have him over to their place as soon as possible; he wanted him to see and read what he is dealing with. In the meantime, David placed extra copies in his vault for safe keeping.

David suggested that Jezalee spend another night with him. She began to cry and said she did not think she could do it; especially knowing what she knows now. David advised her to tell Jim she had been lonely since the children left and wanted to spend another night. David looked at her, put his arms around her and told her she had no other choice; she knew he was right but was still worried. She looked over at Mallory and said, "I know he will want to have sex and I cannot go through with that again," Jezalee states. "Dear, now look and listen to me; after you get back to his apartment from your date night, wait about a half an hour or so, then tell him suddenly you do not feel well. I am sure his feelings for intimacy at that point will lessen," David spoke sincerely. "Knowing him, he will want to take me to emergency," Jezalee said. "Do not worry about that now, you will be fine. We know you can pull this off because of what is at stake. You will need to put on an act and just remember it is for the greater good. Jim is not going to suspect anything; he will be over the moon that you asked to stay over again," Mallory said. "Why would Jim be sneaking around the office and ever find that key?" Mallory asked. "The only thing I can think of, maybe he overheard Jezalee talking with me the day she came in with her divorce documents," David answered. "That is what happened, I remember that day perfectly, he was waiting for me to get finished in your office so we could go out to lunch," Jezalee said she remembered. "Right after you left that day, I gave the divorce documents to Barbara so she could file them away behind the locked cabinet; she always makes sure that no one is around when she retrieves the hidden key. I will have a talk with her tomorrow and see if she remembers who was around that day when she was taking care of that matter," David said.

David directed Jezalee and Mallory into his den where Jezalee could call Jim. Before she made the call, he was asking her not to worry, everything would be okay. Jezalee called Jim at work and the secretary put the call through to his office. She sounded anxious to see him and he said he was looking forward to having dinner again with her after he finished up at work. "Well! The real reason I am calling is, I know we are going out tonight; but I feel so lonely without the children home and was hoping I could stay again tonight," Jezalee asked. Jim was all ears and became immensely happy. "Of course! I want you over all the time, you know that don't you?" Jim answered. "I do not want to overstay my welcome," Jezalee commented. "What did you just say? Did you forget I asked you to marry me?" Jim replied. "I faintly remember that as she let out a throaty giggle." "You can stay, as long, as you want," Jim anxiously said. "Since all that is settled, I will meet you at your apartment around six, if that is a good time for you," Jezalee said. "That is ideal! I am excited about tonight and can hardly wait to see you," Jim remarked. After Jezalee hung up she felt sick to her stomach. David and Mallory could tell that Jezalee was not faring too well! They told her this was one step closer to never seeing Jim again. She let them know she was going to get through tonight no matter what; and hoped Jamerson could find all the information he needed on that low life of a person.

Jezalee told Mallory she needed to get home and take a nap because she did not sleep much at his place last night. Mallory called Bob and asked if he'd be able to take Jezalee home in fifteen minutes. He said he will be right over. Bob dropped off Jezalee, she went to see Helga; she let her know she was taking a bubble bath and then a nap. Jezalee informed her she was spending another night at Jim's. She knew Helga had his number in case she needed to get in touch with her.

Jezalee soaked in a hot bubble bath with lemon essential oil for about a half an hour; dried off then put her favorite silk pair of pajamas on and got under the covers. She managed to fall asleep for three hours; when Jezalee woke up, she felt rested and ready to choose a cocktail dress. She was ready to go out; she just needed to pack a nightgown for sleeping and a casual outfit for the day. She walked over to her meditation area and lit a candle and prayed that she would get through the night and have it all behind her after Jim went to work the next day.

David got a call from his parents, Patrick, and Kathleen; they were calling to see how the summer was coming along. He let them know the children were at Camp and it was quiet on the home front. David asked them how the penthouse was shaping up in Manhattan and they happily said the remodel was finished and they would spend the night there. "How do you like it?" David asked. "It is fantastic! The architect and builder did everything to our specifications and it is more spacious after taking some walls down. We are thrilled with the major changes; the outcome is dramatic and quite a gem if we say so ourselves," his dad replied. "I am so glad you kept that place because it is in such a thriving area near all the things you love most; cannot wait to see it first-hand," David said. "Sounds good! We would love for you, Mallory and the children to come soon to see us and we will stay at the penthouse," his dad said. "Love you guys!" David. said. "Love you too, son!" replied Patrick.

Jezalee had selected Jim's favorite restaurant and knew that would make him happy. Once their meal came, they chatted off and on and the night was going well. After that great meal Jim said he was ready to go dancing at their favorite night club; however, Jezalee said she was nauseated from her meal and if they could go back to his place and dance. Jim thought that was fine and they were at his place within twenty minutes. Once Jezalee got to his place she was feeling calmer and knew what she had to from there. Once they got settled in the penthouse, Jezalee took her shoes off and got them a cold drink. While she did that, Jim changed into some pajamas and was sitting on one of the living room sofas. She walked towards him carrying their drinks, Jezalee sat next to him and knew what she had to do. Jim took his drink, had a sip then set it down on the glass top coffee table. He looked at her very seriously and said, "I came close to buying you a subscription to the Field and Stream magazine," Jim said. She smiled at him and said, Ha! Ha! That is funny! I guess I am never going to live that down. He came closer to her on the sofa and gave her a kiss and ran his fingers through her silky, thick hair and told her how much he loved her. She did not say anything other than, "lets, dance!" They danced for about fifteen minutes then he took his pajama top off then started unbuttoning her dress. She slipped out of her dress, took her nylons off; he said let me help you with your bra and panties. Jezalee was now nude, felt extremely vulnerable, then he thankfully took his pajama top and delicately put it on her as he kissed the nape of her neck. They kept dancing a little while longer, then he turned off the music, he gently took her hand and they walked to his bedroom. He immediately got between the sheets; Jezalee said she needed to use the bathroom. Jezalee went into the bathroom, pulled her hair back in a ponytail, went at a slow pace, took her makeup off, and as she put her face over the toilet, she had a flashback of the photo of him, his wife and son then she stuck her finger down her throat to throw up her dinner. As she flushed the toilet, she was relieved that some food came up. She could hear Jim calling out, what in the world is taking so long? She came out quickly to tell Jim she had just thrown up and would be out in a minute. He could see from the overhead light shining on her face that she looked very pale. She washed her face and hands then brushed her teeth. When she glanced in the mirror, she really did look sick and that was a good sign; she was ready to finish her acting debut. Jezalee slowly walked over to Jim's bed, looked down at him and said she was still nauseous from the meal at the restaurant, and now head a severe headache and was very weak. Jezalee let him know that is what took so long in the bathroom because she threw up twice and had to clean it up. He told her he would take her to the hospital. She said absolutely she did not want to go to the hospital because she felt too weak and tired, to get dressed and sit in emergency room for hours. Jezalee said she just wanted to try to get some sleep and hopefully would feel better in the morning. Jezalee asked Jim if it mattered what guest bedroom, she slept in. He immediately told her she was not going anywhere and to get in his bed. He said he would be across the hall, and he would leave, both bedroom doors open; so, if she needed anything, to call out for him. Jim got up from his bed and got Jezalee situated comfortably. He asked her if she wanted a cup of hot tea or some warm milk before he went to bed, and she said, "Thank You," but she probably wouldn't be able to keep it down. She apologized for ruining their evening and hoped she could make it up to him soon. Jim said he had an exceptional evening out with her and just wanted her to get well. "We will make plans after you are feeling better. I want you back to your normal, healthy self." Said Jim. He bent down and kissed her on the forehead. As Jim left the room, she could tell he was concerned and for one brief, moment she felt guilty. Jezalee laid back on the pillow and had a sigh of relief, she never had to have sex with him again; two times was two times too many. She would never feel guilty again after he stole a copy of her divorce settlement and knew she was very wealthy. She knew he did not love her; it was all a scam and to think he thought she would eventually marry him.

At the O'Malley house, Mallory, and David did not sleep well thinking about Jezalee all night. David had placed a call into Jim just before they went to bed; he had some pressing business in Los Angeles and why not bring Jim along. Since Jim had not answered, he left a message on his machine that the two of them needed to fly into Los Angeles for an emergency meeting. He indicated he was having Bob take them to the airport and he would be picked up at 7:30 a.m. sharp. After David left the message, "You always know what to do in a crisis and this is one for sure. I pray that Jezalee was not too nervous after knowing what we already have found out about this stranger amongst them," Mallory said. "Dear, I have all the confidence in the world that Jezalee pulled it off. If she can pretend to be madly in love with Paul after finding out he cheated on her; never said a word for six months, I think she can handle anything that comes her way," David said. Mallory smiled and agreed.

Jezalee woke up at 6:30 a.m., went straight to the bathroom, looked in the mirror and thought she looked good for someone that had thrown up twice and had a severe headache the night before. She brushed out her hair then put it back in a ponytail so she could wash her face; just as she finished, Jim walked in to see how she felt. He came closer to her and gently kissed the back of her neck. Jim asked how she was feeling, and she remarked, better but still very weak. He said he was making himself some oatmeal, toast and tea and would she like to join him. Jezalee said she'd try to eat and hopefully keep it down. He asked Jim if it was okay with him if she went back to bed after she had breakfast. He took hold of her left hand from across the kitchen table and said, of course! Stay in bed all day and get lots of rest; I will check in on you later. Jezalee asked him why he was going into the office so early. I am not going into the office; I had a message on my machine late last night from David and we are needed in Los Angeles for an emergency meeting and will not be back until after six or seven tonight. As he was telling her, this last-minute change in his work schedule, she said a silent "Thank You" to David for getting him out of town; she would be less stressed out knowing he could not just pop in while she was there.

Jezalee asked if it was okay if Mallory came over. "I would love for her to come over and keep you company while you rest. I am so glad you two are such good friends; she and David are an amazing couple," Jim said. She agreed, I adore them tremendously. "I do not know what time I will be back tonight; but I am hoping you can spend a few extra days with me, that is, if you are up to it. I would love to begin where we left off last night," Jim said. Jezalee agreed! She let him know, no matter how she was feeling, she had a phone appointment with her publisher around one o'clock and needed to be home for the call; she would have Mallory drive her home. Jim said he understood and said they could play it by ear and if she felt better, he would pick her up after he got back into town. "That would be wonderful," Jezalee replied. Jim asked her when the children would be back from vacation. She let him know they would be staying until a few days before school started. "Well! Well! Well! That is great news, we can see one another even more; maybe go on a few mini trips," Jim commented. She smiled then kissed him on the cheek and said that is something to look forward to. Jezalee played along and said, "I hope you will spend some quality time over at my place as well." Jim was all smiles; looked at his watch and had to go, Bob and David would be there any minute. Rest well pretty lady and hope to see you when we get back in town.

Mallory had been ready to come over to Jim's since she jumped out of bed. She was anxiously awaiting a call from Jezalee. A few minutes after Jim left, Jezalee called and told Mallory, "Get yourself over here now and they both chuckled aloud.'' "Oh! And bring a big exercise bag in case we find a lot of items," Jezalee said.

Mallory finally made it to the building and told the doorman she was there to see Miss Albanese in Jim Stark's penthouse. He said he had gotten the message from Mr. Stark to let her up. The doorman rang the buzzer to inform Jezalee of Mallory's arrival.

The first place the girls went to was Jim's closet; Jezalee placed the one photo back into the lumber jacket, where she found it. Afterwards, they headed for the massive library so Jezalee could return the fake book with all its contents; she made sure they were put back in the order Jim had placed them. They both were still paranoid; so, while Jezalee took care of that, Mallory was on the lookout in the hallway just in case David's plan fell through, and Jim would show up unexpectedly. Jezalee, first took, a photo with her polaroid camera of each section of the bookshelves, then started the ordeal of going through every book. The girls would make sure each item they found would be listed according to the order they were in the shell and wrote down what shelf they needed to go back on. The information was listed on the outside of each envelope and then sealed up until they went to Mallory's. Jezalee had found six fake books with items in them, and Mallory needed to get back to her house and make copies and get them back to Jim's so Jezalee could put them back in their original places on the bookshelves.

Mallory decided she had better call David to make sure all was good at his end. The receptionist at their Los Angeles office answered and Mallory asked if she could speak with David and if anyone else was in with him. She said Jim was in with him and was given strict instructions to put any calls from her through whenever she called. When David answered he was happy to hear from Mallory. Since Jim was in the office, she knew he would not be able to hear her talking. She let her husband know she was at Jim's place and Jezalee was sound asleep; while she was sleeping, she had to go back to the house because she had forgotten the six files for the charity auction and needed to make copies for the board members and deliver them while Jezalee slept. David knew by their conversation that they found six more fake books and knew his wife had to get the items copied and back on the shelves in Jim's library. She asked to speak with Jim for a minute and turned the phone over to him. "Hi Jim," It is Mallory; I wanted you to know Jezalee is currently sleeping as we speak, and she did manage to keep her breakfast down. Before she dozed off; she said she was going to call you later in the day. "I will be waiting for her call, thanks a million Mallory, you are a doll," Jim remarked.

After Mallory hung up, she told Jezalee it shouldn't take her more than an hour or so to copy everything and would be back as soon as she was done. Jezalee anxiously waited for Mallory to return so she could get those fake books back where she got them. She could not wait to get home and never see that penthouse or Jim ever again. Even though she knew Jim was with David her nerves were shot and kept pacing back and forth until Mallory returned. By looking at the stuff Jezalee found when they went back, she knew she could not see Jim again. There was a lot of stuff he hid, and this was that much more for the investigator to go through.

Once Mallory arrived back at Jim's they sat down in the living room for a few minutes, and both agreed; it is time to finish and exit from Jim's place. They would be so relieved after they closed his door behind them. They had accomplished their mission and now it is time for Jamerson, to do his magic and do a full investigation on all the people in the news clippings and photos that were found. The girls decided they had seen and read enough that they did not want to try to look for anything else; there was enough evidence there to know that Jim's past was very questionable and would wait to find out what Jamerson came up with. Jezalee knew they must have some hidden meaning since he shoved them in fake books where no one would be looking for them. Mallory said that Jamerson was the best in the business and had all the confidence in him to find out everything he could about Jim and everyone else in all they had found. The fake books were put back in their original places. They did a thorough walk-thru to make sure they did not forget anything or leave anything behind that was Jezalee's. Afterwards, they could not get out of there fast enough. Jezalee just wanted that penthouse and Jim to be a faded bad memory. She gave Mallory a hug and thanked her for being her shadow and helping her so much. They both walked to Mallory's car and sped away.

This was a pivotal moment, with the O'Malley's and Jezalee working closely together to work out a scheme they agreed on; the next step was for Jezalee to call Jim at work. She knew that was a call she was anxious to make, and it was the last call she'd ever make to him. Jezalee told Mallory, she had been deceived by two men in her life, and this was the last time that would ever happen again. Mallory looked at her and could only comfort her by her warm and gentle embrace and say how sorry she was for her going through such an inconceivable situation. They both knew that after what they found, there would be answers and when they came out, they knew Jezalee would have to deal with it head on.

Mallory drove Jezalee home to get some clothes for at least a month; they had no idea how long a process this would take for Jamerson to unravel Jim's past to find all the answers they needed. After Jezalee got her things packed, she called Nina and Joseph over to her house and knocked on Helga's door and asked her to follow her into the living room where Nina and Joseph were seated. She informed them she had to leave unexpectedly to Paris on business and was going directly to a retreat and wouldn't be back for several weeks. She felt miserable having to lie to them; but it had to be this way because of Jim. There was a possibility he would try to get in touch with one of them and that way they have the same information she was going to tell him. She asked Joseph and Nina if they minded staying in the main house while she is away so Helga would not be alone. They said they would take good care of Helga! Jezalee laughed and said to sleep in whatever bedrooms they wanted; just remember my motto, "our home, is your home, always," she also told them it was not necessary to bring any food over from their house unless they just wanted to. Jezalee asked them to eat up all the food in the refrigerator if they wanted to; if not, to pack it up and take it to the shelter where they donate food. She said there is tons of frozen meats and vegetables, take from there before you go spending money. She also left ten thousand dollars in the kitchen safe for Helga and the Johnson's to have in case they needed more food, for an emergency, or to go have fun. She felt so disloyal to her staff because she did not like what she was forced to say to them. Jezalee informed them she'd be going to a retreat in Paris after her business was finalized and would probably be back in a month.

After Jezalee got everything squared away with Helga, Joseph and Nina, Bob picked her up and dropped her off at the O'Malley's to spend a night or two with them until she went wherever David had planned for her. Jezalee made her way into the dining room where

Mallory had laid the rest of all the information and photos out that Jezalee was able to confiscate. They had decided to spread out the rest of the evidence they retrieved that day, and it would be ready for David to review when he arrived home from Los Angeles. Mallory had called David once again and asked what time he would arrive home for dinner. He said he would be home around 7:30 p.m. and was starving. She said she was going to put on ribeye steaks with all the trimmings and he said he was already salivating and could hardly wait to get home.

They decided not to wait for David to arrive before they went through all the items from Jim's place. They were too curious to wait any longer; impatience took over. The girls had placed everything in chronological order; everything fit on the eighteen-foot dining room table. "Good thing we did not use the ten-foot dining room table, there would not have been enough room with all the items you found," Mallory said.

As they read the items listed:

One birth certificate for Christopher Davidson

Born to George and Estelle Davidson, in Holland Michigan———-08-05-1945

Two birth certificates for Robert and Roland Anderson————-12-01-1949

{which happens to be Jim's birth date and year born}

Photo of two baby boys around one year old———————
dated 12-01-1950

Photo of two baby boys with a man and woman————-not dated

Driver's License for a Christopher Davidson————-Issue Date 08-05-1961

Address:162 La Brea Avenue, Los Angeles, CA

Height...5'9''

Weight...140 lbs.

Hair...Lt. Brown

Eyes...Blue

Birth date————————————————————————————
————————————————— 08-05-1945

News clippings of a Mr. Dodge Crocket & Mrs. Kate Crocket,

Burned to death in house which was completely disintegrated—02-05-1964

Couldn't identify body due to no dental records.

Crockets Rented the house from an elderly woman and she had their names on a receipt————————————————————————
————————————————10-01-1962

Photo of what appeared to be a teenage boy————————————
————-dated 1964

Photo of teenage Roland and Angela————————————————
————————dated 1965

Photo of a baseball team group photo with one boy circled————
dated 1965

Photo-high school yearbook-name Roland Anderson-Martin————
————-1966

{adopted by his dad's sister}

Photo—Robert Anderson-Martin/Angela Stewart/Grad.————06-03-1966

Photo of a teenage boy standing by a 1957 Chevy in————————
—————-1966

Photo of same girl-high school yearbook-name Angela Stewart——
—-1966

Photos-Wedding photo of Roland and Angela Stewart—————
09-10-1972

Photo of Roland, his wife Angela and son Robert————————
-12-24-1974

Photo Baby Robert's birthday with Angela and Roland—————-09-
02-1975

Photo says Angela and Roland holding Baby Robert——————-
09-30-1975

Photo Baby Robert's birthday with Angela and Roland—————-09-
02-1975

Newspaper articles on Roland Anderson-Martin————————
——————1979

Newspaper articles on Roland Anderson-Martin————————
——————1980

Newspaper articles on Roland and Angela Anderson-Martin————
——-1981

Driver's license from New York for Jim Stark——————Issued
06-23-1982

Birth date indicated 12-01-49

New clippings——-drowning-deaths-Wife-Angela/Son-Robert——08-
22-1982

Magazine articles on Jezalee:

Town and Country————————————————————————
—————————May Issue 1983

Forbes—————————————————————————————
————————————August Issue 1984

Vanity Fair—————————————————————————
———————December Issue 1984

W————————————————————————————————
————————————————————May Issue 1985

Jezalee and Paul's divorce settlement————————————————
dated 05-25-1986

My Dear Robert, 03-25-1973

It has been two months since I have heard from you; I hope you are
doing better. You mean so much to me and I want you to have a
happy life. You, locating my relatives for me is something I will
never forget, as long, as I live. As far as I am concerned, you will
always be my big brother and hero. We would not have known
anything if you had not found those news clippings; that changed my
life beyond any dream I could have ever imagined. You made all this
happen for me and now it is time for you to be as happy. Please
come live with me and my family; it would mean the world to the
three of us. Having you live in the same town would be good for
both of us. My mom and dad said you can stay with us as long, as
you want; if not forever. There is so much room in our huge,
rambling home; you would have your choice with whatever bedroom
you wanted and would not have to pay for anything. They asked me
to send a message and tell you, they will help you just like they did
for me. They are such an amazing, loving couple and they would
adopt you if you would let them. They are serious about helping
you! You see how much they have already managed to do for me. I
was reluctant at first to go to therapy; but it helped turn my entire life
to normalcy. It was hard at times, but nothing like what we endured
our entire childhood. I still go to therapy once or twice a month to
keep myself in check and it has been an amazing journey; that is

why I wanted you to experience what I have, with this wonderful chance in life I have been given.

I know you like going to the Manhattan Library every day and you have learned so much from all the reading you have done there; you are like a walking encyclopedia. I miss and want you to have what you deserve. My dear Belle and Jude want you to get a great education and they are willing to pay for it. The first moment they met you, they knew you were highly intelligent and were a good person that had been through a traumatic childhood with me.

I think I know why you are reluctant because you feel like you caused those monsters to want to sexually, verbally, and physically abused you and guilt sets in. Believe me! I felt the same way and it is all their sickness. That was the only way they could feel good about their sick selves; they attributed that to power over us. It was a blessing having a highly educated therapist in this field that helped me get through not only the guilt but the pain and suffering that came with it. You are a wonderful human being and I know you don't feel that way; but I want you to. All the abuse has been behind us a long time now. It does go away if you seek help. I seriously do not want you to be stubborn about this.

I feel awful that you were so brave; something I did not have within me. You took more abuse, so I would not cry so much; that told me from day one, you are a very caring person. You have lost your way due to those monsters and you are letting them still affect you. That is giving them the power even after they are dead. You are worthy of a great life like I am having, and I want you to be a part of something special and living here is exactly that.

One of the most wonderful moments of my life was when I walked into the courtroom with my Aunt Belle and Uncle Jude with the name Cathy Crocket and left the courtroom with them, now as my mom, and dad and my biological name Deanna Drake. You could be experiencing this too if you would contact your living relatives.

I do not want to stop typing this letter because it is a form of talking with you. I want you to get over what happened in our childhood. How badly we were inflicted with hate, deception, lies, knowing the

Crockett's were involved in criminal activity, thrived on abusing us, and saw to it we stayed uneducated, and being shut off from a normal, everyday existence.

I hope you come to my college graduation because I need you sitting side by side with my mom and dad. It is in three months; but I wanted to give you plenty of time to think about coming. I would be honored if you were sitting in the audience watching me get my diploma; it would mean everything to me. I hope to get a call from you real soon,

Love, from your sister Deana

After they had looked over everything and read Deanna's letter, they knew Jim was Robert. He was the twin that was obviously kidnapped from the murder scene. They now knew he had an identical twin brother that had survived that horrible night their parents were murdered. They were ready to turn over everything to Jamerson. When they read the letter, they were devastated to learn how the two of them were treated as children. Jezalee and Mallory agreed that Robert could have sociopathic tendencies; however, that would be determined after Jamerson digs deep into Robert's past.

Mallory motioned to Jezalee, why don't we go sit by the pool? I will get some iced tea out of the refrigerator and in the meantime, look in the pantry for some chips to go with the guacamole I made earlier. Let's just think about the beautiful weather and rest our weary minds until it is time for me to cook dinner. It was only 4:00 p.m. and they just wanted to try to calm themselves down after reading and seeing everything that Jezalee was able to find. They relaxed for a couple of hours, without a care in the world. They admitted how lonely it was without the children around but knew that they had so much fun during the summer months and wanted them to have what they deserved.

They were making plans after the children arrived home from their vacations. They wanted to go up to the Castle on the Mountain and spend a few days and decided Labor Day weekend would be a great time. Mallory said she wanted everyone to go up because she loved when there was a huge group. They sat outside until 6:00 p.m. and really enjoyed the quiet and beauty that surrounded them.

Once the gals went back in the house they went directly to the kitchen; Mallory asked Nell if she would join them for dinner; but she said she had a date. "Wait an Irish minute little lassie! When did this all happen and why have you not him before?" Mallory asked. I met him at the weekly Bingo game at St. Mary's; but did not want to jinx it until I knew one hundred percent he was going to show up. You know I am superstitious about such things," Nell remarked. "What may this lad's name be?" Mallory asked. "Ronan O'Reilly," Nell answered. "What does he do for a living?" Mallory asked. "He has owned a Crystal and China Shop for over twenty years," Nell answered. "Really?" As Mallory and Jezalee perked up! Well! "We may just have to check this shop out if you do not mind," Jezalee said. "By all means! he has the most beautiful merchandise," Nell commented. "What is the name of his shop and where is it located?" Mallory asked. "O'Reilly's Irish Crystal and China in San Francisco," Nell answered. "I have a set of Irish China, and crystal goblets from there; I bought them at least eight or nine years ago," Mallory commented. "I remember how excited you were when you bought that beautiful China and crystal; it is a small world after all," Nell said. "Has he ever been married? Jezalee asked. "Yes! Unfortunately, his beloved wife, Deidre, died three years ago from ovarian cancer," sadly, Nell said. "Tragic!" Mallory and Jezalee remarked. "She was his childhood sweetheart, and I am the first gal he has dated since her death," Nell said. "Does he have any children?" Jezalee asked. "Does he ever! Six, and I have met them all," Nell said with a smile on her face. "You are full of great surprises today. How and when did you meet them?" Mallory ask. "Remember a couple of weeks ago when I said I was going over to a friend's house?" Nell said. "Yes!" Mallory answered. "I went to meet Ronan's children and have dinner with them," Nell said. "You have been with us for over fifteen years, and we talk about everything, and this is something exciting that you forgot to fill us in on?" Mallory said with a smile. "I know! But! He is quite a guy and I told you! Superstition took over and now he is not a secret anymore," Nell commented. "Is he coming up to the house to pick you up?" Jezalee asked. "Yes! You will meet him in about ten minutes," Nell answered. Mallory and Jezalee looked at one another, smiled and walked over to Nell and gave her a hug. "It sounds like we need to add a few more people going to Incline Village with us on our next trip," Mallory suggested. Nell perked up and said, "that would be lovely." Five minutes later Ronan was ringing the doorbell and all three of them jumped. "Mallory asked Nell and Jezalee, go sit in the living room while she went to answer the door." She greeted Ronan and introduced herself. "Pleased to meet you, Mallory," Ronan replied. "Nell is in the living room; just follow me," Mallory said. He had brought her the most beautiful bouquet of her favorite flowers, white roses with lavender hydrangeas. Ronan walked into the living room, greeted the ladies; then went directly over to Nell and handed her the bouquet of flowers that he had arranged in an exquisite crystal vase. Nell thanked him, then gave Ronan a gentle kiss on his lips and said how gorgeous they were then took Ronan's hand and had him sit next to her as she sat the flowers on the coffee table. Mallory introduced Jezalee then asked if they would like a refreshing glass of lemonade. "That would be wonderful," Ronan replied. Jezalee and Nell said they would like a one as well. After Mallory served them their drinks, they chatted for about fifteen minutes then the couple left for their date. Once they were gone, Mallory sat there stunned and Jezalee felt the same way. Nell was family and they wanted her to be happy and Ronan was one great looking man and was well put together as Jezalee commented. She deserves a wonderful man, when her husband died ten years ago, we did not think she would ever recover from his loss. It must have been devastating to lose a spouse at such a young age. "I know with the help of your family you certainly played, a crucial, roll in her recover," Jezalee commented. "We tried our best; but no one can take the place of a loss like that," Mallory sadly replied. "That is so true!" Jezalee said.

Just as Mallory and Jezalee were taking the glasses and iced tea decanter back to the kitchen, David walked in from his grueling day in Los Angeles. Mallory asked him to have a seat at the table and at least have a glass of iced tea before he went up to shower and change clothes for dinner. He sat down, plopped his brief case on the table and welcomed the cold drink. "Who was that gentleman leaving with Nell?" David curiously asked. "It is Nell's official first date," Mallory answered. "When did she meet him?" David inquired. "At Church, on Bingo night, of all places and she has kept him a secret all this time," Mallory answered. "Well! You know how superstitious she is?" David commented. "That is for sure!" Mallory remarked. "Jezalee, how are you fairing?" David asked. "I feel much better now; a big weight has been lifted off my shoulders," Jezalee answered. "I know this is something the three of us did not see coming; but trust me, it will all work out in the end. You have been through too much and I feel so responsible for introducing Jim to you," an emotional David responded. "My goodness! David do not think that way! I am a big girl now and I have always thought something was missing after we had dated a few times. I think that is why I never felt truly close to him. He was a diversion from Paul for a few months; then, after that, all I thought of, was Paul," Jezalee admittedly said. "He had all of us fooled! None of us would have ever thought he was an imposter, much less, preying on you for your money and God knows what else he has done," Mallory replied with concern. "That is why I hired Jamerson; he gets to the nitty gritty in every situation. He will find out more than we probably want to know," David said.

Before they went to bed that night, which was late! Jezalee sat down with David and Mallory and could not thank them enough for all they had helped her with. "Lady, we are friends for life and will always help you no matter what," Mallory sincerely said. David let Jezalee know he had left a message on Paul's parents' phone, his brothers at the parish, and her parents to make sure if they did get a call from Jim to tell them she was in Paris on business and afterwards going to a retreat for a month. "I know Paul will not be back until July 5ᵗʰ from Africa; I will leave a message on his answer machine to call me because it is urgent," David said.

Jezalee asked how things worked with an investigator. David assured her Jamerson will take all copies of what we have here and will probably start from the news clippings from the newspapers. He will give it his top priority and will go through each and everything we gave him. Jamerson will research each photo, news clippings, driver's license, the letter, etc. This man leaves no stone unturned. He is highly educated, is a forensic psychologist and is respected in all aspects of the law. I have known him for years; we went to college together. He asked Jezalee if Jim had any of Paul and his family's phone numbers and as far as she knew he did not, unless he managed to find her personal phone book without her knowledge. David said he would make sure that Jim will not know where you are, other than some place in Paris. If he asks, we will tell him you are staying with a friend until you go on your retreat and you do not want to speak with him until you return to the states.

The next morning Jezalee joined David and Mallory for breakfast; they were ready to go over the day's plans. Mallory would drive Jezalee over to her house to get any last-minute items she may have overlooked. As much as David loved his weekends away from the office, he had to go into work on Saturday and Sunday due to the meetings he and Jim were in on Friday at the Los Angeles office. Jim came into work about an hour after David had arrived; he came into David's office, and they went over a few things, and nothing was said about Jezalee.

The gals had gotten Jezalee packed after she had picked up a few more essentials to add to her luggage. She said her goodbyes to Helga, Joseph, Nina and their three children. As she walked away from them, she still felt the guilt of not being able to tell them she was leaving for New York for her safety until they found out more about Jim. She also had informed the security guards that Jim was not allowed on the premise while she was gone. He was not allowed to talk to anyone that lived on the property. After the gals got back to Mallory's, Jezalee was afraid but did not want to show her weakness in front of her friend. She knew how meticulously David had planned out everything with the investigator and they knew the best way to keep her safe. They had no idea what may be uncovered about Jim and wasn't about to put Jezalee in jeopardy.

Jezalee knew it was crucial that she call Jim; she looked over at Mallory and said she needed to do it now and get it over with or she would chicken out. She asked Mallory if she would stay in the room, pen in hand and paper nearby, if she forgot something she needed to say. Mallory said she would be ready in case Jezalee had not said everything she needed to say. She could see that Jezalee had not been her usual self all morning and the quicker she called Jim the better off she would be.

Jezalee and Mallory sat down at the kitchen table and Jezalee dialed Jim's office. David had been in Jim's office going over the imports coming in from Spain when the phone rang. Jim asked Danielle, the receptionist who was calling on line 1, she indicated it was Jezalee. He thanked her! Jim immediately pushed line 1 and said, "Hi Jez," David motioned with his hands as he got up out of the chair to leave. Jim waved him to stay, so he sat back down. Jezalee took a deep breath and said, "I have to leave for Paris immediately to take care of some business." Jim wanted to know what kind of business. Jezalee said she needed to tie up some loose ends with Paul that was overlooked in their divorce settlement. "I thought you completed all transactions during the divorce," Jim was getting agitated and said. "We thought we did!" Jezalee answered back. "I do not know how you two could have overlooked anything, are you changing the terms of your divorce settlement?" Jim said sternly. "Jim, really! That is none of your concern; why do you care so much?" Jezalee spoke with authority and was beginning to get more nervous the longer she stayed on the phone; but was mad more than anything. "I am trying to recover from being sick and I take offense at you questioning me about my personal business; this trip is unavoidable and has to be taken care of immediately. We have known one another long enough and if you cannot trust me now, you never will; in fact, we need time apart to think where this friendship is going and you must know by now, you are treading into dangerous waters," Jezalee furiously said. "If that is the way you feel, fine! Go on your business trip and I will talk with you upon your return," Jim replied in anger. "I do not need your sarcasm or approval for permission to go anywhere! When I have personal things to take care of, they are off limits to you; I am not married to you and maybe I know why I never said yes to your proposal. While I am gone, I have one suggestion for you; do not ever quiz me again and never try to back me in a corner, or that will be the last time you will ever see me and my children again. I am not one of your business deals and I take offense to you asking me anything about what Paul and I did or did not do," as Jezalee sternly put him in his place. Jim sat back in his chair and was tearing up pieces of paper and throwing them all over the floor. She then hung up on him, sat back in the kitchen chair feeling like her blood was drained from her body. Mallory spoke up! "First off, thumbs up for putting that jerk in his place." The palms of Jezalee's hands were sweating like crazy she could hardly keep the receiver in her hands.

David was still in the room and was not quite sure what to say but he had to say something after hearing and seeing Jim's response to the phone conversation with Jezalee. "Jim, is everything okay with you and Jezalee?" David asked. "David, I will never understand women!" Jim answered. "I hear you!" David replied. Jim abruptly sat down in his leather office chair, threw his head back, as he hit the palm of his hand against his perspiring forehead, he then let out a gasp! "I do not know what just happened," frustrated Jim commented. "Jim, what in the world is going on?" David asked, acting concerned. "Well! For one, Jezalee's going to Paris and had never mentioned the trip until now. Secondly, she said she thought we needed some space and then hung up on me," Jim answered. "I guess I am to blame for all of this," David said. "You mean you knew about her trip?" Jim asked. "Yes, I did know Jezalee was going on an emergency trip to Paris and what it is for," David answered. "What is going on?" Jim asked. "Jim, we have known one another for four years and have been working side by side all this time; we have maintained a great working relationship and have acquired a friendship outside of the office; however, I draw the boundaries on, I never discuss anything that is of a confidential matter; believe me! Jim, it is not a big deal, both Paul and Jezalee neglected one important matter and when I was working closely with Jezalee and her attorney, this matter was never addressed. The situation recently surfaced and must be taken care of as soon as possible," David replied. "Jim, why the interest and questions in Jezalee and Paul's business?" David asked. "I do not know, I guess it is a matter of pride, I thought Jezalee, and I discussed everything," as Jim shrugged his shoulders and answered. "Jim, please do not worry about anything, she went through a terrible ordeal with Paul and as you well know she kept his infidelity from their children for over six agonizing months. Two people going through a loss of what was always a strong and loving marriage is understandable that they could not think of everything when the divorce settlement was being written up. Cut her some slack buddy!" David smiled at Jim and said. "You know David, I really appreciate you being such a good friend, to both Jezalee and me," Commented Jim. "Thank you, Jim! I care about both of you and hope everything will get back to normal when she comes back from her business trip and retreat," David replied. "What retreat?" Jim quickly spoke up. "While you were talking with her, she never mentioned she is going on a retreat for a month?'' David asked. "No! She left that out of the conversation," Jim irritatingly answered. "That's a surprise she did not mention it; Jezalee wanted to take advantage of being in Europe while the children are with their father. She said she needed time to herself after working on her books," David responded. Jim thought about what David said for a few minutes; then told him, he just realized she probably hung up on him because he was agitating her, and she did not feel it necessary to tell him anything else.

Jim had a gazed and forlorn look and told David, it had been six years since his wife and son drowned and I had buried the pain deep within. He never want that pain to take over his existence again. He had a wonderful wife and son; they were his world. When he got that call, they drowned, he thought his life drowned with them. He went into a deep depression, sold the places we had lived and loved in; he could not keep anything to remind him of the life he once had. She was his childhood sweetheart; he could not live on the East Coast any longer because that was their place. Everywhere he went reminded him of the life he once had. The best decision I ever made was coming to work for you. When you invited me to your Christmas party, I was not going to attend but to tell you the truth, my doorman, Gary talked me into it. I thanked him later and he was so happy when I told him I met the lady I would marry someday. When you introduced me to Jezalee was the first time I felt whole again. She lit up my dark world and it felt right, I was feeling good about myself. I carried so much guilt over my wife and son drowning, it was all my fault, I was supposed to be sailing with them that day but had an emergency meeting that could not be postponed.

Jim started fidgeting and said it seems as if he can never do things right, with Jezalee. David knew from that emotional speech that Jim was quite the actor and a person who does not have a conscience! David thought to himself, two can play this game and he knew so far, he had Jim fooled. "Jim, I cannot come close to imagining the horror and devastation a loss of the two people that meant everything to you," if you ever need to talk again, I am always here for you," David sullenly said. Both stood up, shook hands then gave a manly hug to one another. "Jim, I am sorry you and Jezalee had a disagreement, but everything will be okay," David said. Jim agreed that he was out of line and was feeling jealous and promised to push it aside and knew Jezalee was right about everything.

Created with Sketch.

The investigator, Jamerson arrived about an hour prior to the couple who would be escorting Jezalee across country. Before they arrived, he wanted to reassure Jezalee they have no knowledge of her situation; in fact, they have only been advised that you have an abusive husband that you need to flee from. They will not be advised of the particulars and are not allowed to ask you anything about your personal or professional life. The moment you meet them, you will be Sarah Sullivan, and remain with that name until we have all the answers. David has gone over what you retrieved from Robert's home, and I will do research from the documents given to me. We will begin to refer to him with his birth, Robert Anderson. You were very brave to obtain this vital information and know that I will do everything necessary to find out who this man is. You will be well taken care of; however, you must stay isolated and never answer a phone, or go out in public. I am sorry to meet you under stressful circumstances; but I feel as if I already know you quite a bit about you through David and Mallory. You are in good hands by knowing them and they have been extremely worried over what was found in Robert's home. David and I have meticulously set everything in place and there will be persons keeping you abreast of everything I unravel.

The doorbell rang and Mallory answered it; she introduced herself and asked the couple to follow her into the living room where Sarah and the men were seated. Jamerson introduced everyone then Mallory said dinner would be served in ten minutes. In the meantime, David and Jamerson took Jezalee's luggage to the rented SUV.

After Jezalee and the couple said their goodbyes, David and Mallory knew they had played their part; but she grabbed hold of her husband and started sobbing. David comforted her and reassured her that everything would be okay. There was one thing that they both had to be careful of and that was not to make any calls from their house or office to Jezalee. The trio left after it was dark so no one could see them. David had spoken to his parents, and they were nice enough to let Jezalee stay at their penthouse in Manhattan for as long as it took to get all the information they needed on Jim, or whoever he was. They knew she would be safe there and they their dear friend Mary would be checking in on her every day, when she went to work in Manhattan.

While Jezalee was riding across country, she had no idea she would be dropped off at three locations. She was not informed that her destination would be David's parents penthouse. It took forty-five hours to drive across country with the couple; one would sleep while the other drove, alternating their driving time. Jezalee was exhausted from sitting in the car for long stretches at a time; but she trusted David explicitly. The couple had been good to her, and she felt bad they had to drive non-stop to one of her destinations, Jamerson arranged to have Jezalee dropped off at a safe house in Philadelphia, Pennsylvania; he knew the lady who ran the safe house, and the drivers would not know that was not Jezalee's final, destination. The couple dropped her off, then an hour later she was taken by car to a farm in Redding, Connecticut, spent the night with a young couple and the next morning after they prepared breakfast for her, a car picked her up and dropped her off at Patrick and Kathleen O'Malley's penthouse in Manhattan.

By the time Jezalee arrived in Manhattan she was relieved of any more traveling for a while. When she arrived at the building, the doorman asked her name and who she was here to see. Jezalee gave him the name David said for her to use; my name is Sarah Sullivan; I am here to see Mary Donovan. The doorman, Oliver called Mary and she asked him to let her up to the penthouse. Oliver asked Sarah to follow him to the elevator as he took her luggage and rode up with her. The next thing she knew, she found herself standing face to face with a very lovely young woman. Mary had Oliver place Jezalee's luggage in one of the guest bedrooms. Jezalee walked over to Oliver, thanked him, and handed him a twenty-dollar tip; he thanked her for her kindness; but he handed it back to her and said that wouldn't be necessary. Before he walked to the elevator, he hoped she had a wonderful stay in Manhattan. Thank you so much Oliver," Jezalee said and shook his white gloved hand.

Mary started the conversation by letting her know that she is a friend of the O'Malley family and was happy to come every day before and after work to check on her. Jezalee told her it was not necessary; but it was so sweet of her. Mary let her know that the refrigerator, freezer, and cupboards are stocked as if she were cooking for an Army; so please cook till your heart's content. "If there is anything else you want or need, I will be happy to oblige," Mary said. Jezalee stopped, stood still, closed her eyes, took a deep breath through her nose, and happily took a whiff of that wonderful Irish aroma of corned beef and cabbage; looks like you have been busy with your culinary skills. "Well! I got some information through the grapevine that you love a good old-fashioned Irish meal," Mary replied. "So true! When I was growing up, I insisted my mom make corned beef and cabbage on a regular basis and she did just that. Thank you for this fantastic surprise," Jezalee said. "You are quite welcome! Whenever you are ready to eat, I will serve us a plentiful lunch," Mary said. Jezalee smiled and said she was ready for that delicious meal. As the two gals ate their lunch, Mary asked her to make a list of whatever she needs, and she will either go after she washes dishes or will be by in the morning before going to work. Mary informed Jezalee she would do the shopping and go on any errands that needed to be done. "You know! This is the first time since I started this journey from San Francisco that I finally feel safe," Jezalee admitted. "I am so relieved you arrived safe and in good spirits," Mary grinned and said. "I will feel a lot better after this is all over," Jezalee confessed. Mary agreed and took their empty plates to the kitchen. She let her know that her husband Eli would be calling David and Mallory to let them know she had arrived safely. Jezalee started to laugh and stated, "David and Mallory are such an amazing couple and have become such devoted friends to me and my children, they think of everything." Mary agreed! "I wish I had never met Robert. If she had my druthers, I would not be lying about being at a retreat, I would be there right now, without a care in the world," Jezalee said. "I know! Wouldn't that be the ultimate treat?" Mary agreed. "Absolutely!" Jezalee responded.

"Before I forget, David wanted you to know that he informed Jim that after your business trip you were going to a retreat. He was concerned Jim would think you would go to Italy and meet up with your family; maybe that will, prevent him from calling them, if he got their phone number," Mary informed Jezalee. "Well! If he did call, there and asked for me they would tell him exactly what they have been told, so I will not worry about that," Jezalee commented. "That is a good thing" Mary replied.

After lunch, Mary gave Jezalee a tour of the penthouse and let her choose which guest bedroom she wanted to sleep in. Jezalee was so at ease after meeting Oliver and Mary, it was certainly going to help being away from home and her children. She knew she had a great support system and realized how blessed she was to have people around her in a crisis of any kind. Mary insisted on washing the dishes while Jezalee unpacked and got settled.

Jezalee asked Mary how she knew the O'Malley's. Mary fondly said she met them in her freshman year at college in 1975; she was a volunteer for a fundraiser off campus at Children's Hospital in Oakland; Mallory headed the entire event, she liked me assisting her and asked to join her in future fundraisers. I proudly assisted her at museums, hospitals, hot lines, shelters, and soup kitchens in San Francisco, Berkeley to Oakland. David introduced me to my wonderful husband, Eli. "Oh! my goodness! It is all coming together now; I know you from conversations with David and Mallory; now that I think of it, you are in some of their framed photos in their family room and David's den. You are that sweet Mary they talk about!" Jezalee was happy to say. "In the Irish flesh! Mary grinned and said. "So sorry it did not click before now," an embarrassed Jezalee said. "That is understandable," Mary quipped with a tender smile. "You have two of the most beautiful children I have ever seen, Sarah and Casey, correct? Jezalee responded. "Thank you! Yes, they are with Eli as we speak," Mary proudly said. "I am keeping you from your family," Jezalee remarked. "Don't be silly! They are having a well-deserved vacation away from mommy and if I know my husband, he is spoiling them crazy good," Mary assured her. "I cannot believe we never were around when you came to visit David and Mallory," Jezalee commented. "I know! We come out once a year and we have missed you each time; you were either visiting other friends or family, or on a trip," Mary replied. "I will make sure the next time you come out that we make a point to be at home and maybe all of us can do some fun things together," Jezalee commented. "That would be wonderful!" Mary replied.

Jezalee asked Mary how she liked the living in Connecticut. "It was difficult taking a California born and raised gal and planting her on the East Coast. It took some adjusting but we do love it here now. I still miss the beauty of the Pacific Ocean; there's nothing more beautiful than Santa Cruz, Monterey, Carmel, Santa Barbara, Malibu, and La Jolla. We also love the San Francisco Bay Area and of course! My favorite people live there. I loved attending college in the Bay Area; and it was great living with the O'Malley's; I had my own luxurious room and did not have to share space with another student. They could not have been any more hospitable and loving; I went home twice a month on the weekends to visit my parents. I was born and raised in Santa Barbara and miss them terribly since we moved here. My parents and Eli's come out three or four times a year; watching the grandparents bond with our children has been such a joy for us. Eli's parents live in Ventura which is close to Santa Barbara, and they always get together and do things; we are fortunate they get along," Mary answered.

Mary called her husband Eli to ask him to call David right away; then call her back so she could say hi to the children. After Mary hung up, Jezalee said she did not need to spend the night in the city; especially since her children were so young. "It is for only two days, and they are probably jumping for joy that mommy is away," Mary said they will be fine.

Mary could see that Jezalee appeared tired so suggested if she wanted to take a nice hot shower or bath to relax before night-time comes, the linens were already sitting out in her room. Jezalee said she was too tired to do anything other than curl up in bed and sleep for about twelve hours. They hugged and said their good nights. As soon as Jezalee got under the covers, she was sound asleep.

When Eli called David, he was so relieved to hear from him and would wait for Jamerson to call him with updates. He and Mallory thanked him and Mary for helping them out in Jezalee crisis. Eli said they would do anything for them and happy to check on Jezalee since she is housebound. Afterwards, David called his parents, and they were relieved Jezalee finally arrived.

Jezalee woke up the next morning at 7:00 a.m., full of energy and wanted to feel free to go about her business in this electric city; she knew that was out of the question. After she took a shower, got dressed, made her bed, she could smell bacon and coffee. She made her way into the beautifully new designed kitchen and there was Mary as busy as could be preparing breakfast. "Good morning Mary, there is nothing better than smelling bacon and coffee in the morning," Jezalee said. "Good morning to you too!" Mary said as she flipped over the bacon. I hope you are hungry! "Yes! Very!" Jezalee answered. "Do you want to sit in the kitchen or dining room?" Mary asked. "The dining room with that spectacular view," Jezalee answered. Mary came over and gave Jezalee a hug and hoped she had a good night's sleep. "I did! That is the best sleep I have had in over a week. Now, if I could walk through Central Park, I would be in heaven," Jezalee commented. "I know what you mean! Central Park is very addictive and seductive; traveling across country without stopping help must have been exhausting," Mary replied. "That is so true; but don't get me wrong, I has been treated wonderfully by all of you; I just want it over; but it has just begun," Commented Jezalee. "It will not be long, as soon as Jamerson puts all the pieces to the puzzle together you will be back home," Mary replied.

After breakfast, Mary told Jezalee she would be off to work then would shop for whatever she needed. Jezalee said she had everything she needed and more. "Well! I thought I would pick up some magazines and newspapers for you to occupy your time; the television is in the sitting room and there is a grand library that Patrick has put together; so, you will not be without literature that is for sure. Oh! One more thing, the O'Malley's will be here tomorrow night; they would have been here to greet you; but they are finishing up a play in Westport, Connecticut and as soon as it is done, they will be here to welcome you personally to their home away from home. Have you seen them perform?" Mary asked. "Regretfully no! I hope to one day soon," Jezalee answered. "Well! They are fabulous on stage; I have seen every play and musical they have been in. I can hardly wait to see them again; they are such an interesting and beautiful couple. Eli and I went to see them in Westport, CT last week and they were outstanding. Too bad the play will be over tomorrow; you would have gotten a kick out of seeing them perform," Mary said. "Maybe one of these days they will come stay with David and Mallory all summer one year and perform on stage in San Francisco," Jezalee said. "That is a great idea! Run that by them when they come to see you," Mary requested. "I might do that!" Jezalee answered.

"Mary, are you still working at the Guggenheim Museum?" Jezalee asked. "Yes, five years and love it!" Mary answered. "Good for you! I was so pleased to hear that you are in the same line of work that I used to do, it is an amazing field to be in and there are no limits as-long-as you have the degrees for different positions," Jezalee remarked. Mary smiled and agreed. "What time will I see you this afternoon?" Jezalee asked. "I should be back around 2:00," Mary answered. "Are you going to have lunch; or would you like to come back here and have a late lunch with me?' Jezalee asked. "That sounds great, I will pick up something at whatever restaurant you would like," Mary answered. "No! Please! I cannot wait to get into the kitchen and throw a meal together, I love to cook, it is very therapeutic," Jezalee responded. "Sounds inviting so I will definitely come for lunch," Mary replied. "Have a great morning, Mary!" Jezalee said. "You, too! Mary, said as she waved goodbye.

Jezalee had always loved coming to New York, but it felt strange not being able to stay in her own place. She knew her tenants who signed a three-year lease were delayed moving into her penthouse; she had asked David if she could have stayed there; but it was out of the question. Not while Jamerson was doing a thorough investigation on Jim. David and Mallory were so protective of her, and she loved that about them; she was relieved that his parents' place being available for her.

Jezalee could not wait to come back to New York when she was not confined. She enjoyed coming here because she got caught up in the allure of this magnificent and magical city. She was thankful that Mallory and she had the same idea coming here for a week when they did; it was a great girl's getaway. Once she settled in San Francisco, Jezalee realized how much she had missed being in America. She thought back to the time when her parents decided to move to Connecticut; she was heartbroken leaving Manhattan. Jezalee always loved telling people she was born and raised in

Manhattan; she knew every inch of the city and to be cooped up knowing there is all that life going on beyond those walls, was a challenge for her. Her parents introduced her to all the places that made Manhattan unique; Radio City Music Hall, Ballet, Opera, Carnegie Hall, all the Museums, Statue of Liberty, Empire State Building, and the list went on. When she and Paul were students, after they went to Harvard; she went to at Yale in New Haven and he went to Columbia Business School in New York, they always managed to spend as much time as they could on the weekends in the Big Apple. They both marveled at how much there was always to do and explore. When they met at Harvard, they loved being in the Boston area, as well; it was a city with great architecture, great people, culturally stimulating.

Jezalee glanced around the O'Malley's penthouse and thought to herself; how lucky she was to be in the surroundings of extraordinary furnishings. It was very modern which normally would not be her taste; but Kathleen had a way of adding old world pieces and just enough traditional to make the penthouse intoxicating to the eye, it was filled with expensive artwork and antiques from their many travels abroad. Jezalee knew that if she had to be cooped up in a place; she could not imagine being more thrilled and delighted than spending her time in their, stunning surroundings. She could not wait for their arrival to let them know how much she loves their exquisite home.

Jezalee was almost finished in the kitchen, that was one place she always felt at home, no matter whose kitchen it was. She had decided to prepare a big meal for her and Mary; she wanted to pay her back in some small way for her hospitality and help in this sordid adventure. Jezalee had made enough food to take a plateful to Oliver, the doorman. Jezalee called down to Oliver and asked him to come up for a minute. When he came up, she handed him lunch wrapped up so it would stay hot for him. Oliver thanked her and said it was so kind of her.

It was 1:45 p.m. and Mary entered the penthouse with her arms loaded down with a variety of magazines, video tapes, tasteful goodies they could explore if their taste buds allowed it. After Mary got settled, she asked Jezalee, "What is that wonderful aroma from the kitchen?" "I have been busy putting together a fat feast for us. We have pork chop ala orange in mushrooms and wine sauce, chicken liver pate with herbs, cream cheese spinach with walnuts in a wine sauce, Carrot-raisin-pineapple coleslaw, carrots smothered in a lemon-orange-maple-brown sugar sauce, lime Jell-O with cottage cheese, nuts, fresh lemon and mixed with French Vanilla ice cream for a refreshing dessert. I hope you currently have the appetite of a trucker or football player, because there is lots to eat," Jezalee happily said. "I am starved and let us eat till our hearts and tummies are content! Mary remarked. "Sounds great to me! This is certainly lunch and dinner combined, too bad we could not go for a walk in Central Park, afterwards," Jezalee commented. "If you get too stuffed you can always exercise some of the calories off in their elaborate gym in the library," Mary grinned and said. "You are kidding? Right!" Jezalee said. "No! That was added during the remodeling, Patrick did not want the gym to be visible; so, it is behind the oversized bookcases and when you push a panel it opens-up to a gigantic exercise room. I completely forgot to show it to you!" Mary said. "You took me through every single room," Jezalee was puzzled. "It is a secret room; after we stuff ourselves, I will show you," Mary promised.

After eating their lunch, Mary took Jezalee to see the ultimate gym. Come! Let me show it to you. As they walked down the long hallway, Mary walked into the library, went over towards the bookcases, tapped the side of one of them and the bookcase moved towards her and Walla! There was the hidden gym. Jezalee gasped! They have thought of everything in this penthouse. I know where I am going to spend an hour or two a day. Thanks for showing this to me! It is something I am interested in doing at my home. My children will go wild over a gym like this.

As the girls sat around the dining room table, their conversations went from life in general, college days, marriage, children, and their friendships with the O'Malley's. They looked at each other and said, "Did we really eat our way to the next size dress?''

Mary was going to spend the night; but Jezalee insisted she go home to her family that needed her. She wanted Mary to embrace every minute she could with her children, and she would feel guilty if she kept her away from them. You need to be there to have dinner with them and to tuck them in bed. Trust me! They grow up too fast; I do not feel right taking you away from the precious time you need to share with them. So, Mary reluctantly left Jezalee and went home to her family with all the leftovers from their luncheon feast.

Jezalee curled up with a good book for a few hours then decided to watch a little television hoping it would help her fall asleep. She wanted to get up early the next day because Patrick and Kathleen were coming to stay for a couple of days. Jezalee looked forward to their company because they were such a wonderful couple. She was thinking back to the first time she met them; they opened-up their lovely estate in Connecticut when her children and she flew with the O'Malley family and stayed two days with them. As she tried to fall asleep her thoughts kept gravitating to Robert; she was thankful her intuition had kicked in to search in his apartment. Jezalee kept trying, to erase her thoughts about him; but her mind was out of control. She desperately wanted to fall asleep with good thoughts; since she could not succeed, she got up out of bed, walked to the living room and made herself comfortable in one of the chairs closest to the twenty-four-foot windows. Jezalee sat for a few minutes but wanted to get closer to see the luminous lights still glowing throughout Manhattan. She went back to the bedroom, grabbed a sweater in case it was cold and walked out on the terrace. Once Jezalee got settled in one of the many patios chairs she relaxed and enjoyed the late, night air. After absorbing the sounds of the city, she pushed the chair to lay back so she could look up at the beautiful, lucid stars; next thing she knew, the morning sun was beating down on her. She placed the chair back in an upward position and went inside.

Jezalee could not believe she had fallen asleep on the terrace and didn't wake up until the sun came up. She looked at the kitchen wall clock, it was 9:00, she knew it was time to get in full speed mode. Jezalee was so excited to see Patrick and Kathleen again, and knowing she would have some quality time with them. She made the bed, took a shower, then later brewed a fresh pot of coffee for starters. By the time she had her daily coffee and a little something, to eat, she was ready to start getting things done. The afternoon had finally arrived and Jezalee had made some hors d' oeuvres to have prior to having a later dinner. Mary stopped by for a short visit after she got off work; they had time to have coffee and pastries while they talked. She thanked Jezalee for forcing her to go home last night because the children were so happy to see her; she felt guilty thinking they did not need her. Mary left about an hour before Patrick and Kathleen arrived. When they arrived, Jezalee was thrilled that they would stay and keep her company for two days. The most difficult time was being isolated and having to lie to her children and her staff about where she was. Her children were so far away and now she could not even speak to them on the phone until they got back to Italy.

The doorman, Oliver, called up to Jezalee to announce the O'Malley's were on their way up. When they walked out of the elevator Jezalee was there to greet them and gave them a hug and kiss. They admired Jezalee for her bravery and were so glad they could help-out while Jamerson found out all he could on Robert. She was a part of their family and such a great addition; they thought she was one of the most beautiful women they had ever seen, besides their daughter-in-law of course! "I cannot believe I am welcoming you into your own home; it feels awkward to say the least," Jezalee said. "Dear! We want you to feel as if it is your place, as long as you need to be here," Kathleen remarked. "Thank you both! Now get in here and let us visit a while before I start our dinner," Jezalee said.

The rest of the day flew by and Jezalee was having the time of her life. She served the hors d' oeuvre's with her special nippy tea drink that people always raved about. Before Jezalee started dinner, they played Canasta, the three of them knew they were not the greatest of players; but they had fun trying. Later that evening Jezalee served dinner out on the terrace and the three of them talked for hours. The next morning, Patrick called his favorite restaurant and ordered breakfast for the three of them. They worked out in their gym, then after taking showers, they decided to watch a couple of movies they had agreed on. Kathleen insisted they order the rest of their meals out while they were there because she did not want Jezalee in the kitchen so they could have extra quality time together. The last day there, they sat around discussing all the places they had traveled and compared the different experiences they had at each place.

While Jim thought Jezalee was in Paris on business, he was trying to figure how he could expedite the two of them getting married. He knew he had to play hard; even thought of asking someone else out on a few dates. He read that if a man seems interested in another woman, it can make a woman jealous; he smiled as he thought of the idea and could not wait to see how it played out.

When Jim went to bed that night, his head was about to explode with so many ideas and knew he was going to get everything he wanted, no matter what he had to do to achieve it. He even fantasized about Alexander having a fatal accident and he would be at Jezalee's side to comfort her with the death of her son. He knew there were so many scenarios that he could come up with, that would bring them closer together. He could visualize her walking up the aisle to him, knowing he would eventually get rid of her as well. He knew now, he had handled everything the wrong way by proposing too soon.

Jezalee, David and Mallory would be overwhelmed at what and how he pulled off being Jim Stark. At times he would have a good laugh just thinking what he had accomplished without ever stepping into the halls of a school. He had Jezalee convinced how much he was in love with her, and he knew how great he was in bed with her. Little did he know that Jezalee thought he was terrible in bed; Jim thought he was playing the Romeo act without a flaw. He did not care what it took to marry her, it was going to happen. If he had to have sex with her multiple times a day, he was ready; he would moan like he was in ecstasy, if she only knew it just brought back visions of the Crockets raping him over-and-over-again. The next time he saw her he would lust after her and convince her of his undying love.

While Jezalee was gone, Mallory took care of her house to make sure the four guards were always on the premises and watched out for any break ins. They wanted Helga, Nina, Joseph and their three children to be safe while in the house without Jezalee. Mallory would invite them over to have different meals with them and Helga and Nina would reciprocate the gesture.

While Jezalee had worked diligently on her two books at home, she got contractual permission to use photos from various Museums around the world for the completion of her one book just a few days before her journey to New York. She finally had the photos arranged in the book. It was finally time to turn over all her hard work to her publisher. When Mary came over that morning Jezalee had all her typed pages and photos spread out on the kitchen table. Wow! "Someone has been busy,'' Mary commented. "Yes! A labor of love and I am finally done," Jezalee replied. "What an accomplishment," Mary said. "Thank you, Mary! I do need a huge favor from you," Jezalee said. "Name it!" Mary responded. "Do you mind calling my publisher in Manhattan and advise her that I am done with both books; I had an emergency in Paris and if she wants you to bring the finished material to her, while I am away, you could drop them off," Jezalee asked. "My goodness! Of course! I will be happy to take everything over for you. If, she asks any questions I will tell her you will be away for a month," Mary answered. Jezalee was so appreciative and thanked Mary for her help in the matter.

As the days went by, all Jezalee could concentrate on, was getting back home, surrounded by her family and friends. Patrick and Kathleen had stopped by to bring her a beautiful bouquet of flowers and the newest magazines on the stands; she was elated they came for a visit, but she also loved the thoughtful and unexpected gifts. They wanted to give her some great news, Jamerson was done interviewing the woman that had been kidnapped a year after Robert. She had given him enough evidence to have the police take over, he had recorded the entire session to hand over to the authorities. She was asked to come in person to the San Francisco Police Station and make a written statement. That was music to Jezalee ears; she told them that she felt sick to her stomach because she had dated that imposter but was so relieved to know she never had to see him again. According to the gal that was raised with him, they were constantly raped and beaten. They were both kidnapped by that sick couple, who constantly killed, conned, stole cars, and robbed people. He did one commendable gesture by getting that girl and him out of that environment. They had lived like that from such an early age, one and two years old; until he set fire to them and the shack. Dodge Crocket got Deanna pregnant, and Robert took her to get an abortion. He confessed to Deanna who he'd killed and why.

Jamerson was quite impressed meeting Deanna; with the therapy, hypnotism and love from her aunt and uncle, who adopted her, she was a success story. Deanna was determined to put what happened to her as a child; behind her. She made up for what she lost as a youth, in spades. Her family was her saving grace and they worked right along with the therapist to make sure she'd have the best care and love possible. She worked years on herself and met a wonderful man, got married and has two young children. Deanna tried so many times to convince Robert to seek help. He went too far, and he needs to be behind bars or in a psychiatric facility. From the times Deanna had spoken to him, she was not sure what to do but she was getting close to going to the police the day before Jamerson luckily found her. Robert, at the time he was confessing to the murders, he said he continually had unrelenting nightmares for years from all the abuse they suffered. Deanna said that was the first time he, spoke of that problem he was having. She pleaded for him to seek help.

Jamerson had asked why they had not gone to the police when they were old enough to know the Crockets were evil people. They told them their parents did not want them anymore and if they even tried to go to the police, they would kill their parents, then kill them. So, they were in constant fear but knew someday hopefully, they would be able to break away. Deanna was named Cathy and Robert was named Chris. Jezalee was stunned that there were people that evil. She was crying for both Robert and Deanna; no child should ever have to experience such abuse. Deanna did say that Robert felt like killing himself many times; but she was able to talk him out of it because she would want to know what she would do by herself. "Did those monsters force the two of them to have sex together?" Jezalee asked. "No! According to Jamerson, Deanna said the Crockets threatened them that the only two people they could be having sex with, would be with Kate and Dodge; the two of them raped both kids, not just Dodge with the girl and Kate with the boy; they crossed over to the same sex," Patrick answered. The three of them decided they needed to get off the topic of conversation and get something that they could relate to.

Days were going by faster than Jezalee anticipated and that was a good thing. She made sure she exercised every day; especially with her constantly eating more than usual. Jezalee had novels, current magazines, daily newspapers, and great company and was appreciative. She would read several novels and asked Mary to pick her up a few more from the library. Mary had picked up the list of books Jezalee asked for and was thrilled over all the reading she was able to get accomplished. Reading put her in a different world, as she figured it did for anyone who enjoyed the art of a good book or novel.

Created with Sketch.

David spoke to Jamerson and had arranged for Deanna to fly to San Francisco and would go directly to the hotel where he reserved a suite for her. David was so happy that she had been found because she was the link that was needed to get that guy behind bars. He asked Jamerson where he was having her stay and he said at the Fairmont Hotel. David said that was a good choice and made sure they bill him. Mallory and I would love to meet Deanna tomorrow after she is finished at the station. He said to meet them tomorrow evening around 6:00 p.m., that should give them plenty of time to get her confirmed statement.

As Deanna was getting comfortable on the plane, she was relieved but sad Robert would soon be behind bars. She knew he was a troubled, man with severe problems and could not kill another innocent person. Deanna knew it was the right thing to do and Jamerson thanked her for all the information and let her know that without her help he would be a free man that is very disturbed. He would be meeting her at the hotel, where she would be staying. The couple that accompanied her on the plane said they had a car waiting for them at the airport in San Francisco and they would take her to the hotel where Jamerson would meet her. As Deanna settled in her beautiful suite overlooking San Francisco Bay, she wanted this nightmare to be over with. She knew Robert would never forgive her; but she had to turn him in because she was afraid, he would do away with Jezalee like he did with his brother Roland and the rest. Every time she thought of the conversation Robert had with his twin brother, it made her blood curdle.

Deanna had put in her statement that one day about three weeks ago Robert called her and confessed everything; he knew he could trust her because of all they had gone through. She listened and could not believe that this man that she knew who saved them from the Crockets would do what he did.

Robert began bragging to Deanna about the macabre murders he had committed, in detail. She froze with fear, realizing he acted as if he had gotten a thrill out of what he accomplished. He had let her know he had changed his name to Jim Stark. He had a false driver's license, passport, and two businesses that he claimed he worked for, which did not exist. Jim was excited to say he was able to walk into the three banks where Roland did business and they thought it was him.

Robert called Roland's office pretending to be a business associate from one of the companies he consulted for. He had Roland's secretary see if he had an opening in a couple of days to come to their firm and she said yes so, he booked a phony appointment, and the secretary booked his flight then called his private limousine driver to take him to the airport. He was finally going to meet his twin brother in person.

Two days later, he knew Roland's driver would be waiting for him; so, he got to the driver thirty minutes prior to his twin brother coming out of his office. He approached the driver and said he came down a little early because he wanted to work on some papers in the car. His driver did not suspect anything because Robert was a mirror image of his brother. He anxiously slid into the back seat behind the driver, took a thin wire and choked him to death. He knew he had to hurry, he slid the dead driver to the passenger seat and drove around to an alleyway and dragged his body into the trunk. Robert was sweating profusely as he was going around the corner and managed to get the job done within five minutes to spare before Roland would come down. He had put a hat on, sunglasses and a phony mustache before his brother entered the car.

Roland greeted Ernest as he always did, got in the backseat, said hi then set his brief case next to himself. Once Roland was comfortable; he realized when the driver spoke it was not Ernest. He asked what happened to his driver and Robert said he had the flu and they called him to replace Ernest until he felt better. Roland thanked him for being on time and taking his driver's place.

As Robert drove, Roland was busy working on some papers; so, they did not speak much. When they got to the airport area Roland noticed he was going in a different way; he asked Robert if this were the right way they needed to go in, and he said it would get him closer to his destination. Roland didn't really pay attention because he was putting papers away that he'd been working on.

Robert stopped the car and Roland looked out the window and asked the driver what was going on, is there something wrong with the car? He proceeded to tell Roland to get out of the car. Robert got out first, as Roland was getting out, he stood facing Robert, he took his hat, mustache, and glasses off. "Brother, you look surprised," Robert said. "You look just like me, where have you been all these years; our family tried to find you for over twenty long and painful years?" Roland said. "Well! I certainly have not been living the dream life you have had." Replied Robert. He asked him if he had been kidnapped and he said yes and told him he had been mentally and sexually assaulted, beaten, and verbally abused by both of his abductors for fourteen long, grueling, and suffocating years. Roland looked at his brother for the first time and was devastated at what he had gone through. "If only there had been a way, they could have found you!" The FBI had been looking all those years as well. They were anticipating being able to obtain some leads, for the mere fact they were identical twins and would always have a photo of him," Roland commented. Robert informed his brother that his abductors never let him go to school and always lived far from anyone. He asked him how long ago he arrived in New York. Robert said he had been there since he was seventeen. "Why are you meeting me for the first time now, I would have been easy to find?" Obviously, you knew I eventually moved here, why didn't you want to call me?" Roland asked. Robert just glared at him and said nothing. "I need to catch an especially important flight in forty-five minutes; so, can we cut this short and set a date and time to meet? Roland asked. "You do not have an important meeting, I called and booked it with your secretary," Robert smirked as he told Roland the truth. Roland was getting nervous; but confused. "Isn't this an interesting way of meeting one another?" As Robert stared into Roland's eyes and said. Roland had no idea who he was dealing with. "Have you enjoyed your life, Roland?" Robert asked. "I have had a wonderful life; he said he was so young when their parents were murdered and never knew he had a twin brother until their aunt and uncle, who legally adopted him, told him when he was a teenager; a psychologist said it was detrimental for him to know everything that had happened. All I was told before I was a teenager; was that mom and dad died in a car crash," Roland explained. This made Robert even madder, disoriented, full of hate, he pulled out his gun and informed Roland he did not need to live any longer, he had a good life long enough and that would be behind him. He also bragged that he had choked his driver to death and would kill his wife and kid within less than twenty-four hours. Roland just gave him a stare and did not know how to approach the situation he was in. He was more than devastated to say the least.

Roland's head was whirling with fright, he had no place to turn or run to, he looked Robert straight in the eyes and tried to talk him down; but he could tell by his demeanor he would be shot soon. Roland did not have a way to defend himself. All that was flashing before him now was knowing that feeling their parents must have had realizing it was the end of their lives. One shot and they succumbed to their tragic deaths. Robert said, "It is my time to have the life you have had all these years," So long brother! Before Robert pulled the trigger that would enter his brother's heart, Roland closed his eyes to see a vision of his family before him, he did not want the last person he would see be the monster his brother was. He had a smile on his face as their images flashed before him; his loving wife and adorable son, who he treasured more than life itself. As he gasped for breath, he whispered goodbye to them; his good life came to an end. Roland slumped to the ground as he took his last breath on earth. Robert pulled the trigger one more time and the bullet went through the dead brother's head. Robert dragged him to the back seat of the car and drove off to a remote place where he had pre-dug Roland's grave, the day before. After he rolled him into the empty grave, he began filling with the wet dirt; he proceeded to get back in the car and make his way towards his rental car hidden in the bushes. Now, he would take care of Ernest's dead body. Robert had bleach, three containers of gas and matches to make sure there was no trace of him being there. Once he lit the matches, saw the vehicle burning, he said good riddance to Ernest, the driver and smiled as he walked away.

The day prior to murdering Ernest and his brother Roland, he rented a car in Manhattan, made sure he wore-gloves-at-all-times. He found the perfect spot to dig his brothers' grave. Once that was done, he sawed off some branches to cover the grave so it wouldn't be visible. He left a note on the car, that the battery was dead. He went afoot to a nearby gas station that was over a mile away; from there he called a cab to take him back into Manhattan and went back to his apartment anxiously awaiting seeing his brother in person the following day.

The day after he successfully murdered Ernest and Roland; he was keeping his promise to his brother. Robert got to the boat hours before he knew Roland's wife and son would be there. He had everything in place, he had put on thick gloves before he boarded the boat. Now! He was ready to get rid of any trace of Roland's existence. He knew that Roland's wife and son would go out early in the morning, on their boat that day, and he was prepared. When they came aboard, Robert jumped out of hiding, they immediately thought it was Roland surprising them and were filled with amazement that he could join them; until he grabbed the boy and made him fall and hit his head and knocked him unconscious. His mom tried to pick up something big enough to swing at Robert but missed and he pushed her down; he then dragged her to the side of the boat where he could tie her up so she could not get away. He then said! Just so you know, I saw Roland yesterday and told him I was going to kill you and your son today. I killed Roland right after that! I let him know, you two were next. Now! You are going to watch your son drown and if you close your eyes; I will brutally beat his body before I throw him overboard. Roland's wife was screaming at the top of her lungs with terror in her eyes, but she did not want her son to have a worse death than Robert had already planned. As she had tears streaming down her face, and crying out loud, she had to watch this monster as she called him, pick up her son's body, turn him upside down while he was now finally conscious enough to yell help mom! Robert just kept submerging his head down in a large bucket of the water he had placed near where he knocked him down. The boy took his last breath a few minutes later; his mom tried to look around and see if there was anyone else in the water that would be able to hear her screams but there was not a boat or a human being in sight. He hurried over to her, hit her head with a blunt object and blood gushed everywhere; so, he knew now he needed to get the boat in motion and go out as far as he could, then throw their bodies overboard. Once he accomplished that, he had to make sure he made a clean sweep of the areas he had been in and around. When he got ready to dive into the ocean, he taped the blunt object that he killed her with, to his back and had to wrap the tape several times around his torso so it would stay secure. He would not leave any evidence that Angela was hit with anything, and it would look as if she slipped on board, hit her head, and fell in. He had gone out five miles, far enough that it would more than likely be awhile before someone spotted the boat. He was exhausted, out of breath after swimming for four hours. He knew he might not have lasted in the ocean for that length of time; but he had been actively building up his strength over the years and was fit. The evidence was still wrapped securely on his back, and he took it off as soon as he was on dry land. He pulled a knife out of his zippered jacket pocket and cut the blunt object from off his back. He was lucky that day because there was not anyone on the beach because the weather was dismal and gray and forecast said it would be raining all day into the next morning. When he got back into Manhattan; he walked through Central Park, dumped the evidence into a garbage can and walked away smiling. He was finally rid of any trace of his brother and his family.

After he confessed to all of that, Deanna was frightened to go to the police for fear he would come after her family. She knew that after killing four people in two days, he was dangerous, and she feared for her life.

In the beginning Deanna did not know a lot about Robert's life; other than enjoying his nice apartment, loving all the restaurants and street vendors in Manhattan. He did not want any friends; he unequivocally told her that she and her parents were the only friends he needed, and he loved them. Deanna would go with Belle and Jude to see him usually four times a year and the four of them would have a great time visiting; he was a great conversationalist with the three of them and was happy to see them. Jude was fascinated that Robert was knowledgeable on any subject that was brought up. Robert was so sweet to them, and he never complained about anything. He was always meticulous about himself and his apartment; he took pride in his surroundings. He always cleaned up after the Crockets and wanted our surroundings to be clean. The Crockets would invariably make fun of him; but he still did. She had pleaded with him to go for help as she did; he was still afraid to discuss his childhood with anyone other than her. Deanna asked him many times to move to Florida with her and her family; but he would not do it. She let Jamerson know that her mom and dad, paid for a beautiful apartment in Midtown Manhattan for Robert from 1967 until he left for San Francisco in 1985. Since he would not take them up on their original offer to do what they did for her, the least they could do was pay for his apartment all those years. Anytime he called her, he was so nice, and sincere about their friendship but knew he was embarrassed by what the Crockets did to them.

Before Deanna met with David and Mallory, Jamerson had taken her to the police station; while they were waiting for her to give her statement, she had remembered one other person he confessed to killing. Jamerson was upset that she had forgotten such an important thing! She apologized profusely and was embarrassed by the oversight. He was sorry he reacted strongly towards her for that one moment. He wrote down the name of the person, turned on the recorder and had her add Charles Dandridge to the list, which at this point, made seven people he killed, which included the Crockets. Once Deanna was called in, Jamerson sat and waited until she was done giving her statement to the police. Officer Robertson came out and thanked Jamerson for all the leg work he had done on the case and all the evidence that Deanna was able to give them.

When Jamerson and Deanna met with David and Mallory for dinner that evening, they found out that Robert had called her about five weeks after the boating accident happened to say he had met Roland and his family for lunch the week before the tragic accident. He proceeded to tell her, after the boating accident Roland could not stay in New York or Cape Cod anymore. After the funeral, everything he looked at, went to or did, reminded him of his wife and son. Roland felt as if he was swimming in a pool of sewage and kept sinking further and further. He asked Robert if they could have lunch one day and he said, "Of course!" They met for lunch the next day and Robert indicated his brother was moving as far away as possible to start a new life. At the time he told Deanna the story, he said Roland had informed him he was leaving in a few days and would not be back. Roland explained to Robert he had a gift for him, and it was only fair because he felt so guilty that his twin did not have a privileged life as he did. Roland handed over six million dollars in cash to him. Robert told her he was shocked when his brother gave him that much money. According to him, Roland also handed over a quit claim deed in Robert's name for both his residences. He had a notary stop by the restaurant so Robert could sign in front of him. He then gave him the keys to both his cars, and he had his housekeeper pack up all his clothes and shoes and they would deliver them to him when he got settled in a new place. At the time he was talking to Deanna, about all this, he told her he was so happy to have finally met his brother. According to Robert, after they ate lunch, Roland asked Robert if it was okay, he called him once he settled into a place. He said that would be great and they said their goodbyes and parted ways. Roland had given Robert the names, addresses, and phone numbers of all their relatives but after Roland left; he did not feel right about having a relationship with any of them because too many years had passed. Deanna told David and Mallory she had really believed Robert because when they talked, he said he was in constant communication with his brother and they saw one another whenever he came into New York; however, when he had called her three weeks ago, he confessed that he killed his brother's driver then his brother. He said he was proud of what he had gotten away with. "What was your reaction when he told you?" David said. "Well, I was stunned but acted like it was no big thing. I got him to tell me where he buried his brother's body and what he did with the driver's body. I told him to be careful because I did not want anything happening to him. I eventually changed the subject and asked when he was coming for a visit because her children kept asking about him. When he confessed to those two murders, he began to boast about how easy it was to murder Roland's son and wife in that order. I did everything I could to not react on the phone. I was mortified at what had become of my true hero from all those years when we were young. After that phone call I was gasping for air, I felt I was suffocating, and was sick to my stomach, every day and night after his call, I came closer and closer to calling the police. I started writing down everything I could remember, so I would have all the information to give to the police. Thankfully, Jamerson showed up before I got up enough nerve to walk into the police station. I think speaking with him was easier to tell him the whole story first." Commented Deanna. Jamerson added that while they were at the station Deanna had mentioned one more victim that she had forgotten about, a Charles Dandridge. Jamerson looked at David, as he slumped over and covered his face with both hands; he saw that he was crying. He asked David if he was okay and he immediately said "NO," far from being okay. Charles was one of my best friends, he worked for me and was killed by a hit and run driver they never found. Jim did this to him! He is obviously the monster the Crockets wanted him to be. Charles was one of the most decent human beings a person could ever meet and have the privilege to know. He was my professor at college and my mentor. He worked alongside me for years after he decided to retire early from teaching. He was a second father to me! Mallory, and Deanna both shedding tears and shaking. Mallory got up from her chair and asked Deanna if she would like to go to the ladies, room and she said yes. She motioned for Deanna to follow her. When the ladies got back to the table David apologized for his reaction; but; to know that Jim Stark, AKA Robert, killed a man to get a job with his company was unfathomable. I befriended Robert like he was sibling I never had; this was devastating news. Deanna thanked them for their hospitality and said she would only be relieved when Robert was sent to prison and prayed, he would never get out. "I cannot imagine he will ever see society again; he will either be in a cell, or in an asylum; he has already confessed to the six murders, and they are going to question him tomorrow about Charles Dandridge," Jamerson said. Before Deanna had boarded her flight to Miami, Jamerson informed her Robert was staying in jail without bail, the prosecution said he was a flight risk. He let her know that the FBI was out at the site with a forensics team, digging up Roland and from what Deanna said in her statement, they saw the limousine that he had torched, and the remains of the driver's body was in the trunk just as she said it would be. They were trying to take samples of any evidence that would help their case; the burned victims, teeth would be the only way they could make a positive identification of him.

When Deanna arrived home her husband Eric was playing with their children, and she walked in his direction and grabbed him for a minute and said she was so happy to be home and in his arms. Eric asked her if there was a date set for the trial yet?" Deanna let him know there would be no trial because he confessed to all the murders, and they have my statement and with the dates and times he called me and confessed over the phone. It is just a matter of the victim's families wanting to have their day in court in front of the Judge. That may take months, depending on how backed up the court is with cases. "While you were away, I was able to hire a manager for our second bakery; so, I will be able to come and go whenever," Commented Eric with a smile. Deanna was thrilled he had finally found someone that could take over the heavy responsibilities so he wouldn't be tied down. They were financially doing great; they paid off their mortgage and car loans and set money aside for emergencies. Her parents had been very generous in getting them started, plus they had set aside money for their college education.

Created with Sketch.

David had been alerted by Jamerson that evening, the FBI, and a SWAT team would be arriving at his office and surrounding the enter building tomorrow morning. I informed them it would be much easier at his workplace, and they agreed. I let them what time you said he usually comes in. So, expect them tomorrow morning any time after 9:00-11:00 o'clock.

When David and Mallory got up the next morning; they were nervous and did not feel much like having breakfast. After David finding out Jim was the hit and run driver that killed Charles; it had been overwhelming for David to even hear Jim's or Robert' names mentioned, whatever he should be called, without getting sick to his stomach. They each had a cup of tea and spoke for just a few minutes because he wanted to get to work earlier than usual. Mallory stood up from the table when David got up and asked him to be careful and stay as far away from Jim as he could, without being suspicious. He assured her he would do just that, and they kissed goodbye. He wanted to get some important business out of the way before all hell broke loose. Jim had come in at his usual time and David went over a few things like he always did. The authorities knew when Jim would be at work, so it was just a matter of time, and they would be walking through the office doors to take Jim away.

That day was the most taxing day David could ever face; knowing he gave Charles' job to his killer. And! To think he had befriended Jim and welcomed him into his company and home; he was basically part of an extended family, so to speak.

It was almost over so Jezalee, Paul, her kids and everyone that helped in this process could feel safe. At 10:30 a.m., Jim was in his office getting a lot of his work out of the way. David was in his, hoping the police would hurry and get this guy out of their lives. Mallory was pacing back and forth in her kitchen and was desperate to hear from David; but she knew not to call yet, in the meantime, Jezalee was trying to visualize Jim getting arrested and going away for good. On July 3, Monday, at 10:55 a.m. California time, the SWAT team and FBI came through David's building very quietly and made their way to the floor David and Jim were on; at this point, they hurried down to where their two offices were. David made sure his office door was open and he motioned to them that Jim was in the next room. They had posted the SWAT team and the FBI at all entrances and exits; when they got to Jim's office, they quickly opened the door and surprisingly he was calm and just asked, "How can I help you?" The one FBI agent looked at him while five others blocked the door. He demanded Jim put his hands above his head, and walk towards the wall, another agent came over and handcuffed him. At this point, he said, "What the hell is going on?" He had no idea they were there for him. Robert Anderson, you are under arrest for the murders of Angela, Robert and Roland Anderson-Martin, Charles Dandridge, Dodge and Kate Crockett, and Ernest Norton; they read him his Miranda rights and carted him off. As they were taking him away, David was in the hall and looked disgusted at him; he called Mallory immediately. She wanted to know when Jezalee would be able to come home. Jezalee could return home until Jim was arraigned and hopefully does not make bail. As David peered out the office window from the 40th floor, he could barely see the SWAT team or the FBI cars and vans leaving with Jim. He knew Jim had enough money to get the best attorney money could buy. He was silently praying that he would not make bail. Even though the Crockets were monsters, he would be charged for them dying in the fire he had started; it would be considered premeditated murder. There certainly was not any evidence that Robert had killed them, much less started the fire, but with Deanna's statement, watching

Robert put the plan in motion and see it materialize, that was enough to initially arrest him. She went over every sordid detail that she could remember while she was held captive by the Crockets. Jamerson called Deanna to inform her Robert had been arrested; he thanked her once again for all her help and he would be call with updates. He will find out more when he is arraigned. Jamerson wanted her to feel at ease because he will be sitting in that courtroom and can't imagine him getting bail.

David called Mallory immediately and said he would have Jamerson find out from some of the guys at the precinct, what would be his odds of getting out on bail. As soon as he is set for arraignment, they can let Jamerson know what Judge will be in court. Mallory asked if that made a difference what judge he gets. David said it absolutely does, plus the fact he is charged with seven murders that Deanna knows of. They have the tape recordings from Jamerson that he took of Deanna plus her written statement; that should be a guarantee he cannot make bail. Let me hang up now and call Jamerson, I will be leaving work in a couple of hours. David put a call into Jamerson and said the authorities just left about fifteen minutes ago with Jim in handcuffs. Jamerson had put a call into the precinct and his buddy said Jim aka Robert was be questioned and booked.

David walked into the kitchen while Nell and Mallory were preparing dinner. Mallory came towards him with open arms and gave him a hug and kissed his whiskered cheeks. David walked over to his second favorite cook and gave her a kiss. Nell smiled then put her arms around him and said thanks boss. While Mallory was sauteing mushrooms, she asked David what was going on with Robert and he said that the District Attorney's office called, and the defense attorney would like to meet with us on Friday and discuss Robert. Mallory commented, I thought he had some high-priced attorney from Broadhurst, Johnson and Strickland law offices. I did too! I did not question him, and we will find out more about the switch on Friday.

Mallory and David went up to their bedroom early. Before they got in bed they sat over in their sitting area and discussed the situation about Robert. They were thrilled that the children loved camp so much they were away while all this was happening. They hoped by the time they came home there would not be anything in the newspapers or television, to alert them knowing anything about Jim. After they finished talking, they took a shower together then got in bed and read a little before dosing off.

It was July 4th, the children were at camp, and the O'Malley's, their staff, and Jezalee's staff barbecued, did a little swimming then went to see the fireworks. Everyone had a great time and wished the others had been home for the fireworks with them.

Jezalee could hear and see some of the fireworks from the O'Malley's terrace. Here she was thousands of miles away from her home and the children were in a different country. Patrick and Kathleen made a point to spend that evening with Jezalee and watch the fireworks with her.

Robert made a call to his attorney, Albert Frank, but he informed him, he was no longer representing him. Robert started yelling on the phone and wanted to know why he changed his mind. The attorney waited until Robert calmed down to let him know his check bounced. Robert was fuming and said it must be a mistake because I have a lot of money in several accounts. Albert proceeded to inform him that according to the Prosecutor, temporarily all Roberts funds were frozen. He went ballistic and told the attorney they cannot do that to me! I earned that money. They know you have earned money since you've been employed for the last four years but according to your bank records, you came to San Francisco with money that you took from your dead brother who was murdered, and you have been charged for his demise. I suggest after we hang up, you make a call to the District Attorney's office and request a defense attorney, I am officially off your case. Robert went back to his cell and was seething; every day all he did was pace back and forth for hours. He was agitating other inmates with his boisterous behavior, so they moved him to another area and warned to keep to himself.

That afternoon a defense attorney, Jesse Stoneridge, met with Robert and informed him that the prosecuting team had enough evidence on him to ask for the death penalty. After they spoke, Jesse read through his case, and I thought he could have him plead insanity. He indicated he would be bringing in a psychiatrist. "No way!" Robert snapped at him and said. "You will definitely be convicted, possibly go on death row and end up dying by lethal gas," The attorney looked at him and said. "Secondly, if you do not let me try this case the way I see fit, you will die. "I am telling you, under no circumstances will I end up in a looney bin." Robert slumped down in his chair and said. The attorney glared into his eyes and told him; he would probably go into an asylum for a-period-of-time but could possibly work his way back into society. Robert told Stoneridge that for fourteen years he felt like he was living in an asylum with two monsters, and he would opt for the death penalty over that. When Deanna and I broke away from the torture they put us through, I promised myself that I would never be exposed to such nutcases ever again. And! You want me to walk right into a place where they constantly drug people, where they walk around in a daze not knowing who they are, much less where they are. The attorney knew from what he read that Robert's life had been a living hell and it may have attributed to him becoming a serial killer. Stoneridge informed him, he still had to meet with a psychiatrist and have his session documented. Will you, at least, agree to that? Robert stood up from the hard-wooden chair and said he wanted to go back to his cell and walked away.

Robert was nervous behind bars, and he paced constantly. Some of the other guys would tell him to knock it off because it was driving them mad. "Do you want me to kill you too?" He would always tell them. "Good luck with that Mr. Death row," they yelled out. He could not seem to fit in with the rest of the inmates, so he pretty much tried to stay away from them as much as possible. His attorney, Jesse Stoneridge had set up a meeting with a psychiatrist and Robert was not pleased; but there were some things he knew he had to do. He had to be there in a few minutes; so, he was trying to calm himself down.

When Jesse arrived with Dr. Pendulum, he introduced them to one another and said he would return in an hour. As the Dr. asked Robert questions, he was sweating profusely and wanted to reach out and strangle him. He would look at him then at the guard on duty and thought he had better be on his best behavior. He knew one thing! He was not going to some insane asylum. He answered the questions with intelligence and let the doctor know he knew what he was doing and would take responsibility for all seven murders they were charging him for. He did confess that there was a seventh one; a Mr. Charles Dandridge and he told him he killed him in a hit and run because he wanted his job. The Dr. asked him if he got the job and he said absolutely. The doctor could tell that Robert was extremely agitated, Jesse had filled him in on the fact that he had rather be on death row then a mental institution. After most of the questions were answered, Dr. Pendulum asked him to write a summary of his childhood, escaping, surviving as a teenager into adulthood. He asked him why he killed each person and was there anyone else he had planned to kill prior to his arrest. As the doctor was putting all his paperwork away, Robert said to him, I did what I had planned out and I accept the consequences. At the end of the session, Dr. Pendulum stood up and thanked him for his co-operation and left. The session had taken over two hours and Jesse remain outside the guarded room until they were finished.

As Robert stayed chained to the metal table that was bolted to the floor, he saw Jesse walk towards the door but paused to have a short conversation with Dr. Pendulum. Jesse walked in, sat down in the chair across from Robert, and asked him how he was. Robert said he was glad that was over, and he wanted to go back to his cell. "In due time," Jesse said. "I spoke briefly with Dr. Pendulum, and he indicated you confessed you would have killed Jezalee Albanese when the time was right. He also mentioned that you wanted to marry her for all her money. You do realize that if she had ever married you, she would have had a prenuptial agreement written up; you would never have been able to get close to her money, dead or alive. Did you know she is one of the richest women in the World! She is a billionaire! She and her husband made their money from scratch," Jesse said. "Yes! I know that!" Robert said sarcastically. "You also indicated if she would not marry you, her son Alexander would have been your next victim then you would be there to console her, prior to killing her," this is sad to know Jesse said. When Dr. Pendulum faxes over the session he had with you, I will review it then go over it with you in a few days. Dr. Pendulum will of course! give his recommendation and the two of us will go over that as well. Robert shook his chains that were around his ankles and said he just wanted to go back to his cell. Jesse said, "no problem! I will get the guard to take you back. The disillusioned attorney walked away for the first time feeling such empathy for a man who had killed seven people. He knew going into this case was going to be tough; every page he read was worse than the next. He read Deanna's statement over and over and wept just visualizing what she and Robert had to endure from toddlers to teens. When he got to his car, he slid in the front seat, but before driving off, he pulled out his worn and tattered wallet that he never wanted to replace because his children had given it to him for Christmas years ago. He opened-up his wallet and pulled out several of the photos he had of his four children and his wife. He stared at their cute, adorable, and happy faces. He and his wife had been so blessed having these four wonderful children. As he kept looking at the photos, he realized that Robert and Deanna never had photos taken and they had lived a life that no one should have to experience. He could tell by Deanna's statement; she came out a heck of a lot better than Robert; if only she had been able to convince him to get the same treatment.

All Jesse wanted to do was go home and see his wife and kids. He knew this was the worst-case scenario of a case for him and whatever was going to happen, it was a no win, no win outcome. The attorney wanted to meet with his employer-friend David and Jezalee, a lady Robert had proposed to. After the attorney spent some time with his family, he went back to the office to put a call into David and Jezalee. David was in his study at home when the phone rang, he answered it and the attorney introduced himself, "My name is Jesse Stoneridge, I am representing Robert Anderson and would like to meet with you and Jezalee at your convenience, of course! David replied, that sounds good, Jezalee will not be back for a couple of days, she is in New York as we speak. "Do you want to set up a tentative date and time, and we can play it by ear?' Said Jesse. "That would be great." Answered David. "How, about Wednesday at 2:00-4:00?" Asked Jesse. "Perfect, Jezalee should be back late Sunday night, this way she can get acclimated back into her schedule and be rested and ready to answer any questions you may have for her." Commented David. "Mr. Stoneridge, would you like to see me before this weekend?" David said. "Yes, I would like that, I have Friday open between the hours of 10:00 a.m. to 2:00 p.m." Jesse replied. "I can come in at 10:00 a.m., I would like to bring my wife Mallory, if that is okay with you," Stated David. Jesse agreed to see them.

Everything Robert had told her was exactly what happened; and the prosecutor now knew that he had murdered seven people. Now that they had the information on Charles Dandridge, they pulled his file and was looking once again at the photos of his car he had been driving. They would check to see if a "Jim Stark" had rented a car during that time and check out all the car rental agencies and mechanic shops. Two days later, Jamerson called David, then Deanna; he found through his sources that if Robert were found guilty, the prosecutors would plead for the death penalty.

David called his parents and Eli to let them know Robert had been officially charged on seven counts of murder. David let Eli know that his parents were going to drive to the city and give that message in person to Jezalee. Since his parents wanted to know all the details; he faxed all the information from the statement given by Deanna. His parents quickly got in their car and couldn't wait to get there with the news; as Patrick drove, Kathleen read the statement and it was terrifying at the least. They called up to the penthouse and Mary answered. Patrick and Kathleen said they were downstairs and will be up in a minute with an important update on Robert.

Mary ran to get Jezalee, who was in the gym exercising. The gals came out of the library and Patrick and Kathleen had just walked in; "Hi, this is a pleasant surprise?" Jezalee said. "We wanted to let you know in person, they have all the evidence they needed to charge Robert with seven counts of murder she blurted it out," as Kathleen was grinning from ear to ear.

Jezalee was absolutely stunned! How did they get the evidence? The girl that had been raised with him came to San Francisco after Jamerson took her statements. Robert had confessed to her three weeks ago to murdering his brother's driver Ernest, Roland, Roland's wife and son, and Charles Dandridge. "Oh No! Charles is the gentleman that David said worked for him was killed by a hit and run driver. He murdered him to get his job and he succeeded. Five innocent lives gone." Jezalee sadly said.

They left Jezalee alone so she could read all the sordid details of each murder; she was thinking how close she may have been to being murdered by him. What a twisted, manipulative, and evil mind. As she read through the statement, she picked up that he was most likely a sociopath. By the time she finished reading what he had done to each victim; she was sick to her stomach and ran to the bathroom and threw up. She looked in the mirror and for a split second saw a frightened woman looking back at her and she broke down in hysterics. Kathleen ran to the bathroom to make sure Jezalee was okay. She stayed with her until she washed her face. Kathleen took her in her arms and said everything is going to be okay. Jezalee told her she was still afraid that he would escape from jail. If he can get away with killing that many people; she wouldn't put it past him he could find a way out. Patrick went in to see how things were and saw Jezalee crying. He asked the girls to follow him into the living and sit for a while. Kathleen looked worried at how she found Jezalee, and she knew that she and Patrick needed to calm her down enough to make her know she was safe at their place, and he could not get to her. Patrick asked his wife if she'd bring her a soft blanket and pillow while he spoke to her for a minute. "Jezalee, you know that none of us will ever let you or your family be hurt by that evil and disturbed serial murderer," Patrick assured her. He had her lay down on one of the sofas and Kathleen had the pillow and blanket; so, they got her comfortable and asked her to close her eyes and try to rest for a while. They reassured her they'd be staying with her, so she would not be alone. She could barely talk but was able to thank them for being there, then closed her eyes and drifter off to sleep.

After Deanna and Robert's excruciating life that they had until they were teens, it appears she weathered through those dark years they were tortured." "Deanna explained to Mallory how much therapy she had gone through for so many years; she would have never made it if she had not gotten the help, she needed so desperately," Kathleen said. From time to time, she begged and pleaded with Robert to seek a good therapist; but he said he did not need one; but she knew better.

While Jezalee was sleeping, the senior O'Malley's called David. They informed David how Jezalee reacted, and they were worried about her. They let him be aware they got her to lay down and she was sleeping now; but she is frightened. He thanked his parents for being there and when she wakes up, he and Mallory will call her, and they will also reassure her, that murderer is not going anywhere. Patrick asked his son how he was doing finding out Robert committed those gruesome murders? Dad, I will not lie! It has been tough to find out we had a murderer amongst us; and a serial murderer at that! Mallory has taken it badly too! We are not going to let any of the children know about this until it is necessary.

Patrick and Kathleen stayed in the library for a while and read the rest of the information Deanna remembered as a small child living with the Crockets; not knowing people had birthdays, and wonderful holidays. The couple never lived in town; so, they were far removed from any social existence. The beatings, and sexual assaults took place at least four or five times a week as they got older. Deanna never fathomed that Robert would turn out to be a killer; she supposed it was due to him always getting twice as much abuse than she received. He invariably took the blame when she made mistakes and they beat him so much he could not move out of bed the next day and his back would be bleeding through his clothes. When those monsters did beat either one of them, they would force them to take off all their clothes so it would hurt worse. They would either use a belt strap or thick rope to beat on them. Deanna has welts on her back; but nothing like what Robert endured. She said in her statement she did not think he should be charged for setting fire to them because of what they went through for fourteen agonizing years.

She remembered one time when she spilled milk all over the floor when she dropped the carton. Dodge ran into the kitchen after he heard something; he saw the milk splattered everywhere. He immediately got the belt hanging on a nail near the refrigerator and said, "Whoever did this will be bleeding to death by the time I get done!" Deanna cried out that she did it; so, he demanded she take all her clothes and underwear off, and he started hitting her with the belt over-and-over again! He ran and told Dodge to stop! Dodge turned to him and said, "you are next if you say another word," Robert yelled out, "I am trying to tell you she did not do it; I did." He stopped putting welts on her back and legs and told her to go to her room and get your clothes back on. She ran as fast as she could and covered herself with a blanket after she got dressed. There were many instances like that; but she did not want to have to relive all of them ever again.

Later that night when they were getting ready for bed, Deanna asked him why he lied; and he said he never wanted to hear or see her cry again. After Robert told her that as they got older, she knew he was her protector, at least at that. He could not stop the raping; but Robert would have rather been raped twice as much just so Deanna was not hurt anymore

Robert eventually told Deanna he had become numb over the years from the constant rapes; he convinced himself, whenever they touched him; he would think of being a piece of stone that was being chipped away and would eventually crumble. When Dodge got her pregnant, he made sure that Deanna did not carry that evil, disgusting man's child any longer than she had to. He knew then and there he had do whatever desperate measures he could come up with; he would have to be strong and make it happen. He knew their only way of survival was to set them on fire after they got drunk. He had overheard them discussing what they were going to do to them; and it was just a matter of time. He knew they would kill them as soon as they were a little older.

Deanna had told David and Jamerson, after Robert confessed to everything, she felt maybe Robert did the things he did because he found his brother who had a life that a child only dreams of having. She was her parents' only child and when he was lucky enough to find her relatives; they helped her a great deal with the issues she had faced. Her mom's brother and sister-in-law, who could not have children, took her in, got her caught up in school with various tutors; this gave her a fresh start in life. There were times that Deanna could not get through the night without screaming out; she would wake up drenched in sweat and be trembling, visualizing the Crockets over her bed ready to yank her clothes off and rape her. Jezalee knew now that the welts on Jim's body were not from being beaten by the enemy in the Vietnam Nam War; it was that evil couple torturing him.

Created with Sketch.

David called Paul's private number and realized he was not returning until the following day. He left a message that it was imperative he call him as soon as he got the message. He explicitly said to make sure the children are not around when he called him back. As soon as Paul and the children arrived at the villa; he said he needed to check his phone messages while they showered and cleaned up. While they were doing that, he went to check the machine and jotted down the messages; when it got to David's, he called him immediately. David answered his private home phone and hoped everyone had a great trip with the children. He said it was extraordinary. David proceeded to tell him that Jim was arrested and charged with seven counts of murder. Paul almost fell out of his chair; he could barely speak. He asked David if Jezalee was okay, and did she know he was arrested. He advised Paul that as soon as Jezalee found evidence in Jim's penthouse they knew there was something very suspicious. I had my private investigator send her to an undisclosed place and she has been hiding out at my parent's penthouse in Manhattan, waiting to hear when he will be arraigned. He will not be getting out on bail because he is considered a flight risk. I would not give any of this information to your family until the children return to San Francisco. I do have a suggestion, while Jezalee will be back in San Francisco in a few days or so, maybe you and Sophia could bring the children back after their vacation is up. "I broke up with Sophia quite a while ago,'' commented Paul. David said he was quite surprised! "I personally cannot possibly be in love with one person and go out with another, it did not work for me,'' Paul said. "I agree wholeheartedly," David replied.

Paul asked David if he had time to spare because he had something he needed to tell him for a long time. Sure Paul, what is it? As David said curiously. I know when Jezalee left me and got the divorce, that no one was on my side, and rightfully so. However, I never told Jezalee what really caused the birth of my second son. David was listening and became intrigued. Paul began, "I usually have business in London every month; in 1979 my nightmare began. I am a man of habits, so I always went to the same restaurant for dinner and would have one drink before going to my hotel suite for the night. That night was not like any other as Paul continued his repulsive story. David was visualizing what it would be like to experience what he went through. By the time Paul was finished, David had tears building up and was outraged that something like that happened to him. "So! David, you can see what I was up against!" Paul said. "I am perplexed why you did not tell Jezalee?" David said. "Believe me, I tried so many occasions, and she shut me down every time; she just would not listen. I decided since she was so angry and no matter what I would say, she did not want to be married to me anymore," a sad Paul said.

Why didn't you let Jezalee know what happened after Jonathan died? Because she was adamant about me never discussing it with her, ever again, I respected her wishes. "You should not have; Paul you are too nice," David remarked. "Paul, listen to me! Get on your private jet to New York, without your children or parents knowing you are going to see Jezalee; tell them you have an emergency business meeting. "I want you to surprise Jezalee before she takes her flight back to San Francisco. As soon as we get off the phone, I am going to call my private investigator that made Jezalee's flight arrangements and tell him to cancel it immediately. Can you be there by tomorrow?" Paul excitedly said yes! "Ok, then, I will call Jamerson. My dad will pick you up or send a driver for you," David said. "My goodness David, that is so kind of you," Paul said genuinely. "Paul, I am so sorry I judged you so severely, it was not right; I should have realized it was not true from what I saw in you as a person when we lived in Paris. It will all be straightened out soon! Keep the faith. I am going to make sure you two reunite," David said. Before Paul hung up, he let David know that the children were going with their grandparents to Sorrento and a few more places until a week before school; so, they will be kept busy. David was happy about that and told Paul, this is your chance to be back together. "I will work my magic charm," Paul laughed with all sincerity. David wanted to forewarn Paul that after Jezalee read the statement of the other victim that was raised with Jim aka Robert, Jezalee had a bad breakdown and thought Robert would somehow escape from jail and come after her. He assured Paul that his parents were there with her and later he and Mallory spoke with her, as did my parents and she is doing much better. When you see her just know she may still be a little shaken up and is fragile over Robert being a serial killer. "I will take good care of her and make sure she understands that none of us will let him come near her," Paul replied.

After David got off the phone, he went upstairs to see what Mallory was up to. He caught up with her to say he wanted to stay home today, and he had something vitally important to tell her and it should be great news to all of us. He called the office and asked his assistant and secretary to forward any important calls to his house and take messages on the rest. By the time he was done with that, Mallory was waiting in the living room; he sat next to her on one of the sofas. "So, dear! What is the great news?" Mallory asked. David began the story and by the time he was done, Mallory was sobbing. He went into the family room and brought some tissue. She was devastated that Paul never got a chance to communicate the true story to Jezalee. Mallory knew that Jezalee had been struggling with her feelings for Paul. David told her what he had planned, Paul would meet up with Jezalee in New York; so, they will have a little time to talk things over and be on a flight to San Francisco together before the children come home. Mallory took her husband's hands in hers and said, "I love you so much," you always take great care of everything, you are my hero." He kissed her on the lips and said, "let us take this upstairs and make sure you put a "do not disturb" sign on the door." "Who can run the fastest up the stairs?" Mallory challenges him said. "The stairs? Are you crazy! I am taking the elevator," as David heads for the door. "I will race you to the elevator," Mallory said.

David went to his den to call Robert's attorney Jesse to inform him that Jezalee wouldn't be back as soon as he thought. Jesse was hoping that they could talk by phone if that were feasible. David left a message on Paul's answer machine to give Jezalee the name and phone number of Robert's attorney as soon as he sees her; she needs to call him.

After Paul hung up from David, he rounded up the children to let them know he was not able to go on the rest of the vacation due to some serious work matters. "Let us call your parents right now and I will speak with them," Paul looked at Gregory and said. Gregory picked up the phone to call his parent's; however, the housekeeper answered. He asked if his mom or dad were home, and she informed him they were out to dinner with his aunt and uncle who lived in town. "Esther, could you please give them the message that we just got back from our Safari and are vacationing in Italy with Paul and

Jezalee's parents; he has an extreme emergency with one of his businesses; but we will continue our vacation in Italy without him. I will put Mr. Albanese on the phone to verify this," Gregory said. Paul made sure Esther made note of the fact that the children were in great company with two sets of feisty grandparents that travel a lot, and they were originally joining Paul and the children on the Italy vacation.

Paul took the children over to his parent's home. When they arrived; the children put their luggage away in their bedrooms. In the meantime, Paul said her had an extreme emergency; but it has nothing to do with any of the businesses. The man you know as Jim has been arrested on seven counts of murder and thanks to Jezalee for finding this information in his home while he was at work. She is not at a spa retreat; she is in New York so Jim could not get to her. She will be staying there until his arraignment and if he gets bail; she will need to stay there indefinitely. Let us pray he does not make bail. She does not know it, but I am leaving tonight and surprising her tomorrow. I spoke with David and told him the whole story about my second son; and he knows what happened to me and how Jonathan was conceived; which Jezalee would not let me tell her. I am going there to try and get my amazing Jezalee back, so pray for us. "Dear, my daughter has never stopped loving you and Jim was just a diversion of sorts; so, go get my daughter and make her happy again," Jezalee's mom, Carolyn said. That is the plan as he is grinning from ear to ear as he hugs and kisses his and Jezalee's parents. "Before I walk out the door, whatever you four do, the children must not know about any of this, including who Jim really is; his real name is Robert Anderson," Paul said. "Oh! My goodness! We certainly will not say anything! Good luck my amazing son, go get your life back," Elene said. Bye all! As Paul walked out of the room, he walked down the hallway to say goodbye to the children and said they would see him after their vacation, if not before. "I will try my best; I am under a tremendous amount of pressure right now and not sure if I will be able to get the problems solved in time to join you; I promise to take care of the situation as quickly as possible," Paul said. "Yes! Of course! dad." He hugged and kissed all the children and told them to have a lot of fun and take loads of photos so he could see all the things they were going to do on their trip. Paul let his dad know that as soon as the plane arrives in New

York, they will refuel and have a new crew to take over the flight. The jet will be coming back to Pisa and ready for their use.

The children were getting ready to embark on a wonderful trip with Antonio, Elene, Carolyn, and Mark. They especially wanted to hear about the history of a few places they'd be traveling to. All the children loved history and wanted to know about Pompeii, Naples, Amalfi Coast and Sorrento.

Mark was happy to give the children a lesson in the history of some of the places he and his family had traveled. All the children sat around, he started with the ancient Roman town when it was completely wiped out by a deadly volcanic eruption; destroying, the inhabitants and structures preserved in a time capsule of pyroclastic ash. Today you can discover parts of the old town that were uncovered after Archaeologists dug up 30 feet of mud and volcanic ash. What is left is a well-preserved ancient medieval town and is one of the most fascinating pieces of archaeology history in the world. "Grandpa, how did it happen?" Alexander asked "Well when Mount Vesuvius erupted cataclysmically in the summer of. AD 79 the nearby Roman town was buried under several feet of ash and rock. The ruined city of Pompeii remained frozen in time until it was discovered by a surveying engineer in 1748," explained Mark. "What took them so long to survey that town," Jessica asked. "Well, I am sure back in the 18th century the town was not much of a thought. Obviously, the surveyor knew some way, through historical reading that there would be an interest in learning why an entire town was gone. The surveyor found the disaster had preserved a part of Roman life. The buildings, art, artifacts, and bodies were forever frozen; so, this showed a unique look into this ancient world. Due to the findings in the 18th century. The site has hosted a tireless succession of treasure hunters and archaeologists. Pompeii is an archaeological site that has been the longest and continual excavated area in the world," Mark commented. "Tell us more!" Alexander asked. "Well! Most of the research has centered around public buildings, breathtaking Villas that portray the artistic and opulent lifestyle enjoyed by the city's wealthy elite. They are trying to see how 98% of the town's population lived a humble existence. Blocks of houses, shops, and all the bits and pieces that make up the life of this ancient city. Just think! After 75 years of work, ⅓ of the city still lies buried," Mark remarked.

Carolyn brought up the Amalfi Coast as well! "Just think how tragic it was for 65,000 people losing their lives in the 14th century due to an earthquake," Carolyn said. "That town subsequently morphing into a modest town of 5,000 population, I had to do a paper in school on this and it was so interesting," Elene remarked. "It is amazing what took place all those centuries ago. Thanks for sharing that with us, after hearing that, I want to know more about world history, it is incredibly fascinating," Adrienne commented.

Early the next morning Antonio was up reading the local newspaper when Mark walked in and asked if he could join him. "By-all-means here is part of today's newspaper if you are interested," Antonio said. "Sure!" Mark replied. They sat and discussed how great it was to have the children on the trip with them. "There are so many great places to see and eat at and it will be so nice to share this with all the children." Mark said.

Paul called his crew with the change of plans; he needed to leave right away for New York on business. He would have the second crew fly the jet back to Italy and have a driver pick his family up, take them to the Pisa Airport and fly them to Sorrento. Paul packed his clothes and accessories what he could in the six pieces of luggage he had at the villa. The crew left Pisa, bound for New York and Paul was a nervous wreck.

Created with Sketch.

Paul was concerned because no one informed Jezalee he was coming; David thought it was best to surprise her. He knew she liked surprises; but he knew her well enough she probably would not be happy with this one. What would happen if she still rejected him? He was basically hoping she would hear him out. The plane landed, he walked off the plane and there stood Patrick waiting to pick him up. He gave him a hug and said welcome to our part of the world; he asked Paul if he had any luggage, and he said my steward was bringing it down for him. After they got in Patrick's car they talked about the latest update on Robert's arrest and how Jezalee was doing. Paul told Patrick how thankful he was for Jezalee being suspicious of this guy and hoped he got what he deserved. Patrick commented to Paul that he was a smooth talker for sure and had everyone fooled. Robert had a tormented childhood and became as evil as the two that tortured him. As they got closer to Manhattan, Paul was not sure this was the way to handle approaching Jezalee; but what alternative did he have? None! This would hopefully give him the opportunity to tell his story completely. He had made reservations at a hotel one block from where the O'Malley's had their penthouse, which would make it easier to just walk over to meet Jezalee. "Are you going to call Jezalee as soon as you check in at the hotel?" Patrick asked. "I am not sure what to do," a nervous Paul said. "Paul, I know this is eating you up, just bite the bullet and call her once you get settled in your suite," Patrick responded. "You know! You are right," thanks for giving me the heads up on that," Paul said as he smiled at Patrick. Patrick asked him if he needed anything; before he drove back to Connecticut and he said no; but thanked him again for picking him up and asked him to give Kathleen his regards. "If all goes well, let us get together for lunch or dinner soon," Patrick said. "I will be shouting from the highest rooftop if Jezalee will hear me out; you and David will be the first to know, and we will celebrate over dinner," Paul enthusiastically said.

Paul got settled in his suite, took a quick shower, and put on some fresh clothes. Patrick had given him the penthouse phone number; so, he got up the nerve to dial it. The phone rang twice and someone other than Jezalee's voice answered. Mary said hello and he informed her, he was Paul and wanted to know if he could speak with Jezalee. "One moment I will get her," Mary replied. Within seconds, Jezalee came to the phone. "Hi Paul, how are you"? Jezalee said in a surprised voice. "I will be better if we could meet and talk," Paul nervous and anxious replied. "Where are you?" Jezalee asked with curiosity. "I am one block away," Paul answered. While she was talking with him, she was experiencing butterflies in her stomach and extremely nervous. Mary was close by and could see how Jezalee was reacting. Jezalee was receptive and asked Paul if he would like to come over to talk now and he said yes. She said she would call down to Oliver, the doorman, to let him up to the penthouse. After they hung up, Jezalee hurried to freshen up and change into a pretty summer dress and redid her hair the way Paul liked it, down and flowing.

Paul could not get out of his suite fast enough. As he hurried down the avenue, he spotted a flower shop and bought her three dozen white roses. As he reached the apartment building, he glanced in a window to see his reflection and straighten his collar on his favorite blue shirt and fixed his hair a little. Oliver opened the door for him; Paul introduced himself then said he was there to see Jezalee aka Miss Sullivan; they both laughed! He walked him to the private elevator that took him directly to the entryway to the penthouse. Jezalee was anxiously awaiting, for him; when she opened the door, she asked him to come in; she could see he had something behind his back, she smiled as he handed her the three-dozen beautiful white roses; one dozen for each child they had together. She gave him a hug and commented that Kathleen had the perfect vase to put them in; she motioned for Paul to take a seat in the living room, and she would be right back. Jezalee opened one of the dining room cabinets and pulled out an extraordinary vase that was multi-colored jewel tones; she walked to the kitchen to fill the vase with water and arranged the lovely white roses in the vase. She placed the roses in the center of the dining room table then walked over to the living room area and sat down.

Mary had left ten minutes prior to Paul arriving. As Paul and Jezalee sat across from one another Jezalee spoke out first, "what was so urgent you flew here to speak with me and what are the children doing without you?" "First of all, I have three things to say, I love you and want to explain a few things if you will hear me out. Secondly, the children are continuing with their vacation with our parents, and they think I have, a business emergency and will possibly take a long time to resolve," Paul took a deep breath to tell her. She looked at him and said she would listen to what he had to say. He began to tell her the whole sordid Gloria story. She got up, motioned for him to move over because she wanted to sit next to him in the chair. Paul held her hand as she sat down, she turned towards him her tear-stained face, and surprisingly kissed him. She could not believe or understand why she never let him tell her the whole story. She sobbed from beginning to end. Paul put his arms around her and said it is all behind us now, we need to be thankful she felt something was not right about Jim or they may not have ever communicated, due to stubbornness. She then commented, "what is the third thing you need to tell me?" He looked her in the eyes, held both her hands in his and began telling her how life had been so lonely without her and hoped she felt the same. She planted a soft kiss on his lips and said she had been wrong in handling things the way she did, and hoped, in time he would be able forgive her. She blamed herself for thinking that he could ever cheat on her with all the love he had always shown her from the moment they met. Paul told her when he came home after that horrible encounter, he should have explained what he went through. He was too embarrassed and did not want anyone to ever know he had been raped by a woman. He felt no one would ever believe him, having the stature he had, that he could not defend himself.

Jezalee asked about Sophia and Paul said I told her he never loved her. They dated and only brought her to your Christmas Party in 86 to make her jealous; but when he saw Jim there, he got jealous of him, and it looked like she had moved on; so, he continued seeing Sophia. "How did Sophia react to you breaking up with her?" Jezalee asked. "She was furious, and eventually thought we were going to get married," Paul said. Jezalee said that sounds like she was completely in love with you. "I never once gave her any indication I had feelings for her in that way; you have got to believe me; the word love never came from my lips to her ears. I had sex with her once as a distraction from you, and that did not work well. I was trying to forget us; but it never happened," Paul said in an intense manner. Jezalee started laughing and Paul asked her what is so funny? "Well! It seems as if we both had the same experience having sex with someone we did not love and was trying to forget about one another," Jezalee said with a grin on her face. Paul came closer to Jezalee and gave her a hug and they both knew they could laugh about that now; but it was not great when they were experiencing having unemotional sex with two people they were not in love with.

Jezalee asked how he knew she was in New York, and he admitted David had called him with an update on Robert then asked him if he could speak to him about how Jonathan was conceived. David felt bad the way things had turned out. He said so many people get divorced over not communicating with issues that make that couple gravitate to divorcing. Jezalee started crying again and knew she had made a horrible mistake in not hearing Paul out. She apologized once again and said she had regrets and had never stopped thinking about him. Her love never fleeted, and it had been difficult whenever they were in the same room together. He smiled at her and confessed he had the same feelings and wanted to come to her so many times but wanted her to be the one. He kissed her as he put his strong and comforting arm around her. They both sat back in the oversized chair and began talking about everything that they wanted to share. He pulled out a piece of paper from his pants pocket and said this is a message from David. She said thanks, read it and put it aside for later.

"If you do not mind, I would like to call David and Patrick, if that is okay," Paul happily said. "It is more than okay, she kissed him again," Jezalee said, of course! that would be great. He went to the phone and dialed Patrick and as soon as he heard Paul's voice; he knew it was going to be good news. "Hi Paul, and what do I owe this call for, as if I did not know," Patrick asked in a jovial manor. "Patrick, everything is better than he could have expected," Paul laughed from happiness into the phone. Patrick expressed his happiness for him and Jezalee and said he had a real keeper there. Paul thanked him and said he was getting ready to call David and Mallory; before they hung up, Patrick asked him if he and Jezalee would like to go out to dinner in the next few days or so?? Paul said we would be delighted. After he hung up from Patrick, he called out to Jezalee and said he was ready to call David and Mallory. Paul asked her to get on one of the telephone extensions after he dialed. David answered, he told Paul he wanted to get Mallory on the phone too! "The more the merrier," Paul happily said. He motioned for Jezalee to join him on the phone; so, she went into Patrick's library where the second phone was. Mallory ran to the phone in their kitchen as David was in his den. The four of them talked for at least a half an hour. Of course! Jezalee was extremely upset that so much time was wasted with being friends with Robert for over three years, she kept saying how stupid, naïve, and clueless she was. The three of them repeatedly asked her to stop thinking that way and know this is a new beginning for them. "Jezalee, maybe it was all part of a plan that was supposed to happen in all our lives; for me to hire Robert, you to meet and be curious enough about him. You took matters into your own hands and look at what you accomplished; all that evidence you found, lead Jamerson right to Deanna. Robert confessing to her, manifested the arrest for the murders he committed. You, who may have no doubt, saved others from fallen prey to a serial killer. Great instincts prevailed, you picked up on it rather soon after you were around him," David praised Jezalee's bravery and forthwith. "I guess sometimes we go through unexpected things in life and do not have the answers until we question why we are the source of the problem." I am just thankful intuition kicked in and I had to get to the bottom of why a person was so void of feelings towards the death of a spouse and a son. Plus! His obsession with me was out of control," Jezalee replied. "I am thankful it is all behind us and we can go on with our lives and realize how blessed to have had amazing childhoods. I know Robert is a serial killer; but I cannot help but have a strong sense of compassion for what he and Deanna were put through. I think of all those dark and lonely years of suffering through the evilness of two deranged people put them through," Paul said with pure compassion. "You are right! So many things in our lives, good or bad, can have a strong impact one way or another. Deanna opened up to therapy; but Robert was too embarrassed to let all his anger, hurt, and fear be known to a stranger, who may have been able to help him heal," Mallory replied with much sadness. "I think we have exhausted this subject and are thankful Robert is behind bars. According to his Attorney, he was forced to talk with a psychiatrist which will hopefully help the healing process begin," David remarked.

"Let us get to exciting things! We have decided to get remarried on July 29th, in San Francisco," Paul happily burst out. Mallory brought into the open that she and David would love to have the wedding on their estate. Jezalee told her it was a big undertaking and would not want her to go to all trouble. "Jezalee, it would be our gift to you if we could do all the work and you two just show up for your nuptials. That way, you and Paul can have an early honeymoon by enjoying yourselves in New York while we take care of everything here. Just let me know the details of what you want, and I will get started," Mallory said with a robust attitude. Jezalee and Paul talked it over and they said that would be fantastic and could not thank her enough for offering. They indicated they would be back on the 23rd, wanted the children to come home on the 26th, and wanted the wedding on the 29th. Mallory said she needed the guest list, which she would have to send the invitations special delivery with time being of the essence. Next! What color scheme, kind of flowers, cake preference, who will be in the wedding party, and what color was her gown going to be? After the girls were talking wedding details the men excused themselves and left the phone. Mallory got all the information she needed for the wedding and would take care of every, last detail. She reassured Jezalee, she wanted her and Paul to relax a few days when they arrived home; and wanted them to only think about the night of their wedding and nothing else. Jezalee was so relieved Mallory offered to plan the wedding; because she had too many other things to think about, especially finding her gown and everyone else's in the wedding party. After David and Mallory said their goodbyes Jezalee and Paul, ran to their bedroom and placed a "Do Not Disturb" sign on the doorknob.

That night ended up being the start of the marriage that should never have ended. Jezalee asked Paul to join her in the kitchen, so she would have company while she prepared something to eat for them. Paul said he was not that hungry but could eat a little. After she was done cooking, they sat at the dining room table so Jezalee could enjoy her beautiful white roses Paul brought to her, while they ate their dinner. Jezalee did not know what to expect when it came time to go to bed; Paul was thinking the same thing. A few minutes later Paul just came right out with it and asked her if they could sleep together, and she was so relieved he wanted to. "What are we waiting for, let us get comfortable," Jezalee softly said to Paul from across the table.

Dirty dishes sitting on the dining room table, kitchen pots and pans with some food left in them. Paul and Jezalee had one thing on their minds and rushed to the bedroom. As they entered the bedroom overlooking the city, they went over to the window, looked out as they held one another in their arms. They both had the same thoughts; they had lost four years of not being together. They looked into one another's wanting eyes, Paul started gently unbuttoning Jezalee's sheer dress, as she took her soft, delicate right hand and slowly unzipped his pants. He had her step out of her dress, tossed it near the closest chair as she was lowering his pants for him to step out of. Paul waited before he removed another article of clothing, he glanced down at her, took one hand, pulled her long raven hair back away from her alluring face, then softly kissed her. As they were kissing, he removed her bra; touched both rounded, firm breasts and could feel her nipples hardening; he leaned down, ever so lightly, placed his head to her breasts, softly kissed them; then ran his tongue over her nipples. As Paul's erection got larger, Jezalee slid his underwear off and kissed his eagerly, growing penis{ or genitals}? Paul quietly said he had waited for so long to be with her and wanted this night to be special. Jezalee whispered in his ear, "I love you" then they began removing the remainder of each other's clothing until they were standing in the nude. Paul dimmed the lights just enough so they could see one another's sensual, nude bodies reflecting from the windows. They slightly stepped back away from the windows, arm in arm, looked out over the city, was mesmerized how, with the night sky and the lights coming from the buildings, it appeared as if there were diamonds in the sky. Paul asked Jezalee to close her eyes, do not move, he drew the drapes closed, walked over to the bed, and turned down the bedding. He walked back over, picked up Jezalee with his Gladiator-like muscular body and arms and gently carried her over to the bed; like a fragile flower, ever so gently, then laid her on her back, carefully climbing on top of her, wanting her so familiar seductive body. She loved the feel of his broad, slightly hairy chest next to her appealing breasts; he gently slid part of his magnetic body off her; so, it was more comfortable to kiss. Their lips were on fire, and they could not get enough of their magical power to attract one another. They made love that night like they thought it would be their last time. After they laid there for a while, they both realized the depth of their love and knew they would never let anyone, or anything ever cause them to be apart. Jezalee was still lying next to Paul when Mary called; she let the answer machine pick up the message.

Paul asked Jezalee to please call her back; she may think somethings wrong since you did not answer the phone. You are right! I never thought of that. They both laughed! While Jezalee was dialing Mary back, Paul could not resist running his gentle but masculine hands down her soft but firm thighs; She said, "Stop! I cannot concentrate.! Mary answered the phone and was glad to hear it was Jezalee. She told Mary she was happy to report that the two of them were getting back together. Mary was elated and said, "I guess I will see you at your wedding. Jezalee quietly whispered, "from your lips to God's ears," then they both led out a giggle or two. Paul turned to face her in the darkness of the room, "I heard that girls," Paul, delightfully said; he took the receiver out of her hand and said hi to Mary and hoped to meet her very soon before they left for San Francisco. She said, "Likewise."

After Jezalee hung up; Paul started kissing her. In the back of her mind, all she could think of was making up for lost time. Paul broke away from kissing her luscious lips, looked down at her, and said, "I bet I know exactly what you are thinking right now. "Really! You think so?" Jezalee said. "Yes! Absolutely, without a doubt," Paul said, so sure of himself. "Well then, tell me, if I say it and it is true you may not say I am right," Paul apprised her with a smile. "I will write down what I was thinking, is that fair enough my sweet?" Jezalee offered a solution. "Ok! Now we are talking." Paul said with a boyish look. After she wrote her thoughts down, she said, "Go for it! Paul gave her a big grin and said, "When we were kissing you were thinking of all the lost time that has gone by, since we have not been together," he picked up the paper and started laughing and said, "I know you, oh so well." Jezalee grabbed his hand and pulled him towards her; he motioned he motioned her to get out of bed. As they stood next to the bed, he lifted her up in his arms and carried her through the bedroom to the bathroom. "What are you doing?" Jezalee asked. "Where are the bubbles?" He asked. "Are you suggesting we take a bubble bath together?" As Jezalee holds onto him. "Absolutely," as Paul lets her down gently. She walked over to the linen closet and handed him the bubble bath. Jezalee asked him to get the tub running with the bubbles and she would be back in a minute. As Paul was filling the tub with hot water and bubble bath, she was getting candles and strawberries dipped in Ghirardelli chocolate. Jezalee approached the antique table closest to the bathtub and set the candles and strawberries down. "What is all this"? Paul came close and asked her. "Just a little something for a romantic mood enhancer while we are soaking in the tub," Jezalee answered. "Do you really think we have ever needed a mood enhancer?" Paul said with his dimpled smile. "No! But it is always extra sensual to feed one other, don't you agree?" Jezalee reminded him. "You are right! But where is the whipped cream; so, I can lick it off the parts of your sumptuous body that won't be under water," Paul asked. "We do not have any, we will need to go shopping tomorrow and get some," Jezalee answered. "Where are the essential oils, you always have?" Asked mister whining Paul. "I did not know my knight and shining armor was going to show up on my doorstep, so bubbles it will have to be," Jezalee smiled and said. Hand in hand, they both stepped into the luxurious bubbles almost overflowing. Paul turned the switch on at the wall so they could listen to some classical music; he lit the candles and dimmed the lights.

They got comfortable in the tub, Paul reached for two chocolate covered strawberries; as he was looking across from her, he came closer to her and handed her a strawberry as he held one for himself. He took his strawberry and put it towards her lips, and she did the same to him; as they fed one another, they both could hardly hold back the urgency to make love again. As they were finishing the berries, Paul had her slide down in the bubbled water a little more and he gently got on top of her; making love in the tub had always been very sensual to them and it was no different now. Paul added more hot water and bubbles and after they both were satisfied, they lay there in the stillness, water calming and bubbles soothing. They looked at one another in the candle lit room and knew they were home again. After laying in the tub for an hour, Paul got out first, then took Jezalee by the hand to help her out. They immediately walked to the shower, got in together and gently washed the film from the bubbles off one another's satisfied bodies. He got out of the shower and took one of the thick, luxurious white plush towels off the heated rack and she stepped out and he wrapped it around her; she did the same for him. They went to bed that night knowing that their lives had been interrupted by evilness, but all was great from here on out.

Paul woke up and looked at his amazingly beautiful wife-to-be. As soon as he moved in the bed Jezalee was awake and looked over at him, her-soon-to-be husband again. Jezalee looked at Paul with that gleam in his eyes and he said, "Are you ready for round two in the sheets?" "You do remember me after all!" She grinned and said. Paul jumped out of bed, went to brush his teeth then came back into the bedroom and opened-up the drapes, saw the sun shining and wanted to make love in the brightens of the day. While he did that,

Jezalee slid out of bed and went to brush her teeth as well. By the time she walked back into the bedroom, Paul was completely under the covers. Jezalee was standing over the bed, she pulled the top sheet off him and said, "my body is telling your body, I want you! So, roll over and let us get some action going!" Paul looked up at her and said, excuse me! "But this man wants a little time to check you out and he loves what he sees!" Jezalee gently laid on top of him, they had held back pent-up emotions for each other for over three years! They were ready to make morning memories.

Both Paul and Jezalee decided, after they got dressed, they would have breakfast out, then take a stroll through Central Park. They had always loved spending time there on the weekends when they were college students and had made-an-effort; anytime they were in New York with their children, they would hang out in the park with them. They walked for hours and on the way back to the O'Malley's, they stopped at a couple of street vendors and had their favorite hot dogs with sauerkraut and had to have a slice of New York pizza. As they were walking down the street, Paul turned to Jezalee and asked her if she had forgotten about something. "You know me better than that, the grocery store is just a block away and they had better have that whipped cream, because I am ready for round three," Jezalee said in her sexy night voice. "Well, well, well! Now you are talking my language, sweet love," an anxious Paul replied and asked why were they on the streets of Manhattan, when they should be in bed or in the tub. Jezalee gave him that look, and he knew they needed to walk faster for what both had in mind.

Once they arrived back to the penthouse, they put the whipped cream away, took a quick shower together then laid nude in the unmade bed and took a short half hour nap as they spooned. When they woke up, they held one another as if they never wanted to have space between their bodies. They gave one another back massages then read parts of the New York Times. As Jezalee glanced at Paul, she could barely contain her excitement thinking how their children would react to them getting remarried. "Are we really going to take the plunge again?" Jezalee asked. "What do you think my beautiful, sexy lady?" Paul smiled at her and said he was ready to go to a Justice of the Peace. Jezalee had a twinkle in her eyes and thought that was a great idea. "You know I was kidding right?" Paul said. "I was hoping because I am not going to be so free with my body if you want some action," Jezalee said with a wanting look on her face. He laid his hands on her gently, slowly, pulled her closer to him and under the sheets they went. Another afternoon engaging in lustful interludes, which included whipped cream.

They had their "where are we living session," Jezalee got serious for a moment and asked Paul where they were going to live? He put his arms around her and said they had many options; their Manhattan penthouse, the San Francisco estate, the Villa in Italy, the chateau in Saint-Germain-en-Laye, the villa in Napa, or buy another place back in Paris, America, or wherever she and the children wanted to live. I will leave that decision up to you, because as-long-as we are all together, I do not care if we are Mars bound.

As they laid there, continuing reading the newspaper, it was all so familiar with what they had always done. They both realized how easy it was for them to start where they left off; when their life was just where they wanted it to be, as a loving couple who had three amazing children and an amazing life with the rest of their families and friends. They knew they deserved to grasp onto their lives they once had and continue down that same glorious path.

While they were still relaxing in bed, Jezalee asked Paul if he minded if she asked him a few questions about Gloria and his son. My sweet Jezalee, I normally would not agree to talk about her; but I know you will never rest until you get answers to your questions. Fire away dear! When you woke up in her bed, what was your first thought? I was nude, jumped out of bed, and I suppose it was an out of body experience and nothing seemed real. I really wanted it to be a nightmare and I would eventually wake up at the horror of that filthy, disgusting woman next to me. What was the place like? I can still smell the cheap perfume, the filthy stench of the room burning my nostrils, to the point of wanting to puke. Did you know what men took you to her room? I did not at first, but when it was time to pay them, I let Gloria know that they would not get paid unless I could deliver the money to them in person. I proceeded to inform them they had better be worried, because I was going to make sure the laws changed for men being raped and I hoped the law would be on my side because I would see to that the three of them would be held accountable in a court of law. I would also bring up kidnapping charges. Do you think the law will change for men? Yes! I have diligently been working on it for several years and we are getting closer. I just hope they will consider past rapes assaults on men and punish the perpetrators. When the time comes, I will be sorry that Gloria did not live to be charged and go to prison. Two men letting a man be raped is deplorable in every sense of the word. It has been tough living with that nightmare for nine years and wished laws did not take so long to go through the system; I would have loved to have seen all three of them in a courtroom setting. "Dear, I feel better knowing that you shared that with me; but the cruelty of it all is incomprehensible and it breaks my heart that you were violated and for a moment stripped of your dignity. One last question, I know you indicated you came home that morning and had every intention on telling me, what happened, why didn't you follow through with your first instincts?" On the way home, I felt strong enough to tell you; but once the children ran to the door and you were right behind them, I could not tarnish what amazing life we had built for ourselves. I was embarrassed and sick to my stomach that I put myself in the hands of three demented people that drugged me. After that happened, I assure you, not once have I had a drink outside our home unless I had a drink from an unopened bottle. Believe me! I have had nightmares a couple of times and I did go to therapy in Paris, and it helped me a great deal. I guess what was so reprehensible is the fact that I could not go to the police, only because I was a man. After Jezalee's questions were answered, she looked at Paul, asked him to lay down in the bed and just wanted their bodies entwined together. She softly kissed him and said how sorry she was that he did not feel he could tell her what happened.

Paul looked at his bride-to-be and asked her to talk about her involvement with Robert. What led up to searching Robert's penthouse? I always felt uneasy that he didn't bring up his deceased wife and son in a conversation; he did not have any photos of them at work, his penthouse, or his wallet. Yes! I went through his wallet. Robert laughed then hugged Jezalee. All this bothered David and Mallory as well. There was a time when he came with us to the Castle on the Mountain, and we decided to take the yacht out for the day, he immediately said he did not like going on boats. We thought that strange when he told us he was supposed to going boating with his wife and son but had a business meeting he could not get out of. What made you keep going out with him? It started out as a diversion from constantly thinking about you. The children liked him, and he was great with them. I did not want the children to be upset if I stopped seeing him; so, I let something materialize unbeknownst to me. I thought I was being a friend to him, and he took it as if I were falling in love with him. When he told me, he loved me I was shocked, there, and then realizing I needed to set him, straight. I could not believe our friendship was undetectable to him; I had sex with Robert once, if you could call it that! Was there anything else that made you shy away from wanting to get closer? Yes! many things, he was always trying to get into my personal business. He was so jealous of you and took opportune times to put you down. He was always pressuring me to marry him. The last straw was when he proposed. I knew then I would see him occasionally in a group setting and once-in-a-while go out to dinner with him; however, from that moment on, I knew I had to find out more about him for my own curiosity. He continually had mood swings at work, out in public, at our home or his. David and his employees noticed a radical difference in his demeanor, and he was talking to himself a lot.

We have been through too much, and just to give those two anymore of our energy is not good for our soul. "You understand, right?" Paul said, somewhat sad. "Honey, I do! And you are so right! We have both suffered too much in the hands of two persons that were tormented in their lives or just, plain sick minded," Jezalee replied. "I am sure that there is one lesson to be learned here," Paul commented. "What is that dear?" Jezalee asked. "To be cautious; it is something that we both should realize with the wealth that we have gained over the years, we can be sitting targets for another Gloria or Robert; we need to be more careful moving forward," Paul answered. "You are so right!" Jezalee agreed.

On a much lighter note! "My love," as Paul affectionately embraced Jezalee, we have not been to the theater in over four years; so, let us venture out to a Broadway play or musical tonight. I will call and get show tickets then call Joe Allen's to make a reservation for an early dinner. We have not eaten there in almost ten years; that night we saw West Side Story on Valentine's Day. Remember couple of weeks later we saw Whose Life is it Anyway. Has it been that long? Yes! I remember when we saw An Evening with Diana Ross the Summer of 76, we came back that same year during the Christmas holidays and saw Fiddler on the Roof and Barry Manilow. There is nothing like a Broadway Play or Musical. I hope we enjoy this one! if it is not sold out. Hey! "Who are you talking to? I know people who know people," Paul said with conviction. "I will believe it when I see the tickets in our hands," Jezalee laughed! "Have some faith my love," as he smiled at her then gave her a loving kiss.

They took a quick shower, got ready to go to Joe Allen's and had a few of their favorite appetizers before they went to see Fiddler on the Roof. They were thrilled Paul was able to get tickets at the last minute because a couple had an emergency and had to back out.

After the play was over, they walked back to the penthouse and could not believe the weather wasn't hot and humid as it normally was that time of the year. Once they got back to the penthouse, they changed out of their street clothes into something more comfortable. Jezalee got them some nippy ice-tea and sat out on the terrace to enjoy the night air and the sounds of the city.

While Paul and Jezalee were having a marriage reunion in New York, their children and the Stanton children were having a grand time in Italy exploring beautiful places. Paul had called the children and his and Jezalee parents and they were having such a terrific time with the teenagers. They let Paul know that the children made them feel so young again and it was great.

As for Jezalee, as far as her children, they still thought she was at a retreat while they would be on vacation. She called them a few days before or after Paul would call them. They certainly did not have any suspicions that their parents were back together, much less getting married again.

David and Mallory were busy while the children were at camp; Mallory would go into the office and help the staff get Robert's work squared away; one good thing about him, he was very meticulous and highly intelligent; so, it was easy to go through the work and divide it up between the staff. Mallory knew the business; so, she took care of some of the crucial issues that needed attention. David had to fill Robert's position and he would be interviewing people in about a week or two. He had such a great staff with some of the people being with him since he started the business. All his staff got together with him when Mallory was there and wanted to say how sad and sorry that they were with how Robert turned out to be because he had everyone fooled.

Paul called Patrick so they could plan what night they would go out; in the meantime; Jezalee and Paul were living their dream life and they were making up for time lost. They had to laugh about the fact they had to pretend they were countries apart and Jezalee was relaxing at a retreat.

Created with Sketch.

Before they headed to look for their wedding attire; Paul called his parents at the hotel on the Amalfi Coast, at one of their vacation tours. His dad answered he phone and Paul informed him, not to let the children, mom or Jezalee's parents know they would be coming back earlier on the 26th. He let him know where they were, and they would be flying into San Francisco on the 23rd and the children will be surprised on the 26th when he'll appear at a dinner Jezalee will have, welcoming, the vacationers home. His pops had been waiting for Paul and Jezalee to find their way back to one another and he could hardly wait for the wedding. Paul told his pops he cannot even tell his mama. The parents knew he was with Jezalee; but he wanted the wedding to be a surprise. He promised his lips were sealed and would not tell a soul. Our wedding will be on the 29th of July at the O'Malley estate. Paul hoped his pops and the rest of the gang would not mind cutting their vacation short; he said he would have the private jet ready for them on the 26th to San Francisco. His pop said, "Finally!" I love you and Jezalee and mum is the word. See you on the 26th at dinner. Ciao Bella!

Jezalee called her favorite Designer, Dani, who just happened to have her thriving business in Manhattan and said she needed a wedding gown and would be getting remarried on July 29th. Dani requested she come in as soon as possible because she needed to get started. So, Paul and Jezalee went out for the day, and he dropped her off at Dani's while he went to his favorite tailor, Georgio, in Manhattan. He had been making suits and tuxedos for Paul for over twenty years, and he knew he would not let him down. While Jezalee was looking through some of the gowns she already spotted one she wanted to try on. Dani's assistant, Muriel had Jezalee go to one of the dressing rooms to try on the gown and as soon as she put it on, she knew it was the one she wanted. She came out to show the gown to Dani to get her opinion, and she dropped her jaw as Jezalee walked towards her. Dani asked her to try on a few more before she made her decision. Jezalee said that gown was her dream wedding gown and wanted it. They both looked at one another and started laughing! Dani told her no one comes in and tries on the first gown and it's the one they buy. Dani always tells her customers "Never" try just one dress on. She was in awe that this gown was unequivocally made for her dear friend Jezalee as she called her. Muriel came out from the back room, cried as soon as she saw Jezalee in the gown. Wow! You are so gorgeous; you make that gown look more extraordinary than it already is. This gown will take your soon-to-be husband's breath away. Dani and her assistant said Jezalee was one of the most beautiful women they had ever seen. She thanked the gals for being so sweet and was dumbfounded that she tried one dress on, and she knew that was the one. Now! Let us discuss the wedding party and what gowns the ladies and girls shall wear. I would love for all the girls to be wearing the winter white/Ivory colors, the same as my wedding gown. "That will not be a problem as-long-as she has their measurement/sizes," Dani answered. Jezalee called Helga and Mallory to get the measurements of everyone in the wedding party right away and fax them over to Dani and Georgio. In the meantime, Jezalee decided tea-length dresses for the younger girls, and gowns for the women. Jezalee called Georgio's, and Paul was still there getting fitted for his tuxedo and would be over to Dani's when he finishes. Jezalee called Mallory to her know she found the perfect wedding gown. Surprisingly enough! No alterations needed; it is ready for me to wear up the aisle. Just as the ladies were placing her wedding gown in a non-see through, zippered bag, Jezalee could see Paul approaching the store. He peeked his head in and asked if it was safe to come in. By-all-means said Dani, have a seat for a few minutes while your wife-to-be finishes getting dressed. He asked Dani if Jezalee had any success and she said she certainly did. She is the most stunningly beautiful woman we have ever seen. Well! I will never disagree with that; she is one in a zillion as far as I am concerned. Jezalee walked out from the dressing room, arm in arm with her gown. She walked towards Paul and immediately said she found the most perfect dress for their wedding. He looked at her, then looked at Dani and did not believe she had found her dream dress that quickly; especially for such a fussy person that his wife was and always has been. Dani and Jezalee laughed, and both reiterated that this is the first time anyone had ever walked in, tried on one dress, and came out of the dressing room and said, "This is the *it* dress! "Honey! Why don't you try on at least a few more dresses just in case?" Paul looked over to her and said. She looked at him, with a certain look, that he knows all so well, that was the ultimate dress. He smiled at her and said, "I am not saying another word because I know once you've made up your mind you never back down," He smiled at her and said as he winked at Dani. "I saw that mister!" Jezalee smiled and said. "I hope to get an invite to the wedding because I would love to see you tie the knot again; and want to see one of my designs going up the wedding aisle," Dani commented. Paul automatically spoke up and said they would be delighted if she and her husband would come. While they were talking, Mallory and Helga had called with the measurements and Dani said while they were already there, she would show them samples of the dresses she thinks would look perfect as an accent to her gown. Paul asked if he was-allowed-to be a part of that and they both thought, why not? Dani asked her assistant Muriel to have another employee help her in the front of the store while she worked with the Albanese's, in one of the back rooms. She motioned for Paul and Jezalee to follow her to one of the sitting areas where she would bring out dresses for them to view. It was a large area with extravagant multi-colored chandeliers hanging from the ceiling, elaborate wall sconces and extraordinary paintings of some of her famous designs that had been recognized all over the world, painted on canvas by her dear friend Andy Warhol. Muriel exited the room for about ten minutes and had several employees bring out dress samples. Paul, being a designer in the athletic world, could see the talents Dani had in the women's fashion world. He agreed right along with Jezalee that one dress was prettier than the next. While they were looking through all the dresses brought out; Paul asked if the girls were hungry because he would like to order some food for everyone still working. Jezalee thought that was a great idea and Dani said that was so sweet of him. Paul rounded up all Dani's employees who were still working and he took everyone's order and said he would call them in. An hour later the food had been delivered from the various restaurants and they took a thirty-minute break to eat before they made some final decisions on what dress and gowns would be worn.

Two hours after having dinner with Dani and her employees, Jezalee made her final decision and Paul thought the dresses and gowns were amazing. They had the sizes in the store on every dress they had chosen for all the females. While they had been there for hours; Paul called Georgio and he had received the measurements for the tuxedos, and everything was good at his end too. Both Dani and Georgio said they would have the wedding clothes delivered to them early tomorrow at the penthouse. Dani bid farewell and said the next time I see you two, will be a special moment for all who gets to witness you two getting married. I am beyond thrilled at you two getting back together. Paul and Jezalee thanked her and all her staff for the extraordinary work, time, and effort they had played a huge part in getting their wedding party dressed to the nines. Dani said to leave Jezalee's wedding gown behind too, because it would be delivered with the rest of the dresses tomorrow.

As Jezalee was strolling down the Fifth Avenue with Paul, they passed so many places they used to hang out on the weekends while they were in college. It was the ideal surroundings they needed before their wedding. Everything was falling into place, and they could not have predicted this Fairytale would have ever come to life once again, for them.

The next morning was just an extension of the days before and they were enjoying all the moments in between. They not only got to go down memory lane in New York, they got to experience the present and think about how fortunate to have an amazing future ahead of them once again.

After Paul and Jezalee got ready for the day, they decided to act like tourists and go to a few landmarks around the city and wanted to venture out to see the Statue of Liberty. Of course! None of this was acclimated until after Jezalee's wedding gown, evening gowns for the women, dresses for the young girls, and the tuxedos for the boys, and men had arrived. Jezalee had Oliver bring the wedding apparel up and place everything in one of the guest bedrooms, Dani had sent over a rolling rack to keep them on until they arrived in San Francisco. Jezalee wanted to look at all the dresses and gowns once again and one by one she checked them out; they were all the right sizes and looked even prettier the next day. A half an hour later Georgio had all the tuxedos delivered. Paul had called Georgio and thanked him for all his hard-working efforts to make it possible to have the men's apparel done. He had also invited him and his wife Emelia to the wedding; and he said they would not miss it. Paul let Jezalee know he had two suites ready for Georgio and his wife and Dani and her husband Octavio at the Fairmont, compliments of them and the hotel would be sending them an invite from the two of them for a three day stay, if they chose to see a little of San Francisco, since they were coming all that way to their wedding. He also reserved another private jet from a friend so Dani and Georgio would not have to deal with commercial flying. He was not sure if his private jet would be available; so, he wanted to make things easier for them since they were coming to their wedding. "You are always full of surprises, that is what I love about you," Jezalee said, as she walked over to kiss Paul. Jezalee called Dani to thank her for all the exquisite gowns and dresses and was looking forward to seeing her and Octavio at the wedding. She was also in hopes they could get together for dinner before they left for San Francisco. She let Dani know they were open to any night up to July 17th, then they would be leaving the next day for Boston. Dani checked her schedule, and they could meet them for dinner on the 15th. They set a time and place and were looking forward to getting together. Paul also called Georgio and wanted to go out for dinner with he and Emelia and they decided on the 16th.

Jezalee had called the Stanton's to let them know they would be back in town on the 23rd and the children would be coming back on the 26th. They are not to know about the wedding on the 29th. Joan was so happy for the Albanese's and was looking forward to the wedding.

Jezalee called Mallory and Helga and thanked them for getting all the measurements to Dani and Georgio so quickly. She hoped that everyone liked what she had chosen for the wedding party attire. Both Helga and Mallory were happy to hear from Jezalee and were relieved they had been lucky to find what they wanted in such a short period of time. Jezalee could not thank Mallory and David enough for having the wedding at their lovely estate. Jezalee commented on what a beautiful and intimate setting it will be. Little did she know that there were over 400 rsvp's and Mallory was in full force with what should be a magical wedding event for her and David's dear friends. Jezalee informed her that they had four more people to add to the invite list; so, she gave them Dani and Georgio's addresses.

Every day while Paul and Jezalee got to embrace the experience being alone, like they started out in life together, was what they had needed. They had been miserable for four years and they were finally the couple they were meant to be. They talked about how their children will react when they find out; they knew all along that their parents were still in love; in fact, everybody did.

They were finally able to leave the penthouse and do some sightseeing before they needed to be back to shower and get dressed to go out with the senior O'Malley's and Mary and Eli Donovan. They had a wonderful day filled with past and present memories made and had run into some old friends from college, they had not seen in years. After their delightful day, they quickly got back to the penthouse and had time to shower and get dressed before it was time to go out. They even had time to listen and dance to some of their favorite music before their dates arrived.

Patrick and Kathleen picked up Eli and Mary on their way into New York; Paul and Jezalee were dancing in the living room when the four arrived. The six of them hung out at the penthouse waiting for their reservation time at the La Grenouille, one of the finest French Restaurants in Manhattan. In the meantime, Jezalee had made some appetizers and Paul served drinks until it was time to leave. Once they got seated at the restaurant, chose what they wanted on the menu; Patrick noticed as Paul sat there, all he could do was stare at Jezalee, capturing her intoxicating beauty. Patrick looked over at him and said, "Hello! Anybody there? Paul laughed! "I heard every word you said." Okay, buddy! What was I talking about? Paul confessed, I am sorry, I did not hear a word you said. I was admiring my ravishing Jezalee. She looked at him as she blushed! Mary and Eli adored Paul and Jezalee and were having a great time with both couples. Patrick and Kathleen were like surrogate parents to Eli and Mary since their parents were on the West Coast; they went out to dinner quite often. Paul thanked all four of them for an amazing night and a special thanks to the O'Malley's for taking them out to such an elegant restaurant.

Once Jezalee and Paul got in the elevator to the penthouse, Paul could not control his desires, he started stripping away at his clothes and asked Jezalee, "Why are your clothes still on?" "Wow! You are one hot, sizzling Italian," Jezalee responded. He was completely nude by the time the elevator door opened to the entry area. Paul picked up his clothes off the elevator floor then gently took her hand and said, "follow me to our lover's den." Once they made it to the bedroom, he dropped his clothes on the floor, turned facing her and looked down at her smoldering face. Her craving lips were waiting for him, as he embraced her in his arms, he softly touched her wanting lips and they both knew their night had just begun. They continued to show their undying, emotional love for one another. After making love, they drifted off while spooning through the night.

Since Paul had arrived in Manhattan, he and Jezalee had a whirlwind of emotions that they had kept hidden inside them for four years and they finally did not need to hide them anymore. They were free from any void that existed within them. This time, without the children with them, they were able to connect as their love redeveloped between them; without anyone taking up time from what they needed to do alone.

Seven days had passed since Paul re-entered back into the life, he so missed with his beautiful Jezalee. They were happy they had decided to stay in Manhattan until July 23rd, that way they still had eight full days to continue their romantic interlude. They made sure that every second of each day and evening was spent nourishing the deep and enriched love they had managed to grow over the years, after meeting one another, being instantly attracted to each other, falling in love, and making a commitment to marriage. They realized they both had made wrong decisions from the event that changed the course of their marriage, and they paid a high price for not communicating with one another. They knew the seed of love they had planted in one another's heart, never stopped growing; it was in dormant until they could nourish it again for one another.

While Paul and Jezalee were in Manhattan, Jezalee heard from her publisher, and she loved the two books that Jezalee had diligently worked on for almost four years. They were finally going out for distribution and her publisher wanted her to come in and talk about the cookbook Jezalee had ran by her. While Jezalee had her appointment with her publisher, Paul had lunch with a few of the guys he went to Harvard with. After hanging out them, he wanted to do a little shopping before he went back to the penthouse. By the time Jezalee was finished at the publishers and was excited to tell Paul the great news about the recipe book they wanted her to put together to get published by the following year.

Paul and Jezalee were extremely happy they had this time together in Manhattan because they were able to see friends they had not seen in several years. They also had dinner with Dani and Octavio and decided to take in a movie afterwards. Paul had really enjoyed meeting Dani's husband for the first time and had a lot in common and wanted to keep in touch. The next evening, they had dinner with Georgio and his wife Emelia and went dancing with them.

They had one week before flying home; so, they flew to Boston for three days. Enjoyed going to some of their old stomping grounds while attending Harvard. They met up with a few friends that lived in the area and decided to rent a car and drive through the New England states on the way back to Manhattan. They had a spectacular trip and wanted to make-an-effort to come back in-the-near-future when they had more time.

Paul and Jezalee had a wonderful and relaxing drive through the New England States and were anxious to get back to Patrick and Kathleen's penthouse. Once they got there, they knew it was countdown time to jetting off to San Francisco where they would reunite their love as a couple.

They had the senior O'Malley's and Donovan's over for dinner the night before they left for San Francisco to thank them for putting up with two lost souls that made it back to one another.

Paul and Jezalee were looking forward to the wedding and hoped that the sixty people they had invited were all able to come and share their night with them. David and Mallory were hoping for the best but were nervous over how many guests were attending.

Jezalee had called her local maid service in town, she used for their Manhattan penthouse. It was a small gesture that she paid for when people leased out their place. She was having them come over to the senior O'Malley's early on the 23rd, several hours prior to leaving for the airport.

Created with Sketch.

It was the 23rd, the maid service had cleaned the entire penthouse, Paul and Jezalee were sitting in the limousine, on their way to the airport. Paul had two limousine drivers pick them up. One took care of all the wedding clothes, luggage, and large metal racks, Jezalee and Paul rode in the second limousine. They had a smooth flight and was happy their wedding day was nearing.

Once they arrived home; Jezalee called Joseph and Nina to come over. They had been staying in the main house and had just moved back to their place once Jezalee called to say she was coming home. As soon as they arrived, Paul and Jezalee hugged and kissed them and said how great it to see them. He then asked Joseph if he could help him reassemble the three racks so they could hang up the wedding clothes. The limousine driver had set the luggage down near the entryway and Joseph helped Paul take the luggage upstairs to the master suite. Jezalee asked Nina to help her roll the rack over towards Helga's wing and she'd take it from there.

They knocked on Helga's door and she was so happy to finally see them together. Jezalee asked her if they could hide the wedding clothes in one of her bedrooms until after the children know they will be getting remarried. She obliged them; and Paul rolled the clothes racks into one of her extra bedrooms. They both gave her a huge hug and kiss and was so thrilled to see her.

Afterwards, Jezalee and Paul had the three of them sit in the living room and let them know the children still did not know about Robert being arrested and they think their dad is away taking care of business problems and Jezalee is still at a retreat in Paris; they have no idea the two of them are getting remarried. They will return on the 26th and we are going to have a big dinner here with all of us and the O'Malley family and staff. We wanted you to try on your wedding attire to make sure they don't need any alterations before the wedding.

Nina and Joseph got the zippered bags with their names on them. They went in and tried on their gown and tuxedo. When they came out of Helga's they walked into the living room. Nina loved her gown and Paul remarked, "you both look like you two are the wedding couple; you look fantastic!" Nina thanked Jezalee for letting them be a part of their special day. Helga could not believe their outfits were a perfect fit. Joseph looked at Paul, "Welcome back Paul; we have missed you immensely." Paul proceeded to go over and give them another hug. Jezalee had the children's clothes too! So, make sure they fit as well; if they do not let me know right away. Sure, thing Jezalee! Helga tried her gown on too and she looked amazing as well and it was a perfect fit as well. Astrid was running errands with her boyfriend, and she would try her dress on when they returned.

After Joseph and Nina went back home, Jezalee called to ask David and Mallory to come over for dinner around 7:00. They were anxious to see Paul and Jezalee and asked if they could bring anything. "Just your beautiful selves," Jezalee said.

After Jezalee hung up she called over the intercom and asked Paul to meet her in their bedroom. "I thought you would never ask," Paul answered. "I know what you have on your mind!" Jezalee commented. He hurried upstairs, pushed open the door, "I thought you would be under the covers or standing nude in the middle of the room by now!" Paul said. "Welcome home my irresistible Italian Stallion," Jezalee said. Paul started taking off his clothes, Jezalee gave him that certain seductive look, and walked closer to him, started slowly unbuttoning her blouse; by the time she started to unzip her skirt, he was nude, and he wanted to take the rest of her clothes off her. Once they were nude, he closed the drapes, while she lit some candles, they walked into the bathroom, took a quick shower together and knew by the time they got in bed, the room would be filled with the scent of the candles. They dried one another off, Paul picked her up and slowly carried his damsel in distress, as he referred to her many times, to their bed. "My Prince is worthy of taking my body for gratification, as I am delighted with blissfulness to seek pleasure from him," Jezalee softly and seductively said. Paul gently laid her down in the bed and said how great it felt to be back in their bed, "Oh! How I have missed and yearned for this," emphatically said Paul. Before Jezalee let things heat up any further she had to confess that when she called over the intercom, she was asking him to come up to help her divide up the closet so he could have a portion of it. He started to laugh and informed her; I do not care if I ever wear clothes again! You say that now but just think of being nude, walking around the house, with friends and family around, down the street or in a board room. "Well! Did I just have a moment of insanity?" Paul asked. "Close to it!" Jezalee answered. "No one is going to see you nude, but me! And don't you forget it," Jezalee laughing said. "I am glad you mistook what I was saying when I asked you up here, heck with the closest today!" Lovingly said Jezalee. "I second the motion," Paul replied as he slowly rolled her on top of him. They were in bed for several hours and experiencing everything they had missed for way too long. After satisfying one another to a world of heated and sensual passion, it was time to get up, take another shower together then go start cooking dinner because their friends would be over in about two hours.

While Jezalee was roasting, baking, chopping, and dicing, Paul was marinating the ribeye steaks and letting them sit until their guests arrived. It was 6:45 and Jezalee had finished in the kitchen and went up to change into her yellow dress, knowing it was Paul's all-time favorite. When the doorbell rang, Paul answered the door and quickly invited David and Mallory in. He had them follow him into the living room and Jezalee had already set out appetizers and drinks. Mallory asked where the lady of the house was, and he said she went to change but will be right down.

No sooner had Paul answered Mallory's question, in walked Jezalee, and all he could say was, "There is my ray of sunshine." Jezalee apologized for not being down to greet them, but she got a later start on dinner and was a little behind. "That is fine with us; we needed time to catch up on things with Paul," David replied.

They talked about the wedding while they indulged in appetizers and a drink. Mallory proceeded to officially welcome Paul back and was astonished to hear what he had gone through and wrongfully judging him with not knowing the whole story. He let them know that he had handled the rape all wrong and no matter what, he should have been up front with Jezalee from the start. I felt, like most men probably do, it is embarrassing; especially of my size, to think I could be raped by a woman. "With all due respect Paul, you had two men that helped her, that's how! You did not have a fighting chance after being drugged and taken to her place. Also, knowing London, did not have a law protecting men from being raped," David commented. Paul indicated he had been tirelessly working with influential people in London for the last several years to get a law passed to protect men as they protect women, who have been raped. "All I can say is, I had nine hellish years having to see that demonic woman once a month in-order-to see Jonathan, and Jezalee having over three and half years dealing with Robert!" Paul replied.

Mallory changed the subject so she could share the photos she had of what their three-tiered wedding cake was going to look like; however, she was not about to show them the actual size, since they think 60 guests are coming and the count was currently up to over 400. Mallory chose an eight-tiered cake and Jezalee wanted it to look like her gown. The designer, Dani had special delivered swatches of the material from Jezalee's gown to Mallory; so, the cake decorator made a mock-up cardboard version of a three-tiered cake; but had decorated the outside with the actual ingredients so they could see what it would look like. Jezalee was astounded the cake matched the design perfectly; it was identical to the materials her gown was made from. The flowers were next; Jezalee loved the Vendela Ivory Roses, White Hydrangeas, and three varieties of Ivory and Cream Roses, her favorite was the Patience Ivory Cream David Austin of England. Mallory had chosen the Chandeliers, and she and Paul loved them.

Jezalee and Paul brought over the O'Malley family wedding attire hoping they liked them. They excused themselves, went to change into what they would be wearing and loved them. They looked amazing, and Mallory loved her gown and David said it was the best tuxedo he has ever worn. They took the children's clothes upstairs and hopefully everything would fit; if not, Dani has one of her lead seamstresses, who recently moved to San Francisco and would be more than happy to refit any of the wedding party's clothes. After the night was almost over, David and Mallory went home and Paul and Jezalee could not run fast enough to get to their master suite. They said goodnight by intercom to Helga and said they may sleep in the next day. She knew what that meant as she giggled and told them to not exhaust themselves too much! They laughed!

The next day Jezalee called Joan and Richard and asked them how they were doing and could hardly wait to see them at the wedding. They both said they had been extremely overworked with their trials coming up; however, expressed, how wonderful it will be to see them get remarried. Jezalee asked them if they were still able to join them for dinner the day the children come home, and they said absolutely.

Paul and Jezalee never left the house and hung around doing nothing but being lazy and resting up until the family arrived from Italy. At one point, Helga even served them dinner in bed; and it was a real treat. Astrid was home and she came up to their bedroom to say hi and she had her tea length dress on to model. She chose to wear the tea length and it was the perfect choice for her. She looked stunning and it was a dress she said she would have plenty of places she could wear the beautiful dress. Later that evening, they got to meet Astrid's boyfriend, Nicholas who would be attending the wedding.

By now, four days before the wedding, everyone had tried on their clothes that were in the wedding, with the exception, of the vacationers and Paul's Harvard buddies. Mallory said if their gowns are any indication of what Jezalee's wedding gown will look like; she's going to wow everyone.

It was girls, night; so, Helga invited Mallory and her staff to come over and join her and Jezalee's staff for appetizers, then dinner at her home. Everyone had finished the appetizers and drinks, and Helga said dinner would be ready in thirty minutes. That was Jezalee's cue to get up and excuse herself and say she had to go to the ladies, room. Helga pretended to be in her kitchen; but she followed in behind Jezalee to help her in the gown. After Helga helped her into the gown; she walked over to the full-length mirror and when she saw the dress in the mirror, it was more beautiful then, she remembered. Helga was crying and flipped over how gorgeous Jezalee looked. "Let us hurry and show it to the girls," Helga said through her tears.

Jezalee walked out of the bedroom, down the lengthy hallway, to Helga's living room, where all the girls were sitting on the over-sized white Damask sofas and chairs. They looked at Jezalee approaching them; she was a vision of pure, ethereal beauty, she had her hair pulled back in a semi-loose bun to get the effect of how she will look at the wedding ceremony. She had decided on a full-length flowing gown, that had a lot of movement, slightly shimmering ivory organza, with scattered miniature French lace with intricate flowers, with tiny Swarovski crystals scattered throughout the full skirted gown, the off the shoulder French lace scalloped bodice with the tiny Swarovski crystals as well, with a wide waistband of lace, with French lace sleeves to the elbow. There was an extraordinary antique brooch to the left of the waist band.

Jezalee was just a few feet away from the girls, she asked them what they thought of the dress. "The word Wow! Does not do that gown justice! You look simply magical, like you stepped right out of a fairytale book come to life," Mallory responded. Everyone agreed it was amazing, incredible, sexy, romantic, and purely exquisite. "The funny thing is! I walked into Dani's and was ready to try on dozens of gowns that day; walked over to start pulling some off the racks, and! There it was, waiting for me!" Commented Jezalee.

Linda was sitting back, taking it all in and asked if she could give Jezalee one suggestion. "Sure dear! Let me know what you think, Jezalee asked. "Well! Do me a favor and take your hair out of the bun and toss that gorgeous mane around," Linda asked. "I see what you mean Linda," Astrid commented. "Aunt Jez, you have got to wear that gorgeous hair down, flowing like your gown does," Astrid nicely insisted. "Raise your hands if you think Jezalee should wear her hair down," Helga asked. It was unanimous! Jezalee asked Linda and Astrid if they would come with her to fix her hair exactly how it should look for the wedding. They excused themselves and Astrid said they would be back in about ten minutes. When they came back, there was not a dry eye in the room! "Now! You see what I was talking about? Not only that! You are a vision, and that gown was designed to wear hair flowing into it; and with your color scheme and décor you are having, it is exceptionally romantic," Linda commented. "Thank you so much for your input and I am wearing my hair down," Jezalee said thanks to the ladies. Helga went with her to get changed out of the gown; afterwards, the ladies had a wonderful dinner. "How many guests are you having?" Nell asked. "All of you of course! And it should add up to around sixty guests," Jezalee answered. Mallory was internally laughing; Nell had been instrumental in every facet of the wedding planning; especially taking care of the hotel accommodations for the guests. Paul and I are thrilled that his brother, Fr. Peter will officiate the ceremony; we were the first couple he married right after he was ordained. This time, after he marries us, he will be at Saint Mary's here in San Francisco for thirty days as a visiting priest.

"Jezalee, you and Paul are explicitly to stay away from our place until just before the wedding," Mallory stood up and said. "All of us are getting ready over here and the men will be at my place," Mallory said.

After girls, night was over, everyone went back to their places and a few minutes after they left, Paul arrived home. He and Jezalee sat in the family room discussing how great it was going to be having the children home and they be a part of their wedding. They were getting so anxious to be getting remarried in front of their family and friends; it was extra special to be able to share this moment with everyone. When Paul went over to David's that day, he took Paul into his den and told him to brace himself because the wedding was way over 60 people. He looked at David and asked how many? David quietly said, "over 400 and was afraid to look Paul in the eyes, when he said it. Paul thought that was great! "Really! Replied

David. Mallory knew your first wedding was small to suit Jezalee because she was too nervous. Paul commented to David that he felt over the years, Jezalee blossomed out of her shyness and does not think she'll freeze up when she walks down the aisle past that many guests. "I pray she does not, or Mallory and I will be responsible," David said. "I would tell her; but this is a special surprise," Paul remarked. "I probably should not have told you," David said. "I am glad I know the surprise and a wonderful one at that," Paul remarked.

That same evening Manny was exited having a sleep over with David and Mallory, he would spend the next day with them until Jezalee had everyone over dinner. When it was bedtime, David carried Manny upstairs on his back, while Mallory was racing behind them. As soon as they got upstairs, the guys went to the bedroom while Mallory went to the linens room and grabbed one of their sleeping bags and extra pillows. Anytime Manny spent the night, the three of them would march into the bathroom and brush their teeth together. David and Mallory taught him their favorite jingle when they were his age, "Brusha, brusha, brusha, new Ipana toothpaste." However, David told him when he and Mallory were his age, the jingle got them to brush their teeth. Manny was smart enough to know he was not brushing his teeth with Ipana toothpaste; but he liked the jingle anyways. Mallory had gotten the sleeping bag and pillow situated near their bed. Manny was content for about a half an hour, he then slid out of the bag, walked over to David and Mallory's bed with his irresistible charm and those doe-like brown eyes and he sweetly asked them if he could sleep in the bed with them. "Absolutely! I do not think Mallory and I could get a good night's sleep unless you are cuddled up in bed with us," David said. "I will be right back! I need to go potty; so, make room and I will return soon," while Manny was in the bathroom, David and Mallory discussed how much they loved that child, he was so full of life, great personality, and curious about all things. A few minutes later, Manny was settled in between two of his favorite people; David and Mallory made up a fairytale story about a brave boy named Manny and within two minutes he was sound asleep.

The day had finally arrived! Everyone would be flying in from Italy and would be arriving early afternoon. Bob had picked up Paul at noon to come have lunch with Linda and him; Manny was having fun with David and Mallory and wanted to help in the kitchen to make breakfast with Mallory. He was especially excited to go over to Jezalee's for dinner because he knew all the children would finally be home.

The Italy vacationers arrived home at 3:00 p.m., Jezalee hugged and kissed everyone as they came through the door. She asked the children to take their luggage to their rooms and dinner would be at 6:00 p.m. Jezalee had the bedrooms downstairs ready for her and Paul's parents or they could take one of the other rooms upstairs. They decided downstairs was great! The Stanton children were staying for dinner and knew their parents would be coming over as well.

The O'Malley children arrived home from camp at 4:30 p.m. As soon as they came through the door, they asked what were-the-tents for. Before any of the children went upstairs to put their luggage away; they needed to inform them that Paul and Jezalee were getting married on their property in three days and their children have no idea they are getting back together. Not one word to Adrienne, Jessica, or Alexander; they will have a surprise at the door after we are assembled over there for dinner this evening. Adam asked where is Paul right now? He is hiding out at Bob and Linda's. Another thing! After he arrives to surprise their children, before dinner everyone will know they are getting married; however, they think 60 guests are coming and in-actuality-between 400. They are not allowed to come on the property until just prior to the wedding.

By 5:45 p.m. everyone that was coming to Jezalee's dinner party, had arrived with the exception, of Paul and Bob. The guests were seated in the living room and the Albanese children started discussing how amazing the trips to Africa and through Italy were. The O'Malley children talked about all their fun adventures at camp and how great it was to have the-majority- of the children be from the Boys and Girls Club. The doorbell rang and it was Bob, he joined them in the living room to hear all about the trips the children had been on. Ten minutes later the doorbell rang again! Jezalee asked her three children to get the package that was delivered because it is extremely big and heavy. As they are walking towards the double doors, Paul is behind one of the tall plants at the outside entrance. The children are looking for a package and do not see anything, suddenly, out pops their dad they scream for joy! He said "hi" children, surprise! The children walked him into the living room. Alexander asked his dad to sit down near him on one of the sofas. The girls went back to where they were sitting; and Paul sat down after he greeted everyone. That was the opportune time for him to get up, walk over to Jezalee, pull out a jeweled box, got down on one knee, opened the box and asked her to marry him. The O'Malley's glanced over at the Albanese children and saw how stunned and happy they were when their dad proposed. Before Jezalee got to answer him; their children, in unison, said "Yes! She will! Everyone stood up, started laughing. and clapping. While they did that, as Paul was placing the engagement on her third finger, left hand, she put her right hand and arm on his back and helped him move closer so she could say a soft "Yes! I will marry you" and gave him a kiss. "Excuse me! Dad, have you been rendezvousing with mom, all this time?" Alexander inquisitively asked. "I sure have and thanks to Patrick and Kathleen O'Malley, we had a marvelous stay in their newly renovated penthouse in New York. All three children walked over to their parents crying and said this is the highlight of our vacation and they asked their mom to stand up so the five of them could have a group hug. "One more wonderful thing to add to all this, your parents will be getting married over at our property three days from tonight," informed Mallory.

The first thing Jezalee noticed when Paul placed the ring on her finger, it was not her original ring, which she had given to him when they arrived in San Francisco. After she had kissed him, she looked down at the ring and said this is not my original ring! "I know! This time, I wanted to design the rings to celebrate our new beginning," Paul stated. Before anyone headed to the dining room, they were anxious to get a closer look at the engagement ring. "Is there a significance in the design?" Mallory asked. "Yes! there is, the emerald cut diamond is 5Karats, representing, Jezalee, me and the three children, he pulled out the wedding band from the jeweled box, with two diamond bands to show they were identical to the band that the 5Karat diamond was connected to. Those three diamond bands represent our three wonderful children," Paul explained. "That is an exquisite wedding set and a clever idea," David remarked. As everyone looked at the rings, they agreed that it was a gorgeous wedding set and Jezalee was even more impressed at Paul's sentimental gesture. "I have missed your insatiable romantic side you have always had!" Jezalee commented. "I will take that as a compliment and be assured that my romantic side has never faded away when it comes to you!" Paul replied. Jezalee let Paul know she would still be wearing her original wedding ring on her right hand, and she wanted him to place those rings on her finger at the wedding before the new set and everyone clapped and thought that was also romantic. After everyone was finished speaking, Helga happily said, "dinner will now be service."

Several hours later, after all the guests had left, Paul, Jezalee, their three children, and all four grandparents went into the family room and discussed everything that had been going on, with the exception, of Robert. The children did ask about Jim, and Jezalee said he was on an extended business trip in Japan. "He is going to have a big surprise when he returns, and he will not be happy," Alexander said. "You do know that I never gave Jim any encouragement of being a couple, right?" Jezalee commented. "Mom, we knew that! But I do not think he wanted to ever believe it, why wouldn't he want you? You are gorgeous, intelligent, and have three of the greatest children on the planet," Alexander replied.

The Albanese children headed over to the O'Malley's the very next morning. The teenagers wanted to hang out in the game room and knew the rest of the house and property were off limits until the wedding. Once all the teens were together, David sat them down and threatened them if one word got back to Jezalee or anyone else in their family staying with them; about how many guests would be attending the wedding; there would be a high price to pay for leaking out the information. She thinks a little over 60 guests are coming and Paul does know but do not discuss it with him because someone with big ears may overhear the conversation. If Jezalee or the grandparents find out, there will be no movies for one month, no talking on the phone to your friends or enemies, no driving any of the cars, for two months and no sleepovers for a month. "Have I made the conditions clear enough? David asked. They said "Yes, sir!" He left the room and told them to have fun.

Mallory called Jezalee in the middle of the afternoon and asked if Adrienne, Jessica, and Alexander could stay over for sleepovers until the wedding. She thought they may want some quality time with their parents for the next couple of days without, having the children there. She ran it by Paul, and he thought it was a great idea, as-long-as they behaved themselves. "You have the sweetest, dearest, kindest, children and we have never had a problem, so I gather it is a yes then, bye!" Mallory said.

Everyone had tried on their dresses, gowns, and tuxedos. Paul had asked David in advance if he would be his best man, since he was the one that was responsible getting them back together. He was honored that Paul asked him; however, David had other plans. Little did Paul know, his longtime best friend Broderick, who he met at college, and had known each other for over twenty years, would be his best man. There would also be four other friends from college that he and Broderick were close to. Eddie, Craig, John, and Bradley were honored when they got the call that Paul was remarrying his sweet Jezalee and could hardly wait to be a part of the wedding party. Mallory had gotten the measurements/sized of all five men and on the lowdown called Georgio to let him know these men needed the same tuxedos without Paul knowing they would be in the wedding. Jezalee had asked Mallory to be her matron of honor, she graciously accepted; however, she did the same thing, she called Natalie and asked her to be Jezalee's surprise matron of honor and she was thrilled. There were two other close friends of Jezalee's from college; but one could not make it due to a family crisis, and the other was in the hospital receiving a kidney transplant. Everyone who was a part of the wedding, which included staff members from both households. Jezalee had gotten close to the O'Malley staff and wanted them to be a part of their wedding also. Paul would be arm in arm with his parents making the same walk, which Jezalee wanted him to have the same experience she would have walking up the aisle with her parents.

It had been two relaxing and wonderful days that Paul and Jezalee had with their parents. It was a throwback to when they first met in college and the six of them would get together. They ate, listened to music, danced, and played scrabble; men against women; each side won a game. Jezalee had three masseuses coming over and gave all of them, including Helga, Nina, and Joseph massages. After they left, they went in the steam room, then the pool. Afterwards, Paul ordered food from several restaurants, and he went and picked it up.

While the Albanese household was relaxing and kicking back for two days; Mallory, David, and their daily staff were checking off lists of things that required last minute attention. They did a walk through each day in the tents to make sure everything was in working order. Bob had hired four electricians, to be on standby, in case there was any unforeseeable problems that may arise before or during or wedding. They added four extra security guards during the wedding and hired a bus company to have eight buses available to pick up all the guests from their hotels, airport, or homes in the area. Each bus had a list of the passengers that be traveling on each bus.

The day before the wedding, the cake arrived, in all its beauty, and the O'Malley's were thankful they had a walk-in refrigerator that was perfect for an eight-tiered wedding cake. The bakery sent over a three-tiered, much smaller version of the cake so everyone could have a tasting preview of the wedding cake. That afternoon, after a late lunch, everyone that had been working so diligently on the wedding preparations; sampled the cake and said it was out-of-this-world-incredible. The florist arrived with the flowers for all the attendees and two for Jezalee; David placed them in the walk-in refrigerator to keep fresh. Mallory called the photographer because he wanted take photos of the interior of both tents as soon as they were decorated.

The first tent was for the ceremony which housed up to 400 guests. There were Ivory, Cream, and Antique Gold-colored Brocade cushioned chairs. A pastel, Ivory, Cream and Antique Gold Karastan runner that the wedding party would be walking down; remainder of the flooring was hardwood. There were nine lightly dimmed chandeliers throughout the tent. There were ten large plant pedestals throughout the room that had extraordinary, large ferns draping down over the pedestals, in Antique Cream, Ivory and Gold. An altar was constructed with an elaborately decorated fifteen-foot arch, adorned with all the exceptionally beautiful flowers Jezalee had chosen. Behind the intricate arch was a magnificent scalloped, drape of the same material as the chair cushions. Up at the altar, surrounding the entire area was antique lanterns, of various heights and widths. Mallory knew, since this was a summer wedding in tents, she knew it would be light out and she wanted the tent material to be blacked out and so the inside of each tent would be soft lighting, candles everywhere and the overhead dim lit chandeliers. They were able to get the look they wanted throughout and had shimmering antique gold organza drapery to soften the tent walls and ceilings.

The second tent was for the reception, for the sit-down dinner, the colors, material, and décor, similar as the first ten, the only difference there were round tables, with tablecloths, and chairs with the same material as the cushioned chairs at the ceremony. The floral centerpieces were on pedestals at a height that were tall enough where the guests could see one another. The arrangements were duplicated with all the various flowers chosen that adorned the entire wedding tents. There were the beautiful lit lanterns arranged around the bottom of the pedestals, to illuminate the tables.

Mallory and David were overjoyed, everything was falling into place and silence was golden amongst any staff or family member. Everyone had helped; they wanted Jezalee and Paul to have the most elegant, magical, and romantic wedding possible. They knew what horrible experiences they both had and suffered being away from one another far too long. Mallory asked them if there was anything she may have forgotten to do, and they said everything is done and all items on the list has been checked off. "This is going to be a wedding that everyone will be talking about for a long time; when the guests walk through the entrance of these tents; it is like stepping into a world of illuminating beauty, everything in both tents are purely magical, romantic, and spectacular," Bob commented. Mallory sincerely thanked him. "Both tents should be in a wedding magazine," Bob said. "That's so sweet of you; I had a wonderful time having a vision for Jezalee, because when I walk through both tents; I feel it looks like the beauty and radiance that exudes from my dear friend," Mallory said. "Well! I have taken a lot of photos and videos, and I am sure they will turn out picture perfect." Bob said.

Mallory asked all the staff members to meet her back at the house after they had made their last walk through the tents. She invited them out for a nice lunch with her and David to relax for the rest of the evening. She thanked them for all the hours they had worked to attain the amazing results in both tents. Mallory let Bob and Linda know that the children would take care of Manny and she already had pizzas and salad ready for the children to help themselves while they went out to eat.

David and Mallory were enjoying lunch with all the staff members from both households; they gave them a token of their appreciation. David handed a seven-day trip to Napa Wine Country; accommodations at a five-star hotel and reservations every night at a different 5-star restaurant. All six staff members were used to being spoiled by their employers but still was always surprised that they were so generous.

After everyone arrived back at their homes, the O'Malley's dropped off Adrienne, Jessica, and Alexander home so they could be with their parents the night before their wedding. After the O'Malley's arrived home, Mallory called Jezalee and asked how she and Paul were doing. She first, thanked her for having their children over for two days; it gave them time to visit with their parents. Jezalee let her know that the first time Paul and she got married; they spent two days with their parents and the last two days was de-ja vu all over again. It was so special! they were so thankful they made it back to one another. "Isn't that the truth, my dear friend!" Mallory said.

Morgan caught up with her mom just as she was going to her room to get ready for bed. "Mom, everything is so pretty for the wedding, but aren't you concerned Jezalee will panic when she sees so many people at the wedding?" Morgan frantically asked. "I know what you mean, it has been on my mind as well, your dad and I just got so caught up in wanting Jezalee and Paul to have something extra special, with everything they went through," Mallory answered. "I have prayed this does not backfire on us, because I do not want Jezalee to be disappointed in the way we handled her wedding," Mallory said. Morgan's mom let her know that they did inform Paul and he thought it was great they would be able to share their wedding with so many of their family and friends. "I hope he is right; you certainly do not want an unhappy bride," Morgan replied.

David and Mallory's parents arrived for the big event; and while they got settled in their rooms, Nell was preparing dinner. After Patrick and Kathleen got settled in their room, David came in and said how glad he was to see them and thanked them once again for letting Jezalee stay in their place during the investigation on Robert. His parents commented on how much they cared about Jezalee and Paul; they were thrilled how things turned out for them. Mallory was happy her parents, Valerie, and Thomas were able to attend the wedding and could spend quality time with them.

While the O'Malley's were having dinner, a few blocks away at the Albanese's, they had finished with dinner and Jezalee was hanging out with her mom, Carolyn and her mother-in-law, Elene. They were having some great girl time. Adrienne, Jessica, Helga, Astrid, Nina, and her two daughters were talking about the anticipated wedding. Jezalee had Nina include her son in with the rest of the guys. Nina had a great idea! She suggested that the guys should spend the night at her place with Joseph, and the girls stay with Jezalee. Jezalee thought that was perfect! She asked the guys to come down because they had a suggestion. The guys thought it was great to spend the night at Joseph's. Jezalee called Mallory to invite her and the rest of the gals to come spend the night and ask if David and all the guys, would like a sleepover at Joseph's. Within the hour, Paul had picked up Gregory and met the rest of the guys back at Joseph's.

The men and boys got their pajamas and started their card games and watched baseball on television. The women and girls got all settled in the family room and were enjoying their girl time together. They were all deciding how they should wear their hair, what color of lipstick, etc. They were looking forward for their makeovers for the wedding. Jezalee asked the girls, since it was unanimous for her to wear her hair down, should she have the hairdresser bother with my hair. They felt that when she washed her hair, blow-dried it, that she would attain the look that she looked stunning in. She said she would call the salon first thing in the morning to tell Gina she was doing her own hair but will pay her anyway; plus! She will be doing her and Paul's mom's hair. "Now that we have all that settled! What other issues need to be addressed," Jezalee asked. "I want all of you to know what my mom has put together, with the ideas Jezalee passed on to her, is the most beautiful surroundings a bride could ever imagine in her dreams," Morgan remarked. She looked over at Jezalee, "You and my mom are an extraordinary duo, and should have started an interior design business, you have such visions when bringing out beauty in everything," Morgan added. "How sweet you are to say those kind words, and I know how your mom is, as soon as I gave her information on what I wanted the wedding to look like, I knew there was nothing stopping her creativity," Jezalee remarked. "I am incredibly lucky to have such a great friend who took on a huge undertaking; even though its only for 60 or so guests, I wanted them to be surrounded by beauty while Paul and I said our vows," Jezalee commented. "Well! now that you two have spoken, I have something to add," Mallory said. "All of us have been waiting with bated-breath for this wedding to take place, I knew I had to jump in to help because David and I wanted Jezalee and Paul to have time for themselves to get reunited and strengthen their love, which, as we all can attest, was never gone in the first place," Mallory stated. Everyone gave out a giggle because they knew they were still madly in love with one another but had been too stubborn to come forward with their feelings.

The gals did not want to stay up too late; even though, the wedding was an evening wedding, they did not want any unwanted bags under their eyes or too tired to wake up and relax before the wedding. The doorbell rang and they could not imagine who that would be this late, so Jezalee buzzed the guard at the front gate if anyone came through that had a code. He said, there had been no signs of any cars or persons on foot, other than Mr. Albanese leaving to go pick up someone. She thanked the guard and as she hung up, Helga had answered the front door and Paul was standing there in his airplane pajamas. Jezalee walked over to him and sweetly asked him what he wanted. He said I will not see you all day tomorrow; so, I wanted to have one last kiss before we tie the knot. By the time they were kissing, all the gals rushed to the entryway, and a few took photos. "This photo is better than the famous photo taken on V-J Day where the sailor grabbed that lady in Times Square and kissed her," Carolyn commented.

The gals all said, "Cute pajamas Paul." "These are my lucky pajamas and knew I had to wear them tonight," Paul remarked. "I hope I did not interfere in whatever you ladies were doing," Paul said. "Who did you bring onto the property earlier?" Jezalee asked. "Checking up on me? I picked up Gregory to spend the night," Paul answered. "Oh! Thank you for remembering him, since he will be in the wedding," Jezalee said. They both kissed one more time and off he went.

The gals headed back into the family room and Jezalee was getting ready to go over the bedroom arrangements. There was seventeen females and fifteen bedrooms. Some gals decided to sleep together, and others had a room to themselves. They said their goodnights and went to their rooms. Jezalee was tired and after having Paul back for three weeks, she had to line up pillows the length of the bed because she could not fall asleep with the empty space with Paul not cuddled up next to her.

In Joseph's household most of the guys were still playing cards, and as usual Alexander won each game. Antonio informed his grandson, when he turns twenty-one, right to Vegas and Monte Carlo, I am taking you. "Pops! You mentioned that once before and it is not going to happen, right?" Paul remarked, "We will have him play the Stock Market instead, I did very well at his age!" Paul said with his eyebrows raised at his pop.

Before Paul and Alexander went to bed, they stayed up in the family room and talked a good hour. Alexander asked his dad how things had been since the divorce. Paul explained it was extremely difficult; not being with the love of his life and moving so far away from him, not being able to be with his dear children, was the worst feeling of loneliness. Paul admitted he was furious with Jezalee leaving Paris the way she did. Alexander made sure his dad knew how he and his sisters hated being so far away from him. Alexander wanted his dad to know that finding out what he and his mom went through was so sad and he felt they both got their egos in the way of communicating with each other. "I am just a kid; but I see and feel the love you and mom have always had for one another. When mom filed for divorce, we were devastated! At the time we were upset, and hurt being informed you had an affair, then you tell us you had a son. Unfortunately, mom did not listen to what you were trying to say to her, and it has affected us all," Alexander said. "I do not want you to be so hard on your mom because; it started with him, and he should have been up front with her. I was coming home to tell her what happened to me; but once I opened the door to my privileged and phenomenal life, I could not bear to tell you're her what had happened to me; if I had, we would still be living in Paris, and she would have helped me get through the humiliation it caused me," Paul sadly said. "We love San Francisco, we have a lot of friends, we are happy; but it has been surface happiness. Inside, we have felt lonely because you were the missing link to our happiness. You were always there for guidance and love; there are many other reasons too! You have been the most amazing dad to us and an incredible husband to mom, the four of us could have ever dreamed of! There were so many things we missed, and we should have been together in every one of them," Alexander said with tears welting up. Paul looked into his sons, tired eyes, and wanted him to know that the five of them will be together and would rebuild what they had, and Alexander hugged his dad and said he loved him so much. On that note! Paul and Alexander hugged and knew tomorrow would bring hope back into their lives. The day of their family healing from what had been and would be an unfortunate road they had traveled for several years. It was to be a moment in time, when two people that never lost sight of the love they had always had as a couple and for whatever reason, they made it back to where they were always supposed to be. Jezalee and Paul had the strength within them to weather the obstacles in their way, push forward and knock down all barriers. They made the effort because their undying love for one another was always there; they just had to keep their strength at full throttle and know, no matter what had happened, what was said and who had entered their lives; they had to find their way back to fulfill their promise to one another. They would love one another the rest of "the days of their lives". Tomorrow they would get back the life they had built together as a loving couple and have their three children at their side.

Paul said it was time to get their beauty sleep for their big day ahead tomorrow; off they went to bed knowing the grand life ahead of them was finally within reach.

Part Four

Wedding Day: July 29, 1989

Wedding Day jitters! David woke up at the crack of dawn, quietly slid out of bed, as to not disturb Adam, and tip-toed by Gregory as he slept. He quickly got out of Joseph's house without waking up anyone. Once he was outside, he ran to his car and drove up to the front of the Albanese's home, went up to the front door and lightly tapped on it; hoping Mallory was awake and downstairs. To his relief, Mallory answered the door, quickly put her slippers on and rode home with him without disturbing anyone.

They wanted to get as much done before Jezalee's pajama breakfast party started around 11:00 a.m. After their morning coffee and roll, they walked out to the first tent, lo' and behold! Joseph and Bob were already at work checking on the lights, and microphone. They wanted to make sure the exquisite French and Italian electric lit lanterns were in working order. While they were doing that, David and Mallory went to the second tent where the reception would be held. They checked out each table to make sure each lantern and pedestals were in the center of the table, where the floral arrangements would be housed. They checked the sound system where, the day before, the DJ had come over to set everything up. When guest would walk into this tent, there would be a large antique board over to the side housed on two exquisite, custom made pillars with the guests, name in alphabetical order. The tables had an antique gold stand with a scrolled letter of the Alphabet; there would be four of Morgan's friends that were hired to assist all guest to their tables according to the chart. David said he would help Joseph and Bob bring over the 50 floral arrangements that needed to be placed on top of the pedestals on the 48 tables and the two pedestals at the entrance of the tent. They had been delivered late yesterday and placed in their walk-in refrigerator, along with the flowers and boutonnieres for the wedding party, the eight-tiered wedding cake, and all the food the caterers brought over that needed to prep the day of the wedding.

Bob and Joseph met up with David and Mallory and said everything was checked out in the ceremony tent and the Grand Piano would be delivered in the reception tent in an hour. While they were waiting for that, they made sure that the generators were all set in case they had an electrical outage. David said he'd help them later in the day when they were ready to bring all the flowers over.

David and Mallory reminded Joseph and Bob that breakfast would be at their home for the men, and Jezalee would have all the gals at her place. They did not want Paul and Jezalee see one another, so they split them up. Someone from Jezalee's house would deliver your breakfasts around 11:00 a.m. In the meantime, come back to our house for coffee and rolls to tide you over until their food arrives. David said he would make sure all the guys got up by at least 10:30 a.m. to make it over breakfast. "See you two later and thank you a million times over for all your expertise in helping us;

we would never have been able to pull this spectacular event off without your expeditious help." Said Mallory.

It was 7:30 a.m., Paul jumped out of bed, got Alexander and Gregory up and the three of them went for a thirty-minute run. By the time they got back, the rest of the guys were up and at the O'Malley's waiting for breakfast. The three of them got to Paul's and they were about to head for the kitchen, when he realized he had to leave and go over to David and Mallory's because he could not see Jezalee until the wedding. He told the boys they needed to leave before he got a glimpse of Jezalee. They quickly turned around and ran over to the O'Malley's home.

When David and Mallory arrived home, they picked up the morning newspaper and took it to the kitchen like they always did. Mallory started a fresh pot of coffee, sat down at the table, opened the newspaper, and was stunned when she saw the headlines, she motioned for David to sit down, and she handed him the newspaper. Suddenly she saw Paul, Alexander, and Gregory walking into the kitchen. She was startled and caught off guard; but tried to be calm. Before Mallory got up, she quickly put the newspaper under the island shelf and asked the guys what they wanted to drink. As she poured their drinks, David asked Paul, how the soon-to-be groom felt. "I feel like the first time we got married, I am as nervous today as I was then." Replied Paul. "Would you three like some fresh, hot rolls, since breakfast will not be delivered until around 11:00 a.m.?" Asked Mallory. "That would be great! I do not think we would last until then, right boys?" Paul asked. "Do you guys mind taking up some drinks and rolls for the rest of the guys, they are in the game room hanging out until breakfast comes?" Asks David. "Sure!" Paul said, no problem.

David buzzed upstairs to the game room and asked what all the guys wanted to drink. "There are three musclemen downstairs, who will be your servers." David informed them. After Mallory had all the drinks poured and three dozen rolls, Paul and the boys brought them up in the elevator on a rolling tray. Mallory let Paul know they had some errands to run and would be back in a few hours. He asked if he could help and they said it was pertaining to your wedding, and they wanted him to relax with the rest of the guys. All the guys were going to hang out there until breakfast was brought over. They started watching sports news, played some fuse ball and sang some

Karaoke to pass the time away. Mallory was trying to hurry as quickly as she could and hoped that Paul and the boys did not notice she was hurrying them because they had a huge situation that demanded her and David's quick attention.

After Paul and the boys went upstairs, they took the newspaper into David's den. They began to read the entire article, Alleged Serial Killer, Robert Anderson, tries to commit suicide in his cell, sometime, late Friday night; a guard found him around 11:00 p.m. The prisoner has been transported to a hospital and is in critical condition. David went in to get Bob and Joseph and the four of them needed to take care of some damage control. They could not let the guests coming to the wedding, divulge what was in the news about Robert. They did not want anything to put a black cloud over this wedding.

Mallory suggested they attempt to call everyone on the list; but needed more people to help. David said he would ask his mom and dad; but they still needed more help. Mallory put in a call to Jezalee and said she needed Linda, Nina, Elene, and Kathleen to come over as soon as possible. "Is everything okay?" Asked Jezalee. Yes, everything is going well, I just need them to help me for a couple hours," Mallory answered. "I will have them take one of our cars and they will be right over," Jezalee replied. "Thank you!" Mallory said.

David and Mallory had rounded up Bob, Joseph, Patrick, Antonio, Linda, Nina, Kathleen, and Elene; they did not want Carolyn and Mark to help because Jezalee might have become suspicious. Once everyone was together, David let them see the headlines and read the article to them. "We have a huge undertaking today prior to the wedding. We need to make calls to everyone on the guest list; we cannot let Paul, Jezalee, or anyone else in our households know about Robert, until after the wedding is over," David.

They made their calls from the O'Malley's, Bob, and Linda's house, and at Joseph and Nina's. They each had a list of 40 names and after three hours, they were almost done; David, Bob, Joseph, and Patrick had to drive separate cars and headed over to the hotels where they weren't able, to talk to the guest but messages at the desk. They had to drive to some of the guests, homes that lived locally, and the outlying areas in the Bay Area. They left a number to call and leave a message on the wedding coordinators answer machine that they received the message. They informed each guest in person, by phone, or left messages, it was most important that the wedding couple not be privy to the newspaper article on Robert.

While David and Mallory had rounded up the people to help with their dilemma, they asked Morgan to make sure all the guys were fed the plates of food that Jezalee had put together for them. Whatever people were helping them said they would eat when they returned. The men came back to the O'Malley home where their food was waiting for them and the women, who helped, went back to the Albanese home to eat.

Before the women went back to Jezalee's to have their brunch, David thanked everyone for helping with something that could have potentially been a disaster. Once they left, the men that helped sat down at dining room table and were exhausted, famished and was so thankful there was a great meal to be had. Mallory was the first done and said she had some calls to make and was taking a nap before the caterers and the women and men from the salons arrived.

David informed Mallory he would help Bob, and Joseph take the floral arrangements out of the refrigerator about 6:00 p.m. and make sure the flowers stayed fresh with the cooling system they had. Patrick spoke up and said he would help too! Mallory said she had the metal carts on rollers, and they held eight center pieces each so it should not take too long. She thanked everyone and went upstairs. Before Mallory went to her master suite; she and David headed over to see how the grand piano looked in the reception tent; when they got over there it was in the perfect spot for the room.

Once Mallory was in the master suite, she got the important wedding calls out of the way then called Jezalee. Jezalee answered her private line upstairs in her bedroom and was happy to hear from Mallory. "Well! Miss Bride to be! How are you doing? Mallory asked. "I am on cloud nine, nervous, happy, and all the above that I went through almost twenty years ago," Jezalee answered. "Is everything going smoothly for you Mallory?" Jezalee asked. "Yes, everything is going beautifully because we have had extra last-minute help and it made things run perfectly; I hope this night is everything you want and deserve it to be, my dear friend," Mallory said with much relief. "With you volunteering to have our wedding, then taking care of all the details, I am envisioning a beautiful wedding; but I do feel somewhat guilty because I know how hard you have worked to get to this day, and it was a daunting task with not much time to spare,"

Jezalee commented with somewhat guilt. "This was a labor of love for two people that have been in a severe storm and weathered through it. David and I wanted both of you, to sit back and relax as much as one can knowing they are getting married in front of family and friends," Mallory remarked. "I am just thankful, it will be an intimate wedding and I know I will be fine, thanks to all that you have done," Jezalee said with conviction. Mallory was thinking to herself! Talk about guilt! What have David and I done! "Dear, you are going to be the most stunning bride, no matter how many people you have at your wedding," Mallory said with a heavy. "With that said, I am sure you need to rest after all the work you have done, I will see you later," Jezalee sweetly said. Mallory let her know, that all the girls would be over at her house around 3:30 p.m., for their makeovers, nail, and hair styles to be done

The men all decided to go play tennis and do some golfing before heading back to Paul's house to get dressed. While they were enjoying the beautiful weather, Jezalee and Mallory were taking well deserved naps. Once their naps were over, Mallory called Morgan to make sure the caterer and her staff arrived and were prepping in their commercial kitchen. She let her mom know everything under control and wanted to reconfirm they could use the counter and island spaces in their personal kitchen as well. "By-all-means! Everything has been taken off all those areas for them to have access for workspace," Mallory replied. "One other thing, dear! Could you please put a large note on our kitchen door for no one to enter or use until after wedding is over," Mallory asked. "Sure! Mom, I will do that now," Morgan said.

Morgan buzzed her mom through the intercom, the photographer had just finished taking photos of the interiors and exteriors of the two tents. He said to give him the go ahead, whenever they were ready for him to come over to take photos of everyone getting ready for the wedding. Mallory asked her to have him wait in the living room and she will be right down. Before she met up with him, she called Jezalee to see if she was up from her nap. Jezalee had just finished taking her shower and Bob left early from the Club so he could bring her over to Mallory's. "I will be there in five or ten minutes," Jezalee said. "Make sure you come up to my room, we will get ready together," Mallory said. "Okay! Sounds good!" Jezalee replied.

When Jezalee arrived at Mallory's, all the other females were getting set up in the bedrooms upstairs. Bob had brought up everyone's wedding dresses, gowns, and accessories; then, went to the Country Club to pick up the men. He had taken all the boys and men's clothes for the wedding, over to Paul's house and set them up in different bedrooms to get ready. Four barbers were on their way over to give the boys and men hair trims and clean shaves. Bob had taken over the tuxedos and accessories to the five alums from Harvard, who would be a surprise in Paul's wedding. He needed them to try on the wedding apparel to make sure everything fit by the measurements they had given Georgio. David had gotten them a suite at the Fairmont Hotel, for a few days; but they would be escorted over to the Albanese estate and get ready in Helga's wing. Helga was the only one in the wedding party that knew they would be in the wedding. Joseph had gone over to get them as soon as the women went over to Mallory's. The men would have no idea the five men arrived, by Joseph sneaking them in at the back entrance of Helga's wing and the doors were locked, just in case, someone was roaming around the house.

Once Jezalee was set up in Mallory's bedroom, they were getting ready for their makeup to be applied then they would have their hair and nails done. When her hairdresser arrived; Jezalee showed her wedding gown to her, and she agreed her hair down was going to be stunning. While they were getting their makeup applied, their gowns were being steamed.

Every bedroom was occupied; the females had taken over and were getting complete makeovers to look their wedding best. Their clothes had been professionally steamed and their garments and accessories laid out when it was time to get dressed.

When Carolyn was finished with her hair and makeup, she came to see Jezalee. Jezalee looked up and saw her mom come through the door. "Mom, you look exceptionally beautiful; I love your hair and the gown looks amazing on you," Jezalee complimented her. "You came at just the right time; you can help me in my gown," Jezalee said. Mallory took the gown off the rolling rack and carefully handed it to Carolyn. Mallory stood by in case Carolyn needed any assistance. Carolyn asked Mallory to take one side of the gown, that way it would be easy for Jezalee to step into it. After they got it zipped up in the back; Jezalee faced them, and they both started crying. "Stop! Your makeup is going to mess up your gorgeous faces," Jezalee commented. "You are a vision of pure happiness, and I am so thrilled this day has come for you and your beloved Paul remarrying," Her mom said as she took another look at her beautiful daughter. "Thank you! Mom you are the sweetest, dearest mother a daughter could have," Jezalee replied. "Mom, I have only one request at my wedding," Jezalee emphatically said. "What is that! Dear?" Her mom asked. "I want you to walk me up the aisle too! Not just dad," "Really!" Her mom asked. "Of Course! I think that should have always been the tradition; you may have gotten pregnant by dad, but you carried me inside you for nine months and gave birth to me," Jezalee uncompromisingly answered. "So! I will not walk up that aisle without you both at my side," "I would be honored and proud to walk with you my sweet child," Her mom replied. "Thank you, mom!" Jezalee said. "While we are together, I have something old for you to pin it under your gown or maybe on top of your Bible when you hold it," her mom said. "Oh! Mom, it is grandma's antique brooch, it has always been my favorite piece of jewelry. She always wore it to Sunday Mass," Jezalee remarked. "Do you remember me telling you that your grandpa surprised her with this gift on their wedding day?" Her mom asked. "Just knowing that grandpa bought that for her to wear on their wedding day is even more special; I am going to remove what the designer made at the waist and want to have the brooch there instead, it is too gorgeous, not to show off." Jezalee said answered then hugged her mom. "I will make sure I give it back to you right after the wedding, I would not want to lose it," Jezalee assured her. "Do not be silly! This is something old and I want you to have it," her mom replied. "Mom, I could not have gotten a better start to my wedding, with this gift, I will cherish it forever," Jezalee cried. "Now! Of all people! You most assuredly are not allowed to cry?" Mallory stated.

Everyone had their makeovers and looked like a million dollars! They came rushing in to see the-end-result of Jezalee in her gown. There was not a dry eye in the room. "Jezalee; you could not have chosen a more perfect gown, and your hair is absolutely gorgeous," Astrid spoke up as soon as she saw her. What is that in your hair, it looks so pretty? Linda asked," "When the hair-dresser saw my hair, she loved it just the way it came out after I washed and blew it dry; but she had this idea of adding just a slight touch, here and there with this shimmering gold she had, and I thought it was a nice, subtle touch," Jezalee answered. "It looks amazing against your silky, black hair," Linda replied. "Thank you, Linda, you are the reason my hair looks good today," Jezalee said.

Alexander knocked on Mallory's bedroom door, and said he had something blue for his mom. The ladies said to enter so he walked in; did not see his mom. They said she would be right out; she is in the closet putting on her heels. When Jezalee walked out she was surprised to see Alexander. "Mom, I do not know how you do it; but you get more beautiful every day. Dad is going to cry his eyes out when he sees you coming up the aisle in that dress; you have never looked more radiant," Alexander said. "You are such a dear heart and so complimentary, thank you my sweet son!" Jezalee replied. "He handed his mom the melody and lyrics he had written and said he was hoping he could play it at the wedding; this is your something "Blue" on colored parchment paper," Alexander said. "Thank you! My dear son," Jezalee responded. Adrienne and Jessica had "Something borrowed, 2 anklets with their names engraved on them; one for each ankle, under your gown," Adrienne said. "These are perfect, my dear incredibly sweet loving daughters! I remember your dad buying them for you five years ago, Christmas," Their mom replied. As she had the girls put them each around her ankles; her mother-in-law, Elene said she had something new for her wedding. She handed Jezalee an Antique Hand carved wooden box and inside was a beautiful Antique Ivory Leather Bible for her to carry up the aisle. "I was informed that you were going to carry a Bible instead of a floral bouquet and I thought this would match your gown and wedding décor better," "it is gorgeous, I will treasure it forever, thank you my lovely Elene," Jezalee said.

Jezalee looked around the room and let everyone know how much each of them meant to her and thanked them for being an integral part of her life. "I now have my traditional items, something old from my mom, something new from my mother-in-law, something borrowed from my daughter's, and something blue from my son. You have made this day so special for me and I cherish your thoughts in these beautiful adornments, that will go up to the altar with me; I am so blessed," Jezalee loving said as she hugged and kissed each one.

The photographer had gotten amazing photos of the guys and gals, while they were getting hair trims, shaves, makeovers, last minute touches of getting dressed, and took photos most of the wedding party outside. He photographed Paul and David; but the groom had no idea there would be later photos with his five buddies from Harvard. The photographer had taken photos of the Harvard alum while they had been getting ready, and Paul had no idea all this was going on in Helga's suite.

It was time! Ave Maria, sung by an opera star, who was a friend of the Albanese family, who officially performed San Francisco Opera House, and Alexander on piano, was playing as the guests were being seated. The maid and matrons of honor, flower girls, and ring bearers were outside the tent, waiting for the arrival of Paul and his parents; they were going to be the first to walk up to the altar. The music changed to Canon D, by Johann Pachelbel, that was Paul and his parents, cue to walk up to the altar; when the attendee drew the drapes back to enter, he and his parents gasped at the beauty of the room, all four hundred guests were standing; and in a distance, Fr. Peter was at the altar waiting for his brother and parents to walk slowly as the guests unconventionally stood and applauded Paul. As Paul arrived at the altar, he hugged and kissed his parents, he placed both his hands to his mouth, threw a kiss to the guests still standing, walked over to his son at the piano, kissed him and said a few words, then turned around facing his brother, walked up to him, hugged, and kissed him. They said a few words and Paul took his place, facing the guests, they sat quietly.

The groomsmen, best man, the matrons, and the maid of honor took their places, their cue was when the attendee drew back the drapes and Alexander performed, Suite No. 1 Op. 46: Morning Mood played on piano, as the wedding party walked up to the altar. As they were coming up the aisle, Paul was surprisingly shocked when he saw five of his Harvard buddies in his wedding, he was in tears of joy as he nodded his head when each got to the altar and stood next to him, grinning from ear to ear. The wedding party is standing to the right and left of Fr. Peter, knowing any minute the music will begin for the ring bearers, flower girls and Jezalee with her parents will enter the tent last.

Jezalee and her parents, Mark, and Carolyn were standing outside the tent; checking their daughters perfectly flowing gown, every strand of her raven, silky hair was in place, her makeup was flawless on her radiant and gorgeous youthful face. Her mother handed her the new, engraved Bible with the wedding date, Paul and Jezalee's name in gold, from Elene and Antonio, she would be holding with her Swarovski crystal rosary Paul had given to her on their first wedding day, she had two ivory and cream roses, a symbol of the two of them, which she would dry as a keepsake, and inside, between the pages, she had placed the song her son, had composed for her. Before their cue to enter the ceremony, she and her parents held hands, bowed their heads, and said the Lord's Prayer. Mark made sure his wife's gown, makeup, and hair was perfect, as well as his daughters. Carolyn glanced at her husband's tie and Boutonniere to make sure they were on properly and that his shoes were not scuffed. Carolyn then spoke to the children and made sure their clothes were perfect. As soon as the music started, she had them stand in front of them.

The drapes opened, guests stood as Alexander at the piano, Adrienne and Jessica were singing, "If Ever There Was", written by Alexander. As the ring bearers, one had the brides' rings, the other had the grooms ring, and the two flower girls followed; Paul was already in tears. Jezalee looked at her parents, the three slowly entered the massive, magical, illuminating room filled-to-capacity. She stopped for a moment, amazed and admiring every inch of space that was befitting a Fairy Princess or Queen who had stepped into a magical kingdom filled with her fantasy dream coming alive, she took a deep breath, clenched her bible, looked at all the people there to take witness of hers and Paul's wedding. In a split second, she realized one thing! She was exhilarated by all the guests there to celebrate their momentous Nuptials. Then! She froze and both her parents whispered in her ears. Her dad said, "All these family, friends, co-workers, and staff are here to witness you and Paul celebrating your love for one another, it's all wonderful." Her mom looked at her as a couple teardrops fell from her eyes, she then took her daughter's shaking hands holding the Bible, Rosary, and roses, and said, "My dear, sweet, beautiful daughter, you are beginning a new chapter in your lives; and sharing your commitment to love one another in front of your guests you know and love, is a testament to your strength. You walk up that aisle to the man you love, with pride, devotion, commitment and most of all, love." After her parents spoke, her mom had a handkerchief to blot off her tears and made sure no touch ups were needed.

As David and Mallory were watching from the altar, Jezalee walking slowly up to her future, they both had the same reaction when she stopped, and her parents were whispering in her ears. They both got the same sick feeling that she was upset there were so many guests. They both had the same thoughts, as they were on opposite sides of the altar. They owed Jezalee a huge apology for going over her head and crossing the line.

As Paul was watching his exquisite bride at the entrance, when she stepped into the drape drawn tent, he saw this amazing vision of the most beautiful woman in the world, and she wanted to marry him. Then! When she did not proceed forward, he knew that she was thrown off with so many in attendance; he was ready to sprint down the aisle to tell her, everything's going to be okay, and he would walk up to the altar with her and her parents. While he was thinking about all that in a flash flood moment, their children kept performing. Jezalee slowly began walking up to the altar with her parents. Paul watched every step she took, the closer she got, the more beautiful and radiant she looked. Her hair cascading past her sexy shoulders, and the gown was something out of a fairytale, that a Princess or Queen would be wearing to meet her one and lonely love, Prince Charming, or her King. Jezalee and Dani were right! This gown was amazingly and was one hundred percent the, IT GOWN! and had to have an IT women wearing such an incredible gown, which was his Jezalee.

Jezalee tried to look around at the guests as she walked up the aisle; but her eyes were mainly on her wonderful and extraordinarily handsome husband-to-be. Paul never stopped looking at his exquisite wife-to-be once those drapes were opened. As Jezalee slowly walked up the aisle, he saw an ethereal-like angel that stepped out of a perfect world of innocence. As the surrounding décor euphorically enveloped her, she was coming to, a place of love and devotion from the man that cherished her for who she was. She in turn would take his giving hand in hers and show him the way to the everlasting love and devotion two people can lovingly share together as one. As Jezalee kept looking into her knight in shining armors eyes, from afar, she felt her future be one of undeniable love from a man that stepped out of the pages of a world only known by the two of them. As she and her parents made it to the altar, Paul walked over to the three of them, looked into his bride-to-bees eyes, knowing both-of-them had tears of exultation. The four of them hugged and kissed one another, and her parents wanted to say something to Paul. Her dad said, "May you and my daughter be as happy, if not happier the second time around. You are the son I never had; I love you." Her mom said, "I love you, Paul! You found your way back where you always belonged." Jezalee's parents walked slowly way from the altar and sat next to Paul's parents. After they finished and her parents went to sit down, Jezalee took a stride over to Joseph and Elene and gave them each a kiss on the check and a hug. She then walked back to the altar and walked close enough to her brother-in-law to give him a kiss and hug as well; before he had them say their vows.

Paul's brother was beyond rejoicing in his soul to be officiating the wedding with two of the people he loved most in his life. He could see the internal love oozing from them, then looking out at the packed tent with all the people that had been an important part of their lives. He was ready to begin the ceremony! He introduced himself, I am Fr. Peter Albanese, the brother of Paul; I am thrilled and fortunate enough to marry two of my favorite persons once again! The guests gave a soft laugh. Before Peter started with their vows, he had some wonderful short stories that made the guests laugh and cry; he was quite an orator and people were always mesmerized by his presence. There was not a better person to be officiating this magical wedding for this amazing couple. Fr. Peter looked out to the guests and said, "I know we better get this wedding ceremony started so all of you can celebrate the reuniting of two people that are dear to all of us in this room tonight. Paul and Jezalee, would you please face one another; as they looked into one another's eyes, they held their hands together and were ready for everyone to experience the love they have always had. Fr. Peter requested that Adrienne, Jessica, and Alexander join them at the altar, while their parents said their vows.

Before Fr. Peter started with the traditional vows, Jezalee spoke up and asked if she could say a few words. Fr. Peter was caught off guard with her request because he remembered how shy she was at their first wedding. He smiled and said, "Of course, Jezalee."

Jezalee, kept holding on to Paul's masculine, but soft hands. "I knew the moment I laid eyes on you; you were the one! I instinctively knew I would marry you. I called my parents as soon I could locate a phone. We started out as friends, but I had other thoughts, and was just waiting for you to catch up to me. How could I not fall for you? 6' 4'', incredibly handsome, extremely intelligent, over achiever, personality that could win over an enemy, and Italian, on top of all that. After you showed signs of possibly having a future with me, I knew it was just a matter of time! Paul! You have been the center of my universe and have always been the person there if I felt weak, you always gave me strength, and still do. You are a man without scruples, a devoted Catholic, a man of morals, fortitude and are always the calm before the storm. You are a man of great conviction, unending loyalty, and a friend to all. I have been blessed in this life to find YOU, the love of my life. You are a man that never stands still if someone falls. You have been my friend, my husband, my lover, a doting father, a loving son, and a best friend and loving brother, and you never failed at any of those. You have always been my knight-in-shining-armor.

Paul was taken aback and knew he had to say something, Jezalee had been strong enough and he needed to say how he felt about her. He was probably more nervous, mainly because her words were very unexpected. Paul continued holding her feminine, soft, slender hands, looked into her dromedary emerald-green eyes. My dear Jezalee, the first day I saw you, I recognized your beauty, and that drew me in. Within a week, of meeting you if nothing else, I knew we would be lifelong friends. It did not take long for me to see and feel the love you had for people and life itself. The weeks and months that followed, opened-up my curiosity to know more about you, hear your intelligence, your sense of humor, your ambitions. You were always filled with so much joy and it was infectious. When I would look at you, I not only saw your outer beauty, but your inner beauty that made you the person you have always been. The more we saw each other, I could see endless amounts of attributes that came natural to you. I was certainly saying my prayers every night, the good Catholic that I am, hoping I could be worthy of your love, so I could put a ring on your finger. My parents always encouraged me, not to rush to find love because it would come to me when the time was right. Your love struck me like a lightning bolt. Over the years, you have invariably been an angel at my side, my great listener, always humble, endearing, quite the comedian, selfless by nature, a devout Catholic, helping others, your patience is a virtue, you have been with me every step of the way through college, finding out what interests we had and building and nurturing our personal relationship. You are the light into my soul, the beat of my heart, you bring the best out in me, and you are the only woman I have ever loved. You have always been my friend, my lover, my wife, a mother to our three wonderful children, and a devoted daughter to your amazing parents. There is no romance in my heart, soul, and mind, unless you are in my life.

Fr. Peter looked at Paul and Jezalee and said, "Thank you both for your sincere and loving thoughts of one another, and now I will recite the traditional vows. After he had them repeat after him, the two ring bearers came forward with the rings. One stood next to Paul, with Jezalees rings, the other was standing next to Jezalee with Paul's ring. As they exchanged their vows, they went through the ceremonial part of placing the ring{s} on one another's, third finger left hand. Paul also placed her original wedding ring on her third finger, right hand because she expressed how she would always treasure their first marriage vows with her ring. Fr. Peter looked at them and said, now that you have said your vows and spoke so eloquently about the love you have for one another. "I now, pronounce you husband and wife, you my kiss your bride." Everyone stood up, applauded, whistled, and stomped their feet against the hardwood floors as well. Everyone was uproariously happy for these two reuniting. When all the guests assembled outside, there was sparkling gold confetti when the bride and groom came out from the tent.

While the photographer was taking outside photos of the wedding party, the attendees were seating the guests in the reception tent. Once the photographer had gotten the photos he wanted, outside, he went in the tent, waiting to take photos of the bride and groom as they walked through and were announced to their guests. Everyone stood up and applauded the remarried newlyweds. They walked through the crowd of guests to the wedding table and the rest of the wedding party followed. Once they were seated, Paul rushed over to his best friends from Harvard and let them know how great it was having them in the wedding. Jezalee went over to talk with the guys too because she had hung out with all of them in college; they went on a lot of double dates and as a big group. After they spoke to them, they went down the line at the wedding table and to talk to each person, then they waited for David and Mallory to be last because they had more to say to them. "That was some serious change in the wedding list! Thank you from the bottom of my heart because it is amazing seeing the people we care and love," Jezalee said wholeheartedly. "We were worried when you paused at the entrance. We thought you did not like the large gathering," Mallory said. "Quite the contrary! I stopped because I was overwhelmed at the beauty of what you put together and wanted to process it in my brain to always remember that moment in time forever. I was never mad! It was just the opposite. I also froze, knowing what I put Paul and I through; but my parents were reaffirming me that everything is wonderful," Jezalee commented.

As the caterer and her team of assistance started bringing the food in, everyone was seated and enjoying their meal as they had conversations with their table mates. The DJ played soft, classical music as everyone ate.

Jezalee and Paul got up and to talk with as many guests as they could and at one point, Paul grabbed a microphone and when he spotted a person he would talk from the microphone, and it worked out well with a lot of the guests. Jezalee liked that idea and did much the same. Everyone was having a grand time and when Jezalee and Paul's parents saw the two of them walk around, talking to guests, then with the microphone, they could see the happiness enveloping them and they were four proud and relieved parents that this day had come. "They certainly know how to work a crowd and not have any boring moments," Mark said.

After everyone ate, they knew the first dance was going to come next; so, the ladies and men lined up outside to use the custom-built restrooms, so they could hurry back in to watch Paul and Jezalee take that first dance.

While people were using the restrooms, Paul and Jezalee decided met up with the Stanton's, all their relatives that came from out of the country, Alan and Elaine's family, Natalie and her family, the list went on and on. Once the people went back to their tables, they knew they better get ready for their solo dance.

The bride and groom walked to the dance floor and melted into one of their favorite songs; the lyrics, and melody were amazing, and no one would ever be able to replicate the incredibly emotional voice of the singer. After the song was over, Alexander came up to his mom for the second dance because his grandpa Mark thought he should be next, instead of him. Jezalee said that is great and after they danced, she went over and got her dad to dance, then she went over on got Antonio to have one dance with her as well. He took her back to Paul, after his son had a dance with his two daughters, his mother and mother-in-law. He prompted the DJ to play the next couple of songs for he and Jezalee. They danced to a couple more of their favorite songs, then decided to walk around and talk with more guests. Jezalee and Paul wanted to hear Alexander at the piano, while his sisters sang the song he had composed for his mom. Afterwards, everyone gave them a standing ovation. The DJ resumed the music and people started coming out to the dance floor.

People were still dancing when the cake was brought over. When they rolled that eight-tiered wedding cake into the reception; jaws dropped, cameras were going off like royalty or a celebrity had just walked through. The cake was exquisite with its layers of what looked like shimmering gold lace with tiny beads on two tiers, three had what resembled a rosary made-out-of-pearls, with the crosses hanging down. The other tiers had beautiful antique, embossed designs. At the very top, they had their initials scrolled and below that was the third layer showing the rosary with the cross, made in the shape of pearls.

As the night went on, David and Mallory knew by the end of the evening, they were going to reluctantly be forced to inform Jezalee and Paul about Roberts attempt of suicide. They both knew it was the last thing they wanted to bring up on their wedding night; but there was not a choice in the matter.

While David and Mallory were dancing, they looked around the room and were so pleased that everyone appeared to be having an exceptionally great evening. After the cake was cut and eaten; a lot of couples were still out on the dance floor and several times the guests had started a conga line and even started the limbo. Some of the guests would go up to the DJ and request songs to dance the Charleston, the twist, the mash potato, and the younger generation was getting a kick out of the different dances the older generation came up with. There was music to satisfy teenagers to octogenarians; and no one frowned on any of the music played. It was an evening for anyone and everyone to be applauding how the entire evening had been a huge success.

Most of the children left the reception around 11:00 p.m. and headed over to the O'Malley's house to play games or try to get some sleep. Before they left the party, they checked out with their parents and said they would be hanging out in the game room. Mallory had brought in extra sleeping bags, pillows and blankets and had Nell leave some snacks and drinks out; in case they got hungry.

While the children were settling into the game room, people were still in conversations with friends they had not seen in a while, or they were dancing. It was 2:00 a.m. before the last few guests left; Paul and Jezalee were glad some of their family and friends stayed longer so they could get a chance to have to visit with them before they left the reception. They had made the effort and succeeded in talking to every guest before they left, and they were happy it worked out as well as it did.

After the last couple left; Paul and Jezalee walked over to thank their dear friends once again for the extraordinary wedding and reception they surprised them with. They were overjoyed that they even thought to invite all the people they knew and loved over the last twenty-five years of their lives. David and Mallory were elated that they loved what they had accomplished in such a short period of time. "Our wedding you put together, looks as if it took a year to plan and execute to perfection," Jezalee and Paul both remarked.

David asked them if they would sit a few minutes because he had something of extreme importance to share with them. Paul and Jezalee looked at him with worried looks and waited for what David had to say. With a heavy heart, Mallory and I did not want to mention this on the night of your wedding; however, we are pretty much forced into showing you the newspaper headlines today indicating that Robert tried to commit suicide in his jail cell. We had to contact all four hundred guests to make sure they did not bring it up at the wedding. We wanted to keep it from the children as well. Jezalee and Paul were stunned! They asked what condition Robert was in and they said, according to the newspaper, he is in critical condition and do not know if he will make it. Paul looked at Jezalee and pretty much felt they needed to tell their children; so, they did not hear it from someone else. Mallory let them know that all the children were at their house having a sleepover and maybe they should check in with them to see if they were still awake. The four of them made their way to one of their golf carts and David drove it to their main house; they went directly to the game room, where most of the children were already asleep. The Albanese children were still awake and talking with Morgan. They asked the children to come down to David and Mallory's bedroom so they would not wake up anyone. David began to inform them why Jim had been arrested and his real name was Robert. David proceeded to show them the newspaper headlines about his suicide. "Mom and dad, I feel so sorry for the life that Robert had; he never had a chance to live and be surrounded by goodness," Alexander spoke up. "I feel the same way; after all that you told us about his childhood and how he helped out Deanna, I have to know deep down he had a good soul," Adrienne commented. "He had a tragic life and never recovered," Paul sadly said.

Even though Jezalee and Paul had to be informed about Robert; once they spoke to their children about it, it was off limits. Nothing was going to ruin their wedding night. Not only was it magical at their wedding, the same held true for that night with Paul and Jezalee in their marriage bed, as they called it. The passion continued as it did when they were first newlyweds. The last twenty-three days, constantly being together, and was a continuation to their rendezvous in Manhattan. It had been a testament to their undying love for one another.

Paul and Jezalee woke up rather early the next morning. They were still recuperating from their spectacular wedding. It had been a night filled with seeing family, friends, and business associates at the most beautiful wedding they could ever imagined having. Mallory had outdone herself once again! Everyone that came up to them said it was the most magical night they had been a part of.

Created with Sketch.

Paul asked Jezalee if she would like to fly over to Florida to meet with Deanna and her family. She thought it was a stupendous idea; she wanted to hear first-hand about her and Robert's life together. Jezalee called David and Mallory to ask them what everybody was up to. They let her know that the grandparents left on a sightseeing tour of California. The children were swimming, enjoying the summer weather and were catching up on what they did on vacation, and just relaxing. Jezalee let them know she and Paul were going to call Deanna and see if they could meet with her. They both agreed that was the right thing to do.

As soon as Jezalee hung up, she called Deanna and her husband Eric answered the phone. After Jezalee and Deanna spoke for a few minutes, she agreed with Jezalee, it would be nice to speak in person. Jezalee asked if it would be okay if Paul came along and she said she would not want the newlyweds to be apart, as they laughed. They decided, the next day would be ideal because Eric had planned to take their children to a double-feature movie, and she would be home alone most the day.

Jezalee called Mallory back to let her know she and Paul were going to Miami. Mallory was happy Deanna wanted to meet with her; she then said she had an idea and wanted to run it by her and Paul. Mallory invited them for brunch and Jezalee said they would be over in about ten minutes and they, were starving.

Once Paul and Jezalee knew Mallory had a plan, they were curious what it was about. David went to the front door when the Albanese's arrived and invited them in. Well! How are the new bride and groom? They simultaneously replied "Amazing." David had Jezalee and Paul go into the living room, Mallory walked in a few minutes later with a tray of iced tea and lemonade and set it down on the coffee table; she went over and hugged both newlyweds then sat down next to David. She let them know that brunch was ready, and they would be eating in about fifteen minutes.

Jezalee was anxious to find out what plan Mallory had up her sleeve. "Okay dear friend! We have waited long enough, what is your plan?" Jezalee curiously said. "Well! As soon as you mentioned you and Paul were going to visit Deanna I thought, why don't David and I take the children back to Italy and let them finish their vacation," Mallory suggested. "That sounds great! I am sure the children would love to finish up the rest of their summer vacation and I hope that includes your three as well. I kept the hotel reservations at each place they had planned on going to; but you can also stay at our villa as well. There are two guards on the property, and I have a caretaker and his wife that live in the west wing and take care of our home when we are not there. They will cook your meals if you choose to stay there; their names are Rosa and Franco, and they are a delightful couple that had worked for our Sauce Company and after their children went off to college they decided to retire; but I asked them if they would be interested in watching over our place in Pisa and they could not pack up their offices fast enough and move to the villa. Whatever days you want to stay there instead of going to a hotel, just let Rosa and Franco know, I will give you their private number so you can let them know," Paul spoke up with enthusiasm. He then called the Stanton's from David's den and the Stanton's agreed to let their children finish their trip through Italy. When Paul came back to the living room, he was happy to inform them the Stanton children would be joining the rest of the gang. Paul asked David and Mallory if their children wanted to come, and they wanted to surprise them once they got the particulars settled and when they would be leaving.

"The jet is available now," Paul said. Jezalee reminded Paul they are committed to seeing Deanna tomorrow. "Oh! That is right! I know what we will do! Let us have the crew fly us to Miami this afternoon, drop us off and they will fly to New York; spend the night there, refuel the next day and return to San Francisco. We will keep our appointment with Deanna for tomorrow, visit with her; afterwards, we will stay at a hotel in Miami until you all are finished with your vacation in Italy or wherever else you want to go. Jezalee and I have never had the opportunity to visit Miami, and this will be a perfect time for us to do just that. We will get our salsa groove on and have some fun the Miami way. The jet will stay at the Pisa Airport at your disposal. Once the crew drops you off; I will have them stay at one of the hotels nearby and whenever you want to go somewhere; they will be ready," Paul said. "When do you two needs to come back?" Jezalee asked. David said he was taking a month off; but needed to be back to go on a road trip to take Morgan's car to Princeton. "I have an idea! I do not know if you would be interested in having her car transported; but if you are, my friend owns a transporting business," Paul suggested. David thought that was a terrific idea and got his number from Paul. He said he would let the crew know that when they were finished in Italy, they would fly into Miami to pick he and Jezalee up and they would all go home together.

Paul also suggested, when they arrive back in San Francisco, the jet will be available for to fly to Princeton; no sense in taking a road trip, they would be able to have more time getting Morgan settled in and ready for college. "That is so generous of you to suggest that we use your jet; but we do not want to put you out," David replied. "After all you have done for us; this pales in comparison," Paul remarked. "It is settled! You two are going to use the jet to fly to New Jersey and have a great time with Morgan, end of conversation," Jezalee spoke up. "Well! We got one more thing settled! Now where is that brunch you promised us?" Paul asked.

Mallory went out to call all the children in to give them the good news. Once the children gathered in the living room, their parents asked them if they would like to continue their vacation in Italy; they were jumping for joy. "Can the Stanton's come too?" Adrienne asked. "That has been taken care of and Morgan and her siblings are coming too!" Paul answered. Adrienne and Morgan were jumping up and down and could hardly contain themselves. Adrienne asked David if she could use his den to call Gregory and he said of course! They looked at the children and told them, they would be leaving in a couple of days for Italy. "I am going up to pack now," Adam shouted out. All the children decided to do the same thing.

Jezalee called Helga, then Nina from the O'Malley house to let them know and she and Paul were leaving for Miami in a few hours and the children would be leaving in a couple days with the O'Malley's to Italy. They were having brunch now and would home to home in about an hour.

Right after Jezalee got off the phone, Patrick O'Malley called and said they were having such a great time with the other grandparents and would not be home for dinner; they decided to eat at the Fairmont Hotel. David filled his dad in on what was going on and asked him to let the others know Paul was getting the jet ready for departure in two or three days for Italy, if they wanted to go back to Italy with the rest of the group. Patrick asked Kathleen, Joseph, Elene, Carolyn, and Mark what they wanted to do; they decided they wanted to get some sightseeing done in California while the six of them were together.

While they were all together, Alexander asked his parents, when they returned from Miami, if they were going on a honeymoon. "That had certainly been the initial plan; however, your mom and I had decided it was going to take a few trips later," Paul answered. "Your father and I had kind of an early honeymoon, for twenty-three glorious days and nights in Manhattan, we decided against a planned honeymoon, we feel as if our marriage is one big honeymoon, and we want your dad to get acclimated back into our family life as a full-time husband and dad," Jezalee said. "That is certainly understandable," Alexander, and his siblings agreed. The children could not wait to be a family like they used to be. Paul also added that he wanted to get better acclimated to the area, the estate, and needed to take time to check their vineyard and winery in Napa. He walked over to their children and let them know, the most important part, is being with the four of them because he had a tremendous void for the last four years. Jezalee walked over to the four of them and said "Amen" to that.

The grandparents were thrilled they had time to spend traveling in California. They had decided to rent a van and drive to Napa Valley, they stayed a few days at Paul and Jezalee's villa at their Winery-Vineyard. Next stop was Tahoe then they headed down to Santa Barbara.

After Paul and Jezalee had brunch with everyone, they said their goodbyes went home and packed. The children went home with them and packed their clothes for their Italy trip. Afterwards, the children knocked on Helga's door and said they wanted to help her in the kitchen when it was time to start dinner. Helga would later be preparing dinner for her daughter, Nicholas, the rest of the staff and their children.

Paul got a call from one of the crew and a driver would be there in thirty minutes. Paul brought down his and Jezalee's luggage and set it by the front door; they said their goodbyes to Joseph, Nina, and their children, then came back to the main house to say their goodbyes to Helga, Astrid, and Nicholas.

PART FIVE

MIAMI BOUND

Before take-off, the pilots and stewards came out to congratulate Paul and Jezalee one again for getting remarried. Mallory had invited all his crews and their families to the wedding and thanked them for coming to the wedding, which meant a lot to the Albanese's.

After the jet took off, Roger came back to ask Paul and Jezalee what they would like to eat and drink; they just wanted a drink. They decided to read the newspapers; when they opened to the front page, there was another article on Robert. He was released from the psychiatric hospital; returned to jail and would remain on an intensive suicide watch, which involved guards and staff-intensive overseeing. Robert was placed in an environment where it would be difficult for him to hurt himself; a padded cell and wearing a safety smock for his protection. He would be given only finger foods because eating utensils were forbidden until he had a full recovery. Robert would be re-evaluated by a psychologist who would do a suicide screening and assessment. The articles also indicated that Dr.

Pendulum came in to access him and Robert said he had tried to commit suicide because he did not want to ever see a Mental Institution. If that happened, he forewarned him that he would try killing himself and he would not survive the second time. The article said that his Attorney Jesse Stoneridge and Doctor Pendulum discussed the case with the Prosecuting Attorney and after reading all statements, they took the Death Penalty off table. The District Attorney would ask the court for five life sentences without parole. In the articles it also mentioned the reason he did not receive seven consecutive life sentences without parole, was due-to-the-fact that he and another victim had been kidnapped by a couple named Dodge and Kate Crocket. This couple had mentally, physically, verbally, and sexually abused these two children for over twelve or thirteen years of their lives. The female victim was impregnated by Dodge Crocket and that was when Robert knew he had no other way out but to set them on fire while asleep and run for their lives. They both knew it was a matter of time, that the Crockets would have killed them both.

Paul and Jezalee were happy to know that Robert would probably be behind bars in a prison cell or in an isolated room at an institution the rest of life. Jezalee thought he would have been institutionalized instead of prison because of what he endured as a child. Paul felt a little differently because of basically Robert murdering Charles Dandridge to get closer to Jezalee and he wanted to marry and murder her. Jezalee said it would be up to the Judge to make the final decision and she hoped it would be soon.

When the Albanese's arrived in Miami, Jezalee called Deanna to let her know they had arrived in Miami and what hotel they were staying at. Deanna gave her their address and was looking forward to meeting them the following day.

They loved their hotel and accommodations and knew they had come to the right place. They had dinner brought up to their suite that night. They talked and kissed for a few hours in bed; they were so excited over their life and how it had come full circle. They knew how blessed they were to find their way back into one another's arms again. Before they fell asleep that night, they made love as their bodies were enraptured as one; that penetrating pleasure they would arrive at when they made love; this was a love that was unexplainable; but attainable and they never lost the passion after all the years that had passed since they had met, fell in love, and started their life together. They fell peacefully asleep in each other's arms.

Once Paul and Jezalee arrived at Deanna's home; she invited them in, they met her husband Eric and their two children, Martin, 11 and Elizabeth, 8. Eric said he had taken the children to the movies while the three of them got acquainted and talked.

Deanna was so happy to finally meet Jezalee and congratulated Paul and her on their remarrying. She knew that Jezalee had received the statements she gave to Jamerson and the police. The first thing Deanna noticed about the couple was their extraordinary looks; they looked like they had just stepped out of a photo shoot that would land them on the cover of an elite magazine. The first time they saw Deanna come towards them, they both had the same thoughts; here is this pretty woman, who you would never have suspected that she had been tormented for a dozen years. She had endured so much trauma; but by the grace of God, Robert's bravery, got them away from that life of hell. They praised Deanna for working so hard getting her life to normalcy; she was to be commended with all the efforts she put into focusing on what mattered in life.

Deanna had a lot of questions for Jezalee and apologized for Robert coming into Jezalee's life and finding out what his intentions were; she started crying and was in so much pain over what Robert had turned into. "Deanna, please do not shed tears, I look at it this way, I am standing before you, unscathed while Paul and I are hoping this will be the start of a friendship," Jezalee said. "Thank you for saying that; I am just torn up over my hero turning into a serial killer. Me and my family had such high hopes for Robert," Deanna remarked. Paul asked her where she kept her tissues and went into the restroom to bring the Kleenex box to her. Deanna thanked Paul and he gave her a hug and told her he was so sorry she went through so much. Deanna began to tell them the good side of Robert as the little boy that she grew up with. Robert had taken such great care of her; at least as much as he could get away with. Jezalee remarked that she could not fathom two innocent children being treated the way they were, she wanted to assure Deanna that she would not ask another question about their childhood because she knew it had to be too painful to look back and talk about it. Deanna made sure that Jezalee would understand she did not have a problem talking about the childhood she was forced to have. She made sure she let Paul and

Jezalee know what a gentle soul Robert had been the entire time they were raised together; but there was so much more that he went through than she did. Robert was the reason they found her family and were reunited. Deanna wanted them to also know that she was fortunate enough to have an exceptional Aunt and Uncle, who adopted her. She cherished them for all the love and care they bestowed upon her. They made sure they found the best professional care she so desperately needed to be able to be a survivor. She knows she would never have gone to the extreme existence Robert chose; but Deanna knew her life wouldn't be as grand as it had become without the constant nourishment she received from her family. Paul sat back and listened to her and was so impressed with what she had accomplished with never attending a school during her vital, informative, and impressionable years. He was devastated at the life two children went through; he had realized how brave Robert had been for both-of-them. Paul was a religious man; but felt that Robert had no choice but to end the miserable lives of the Crockets for his and Deanna's survival.

Jezalee had listened, as Paul had, to Deanna's recollection of both Robert and her childhood and it was nothing but a miracle and a lot of Robert's determination of freeing themselves. After Deanna was done with her story; she wanted to know every detail of what Jezalee had experienced with Robert. She was embarrassed that he had put so much pressure on this wonderful person; knowing he probably had plans on murdering her after they married. She was curious why Paul and Jezalee ever got a divorce and what got them back together. Since Deanna had opened-up her heart and soul to them; Jezalee started the story and Paul told her all the circumstances that led up to their divorce and how they got back together. Deanna was overwhelmed at what had happened to Paul and cried when he explained the one night of terror he woke up from. As it was! It stayed a nightmare dealing with Gloria until her demise.

Deanna and Jezalee wanted to see Robert together. Jezalee would contact Robert's attorney Jesse when they returned home. Before they left, Deanna's husband Eric and their two children had arrived home after having a great time at a double feature movie. Eric had stopped by and picked up Mexican food and invited Paul and Jezalee to join them before they went back to their hotel.

Paul and Jezalee had a great time visiting Deanna and her family and enjoying a meal with them. They invited her family to come and visit them in San Francisco whenever it was suitable in their schedule. Before their taxi arrived; they informed Deanna and Eric they were staying in Miami for probably two weeks on a vacation, to experience some of the spirit and nightlife of Miami. They said they would love to get together with them for dinner and maybe invite their parents as well. Eric and Deanna thought that would be great and to give them a call whatever evening they had open.

Just as Paul and Jezalee said their goodbyes, their Taxi driver arrived and took them to their hotel. Back at the Drake's home, Deanna was discussing with Eric how glad she was that the Albanese's, had come to visit. She told him everything they discussed; and he was shocked when he heard what Paul had experience.

Created with Sketch.

After Paul and Jezalee were settled in at their posh suite at a high-end 5-star hotel; later that evening they left a message at the hotel where their parents and children were in Italy. They also called down to the concierge and asked if they had a list of the best nightclubs, restaurants, shops, theaters, and other places of interests, in Miami; and he said he would have his assistant bring it up. Before they went to bed that night, they read through the brochure and had marked the places they were interested in.

The next morning, they could not wait to go exploring different areas and trying some of the Latin cuisine. They had the greatest time going from one shop to the other, a different restaurant for all their meals, and the nightclubs were the hottest place in town to hear the best Latin music. They salsa danced every night and joined in Karaoke singing; Jezalee would not do it by herself; so, they did it as a duet. They walked the beach near their hotel and swam in the ocean by day and tried all the finest restaurants, and the liveliest nightclubs by nightfall.

They remembered the Mariel Boatlift in 1980 bringing 150,000 Cubans to Miami, the largest transport in civilian history. Here it was 1989 and they both thought this place was going to explode even bigger one day into another go-to place with the Cuban-Latin influence. They could for-see massive expansion in the night life while they were checking everything out. They envisioned a subtropical paradise with an influx of Cubans, Haitians, and Nicaraguans. They could see how the beautiful and multi-cultural Latin influence was everywhere and it was amazing. While they were there, they wanted to overindulge in the lively music, extraordinary cuisine, and amazing dance techniques. While Paul and Jezalee were there, they could not help but join in and be a big part of this exciting multi-cultural experience that gave one so much life within.

After being in Miami for a week, Jezalee called the Drakes, they got a sitter, called their parents, and two days later Paul had the concierge call for a driver so they could have a night on the town. When the Albanese's arrived at the Drakes home, they had the driver wait while they went in to meet Deanna's and Eric's parents; they had a couple of gifts for Martin and Elizabeth. After they watched the children open their gifts, the eight of them said their goodnights to the children and sitter, and off they went for some Miami night life fun. Paul had made reservations at the best restaurant, then off to several nightclubs, then ending the night at another restaurant known for their desserts. The four couples had the greatest time together, and Paul let them know, this was not their last trip to this beautiful and lively city. Jezalee also pointed out to Deanna and Eric's parents, they were giving them an open invitation to come visit them; also let them know, if they ever wanted to take a trip to Pisa, Italy or Paris, France, they would make-arrangements, with their caretakers, and staff, to use their villa while they were in Italy or their chateau in Saint-Germain-en-Laye, outside of Paris. Deanna, Eric, and their parents could not believe the Albanese's hospitality was so forthcoming. "We may just take you up on your gracious offer one of these days," Remarked Deanna's father, Jude. "We hope you do, and if my private jet is available, it will be at your disposal, as well," Paul assured them. When the three couples were out with the Albanese's, at the restaurant, Paul took a mental note what wines they preferred. As soon as Paul and Jezalee got back to their suite that evening, he made a list of their finest wines from each of their wineries to send a case to Deanna, Eric, and their parents.

Paul and Jezalee got comfortable in bed that night; they reflected on the sunny and enchanting days, with magical and intoxicating nights they had experienced in Miami. They were ready for more for the next couple of weeks.

Jezalee woke up before Paul the next morning and had ordered breakfast and asked restaurant to bring it up in about an hour. She quietly got back in bed and started kissing Paul. Paul immediately woke up and Jezalee got back in bed, gave Paul another kiss and he immediately kissed her soft lips. They could not keep their hands off one another; they were like two bunnies trying to mate. After their romp in bed, Paul gently picked Jezalee up from the satin sheets and carried her into the shower. As the warm water trickled down their bodies, he slowly lowered his head and brushed his lips against her, ever so gently in a tantalizing way. They proceeded to wash one another's sensual bodies and made love standing up as the warm water trickled down their bodies.

Once they were finished in the shower, they quickly dried each other off, then got dressed. While Jezalee was putting her make-up on and brushing her hair; there was a knock at the door, Paul answered it, and their breakfast had arrived. Paul walked into the boudoir and let Jezalee know their breakfast was ready. They sat down to breakfast and looked over The Miami Times of America, San Francisco Examiner and New York Times while they ate. Two hours later they decided to do a little shopping in the Miami boutiques and talk to some of the local people.

The next several days were spent renting a car, driving to more sights throughout Miami, soaking up some sun on the beach, and buying gifts for everyone. After they were done with everything, they decided to spend the rest of the time relaxing in their hotel suite, having the rest of their meals at the hotel, and utilize some of their time at the pool and the rest of the amenities the hotel had to offer. When the bellman brought up the last of the brightly colored wrapped packages; he gave them a grin and asked if they were having a Quinceanera party. They laughed simultaneously and answered, "No! these are presents for family, friends, and office staff back in California," Paul answered. "Wow! That is quite generous of you," the bellman smiled back and commented. As the bellman took out the last emptied roller cart, Paul handed him a tip and thanked him for such great service.

While Paul made a few business calls to their California Winery, and checked in at his San Francisco office, Jezalee took a quick shower and changed into a bold and trendy, de la Prada outfit that her dress designer, Dani, in New York had picked up for her when she was in

Madrid last year. Jezalee had not purchased any new designs of de la Prada since her first showing in Madrid venue LOCAL, 1981, it was the peak of the Movida Madrilena. Prada and another designer, Pepe Rubio, were involved in the counter-culture movement. The Movida was their freedom after the sad, gray era of their dictator, Franco. Paul and Jezalee had purchased a vineyard-winery in Madrid that year and just so happened to read about de la Prada. Jezalee immediately called to see if they could obtain tickets for the Movida and as luck would have it, Paul had met a gentleman in Paris at a fundraiser, who was one of the persons running the event in Madrid. Jezalee, mostly wore clothes that were timeless, sophisticated, and usually not too many prints; however, there was something about de la Prada's bold, colorful, and av-ant-garde designs that she particularly wanted to wear while they were in Miami. As she walked towards Paul, he looked up and said she was a vision of a color wheel in motion. "Wow! That is an amazing abstract expressionistic print and looks like you stepped out of a pop-culture magazine," Paul said with a mellifluous sound. Jezalee walked closer to Paul, bent down, and gave him a kiss. After the kiss, he got up from the chair, gently grabbed her and said, "I really need to expand my wardrobe after seeing this dress; maybe I should go down to one of the boutiques in the hotel, and hope they have some bright-colored suit for me," Paul remarked. "Hon, that is a brilliant idea! Why don't I go check them out while you finish working?" Jezalee harmoniously said. "Dear, are you serious?" Paul asked. "Absolutely! Let me go see what they have," Jezalee answered. She grabbed her purse and off she went, hoping they would have a suit to compliment her dress. An hour and a half later, Paul had just finished his business calls, Jezalee arrived back with her arms loaded with a few packages, three shirts, and three suits for Paul to choose from. She walked into their bedroom suite and hung the clothes up in the closet, waiting for Paul to get finished with his shower. Jezalee walked into the bathroom; Paul saw her in the mirror, turned around and gently put his arms around her, drew her to his body and kissed her slightly perfumed neck, then her sensual red lips. She then asked him if he was ready to try on what she found in the hotel Boutique. Jezalee warned him he would probably need to put on his sunglasses because the suits were blindly bright. She said she would stay in the bedroom and watch him model the outfits. He tried on all three and Jezalee stood next to him, and they both agreed the scarlet red suit, with the canary yellow printed shirt was complimenting to her dress. They both looked in the mirror and laughed! Not that they were funny looking in the bold clothes; it was just so far from what they normally would wear. Jezalee looked up at Paul with those eyes that were telling him, it was time for romance. She started undressing him, one item at a time and once she had him completely nude, it was his turn to begin undressing her. It was late afternoon, a love-making delight and knowing they had both pleasured one another to the fullest of their desires. They laid there for about an hour after their bodies had connected and consumed one another into a sexual euphoria.

Paul and Jezalee got up from bed, took their shower together and got dressed for the evening for fine dining, dancing and just enjoying their time together. As they walked out of the elevator, people turned their heads when they walked by; the concierge walked over to them and asked if they would not mind if he took a few photos of them for the hotel's brochure coming out in a few months. Jezalee wanted to know, why they did not photograph models instead. "I cannot imagine any two models look more stunning and handsome then the two of you," the concierge remarked. They were assured they would have a few models as well; however, after seeing the two of them come and go over the last two weeks, he wanted to have at least one couple that were guests. The concierge asked them if it was okay if he took a few more photos tomorrow before they left. "Now! Just so you know, we will not be dressed in such bold outfits tomorrow," Jezalee informed them. He laughed and said, "whatever you wear will be great." We will see you in the morning around 9:30 a.m. before we take off for Pink Sands Beach.

The next morning Paul and Jezalee woke up at 7:00 a.m., got ready for the day, had breakfast sent up to their room. They were ready to leave by 9:00 a.m.; they went down to the lobby, saw the photographer speaking with the concierge. As soon as the concierge spotted the Albanese's, he waved them over and said they were ready to take a few photos of them. Paul and Jezalee were flattered the hotel wanted to photograph them; but they had to also laugh about it. Out of all the guests that walked through the doors of the hotel, they chose them. Their photo session only took thirty minutes and the photographer said he would send them copies of the proofs and wanted to get their approval of which poses they liked the best.

Paul gave the photographer his business card with his San Francisco address and said they looked forward to seeing the end results. The concierge came over to the Albanese's, thanked them for agreeing to being a part of the brochure and as soon as it was ready for publication, he would send them a copy. He asked them how long they would be in Pink Sands Beach, and they said they between three to seven days, then they would be back to the hotel to finish up their vacation. The concierge said their rental car was ready and hoped they had a great time.

When they got in the rental car, they were looking forward to exploring Pink Sands Beach and decided they would probably stay for a few days if they liked it. Pictures did not give the beach justice, the water was the most brilliant turquoise with gentle waves, with surrounding coral reefs. The unique pink sand was formed from a tiny animal with a reddish pink shell. The shells would break up by the strength and power of the waves; then blended into the white sand. They ended up staying a week at Pink Sands Beach. They road horseback, along the beach then rented bicycles to ride through the beach area. They were having a marvelous, relaxing time and knew they had found another piece of heaven in this extraordinary world.

They got back to the hotel from their excursion to Pink Sands Beach, and only had one night left before they would be headed back home. Before they checked out of the hotel, the concierge had the proofs from their photo shoot, and they turned out great. The concierge, photographer, and the Albanese's, agreed on the photos that should be in the brochure. They thanked them for being receptive to the photo shoot and was looking forward to seeing them again soon. Paul assured him them they would be traveling back to Miami when time permits. Jezalee added that it was an exhilarating place that is on the top of their traveling musts and was so happy to be exposed to such amazing people, music, food, dance, and an incredible culture.

PART SIX

Paul and Jezalee boarded the jet in Miami and were so happy to see everyone. They discussed what they did during their vacations; but were anxious to get back home to their normal day-to-day routines.

After the families arrived back in San Francisco; the children were preparing for their first day back at school and college; by doing some last-minute clothes shopping. David and Paul were both back, full throttle ahead at work. They got together, over at David and Mallory's for an outdoor barbeque and the following weekend, after Mass, Paul and Jezalee had everyone over for an afternoon sit-down Italian feast.

David, Mallory, and Morgan boarded the Albanese jet; bound for their daughter's first year at Princeton. Nell and Linda getting were Erica and Adam ready for school to start before their parents got back from getting Morgan settled in her apartment near Campus. The staff, who had children, were getting them ready for the new school year as well. Paul and Jezalee were anxiously getting their children ready for school; they hung out around the house and wanted to have some alone time as a family once again. This was the first time, in four years, that the Albanese's and their children, were back to their family life as it used to be.

Everyone was back to their daily schedules; Paul was working crazy hours with several of their businesses, Jezalee's two books had been on the best sellers list for over a month. She was exhilarated just thinking about eventually publishing a cookbook. After they had gotten back from Miami, Jezalee started going through all her accumulated recipes and menus she had experimented with from the past twenty odd years, and knew she had enough recipes to put together several cookbooks. She knew she wanted to have one cookbook that was all about the perfect menu and was relieved she had kept all her recipes and menu planning since the first time she cooked her first meal for Paul.

Adrienne was ecstatic that she got into Stanford and had some classes that coincided with Gregory's; so, they were able to usually have lunch together every day. Alexander and Jessica had the classes they wanted; but missed seeing their sister on campus.

Deanna called Jezalee and wanted to thank her and Paul for not only coming for a visit to meet with her; but taking Eric, her, and their parents out to dinner. She also wanted to tell Jezalee she was available to come to San Francisco and would like to set up a date and time when she would like to go see Robert together. Jezalee said she would call his Attorney Jesse Stoneridge and hopefully; he can make that visit happen for them.

Paul asked Jezalee if she was absolutely, without a doubt, ready to face Robert. She said she did not want Deanna to go there alone and wanted to be supportive for her and yes! She did want to talk to him one last time. Paul concluded that if she thought it was necessary, then by-all-means go and see him face to face.

A week later Jesse was able to get clearance with the police station for the gals to meet with Robert. Paul had sent his private jet to fly Deanna to San Francisco and he had Gregory pick her up at the airport since he was working that day. He drove her to the Albanese home where Jezalee and Paul were waiting for her arrival.

When Deanna arrived at the estate; she asked Gregory, "Do they always have guards at the entrance?" "Yes! they are one of the richest couples in the world. They are so down to earth and like one of us; it is not a rag's, to riches scenario, by any means! They both went to Harvard, Yale, and Columbia Universities; but he took some of the money he made from being a young athletic designer and put it into stocks and made quite a bit of money to start other businesses from the ground up. When I first met them, I happened to be his driver one day and they invited me into Jezalee's home, this was before they got remarried," Gregory answered. "Wow! That is, an amazing story," Deanna said. "Well! They both are amazing and quite the entrepreneurs; enjoy your time with them because they are my favorite people, next to my parents," Gregory admitted. "Thank you for letting me know a little bit about them, it is refreshing to know that people with that type of wealth are like your favorite next-door neighbor," Deanna replied. Gregory gets out of the limousine and gets Deanna's overnight bag and said he will take it up to the door for her. She says thank you! And follows behind him. "Gregory, have a wonderful day!" As Deanna said goodbye. "You, as well, Deanna." Gregory replied. She rings the doorbell and Jezalee answers the door, she sees Gregory about to get into the car and yells out! "Gregory come here hon." "Hi Jezalee! How are you today?" Gregory says. "Please stay for dinner," Jezalee asked. "Sure! But you three probably want to visit," Gregory answered. "Don't be silly! Come eat with us," Jezalee insisted. He parked the car over to the side and went on in the house.

Jezalee welcomed Deanna to their home and Paul was finishing up a business call but would be with them in a few minutes. She took Deanna's luggage and left it in the entryway while she had them follow her into the living room. She asked them to please sit down and if they would like a drink and they both said no thank you. She sat down, then asked Deanna if the flight was okay and she said it had been wonderful and the stewards and the pilots were so attentive and sweet to her. Good to hear! Jezalee said Paul had hand-picked his crews and they had really enjoyed them when they traveled. "Your home is like looking through the pages of "Architectural

Digest," Deanna said. "That is so sweet of you to say," Jezalee replied. "Their chateau in France has been in that magazine as well," Gregory said. "I can certainly see why," Deanna replied. Just as Jezalee was about to say something, Paul walked in to say "hi" to them. He sat down next to Jezalee, after he had welcomed Deanna to their home then asked Gregory if he was able to get all his classes at Stanford and he luckily had. "Do you occasionally see Adrienne on campus?" Paul asked. "Yes! We usually have lunch every day and manage to get some studying in together before our next classes," Gregory answered. Paul let Deanna know that Gregory and their daughter, Adrienne had been dating for a year now. "That is wonderful that you are going to the same college and can see one another on campus during the day," Deanna commented. "If you do not mind me asking, what college do you both attend?" Deanna asked. "My goodness! I do not mind at all! We attend Stanford," Gregory replied. "This is one young man that is paving his way to an amazing career as a surgeon; he consistently receives straight A+'s in every class and I like to brag about it because we are fortunate enough to know and adore him," Paul spoke up. "That is quite an accomplishment, your parents must be so proud," Deanna replied. "Well! I appreciate the compliments and I can tell you! I love college so much and I do the best I can," Gregory said. "With that said, why don't you three follow me into the kitchen while I help Helga with dinner, and I have some appetizers waiting to be eaten, while we wait for the rest of the gang to arrive home," Jezalee said.

Paul, Gregory, and Deanna sat around the kitchen table as Helga and Jezalee cooked up Chinese Cuisine, at Alexander's request. They were enjoying the spring roll appetizers while they watched the ladies prepare dinner. Alexander and Jessica arrived had home from The Boys and Girls Club and Adrienne showed up about fifteen minutes later. Paul introduced the children to Deanna, and they kissed their parents, Helga, and Gregory, then went to wash up for dinner. Dinner was served in the dining room thirty minutes later; everyone enjoyed their meal and great conversations.

After dinner, Deanna offered to help clean up and Jezalee said the children will do that tonight while she showed her to her room. She gave Deanna the option of an upstairs or downstairs room; Deanna preferred downstairs. She let her know Helga was downstairs if she needed anything to knock on her door or use the intercom to reach them upstairs. Jezalee took her to one of the guest bedrooms downstairs and told her to make herself at home and she had all the fresh linens sitting out for her and a vanity with a variety of soaps, lotions, and perfumes for her to choose from. "I feel like I am at a ritzy resort hotel," Deanna commented. "Anyone that comes through our front doors, deserve to feel like they are family, and that will always include you and your family as well," Jezalee remarked. "That is beyond sweet and generous of you Jezalee," Deanna said. "Well! thank you!" Jezalee said. "After you get settled, join us in the family room, it is to your right and down the hallway, I am sure you will hear us," Jezalee said.

Deanna joined them in the family room and Jezalee said there was a few people that wanted to meet her tonight and they would be there in about ten minutes. Deanna looked puzzled and gave Jezalee and Paul a smile, lowered her eyebrows and shook her head. "Do you remember most of your conversations with Jamerson?" Paul asked. "Yes! I sure do!" Deanna answered. "Well! He will be here tonight with a few people that we all feel you would want to meet," Paul responded. She still was not sure who they might be; but she knew that they had her best interest and would wait to see who shows up.

Jamerson arrived with the mystery guests and Paul answered the door and invited them in. Jamerson introduced them to Paul, then they followed him into the family room. The children went up to their rooms and Deanna and Jezalee were waiting for the surprise guests to walk in. As soon as Deanna saw Jamerson, she got up, walked over to him, and gave him a hug. She looked behind him, there were five adults standing there waiting to meet Deanna and Jezalee. Paul asked everyone to please have a seat. Jamerson began to introduce Roberts two grandparents , from his dad Lucas's side, then introduced his grandmother, from his mother Mary's side. His grandfather, from his mother's side, died a month. Then, the last two were his Aunt Janie and Uncle Stewart, who adopted Roland, after the murder of their parents. Jamerson let everyone know that they had been looking religiously for Robert for over twenty plus years without one lead. When Jamerson informed them of the life that Robert had after he was kidnapped, they realized why there were never any clues because the Crockets made sure they never let he or

Deanna be seen in public without a disguise on and they never were allowed to go to school. Deanna and Jezalee broke down in front of them as did, Robert and Roland's family members. They intensely regretted that he never wanted to look them up and come home. They were always there for him and would have done everything in their power to make sure he got the therapy that Deanna had received to try and recover from such a horrifying life they were thrown into by the monsters that murdered Lucas and Mary. Roberts family said they would be in that court room the day the Judge sentences Robert and they regret that night of December 24, 1950. Janie spoke up and said, if only her sister and brother-in-law had taken them up on spending the night with them, they would never have been on that road to meet their demise. Roberts family knew in advance that Jezalee realized something was off about Robert, and without her and Deanna they would never have known who murdered their Roland, Angela, and little Robert Jr., who had been named after his uncle they never found.

It was an emotional-few-hours; after Jamerson took Robert's family back to their hotel; Jezalee, Paul and Deanna sat and talked for a while. Deanna was so happy to meet all of them but still could not get over the losses they had to bear. She and Jezalee could not stop crying! Paul had tears off and on too and it was most difficult seeing the grandparents, all in their 80's finding out and trying to grasp the fact that their own flesh and blood, went through a life of constant torture; then not wanting to find his family who longed to have him home. They knew that Roland had such a great childhood and knowing that Robert did not, was unbearable for them to comprehend that he did not want to find them.

The next day, after the children got off to school, Jezalee prepared breakfast for her and Deanna. Helga usually joined them; but after she made breakfast for Paul and the children she went back to her wing and wanted Jezalee to have privacy with Deanna. Paul had an early meeting at the office and would not be back until time to take the gals to visit Robert. While the gals ate breakfast, they both admitted they were nervous about seeing him. They knew they would not be his favorite people to see but they had to tell him how they felt.

When Paul arrived home, the gals were ready to go see Robert. He drove them to meet up with Robert's Attorney, Jesse, before they would see him. They wanted to know what kind of mood he was in and were still a little nervous. Jesse warned them, Robert was never in a good mood and wanted them to know he may flare up at them. He gave them advance notice that he was in restraints to prevent him from trying to commit suicide again. He was watched around the clock and becomes extremely agitated, which may cause limited time with him.

Paul waited in a separate room and would be there as-long-as they could meet with Robert. Jesse came through the secured private area that leads to a room where Robert was waiting to see Jezalee and Deanna. Jesse told the gals he was shocked that Robert agreed to see them. When the gals walked in, they saw Robert much thinner, his skin was washed out, and his ankles were both in heavy chains, bolted to the floor and he was wearing his therapeutic restraints. There were two guards in the room at all time and Jesse was there, sitting over in the corner. Deanna and Jezalee sat down in the chairs that were provided and Robert said hello to them and smiled. Surprisingly, that was the first time Jesse had ever seen Robert smile. Jezalee and Deanna greeted him, and he told them he was happy to see them; they both tried not to appear shocked at his demeanor because they were expecting him to come across belligerent; but that was not the case. As Jesse sat in the corner, he was shocked at Robert being so cordial to the ladies. Deanna spoke first and told him she was so happy to see him too! Jezalee was a little more reluctant; but she said she was glad that he would see her. He looked at them and said he knows how badly he had hurt so many people and knew he could never make things better. He apologized to Jezalee saying he was embarrassed leading her on in his deceptive manner; it was nothing against her, but he had never been able to love anyone other than his dear sister Deanna. The only four people he ever trusted was Deanna, her parents Belle and Jude and David, whom he respected as his boss and as a friend. Jezalee and Deanna were trying to hold back their tears, and the one guard looked over at Jesse and saw tears coming down his face. Jezalee responded by saying, she wished, with all her heart that his life had been different for him. Over the years that she was around him, she knew something was off but could not pinpoint what it was. She did apologize for spying on him and finding all the items he had hidden. "That is why you wanted to spend the night! Now it is all coming together, you are quite the female version of Sherlock Holmes. Not only were you good at that; you are the most beautiful woman on the planet; and the most amazing lady I could have ever met in my life. I would have given anything to have been in a right state of mind to love you the way Paul does. That was what I was jealous about, I did not know how to love you, or for that matter, anyone other than Deanna and her family. I was raised with Deanna, so I knew and will always love her like she is, my sister. I want you to know that I cared deeply for you and your children; but my mind wanted to destroy you because I could not be like you and your family," Robert said to Jezalee with tears streaming down his face. "I sincerely wished your life had been the way it was meant to have; a loving family you were born into, sharing a life with them and your twin brother Roland. After reading what those monsters did to you and Deanna, was something out of a horror movie that she will never get over how badly they were treated. Jezalee let him know that he did the right thing by setting them on fire; if he had not, they would have eventually murdered Deanna and him. It is difficult to see you this way; but completely understands why he ended up there. Life has not been fair to you, and I hope you understand that killing all those people did not change you, it made you be a product of your environment with those two sick and demented people you were forced to live with. My children and I got to see some of the good side in you and I thank you for that; I just wished you had gotten professional help; he may have saved a lot of lives, including your own," Jezalee said.

Jezalee began to tell Robert what had happened to Paul that horrible night when he was drugged and raped. As she briefly told him that is how Paul's second son, Jonathan was conceived. Robert sat there with actual tears streaming down his face. He looked at Jezalee and said, "I am so sorry he was a victim just like Deanna and I were," Robert said. Jezalee wanted to set the record straight; that her husband was a victim and was not aware that the sexual assault had happened. It disrupted their marriage; but he told David his story and he thankfully was the catalyst that got them back together. "What a horrible person that woman and two men were. It is strange how things happen; I would have never gone to San Francisco if I had not seen you, in several magazine articles. If Paul had not been victimized, you and your family would have more than likely never have moved to America. Our paths would have never crossed. I have one last thing to say to you dear Jezalee, as-long-as I am on this Earth, I will regret I thought about killing you or Alexander. Deanna and her parents were right all along; I desperately needed help but was too stubborn and embarrassed to meet with a therapist. In jail, I have had no option; and I have to say that Dr. Pendulum has worked with me on-a-daily-basis and I see the difference in how I feel and the horrific things I have done. He admitted to Jezalee, one night after visiting her, he went home and was getting ready to shoot himself because he was upset; but he heard her voice on the answer machine and dropped the gun on the floor," Robert said. "Why did you want to kill yourself that evening?" Jezalee asked. Robert sadly bent his head down and did not want to make eye contact with her or Deanna. He began to tell them the horrifying nightmares he had from living with the Crockets all those years; they were coming more often and with being rejected by Jezalee had pushed him over the edge. Jezalee promptly spoke up and explained to him that if he had been under some therapy, it may have saved him from all of what had taken place. "Robert, after my divorce, I am not regretting that we met one another; we had some nice times together; and my children had considered you an uncle. She hoped he understood what she had been going through and if she knew then, what she knows now, she would have gotten him help whether he wanted it or not," Jezalee commented. "That is the Jezalee I know and adore," Robert thank her for coming here with Deanna.

Jesse interrupted for a minute and asked if the ladies had any Kleenex to wipe the tears off Robert's face. Jezalee got some tissue out of her purse and handed it to Jesse. Jesse walked slowly around to Robert, dabbed the tissue in the glass of water sitting close to Robert and cleaned his tear- stained face. Robert kindly said thank you and looked at the girls and tried to put a smile on his face.

Robert looked at Deanna and let her know he needed to confess to her and her parents; he did find his entire family; which included both sets of his grandparents, Roland, and their aunt and uncle, that adopted his brother. He watched each of them from afar and tried to get up enough nerve to say "here I am." Robert could not face them!

He knew he was too broken and never wanted them to know how he had lived with the two people that murdered his parents. He did try several times to knock on one of their doors; but finally walked away and never looked back. This was just after he left Deanna in Miami and moved to New York. Two days after Robert got settled into his amazing apartment, he flew to California, with the intention of meeting his family; but backed out from his humiliation setting in.

Deanna was more than shocked when he told them he had found his family and would not see them. She knew that his life would have been better if he had given them a chance. She looked at her brother Robert, as she called him, and said she was thankful he had someone to tell his story to and how he felt about his life as it was. She let him know that she had met his family last night and they are wonderful people; and he should have given them a chance to love him in the flesh. Even though she had never met Dr. Pendulum she praised him for helping him discover the person he was deep in his soul. He began to cry and tell her the Doctor helped him understand what can happen to a child when they have been continually sexually and verbally abused, day after day and in all those formative years. "I know it is too late for me because, here I sit! After killing five innocent people, these people had families that loved and cared about them and I took that all away because of my mixed-up sick mind," Robert admitted. He turned and looked at Jezalee and said, "That is why I never went to Mass with you or anyone; I felt there was not a God; because he never saved me and Deanna from that evil couple," Robert said to Jezalee. "I understand completely," Jezalee remarked. Deanna said the only thing that saved her from a mental breakdown and probably ending up in a Mental Institution for the rest of her life; was Robert locating her aunt and uncle. They welcomed her with open arms and had also been looking for her since the day they found out she was kidnapped from her parent's murder scene. It had been excruciating years, for Belle and Jude trying to find her, in hopes she was still alive. When Robert and Deanna showed up on their doorstep, it was a moment in time, Deanna, and her family will never forget. They had hoped the same for Robert, but he was adamant about being alone in New York. "We should have never listened to you; we should have done an intervention to save you," Deanna burst out crying. Jezalee started crying once again and looked at Robert and the tears would not stop.

Robert was trying to calm himself down in-order-to be able to speak; he could not wipe the tears away because of his restraint wrapped around his entire upper body. He was finally composed enough to speak and said, "Deanna, I do not know how long I have left on this Earth; but know one thing! I am filled with regret every day I sit in my cell and know that I should have listened to all of you and would have hoped I turned out half as great as you have; and could have had a normal life with a wife, children and maybe a dog or two. Jesse was still captivated over the conversations between the three of them; as he looked over at the two guards, he saw tears from one of them.

Deanna said she was hoping Robert would keep meeting with Dr. Pendulum, because he was the only one that can guide him, out of his dark hole, and hopefully, not have feelings of guilt about what he experienced. She wanted Robert to know he was an amazing human being, and she will always love him. He looked at her and Jezalee and said, "I thank you both for coming to see and speak with me, I will be forever grateful, and know I am becoming a better person in here, than I ever was out there in society." Jezalee and Deanna walked away with uncontrollable tears and said their goodbyes. As his eyes and cheeks were burning, he watched them walk away; all he could think of was the tracks of his tears streaming down his face.

Jesse looked over at Robert and finally, for the first time, witnessed his vulnerability; where he could see a man that could hardly contain his emotions. Robert knew that he had tried, with all the strength he had within him, to not show he was an emotional wreak; but he could not hold it in. Jesse said his goodbye to Robert and thanked him for seeing Deanna and Jezalee. "I thank you for bringing a lot of amazing sunshine into my life today," Robert surprisingly remarked.

The gals caught up with Paul as they saw him sitting in a waiting area all by himself. He took one glance at them and knew he had better not say anything at that moment, he could tell they had both been crying a lot. Jezalee asked Deanna if she would like to go have lunch and she said that would be nice. Paul took them to a French Restaurant in the city and as they waited for their menus, he asked the gals if they had a good visit and they both said better than expected then they simultaneously burst into tears. He apologized for making them cry and would change the subject. Jezalee let him know that Deanna and she saw a different person in there and his attorney was making sure he met with a Dr. Pendulum every day until he was off suicide watch and out of the restraints, they had him in. Deanna spoke up that Robert finally admitted that he should've gotten help when she pleaded with him. When the maître'd brought over the menus; Paul could tell the gals were probably just going to lunch to appease him; but he did not say anything to them. He would just let them order something and if they did not want to eat anything that was okay. When their meals arrived, the girls did try to eat some of their meal, but they were in a different state of mind after meeting with Robert and he fully understood.

The next day Deanna flew home in the Albanese's private jet and was so happy she got to visit Robert before he was sentenced. She was also glad she was at Paul and Jezalee's when Roberts family came to meet them. Now! All they had to do now, was wait for the date Robert would find out his future.

Created with Sketch.

Everyone was anticipating Robert's sentencing; however, life went on and they tried to keep from talking about the what if's, of his sentencing. He would finally be standing before a Judge and find out what his future would be. Since Jezalee and Deanna had visited him, Jesse had seen to it that Robert continued his sessions with Dr. Pendulum, and he was finally taken off suicide watch and the therapeutic restraints removed. It was a long time coming; but Jesse had to keep Robert safe from himself. They kept him away from the other inmates and he finally asked to speak to a Priest.

The day of the sentencing, Tuesday, September 19, 1989, Jezalee, Deanna, and their families were in attendance, as was all of Roberts family which he had never met. David and Mallory were there, along with Charles Dandridge's family, and Ernest Stafford, the driver's family, and Roland's wife, Angela's parents, and other family members.

The Bailiff brought the Court to order when the Honorable Judge Bartoli appeared. Everyone sat down after the Judge was seated. He called the room to order and asked Robert Anderson to stand. Jesse stood as Robert did, waiting for the Judge to speak. The Judge asked how Robert Anderson pleaded and he said, "guilty your honor." The Judge proceeded and asked him to please sit down.

He addressed Robert and explained to him there was quite a few people here today to speak before the court on how they were affected by the murders that took place on their family members.

Ernest Stafford's family came forward and spoke a little about Ernest and the loss of an amazing human being's life, at the hands of Robert Anderson. They unequivocally pleaded with the court not to spare any leniency and this serial killer needs to be sentenced to life in prison.

Charles Dandridge's wife stood up with her family and said she understands what Robert did, is a travesty. The loss of her husband and their children's father was unbearable at times. He was a man of respect, compassion and always believed in the truth will set you free. My family and I know that Robert acted out of not understanding what a person's life meant, because he was never exposed to forming the essential tools to know right from wrong. I beg the court for Robert to be able to seek extensive therapy and be able to live a normal life and prosper. I not only speak for myself and our children; I am speaking on behalf of my husband because he would never want someone who has suffered as much as Robert did from a kidnapping, continually being sexually and verbally abused, beaten, and humiliated for thirteen years. I beg the court to use compassion and leniency in his sentencing.

Jezalee and Deanna had their moments in front of the Judge and they both expressed what they had gone through with Robert. They knew he made a bad judgment call when he did not let his grieving family know he was alive. He was too embarrassed to confess what the Crockets did to him. He was fifteen and Deanna was fourteen when they escaped, and Robert was forced to set fire to the Crockets for their own survival. They never had the opportunity to attend school, meet other people.

Deanna informed the Judge that Robert took great care of her like a normal adult would have. They searched every day for over two years, until he found her aunt and uncle, who later adopted her. If it had not been for Robert, she would not have the wonderful life she has today. We both had severe trauma from those two monsters, and I would have never made it without extensive therapy for several years.

The last people to speak was his immediate family, they came forward together; they looked over at Robert, they had tears as they looked at him. They knew he was a wounded soul and had been so broken from being around two people filled with hate.

Roberts Aunt Janie, and Uncle Stewart, addressed the Judge in hopes he would find it in his heart and moral sense to show leniency on Robert due to the circumstances that led him to this courtroom today. He never knew he had a family waiting to find him and bring him home. He and Deanna were told by the Crockets that their parents gave them up and never wanted to see them. They did not know the truth until Robert found the clippings, prior to escaping. Unfortunately, his captors, made sure the clippings did not show where the murders took place or the names of the victims. They did not want to take any chances of them knowing the names of the deceased parents because it would lead to their remaining family members. They forgave Robert for murdering Roland but once they saw the evidence, spoke to Deanna, who shared the same horrifying experiences he did, they could not in all consciousness hold him accountable and live with themselves.

The three grandparents, stood up, walked to where the speaker was and individually addressed the Judge and without a doubt; they three agreed Robert was punished every day, from December 24, 1950, until he and Deanna escaped a life of hell on Earth in 1964. He should not be tried twice for the crimes he committed. They felt he served his time by being kidnapped, continually torched, and raped day after day, for fourteen years. Robert not only has bodily scars; his mind has been scared from all the abuse as well. After what he went through, he deserves to get help and try and live a normal life. We plead with the court to confine Robert to a special facility that deals only with people that have been continually abused during their entire childhood. We want our grandson back and hope to be able to see him as often as possible.

"I was ready to sentence Robert Anderson today; however, I have heard compelling and most gripping statements that I need additional time to review in my chambers. I have reviewed all Roberts sessions with Dr. Pendulum; however, I am going to have one of Dr. Pendulum's colleagues, set up some additional sessions; so, I can review a second opinion, as well. I will review each person's statement and will take everything you have said into consideration, along with what he is done to his seven victims," Judge Bartoli commented.

The Judge hoped he would hopefully be able to give his ruling within a few weeks. The attorney's will be notified accordingly, and we will all meet back here and at such time I will give my sentencing for Robert Anderson.

The Judge made it clear that Robert was not eligible to post bail and would remain in custody until his sentencing. The Judge thanked everyone for participating and left the bench. Robert went back to his cell; but before he did, he had one more glance at the family he never knew and shuffled out with the heavy chains weighing his ankles down. As he shuffled to his jail cell, his eyes filled with tears and feeling out of sorts, he knew he needed to call for Dr. Pendulum and the Priest that came by to see him on a weekly basis.

After everyone cleared the courtroom, they stayed outside the doors and wanted to give their condolences to Deanna after hearing about her harrowing experiences all those years. Roberts family asked if they could get her phone number and address to keep in touch with her and she was delighted they asked.

David and Mallory went over to Charles' family and was pleased they had shown up; but knew how difficult it was for Mrs. Dandridge to address the Judge. Mrs. Dandridge hugged David and Mallory and said she knew it was what Charles would have wanted her to do. She knew in her heart of hearts Robert was a very disturbed man and the reasons were certainly spelled out in the Courtroom. As David and Mallory said their goodbyes, they were filled with pain, sorrow, and tears over the entire courtroom statements.

Jezalee and Paul walked over to David and Mallory and said they were glad that was behind them. Both David and Mallory let Jezalee know that they knew how difficult it was to get up in front of the Judge. After the O'Malley's, Albanese's, and Deanna said their goodbyes to the victim's families, they walked to David SUV, and he asked them if they were up for a nice late lunch of their choice. Paul asked Deanna if she would like to spend one more night, to relax and rest up, before flying back home. Deanna was relieved that Paul invited her to stay an extra evening, because she was not mentally ready to be with her children. Deanna immediately said she would love to stay one more night, because she felt she was not in the best state of mind to see her children. Deanna thanked Jezalee and Paul for their gracious hospitality and knew after a good night's sleep, she would be ready for her family. David said she could use his car phone as soon as they got to a restaurant. Once they arrived at the Fairmont Hotel Restaurant, everyone got out, Deanna walked to the front passenger seat and got in. David handed her the phone and told her to take her time because they would wait for her in the hotel lobby. Deanna spoke to her husband Eric, and he agreed that staying one more night would be good for her. She also let him know he did not need to pick her up at the airport because one of the pilots would be renting a car and she would have a ride.

Once Deanna spotted the O'Malley's and Albanese's, she walked over to them and thanked David for the use of his car phone. "Is Eric okay you staying one more night?" Jezalee asked. "Yes! He thought it would be best as well," Deanna answered. By the time they arrived home, the children were home from school. Nell had prepared a wonderful Irish meal for the O'Malley's and Helga had prepared a great Southern home cooked meal that Adrienne requested for the Albanese's.

During dinner at the Albanese's, Gregory had driven Adrienne home and she invited him to dinner; he was all in for homemade Southern food. Deanna was so relaxed around their family and knew she wanted to keep in touch because they were such wonderful people.

After dinner the children finished their homework, they came down and said their goodnights and went to bed early. Paul, Helga, Jezalee, and Deanna sat in the living room discussing children, the different businesses that the Albanese's owned, and wanted to know about the bakery business that Deanna and Eric owned. They felt fortunate they were becoming well known in Miami and had their two locations and expected to open-up another one by the end of the year.

Jezalee could see that Deanna looked tired and asked her if she needed to go to bed; if not to stay and visit longer. Deanna was exhausted and excused herself for the evening and thanked them for everything.

Helga and the Albanese's; went to bed about a half an hour after Deanna did, everyone was completely drained from preparing for Robert's Courtroom statements and then they would not find out until the Judge reviewed everything.

Paul and Jezalee went to their children's bedrooms to kiss them goodnight; and they each had looked up at their parents from their bed and told them what a wonderful feeling it was to be a complete family again. "Was this something the three of you rehearsed, because you three said the exact same thing?" Paul commented with a smile. Jessica was the last one to kiss goodnight and confessed they had each decided to say the same thing. Paul and Jezalee laughed and knew the children were back to their old selves and it felt amazing.

Once Paul and Jezalee showered and got their pajamas on, they laid in bed for at least an hour discussing the possibility of taking a few mini trips during next year, which would include the children as well. One thing for sure, they were going to their Napa Vineyard/Winery immediately and start construction. The six-bedroom Italian villa needed remodeling; it had spectacular views but the way the architect designed it, he had not taken advantage of the land's surroundings; which meant, they needed to change out the windows to make them three times larger, to utilize seeing the beauty of the land from the villa. They also wanted to go visit their other vineyards and wineries in Europe to see if they needed any updating. Paul checked in with his managers on a weekly basis with all their businesses; he was a hands-on person and never wanted anything slipping through the cracks. They both knew they had great people working for them; but always wanted to keep abreast of every detail.

Deanna flew home the next morning, felt rested, enjoyed spending extra time with the Albanese's and thanked God every day for her life being what it was. She was happy that the next Court appearance, Eric would be coming with her; the Albanese's; already invited them to their place when the date was set.

The weeks were flying by, David and Mallory noticed how wonderful it was to see Paul and Jezalee back to how they remembered them, when they lived in Paris. David and Paul were always surprising both families and staff with weekends away; especially since there was a private jet readily available at any given time and there was the Incline Village, Castle on the Mountain, that they immensely enjoyed.

Created with Sketch.

It was the middle of September, the Albanese's received their long awaited, invitation from the Vatican, for Peter's Consistory Ceremony, becoming a Cardinal. Peter's parents, Antonio and Elene, Paul, Jezalee, their children, Jezalee's parents, Carolyn, and Mark, and his aunts and uncles were invited for this auspicious occasion. Peter would officially become a Cardinal on Sunday, December 03, 1989.

The Albanese's called Peter as soon as they received their invitation and asked him if he was nervous. Peter had a very charismatic presence and had nerves of steel; so, he told the family he was looking forward to the ceremony and was just anticipating seeing them in the audience.

Paul asked Peter if he would be in Pisa to have Thanksgiving with the family and he said he would not miss it. He let him know they would fly over for three days to be with everyone because they wanted to see him before the ceremony at the Vatican. Jezalee was happy about the date for Peter's ceremony; it was after their Halloween Party, and before their Christmas Party.

Jamerson called all who were affected by Robert and gave them the sentencing date of December 11, 1989. Deanna, Jezalee or the O'Malley's were not attending. He knew that Roberts family would be in attendance.

Knowing Paul would be going home for Thanksgiving, to Pisa with his family for the first time, after the wedding; he could feel the normalcy and gratitude of it all. With the Halloween and Christmas Party's coming up, and experiencing Jezalee planning the extravaganza, he did get that certain feeling of what it was like watching his wife create something right before his eyes. He had always been in awe of what she could come up with in a moment's notice; but to have a month or so to plan, was even more extraordinary.

When Fr. Peter told his Congregation he was leaving, they wept and knew their Parish, would never be the same without him. He had given so much of himself to the Church and the Community. All the parishioners decided to have a party the day after Thanksgiving and Paul, Jezalee, their children, and all the rest of the family in Italy would be a part of Peter's farewell party. Not only were they going to miss him being their Priest; but his talents as well; he had raised a significant amount of money for the poor families in their area with the sale of his oil paintings over the years. During the party, one of Fr. Peter's Deacons stood up and said, "On Sunday, December 03, 1989, our beloved Priest, Fr. Peter Albanese, 45, becomes a Cardinal in Rome, Italy, at the Vatican. He will reside at the Vatican, as one of the papal advisors. Fr. Peter was our Priest for fifteen years and will be missed by all of us. We wish him good health, a long life, and embracing his new calling to the Catholic Church.

Thanksgiving had been wonderful in Pisa and spending a few days with Peter, plus, attending his farewell party was fun but sad for Antonio, Elene, the rest of the family, and the whole community. This would be a huge void for Peter's parents, since they attended Mass every morning to see Peter.

Once the Albanese's, were back home, and the children returned to school; Jezalee knew the planning of the party was going to be full speed ahead. The invitations had gone out November 1st, and she had ordered all the twenty-foot artificial Christmas trees for the first floor; they had arrived Tuesday, December 5th. The freshly Christmas cut trees, would arrive on Tuesday, December 12th; Jezalee had purchased enough exquisite ornaments over the past twenty-five, plus years, that would adorn all the freshly cut trees that would be in the family room, each bedroom, and the foyer. The children always had friends over to help decorate the trees in their bedrooms. Jezalee and Paul would spend a quite evening alone, listening to Christmas carols in their bedroom while they decorated their tree. Everyone in the family, including the staff and their children would help decorate the tree in the game room. The family room tree was left for the five of them to decorate. A holiday decorating company would be coming come in to decorate all the artificial trees throughout the house. Jezalee had planned the menu and had most of the food would be catered; except for she and Helga always adding their favorite Christmas recipes to the party menu.

Occasionally when Paul had a few idle moments to spare, he would wander through each room of their massive estate in San Francisco, never thinking they would go through a divorce, sell their Paris estate, Jezalee and their children would move to San Francisco, he would live in a hotel in Pairs. Their divorce was the longest, dreadful, and loneliest four years of his life. Sure, he was able to come as a visitor to her one Christmas Party, and he would have them at the Pisa villa, and the chateau in Saint-Germain-en-Laye; but it was not the same while being divorced; it was strained, lonely, uncomfortable, and feeling out of sorts. This was the first Christmas he felt life was back to where he could feel the love, respect, passion, and the unity of his family. There was one room Paul gravitated to more than the others, the family room; he would glance up at the extraordinary family portrait Jessica had painted. Seeing Jonathan in the portrait was difficult at times; but other times, it was such a gift to be able to see him up there with the rest of the family. He came into their world in a horrific way and had a monster of a mother. He was just thankful he had some time with Jonathan and had wished he had gotten him away from his mother before the tragic accident. He knew if Jonathan had lived, Jezalee would have welcomed him with open arms, with a heart filled with love, and a carrying soul. That always gave Paul comfort when he was saddened about Jonathan's short life.

Created with Sketch.

The Albanese family were relaxing on their flight to Rome, they decided to play a few board games, then take a long nap before arriving. They could hardly from the anticipation going to the Vatican and seeing Peter becoming a Cardinal. When they were informed, he had been one of the Cardinals residing at the Vatican as a papal advisor, they knew it was quite an honor for that to be bestowed to a new Cardinal.

It was finally Friday, two days before they would experience Paul's brother becoming a Cardinal. The jet was ready for the family to fly into Rome, where he had already secured three suites at the nearest 5-star hotel for the family. His and Jezalee's parents arrived there on Thursday to meet up with some relatives and friends they had not seen in a while.

Everyone woke up rather early on the day of Peter's special ceremony at the Vatican. They hurried to get ready to have breakfast in the hotel dining room; everyone either had butterflies in their stomachs or could not eat; or eating too much because they were a nervous wreck for Peter. Paul was rather calm and stood up to say a few words before their breakfast arrived. He wanted to make it clear what a propitious occasion this was for them to be able to attend. It is a very ceremonial and reverent moment, with all its pomp and circumstance. Paul wanted his family to know that his brother has been this special and amazing person his entire life and his devotion to his Religion has set him apart from others. He has worked tirelessly to be bestowed this honor today by the Pope. At one point he confided in Paul that he was not going to accept the appointment; but he knew in his heart that he had be able to do good no matter where he was. He left his Parish with a heavy heart in pain; he was close to everyone that attended Mass on a regular basis and always welcomed people just passing through. It would be a huge void in his life because he treated them like they were his family. He knows it will be far from what he was used to; but he considers the Pope a wise man and would not have appointed him if he thought he would be unhappy or to not fulfill his obligation as a Cardinal.

The Albanese and Marino family arrived at the Vatican and were taken to a special room where the Ceremony was about to take place. As they sat in their velvet covered chairs, in walks Peter, with his red zucchetto {skull cap}, cardinal cape over his red and white cassock. As he approached the Pope, he knelled down in front of him and the Pope placed the three cornered, red birettas on top of his head, leaving the zucchetto underneath. The Pope said his speech, then blessed the new incoming Peter as a Cardinal, to the highest rank in the Catholic hierarchy. Everyone in the Albanese and Marino family were in tears of sadness because they would see less of Peter, and tears of complete joy at what he had accomplished. After the ceremony there was a huge reception where all the guests were invited. Everyone in the families were in awe of the reception given for the newly appointed Cardinals.

By the time the Albanese's and Marino's flew back home to their civilian lives, as Alexander called it; they were still reminiscing on the ceremony they witnessed watching Peter becoming a Cardinal. They still could not get over him being in Rome, at the Vatican. They were trying to imagine what he had be doing when he first got there; but they were extremely proud of Peter. His parents would feel the biggest voids, not seeing him every morning at Mass.

Created with Sketch.

A week went by, it was Roberts sentencing, Monday, December 11, 1989. While most people were going to Christmas tree lots with their families, to choose that perfect tree, making homemade cookies, listening to their favorite Christmas carols, decorating their tree, and shopping for the perfect gifts for their loved ones. Robert was sitting in a cell awaiting the Judge's decision.

Deanna had expressed to her husband, Eric that she was saddened that Robert never wanted to see her again. He knew his wife was not going to the sentencing; but for him to disown her from coming to visit him was cruel since they had always felt like brother and sister. Deanna did know that Robert's/Roland's and Angela's family would be there; she felt so sad what those families had already endured was tragic.

Robert was escorted into the courtroom with his ankle and wrists confined to the heavy steel chains; he glanced towards the people that were there for his sentencing. Robert's Attorney, Jesse hurried through the double mahogany doors to the courtroom, before, the Judge came from his chambers.

Judge Bartoli looked around the courtroom and realized it was a lot less than half the people that were originally there, who had given their statements. He spoke a few minutes to the people seated in the courtroom then addressed Robert Anderson and his attorney, Jesse Stoneridge. Both men stood facing the Judge; he asked Robert how he pleaded, and he said, "guilty your honor."

The Judge read off each victim's name, and date that Robert had murdered them. Judge Bartoli informed the court he had gone over all court statements from, the victim's families, read all documentation from his sessions with Dr. Pendulum and Dr. Salinger. The Judge indicated that both Dr. Pendulum and Dr. Salinger came to the same conclusion.

Judge Bartoli asked Robert if had anything to say before sentencing. Yes, your honor, "With a heavy heart and a broken soul, I am ready to face my family to let them know that I did not start out in life to become a murderer. When those demonic people did things to me and Deanna, I knew it must be wrong. I hated them so much and they had all the power and they tricked us into thinking our families had given us up. When Deanna got pregnant at 14, I knew the only way to rid us of those-two-evil monsters, I had to take drastic measures for our survival. When I set them on fire, I thought that Deanna and I were finally free. I never knew that deep down I was becoming a younger version of them, and I did not know how to control it. I had a twin brother I never got to know because by the time I met him, I had terrible thoughts and envied him. Deanna and I lived a tragic and sick existence for such a long time, and I ended up being the week one, never thinking that would ever happen. As the years went by, I was eaten up with guilt with what we both experienced. Our childhood has haunted me the rest of my life. I tried to analyze why I had such thoughts and knowing how much I hated those two monsters who kidnapped us. I started out feeling on top of the world when we escaped the life we had; I was doing well then once we located Deanna's family I felt like an outsider; and it certainly was not because of the way they treated me. They wanted to take me in and get the same help Deanna would and did receive. She is thriving from her extensive therapy. I had every opportunity to get help, and I refused. Anyone sitting in this courtroom today because of what I did to their loved one's; I regret killing them and leaving them without the loved ones they once had in their lives. I, not for one second, regret setting the Crockets on fire. We never knew that a normal, loving, and innocent childhood ever existed. I am overwrought with anger, and overwhelmed with embarrassment standing here, knowing that these family members will never be the same because of me. I want the families and the court to know, no matter my sentence, I will be a model prisoner, knowing that I will have a better life in there, than I did on the outside.

Judge Bartoli asked Robert if he was finished, he said yes, your honor. The Judge asked Robert to stay standing. Judge Bartoli looked down on his paperwork; then sullenly looked Robert in the eyes and began the long-awaited sentencing. "Robert Anderson, after carefully reviewing what was set before me, I sentence you to five life sentences, without parole; however, after you have served ten years, in the San Quentin Penitentiary, you have one chance to go before the board to be released after ten years of being incarcerated. I want each of the victim's families knowing, it has been a thought-provoking experience to come to a decision; however, knowing these murders were premeditated and, with all conscientiousness, there was only one sentence I could decide upon. Robert Anderson, you will be escorted out of the courtroom, and a prison van is awaiting your departure to San Quentin Penitentiary.

The victim's families had hoped the Judge would have sent him into an institution for further psychiatric help; abut they understood why he came to his conclusion and hopefully Robert could get out in ten years. After the families made their way out of the courtroom, they gathered around in the lobby area and realized they were feeling sorry for him; but knew the Judge did the right thing because they were all premeditated murders.

Jamerson was in the courtroom; he immediately placed a call to Deanna, Jezalee, and David to let them know what Roberts's sentence was. Deanna was of course, devastated at how Robert's life had turned for the worse. She called her parents, Belle and Jude and they were saddened to know that Robert had put himself in a dark place and hoped he would eventually be freed. As for Jezalee, she had certainly felt sorry for Robert; but every time she thought back to him, contemplating, killing Alexander and her, made her wake up and realize, he needed to be behind bars.

Jezalee called Mallory, who had just gotten off the phone with David and heard about the sentencing. They both agreed it was a good day for many reasons; Robert would be behind bars for at least ten years, if not for life. They could finally feel free of his sickness.

As Robert sat on the bus, he was temporarily fixated on the passing vehicles, and curious as to where they were going. There he was, on an uncomfortable, wore torn seat, with its springs coming through the aged leather. On the way to San Quentin, in the bus, with his wrists chained to the metal part of the seat in front of him, and the chains around his ankles were attached to the metal legs. As Robert got closer to the prison, he was hyperventilating, chains around his ankles and wrists were making him claustrophobic; but it would come and go as his thoughts did.

As Robert stepped off the bus, he looked around at the sprawling prison, which was built on first class Bay property, with a backdrop of San Francisco Bay. From what he had read about the area, the prison was sitting on a valuable piece of land.

Once he arrived, everything was methodically done, step by step. He entered the Receiving and Release area to receive his identification card and prison number that would follow him, for his whole incarceration. After he left that area, he went through a myriad of questions at the intake desk. Before going to his assigned cell block, he was unshackled by the Transport Guards, he had to strip completely naked, tossing what he wore into a bin and follow the footprints on the cold, Clorox smelling concrete floor. He reached a spot where there was a line of Correctional Officers lined up, and he had to stand in line with the rest of the incoming inmates who got off the bus. He was told to run his hands through his hair, show them the inside of his mouth, lift his head so the guard could see up his nostrils, his ear canals were checked, he had to lift-up his penis, sweep underneath with his hand, bend over, spread them, then squat and cough. He was asked if he wanted to take a shower or wait until the next day. He decided to wait for a shower for the following day. Once that was over, he was handed a pair of boxer shorts and they put him in a holding tank while they got his information into their system. Robert was then called up by a higher-ranking staff member. Here, he was asked what affiliation he was, in-order-to get housed in a proper cell and unit for him. He found out if you are white, you go with the whites, unless otherwise specified. After that, he nervously waited around the "holding intake" for the rest of the inmates to get booked and then he still had to wait until other inmates came from other counties. While waiting with the other inmates, they each received a sack lunch and received their property that they brought from the jail they had been in. He got his prison blues, as they called them, and a bedroll. By the time he and the other new inmates were booked, they were taken to their unit and cell. Robert had no clue that entering the gates of hell would take until nighttime to be processed.

After the ordeal of his entrance into the prison world of convicts; the guard walked beside him, which seemed a mile, taking Robert to his assigned four-by-nine-foot cell. As soon as Robert saw the room, he noticed there were bunk beds, and asked, "why two beds?" The guard informed him he would be getting a roommate soon. Robert was beyond livid! He wanted to say something; but he learned from being in jail, the less you say or complain about, the better things will be. The guard let him know, he could choose the top or bottom bunk before the other Cellie arrived. After the guard went through the list of rules and regulations, he advised Robert prison was never a quiet place and takes some time getting used to it. Before the guard left, he handed the typed-up list of rules and regulations for him to keep. This place is about locked gates, doors, and cells. They have a saying amongst the inmates, called "ear hustle," you may hear that term used; all it means is inmates talking amongst themselves. One last bit of information, prison is about survival, try to stay under the radar of the troubling and vicious inmates," the guard nicely warned him.

After the guard closed and locked the cell door, Robert read over the list and knew he was getting half the space in this closet sized cell. It was a far cry from the master suite closet he had in his penthouse, which was a fifteen-by-twenty-five-foot space with all his designer clothes and shoes. This was a major adjustment and would be difficult for him. He knew, to get on the good side of the incoming prisoner, he would let that guy take the lead in what area he wanted in the cell. They at least had small lockers to put their personal items in, and a separate section for their toiletries. Robert noticed on the list that he could buy rubber sandals for the shower, because no one was allowed, to go barefoot. He could not understand why they did not issue them when they received their uniform. Robert realized being incarcerated the rest of his life was going to be a huge undertaking and regrets would mount up. He was thankful that he at least had a chance, after ten years to be paroled. Robert was hoping his Cellie, as they call a roommate; would not be there for a few days, so he could somewhat adjust to the living conditions by himself.

Since dinner had been served while Robert had been in processing, the guard brought him his first hot meal and informed him, he could go to the mess hall three times a day, choose what he wanted to eat from what they were serving and could stay there or go back to his cell to eat. After the guard left, he looked despairingly at the food and knew this would be difficult to consume; but needed to keep his strength up. He had put himself behind bars and this would be just the beginning of what he left outside these prison walls. The last twenty-five years had not prepared him to live like this the rest of his life. He knew that he had to mentally try and deal with what he got himself into and would go to the library and start checking out books, since reading always helped him with his anxiety.

Once Roberts, Cellie joined him, he was happy to know the guy did not smoke and wanted the top bunk. That was music to his ears, because he was hoping he could keep sleeping on the bottom bunk. He was a quiet man about fifty, had been at San Quentin for five of his twenty-five-year sentence. His name was John and had asked to be transferred where someone did not smoke and talk incessantly.

December had been a full month, Peter becoming a Cardinal, Robert going to San Quentin, and the Christmas soiree at the Albanese's home. Everyone and anyone had showed up for the spectacular event and it was a night to remember.

The O'Malley's invited everyone up to the Castle on the Mountain for New Year's Eve. That meant whatever staff that had stayed around for the holidays would be coming, and the Stanton's were always a welcome addition to their trips, as was Nell's boyfriend, Ronan.

David, Paul, and Richard were becoming close friends and would have their sons, joining them on weekend trips to camp out, play a little tennis, basketball, or soccer. All three men were very athletic and loved sports. They took the boys to ball games, went sailing, to movies, and liked playing pool with them as well. As for their daughters, they would go to their father-daughter dances, take them skating, to the movies and take them out to lunch or dinner. While the men did all this, Mallory, Jezalee and Joan would go shopping, meet up with other lady friends, go to Museums, Musicals, and Plays.

After Robert had been in prison for two years, they appointed him clerk in the library; he was finally in his element. Once he wanted to check out a book for the first time, he had always heard that a prison library was a place the inmates could come and go; but not at San Quentin, there was a clerk on duty, and he was behind an enclosed area with a window. Outside the window area was a catalog of the current books available and where you signed out for a book. Shortly after Robert started, several magazines were added to the library list. Every month he would thumb through them to see if Paul and Jezalee were in any of the articles. After about six months working in the library, they were on the front page and the article talked about the two dynamic entrepreneurs. He read the article several times and knew it was bringing up memories of Jezalee and he knew how obsessed he was over her, to a point of sick-minded. He still had those feelings; but he kept those to himself. He knew he was an intelligent man; but with deep-seeded problems, knowing he had no control, and it was frustrating for him. Through all the therapy he had, he kept certain things he would never divulge to anyone. He knew if he said too much, he would never have a chance getting released in ten years. He heard from other inmates that no lifer inmate had ever been approved to leave after ten years, so ne k new his chances were slim to none.

Robert was doing the best he could, with what he was dealt with. There were things that irritated him in prison, it was never quiet; but one thing was for sure, they may lock up his body but never his mind. It was, a complex environment, to be in, there was one neighborhood of prisoners that were actively elevating their lives, so once they left prison, they could live productive lives. There were other neighborhoods much more difficult in the prison and were always breaking out fights. He and John were thankful they were in the more subdued part of the prison and stayed away from the troublemakers. Robert still had nightmares and his Cellie asked him what they were from. After the extensive therapy he was still getting at the prison, he was able to talk to John about his life and what had happened those excruciating fourteen years. John was gasping at one point and could not believe that two human beings could do what they did to Robert and Deanna.

One night John and Robert were talking about the prisoners that had unsuccessfully escaped from San Quentin, they both laughed at some of the stories and said, "What were those idiots thinking?" That night after they hit their bunks to get some sleep; Robert stayed awake thinking of how he could get out of prison. He was going to start spending more time in the exercise yard and trying to figure out if there was any way he could escape from there. Robert vacillated over the idea of John escaping with him; but was it too risky if he mentioned it. If he said something to John and he did not want to do it, he could get him in trouble and lose some of his privileges, and certainly would not be eligible for parole in ten years. His mind was spinning with thoughts of how to escape. He was thinking he could offer John five hundred thousand to escape with him; but he did not really want to part with any of the money he had hidden in San Francisco. He felt he had made the wrong decision to be the clerk in the library; it may have been better to be on trash duty; or something where they used the gates to open every day.

PART SEVEN

1993

The years went by with much anticipation of children graduating from, elementary, junior high, high school and college. It was 1993, Adrienne had graduated with honors, being at the top of her class from Stanford; Gregory had graduated at the top of his class, with honors at Stanford the year before and had been accepted into Harvard School of Medicine. Adrienne was finally joining Gregory at Hartford, after a year of their long-distance relationship. She had been accepted into the Masters' Program in the Psychology Department and had started Harvard. Her parents helped her find a nice apartment not far from campus, which was down the street from Gregory's. Gregory had come over to see Jezalee and Paul while they were in town and the four of them had a great time the few days they were there. While they were there Gregory asked Adrienne's parents for her hand in marriage and they both could not say yes fast enough. He showed them the ring and thought it was magnificent; they could tell that he had saved a bundle of money to purchase just the right ring and they were so proud of him. His parents had come out the night before he was to propose to Adrienne and he wanted all four of the parents there, in-close-proximity of where he was going to propose to his one and only. The night of the proposal they went to a 5-star restaurant, after they ate, the six of them danced and once the parents left the dance floor, they brought out a video camera and started taping them. Gregory started walking towards the love of his life and got down on one knee and proposed. Adrienne of course! Was crying happy tears and was shocked beyond words. The parents kept waiting for her to say yes; but they beat her to it, and she started to laugh, then she looked down at the love of her life as he was still kneeling, and softly said yes.

Jessica moved to Los Angeles in 1990 and had been living her dream, going to UCLA, enriching her art techniques. She had a lot of friends from her classes; however, she noticed one-particular guy who caught her undivided attention. Mateo came over and asked if he could sit at her table, while he ate his lunch. She looked up at him and could hardly contain herself; but she managed to get the word "yes" out, without making a fool out of herself. Over the next few weeks or so, they managed to get to know one another, and were both pleasantly surprised that they had a lot in common. He was born in Milan, Italy and had moved over to America, with his parents and siblings when he was 9 years old. They lived in Santa Barbara, his father was a composer and had written several famous scores for block buster movies; his mother was a fashion and jewelry designer who was well known amongst the elite. Mateo and Jessica hit it off immediately; she could finally use her Italian to talk to someone. He and his one brother, Romeo were roommates, and lived close to campus. His brother was in his last year at ULCA and would be taking off for Milan, where his fiancee lived. Matteo had been accepted into the UCLA School of Theater, Film and Television, and wanted to someday be a director.

Alexander was accepted into the Juilliard Performing Arts School, and the University of Music and Performing Arts in Vienna. He had taken a year off after High School and was having a tough time deciding what Performing Arts School he preferred. During that time, he kept studying all the great Composers, and played their pieces 8 to 10 hours a day. Alexander wanted to be clear-headed before he decided what school to attend. He would research information on both prestige's schools and make his decision when he knew which one would be ideal for him. After constantly working on his favorite pieces, in 1993, he finally had decided he wanted to go to the famous Juilliard School, and he was one hundred per cent sure this was his destiny.

Once he arrived, he knew this was the place to be and would expand his talents further. Since he had not attended a college prior to being a student at Juilliard, he was required to live at the Meredith Wilson Residence Hall. He could hardly contain himself, and once his vacation with the family was over, he would be fulfilling part of his dream.

The last few years, Jezalee had managed to put together two cookbooks, which both became number 1 sellers. Her Historian books were in its second edition and was happy they were still doing so well. She was exceptionally thrilled that most of the museums throughout the globe sold her books in their gift shops.

Jezalee and Paul were getting ready to celebrate their nineteenth anniversary {it would have been 23 years if they had not gotten a divorce} by taking a trip around the World and would visit their children in their new places while in school, visit all their family, friends, and acquaintances. At some point, their children, with their significant others, if they had one would be joining them in Japan for a month vacation.

Paul and Jezalee still had their beautiful estates, properties, and businesses. They had been spending a lot of time at their Villa in Napa; especially after they had renovated it. All their Wineries, especially the one in California, was winning Awards across the Globe. Their other Wineries were doing exceptional, as well. Everyone always teased Jezalee because she never drunk alcohol, other than for using their finest wines from all their locations in her recipes.

Paul was still designing athletic wear for Italy. Their Albanese International Sauce Company was still number 1. They sold their interest in the diamond minds and used that money to open-up a Center for Families in Need in San Francisco, Los Angeles, Chicago, and New York.

David and Mallory's Import-Export business was thriving, and they had invested in the Albanese Sauce Company, and in their California Winery. Mallory was running the San Francisco Center for Families in Need, and hopeful that with this center, it would make a difference in the community. She worked tirelessly there, as did Jezalee, Joan, Helga, and Nell. With most the children gone, they had the extra time to give to the Center.

Astrid and Nicholas got married the year before and had a huge garden wedding on the estate in Saint-Germaine-en-Laye; it was where she had always dreamed of have a romantic wedding. She was now finishing her master's degree; and had a great job at a brokerage firm in Chicago. Her husband, Nicholas was also working towards finishing his master's degree as well. and was teaching High School in the city.

Morgan had graduated from Princeton and decided to stay back east for a while, to see her grandparents more often. She had a boyfriend for 2 years at Princeton; but he had graduated a year before her, and they were not serious enough to keep a long-distance relationship. They remained friends and wished one another well. She was still trying to decide what she wanted to do and thought she may switch majors and continue going to Princeton.

Adam was in his second year at University of California Berkeley; joined a fraternity and had a girlfriend, named Deirdre, whose family was friends of some of their relatives in Ireland. She was in a sorority, and that is basically how they met, at a fraternity party. He wanted to be a history teacher and hoped one day to work up to being a professor at a prestigious university.

Erica was still living at home and had just graduated High School. She felt so lost at home without her siblings around; but Manny hung out with her, and she constantly had her friends over. She had applied to several schools and got in at University of California Santa Barbara, which had been her first choice, her best friend had gotten in there as well.

Mary, Joseph, and Nina's daughter was accepted at the Parsons School of Design in New York and was in her second year and loved it. Her family came out to see her as often as they could. The Albanese's let Mary, live at their penthouse in Manhattan while she was going to school. They had decided not to rent it out anymore and wanted it to be available for any of the children while they were going to college; plus, the parents could stay there when they came for a visit.

Joseph Jr., son of Joseph and Nina, had just graduated high school, along with Erica. He had been accepted at MIT, the top college for Architecture in the world. He had been encouraged by Paul and his dad for several years to study hard, because they saw his talents and knew he would make it into MIT. He had a girlfriend the last year in school but was nothing serious; but they wrote and called one another from time to time.

Janine, daughter of Joseph and Nina, was going into the 8th grade; but knew she would be so lonely without her siblings at home. She had decided to join the choir and drama club since she was a good singer and was interested in acting. Her parents were not too worried for her, Manny came over a lot to hang out and she had a lot of friends that would help her from her loneliness.

Manny, the son of Bob and Linda, was just entering high school, he had lost his shyness and gained quite a personality the last few years. All the girls constantly following him. He was handsome, tall for his age and quite an athlete; however, he had been around enough people to know the importance of education and he was serious with his studies and was a straight, A student, and did not have time for the "likes of girls," as he would say.

Created with Sketch.

Paul and Jezalee had been traveling for months; they called the children to let them know they were on their way to Japan and would have the jet ready for them once they were ready to board. Jessica had already arrived by commercial air lines and went straight to the penthouse in Manhattan, where Mary was living. Alexander, Adrienne, and Gregory had already arrived two days earlier and were excited about meeting up with Paul and Jezalee.

The siblings and Gregory decided to wait five days, because they wanted to have a little fun in New York while they were all together. Paul and Jezalee thought that was fine, this would give her and Paul some extra time to relax and enjoy the Japanese Culture and visit friends that lived there.

They had been to a lot of places in the last two months; but there was such a fascination about the people, the architecture, and the cuisine, that pulled them into the Asian Culture. Jezalee always remembered reading all the Pearl S. Buck novels, where she became intrigued by their Chinese culture. Knowing that Japan is rich in culture and history, as China was, she always wanted to go to both places. She and Paul had been to Hong Kong, China about ten years ago and knew one day they wanted to explore Japan. That time had finally come and knew that the children would love this country as much as they did.

By the time their children arrived, Paul and Jezalee were looking forward to showing them the sights. Paul and Jezalee had a huge suite with five bedrooms. Since there was a thirteen-hour time difference from New York to Tokyo; it would take a day or two to get acclimated to the time change. They had booked the two suites for 2 to 3 weeks; so, they had plenty of time to rest up first then see the sights.

After two days, of rest, everyone was ready to explore the beauties and mysteries of Japan; it was a country that was heavily populated in the cities; but so invigorating. They tried to get all their tourism in before sunset then choose a different restaurant every night they were there. Paul and Jezalee had friends that lived in Tokyo and were anxious to take them to the five main islands in Japan, which were Hokkaido, Honshu, Kyushu, Shikoku, and Okinawa. Marie and Bert took them to see historical temples and shrines, nearby castles, they took the whole family around to special, out of the way places, to join in festive dancing with the local people, went to a couple of festivals in each of the islands. They went hiking and saw Mt. Fuji from afar. The last main island was Shikoku, and it was located between the Seto Inland Sea and the Pacific Ocean. They had done a lot of sightseeing there and wanted to see the Sambaitani, Fudo, Nagasawa, and Nikobuchi, and the Dodoro Waterfalls.

They had loved the scenic beauty and splendor in some of the most miraculous places in Japan. They were traveling through the majestic mountains of Shikoku, then decided they would stop to eat down along the riverbank, looking up at the beautiful mountains that surrounded them. Marie and Bert, the Albanese's friends had lived in Japan for ten years, due to Bert's business and was so happy that they were able to take time out to guide them to the most spectacular parts of Japan.

Everyone had their food and started eating, Paul stood up to go over to get a couple of drinks for he and Jezalee, and Alexander saw his dad fall to the ground. Everyone raced over with Jezalee; they first thought he had a heart attacked. They were in an unpopulated area and Bert knew they expeditiously needed to find a doctor. They looked around and could not see anyone; it was continuous lush green mountains and hillsides with no one around them. Paul was unconscious and was losing a lot of blood. Gregory ran to him, tore open his shirt and took his white t-shirt off and pressed light to his chest. He looked at his face, neck, arms, then his legs. He let them know he had been shot in the chest and needed to get him to a hospital asap. They left the food and drinks, got in the van quickly, while Gregory, Alexander, and Bert carefully carried Paul to the back of the van, Gregory stayed back with him. as they drove away. Bert went to the nearest place of business and let the man know that someone was shot, and they needed to get him to a hospital asap. The proprietor called the local police, and they had a helicopter leave immediately and they alerted the hospital they had a gunshot victim losing a lot of blood. Gregory rode in the helicopter to watch over Paul. They were at the hospital within ten minutes. Jezalee, the children, Bert, and Marie got to the hospital, as soon-as they could. Gregory let them know Paul was in surgery and it may take several hours, depending on the damage the bullet caused. Jezalee and the children were crying, they could not understand who would shoot Paul; was it some random hunter, out for a thrill in shooting someone, or had someone followed them? Gregory reassured the family and their friends that they had a team of specialists trying to save Paul's life. Three hours later, the main surgeon came out and informed the family that Paul had a close call; but the human body is a remarkably resilient machine. What the doctors expected to be a fatal outcome, turned out to be non-fatal because, by sheer luck, the bullet missed everything critical on its path through the body. Everyone was stunned at the news and were so relieved. By the time Paul was in recovery, there were four policemen to guard him. The Dr. said he must have some angel on his shoulder, because he had never seen anyone survive a gunshot wound from where it entered-into his body. Everyone gathered around Jezalee and comforted her. Bert and Marie were devastated at Paul getting shot and knew he came close to dying was unfathomable. They knew of a hotel just a few blocks away and was going over to get a couple of suites for as long as Paul was in the hospital.

The surgeon, Dr. Takahashi indicated to Jezalee, he wanted to keep Paul in the hospital for at least a week. He assured her they had police guards there to keep Paul and the hospital safe; he indicated that the policemen are on foot, scouring the entire riverbank, hills, and mountains. They are going door to door asking people if they saw anyone around the time Paul was shot and no luck with any information yet. She thanked Dr. Takahashi for saving her husband's life. He let it be known, the bullet saved his life by not traveling to places in the body where they may have had a difficult time in saving Paul's life. The doctor asked her if she may have known the assailant and she responded and by telling him, Paul has no enemies and furthermore, she could not think of one person that would want him dead. Well! let us take all the precaution we can; I am going to have him placed in a more secure area of the hospital, and the police will be in and outside his room for protection. I want you to be able to go and get some rest and know that your husband is well protected here. She thanked him once again then he walked her into the recovery room, and Paul was still out. Dr. Takahashi had her wait until they moved him to a private and secluded room with bars and locks on the windows and a steel entry door. "I feel like I am in the middle of a James Bond movie," Jezalee smiled at the doctor and said. He walked closer to her and gave her a hug; not usual for someone of his culture. "I went to Medical School at Harvard, I did pick up some of the nice western ways," he looked at her and said. "My husband and I graduated in 69,'' Dr. Takahashi when did you graduate?"Jezalee asked. "We could have passed one another on campus, I graduated in 71'," he answered. "Are you sure I cannot stay with my husband, just for this one night?" Jezalee asked. "It is not our normal regulation; but since we are Harvard Alumni I will bend the rules this one time." Dr. Takahashi looked at her, grinned, and said in a comforting manner. She hugged him and felt more at ease since she was going to be able to stay. He immediately had an extra bed rolled into Paul's room.

Once Jezalee knew she was staying; she went over to the waiting room where everyone was waiting to let them know she was going to stay with Paul, in his room for one night and that they have four policemen to guard him, and more at every entrance and exit of the hospital. She asked them to go back to the hotel and she would see them in the morning. Bert and Marie said they would take good care of the children. Before they walked away, "That was some medical work back there at the river, she started crying and hugged Gregory; you helped save Paul's life, and Dr. Takahashi was impressed at how quickly you were able to check Paul's vitals, and stop him from bleeding out, you are going to make, one fine doctor," Jezalee said. As they left, Jezalee hurried over to the doctor, and he took her to another wing of the hospital and her bed was set up for her to hopefully get some sleep. The officers spoke English and let her know how sorry they were and hoped Paul had a full recovery. They told her they would be in the room watching over her as well during the night.

That night, as Jezalee lay in the hospital room, near Paul, while the two officers stood only a few feet away from them, and two outside the door; she felt their lives were so volatile. They left a dim light on, and she asked them if they had ever been in a situation like this. They looked her way and told her, unfortunately they both had.

The next morning, Paul woke up and had no idea what had happened. The officers wished him a good morning and let him know he had been shot in the chest and was rushed by helicopter to a nearby hospital. Just as they were talking, Jezalee woke up, jumped out of the hospital bed, and went over to give Paul a kiss. Paul was perplexed at what happened and was feeling the pain in his chest. Jezalee let him know that a Harvard Alumni saved his life. Just as Paul was going to ask her his name, Dr. Takahashi, walked in to check on him. The doctor immediately introduced himself and let him know they got the bullet out and he had never seen such miraculous luck. He examined the chest area and his vitals, and he informed Paul, he needed to stay for another 6 days for extra precaution for any unforeseen infections that may occur. "First off, Dr. Takahashi, it is nice to meet you; I wish it had been under different circumstances," Paul said. Dr. Takahashi agreed and gave he and his family an open invitation to join them after his recovery if he was up to it. Paul let him know that was a generous offer and once he was out of the hospital bed, they may take him up on it.

Jezalee had left the hospital with one of the officers so she could go to the hotel, take a shower, have breakfast with the children and bring them back to see their dad.

A week prior to shooting Paul, Robert had escaped from prison. He found it rather easy; all he had to say to any of the guards, which he had befriended for the last couple of years; he needed to pick up some books from the nurse's station that they were finished with. He had been down to the nurse's station on a few occasions delivering the books they requested and was there when a doctor or nurse would leave out the exit door; he paid close attention to them punching in the code as they left at night. The station was ten feet from his freedom. There was a door leading out to the parking lot and he darted out of there as soon as the coast was clear. Robert found a car that was unlocked, car jacked it and drove it to a hidden out of the way area to change the license plates, which he had stolen from the prison and hid down his pants. Once that was done, he had his money he was issued to buy things he needed from the commissary; but he had been saving every dollar he could for his escape.

Robert went across the Golden Gate Bridge to San Francisco without getting stopped by the authorities; once he arrived there, he went directly to the cemetery where he had emergency money hidden, along with his original California drivers license, birth certificate and passport that he had made under the name of Christopher Davidson when he first arrived in Los Angeles with Deana. He always renewed his license just in case he had to fall back on using that name for one reason or another. Luck would be on his side because he had renewed is license a year before he went to prison and he still had a couple of years left before it needed to be renewed again.

When Robert first arrived in San Francisco in 1985, before he started his position with David's company, he opened up a bank account, then paid cash for his penthouse in the city. When he arrived, he had 6 million dollars and buried 3 million of it. Robert decided a cemetery would be the best place to bury the money and his documents for safe keeping. He found the perfect spot behind a mausoleum site surrounded by trees, shrubs and rose bushes so when he had to dig up a 1 foot wide by 4 feet deep, he would not be conspicuous. He had bought a heavy metal, waterproof miniature safe, placed his money and documents in it after he secured them in heavy plastic and taped them up.

Being relieved that he was a free man, he headed straight for a Thrift Store to buy the best second-hand clothes he could find. He had enough money to buy a few things but knew he had to dig up his hidden money to get a cheap motel for one night. He knew he needed to buy nicer clothes; but that would have to wait. He found everything he temporarily needed in the Thrift Store; he bought a pair of western boots, a cowboy hat, a pair of sunglasses, 6 pair of socks, two shower curtains, four pair of gloves in two different sizes, garden tools and a shorthanded shovel, a purse with an opening without a zipper, and a set of four stainless steel silverware. Luck would be on his side again, there was a windbreaker jacket on the passengers side of the car and he wore that to hide his prison shirt with his number on it, and rolled up his prison pants to look like they were shorts. When he got to the cashier he asked her to place the purse and the silverware in a separate bag because they were for his mom. Once Robert left the shop, he hurried to the car to change clothes. He wanted to make sure he was not going to get his fingerprints on anything. He he took a fork from the bag; used it to retrieve the purse by taking it out of the bag by lifting it from the handle with the fork. He then took off his soiled prison shirt, and placed it in the purse, he took the fork to retrieve his newly acquired shirt out of the other bag. He did this until he had his pants, 3 pairs of the socks on, boots, cowboy hat, and his sunglasses on. He purposely bought boots two sizes too big in case he left footprints anywhere. Robert would later burn them, leaving no trace of his prison clothes, and shoes. He knew time was of the essence; however, he needed the money out of the hole so he drove to the nearest neighbor close to the cemetery and waited until it was dark. Once it was late, he headed over to the mausoleum and started digging up his safe. After he ran out of the cemetery with his safe in his hands; he drove to a 24 hour market where he bought Kotex pads, hair dye, nail polish, polish remover, a few candy bars, and popsicles. and got out of there as quickly as he could. He did not want to go in and just buy hair dye; he wanted it to look like he was shopping for a wife. He was smart to keep his California driver's license active; he would remain Christopher Davidson until he could obtain a new driver's license and birth certificate; he certainly was not going to use his Jim Stark identification either; it had been twenty-nine years since he and Deanna went to Bullet, and eleven years since Bullet made his Jim Stark identifications, and was hoping he was still active in the forgery business. He kept his name and phone number all those years and was praying he could use him again. Robert had decided before he escaped from San Quentin, he would prefer Alaska then some island, where almost all escapees go to live. As soon as he killed Paul, he would be starting a new life, once gain.

In the meantime, before he would fly to Tokyo, he had to change his identity as much as he could. He checked in at a half-way decent hotel, grabbed a local newspaper, and sure enough, there he was plastered on the front page. Escaped convict on the loose; anyone seeing this fugitive, call 911 or your local police. He was hoping that the elderly man at the front desk at the hotel would not see any resemblance with what he was wearing and having the sunglasses on. After checking in, all he could do was hope that he got away with it for the night.

When Robert decided to finally try to go to sleep, he took the two shower curtains and laid them down on the unmade bed to sleep on. He slept in his newly acquired clothes and boots. He did not want to leave a trace of him being there. Robert tossed and turned all night, and at one point, woke up completely soaked. He made sure he had placed the do not disturb sign when he had arrived; he did not want to have anyone coming into the room until after he left. He had a pair of rather thin gloves from the box of dye, wrapped toilet paper around each finger, then slid the gloves on, then slid a pair of the second-hand gloves he purchased. He had not touched anything with his bare hands. Before he dyed his hair, he made a few pinholes, in the plastic shower curtain then placed it in the sink, over the drain, that way none of his hair would fall into the sink, he made sure. He also dyed his eyebrows; so, the hair matched. Once he was done with that painstakingly ordeal, he washed the dye off the gloves and padded them dry as much as he could using his prison pants. He knew he had spent enough time at the hotel and needed to be gone to make sure Bullet was still in business. Robert went to check out, and thank goodness there was someone else attending to the desk; because he did not want the night clerk to notice his eyebrows were darker. There was a young teenage girl, and she processed his payment. She did ask him if he was a real cowboy and he said, with a drawl, he was on the rodeo circuit and that's about as much cowboy as man can get, as he walked away and tipped his hat to her.

After leaving the hotel, he hustled to the nearest pay phone hoping Bullet was still in business. Sure enough! Bullet answered. Robert asked him if he could make another fake birth certificate, driver's license, and passport? "What! Are you tired of being Jim Stark?" Bullet asked. "Pretty much! I have exhausted Jim, and no one likes him," Robert answered. "I will do whatever you need," Bullet said. "Well, I hope a third times a charm," Robert remarked. "I have heard that saying, and for your sake, I hope it is true," Bullet replied. "Can you come to Oakland; I can meet you at the airport and pay you handsomely?" Robert asked. "What does handsomely mean in terms of dollars?" Bullet asked. "How does a hundred thousand dollars sound," Robert answered. "It's a deal; but I prefer to drive up after I get off work," Bullet responded. Robert knew what he meant and thought that was a much better idea and he would get two hotel rooms at the Claremont Hotel under the name of Christopher Davidson. He gave him the address and phone number of the hotel and to let him know an hour before he would be arriving. Before he hung up, he had a brainstorm, "how would you like to go to Tokyo on a mission with me?" Robert asked. "How long would I be gone and what else would I have to do?" Bullet hesitated for a minute then asked. "We will talk more when you get here," Robert answered.

Before Robert got to the hotel, he had his matches, lighter fluid, prison clothes and shoes, the large purse he had gotten at the Thrift Store, along with the silverware. He found a park where he could get rid of all of it. They had barbecue areas and large metal trash cans, so he made sure the articles of clothing were dry then threw everything in with them in the can, dossed it with lighter fluid and lit a few matches, and it was burning fast. He kept looking around to make sure no one saw him, and it was all clear. He made sure the articles were in ashes; he was glad the purse was made out of a fabric that burned easily; once that was done, he then went over to several of the barbecue pits where people had not cleaned up, scraped the ashes into the bag he kept, then dumped them in with his ashes. No one would think it was anything other than ashes from cooking. So far, he had been lucky and hoped it stayed that way.

Three days later, Roberts new name was Clarence Russell, born, January 5, 1952, in Seattle, Washington. He had his new birth certificate, driver's license, and passport. He was ready to take the next step. He thanked Bullet for doing another great job for him and handed him an extra twenty thousand and said he hoped he never retired; in case he needed him again. Robert told him, he did not like traveling alone, and he was on a mission and wanted a traveling companion. He explicitly let Bullet know they would act like two buddies going on vacation. Robert said he would make it an even two hundred thousand if accepted his offer. Bullet grinned and said he was on board as-long-as he did not have to hurt or kill anyone, and no drugs involved. Robert said all he had to do was be there as a friend and nothing else.

Now, the new Clarence knew it was time to go take care of why he escaped in the first place. While he purchased their round-trip tickets to Tokyo from the Oakland Airport, back to Oakland.

Robert did what he came to do, he and Bullet had to hurry to the Tokyo Airport so they would not miss their flight to Oakland. Before they boarded their flight, Robert grabbed a few newspapers to see if he could find out anything about Paul's demise. He had no idea that due to what happened, the Japanese authority were not letting that incident leak out to any newspaper; they wanted the assailant to think Paul could be dead or he may have survived. Robert came-to-the-conclusion they did not put incidences that happen to vacationers in the newspaper. He knew in advance he would not be able to bring a rifle on the plane. He had been fortunate enough, since he had traveled several times to Japan on business with David, he knew where to buy a rifle if he ever needed one. Once he got the rifle, the rest was easy.

Once Robert and Bullet landed back in Oakland after their trip to Japan, they hailed down a taxi to take them to the Claremont Hotel, which Robert had booked for the week. They spent one night at the hotel then left on the road for Los Angeles. Bullet dropped Robert off at the nearest entrance at LAX airport and thanked him for being so generous. They both had agreed it was best that Bullet did not know where Robert was going; but knew that if he ever needed Bullets' assistance again, he had his number. They said their goodbyes, Robert waited until Bullet was out of sight to make his way to the terminal where he was in line to board a plane for Alaska.

After Paul was discharged from the hospital; He and Jezalee spent a lovely evening with the Takahashi's, James, and his wife, Ikuko; but she went by Cookie. They talked about Harvard and surprisingly, they knew some of the same people. Both their children were in the States and going to Harvard as well and both wanted to be doctors. Jezalee gave Cookie their phone numbers at their home in San Francisco and Pisa and gave them an open invitation to come stay with them when her husband was not saving lives.

When they got back to the hotel that night; the children had gotten a call from David and Mallory, who had been on vacation in the Cayman Islands with the children and found out when they arrived home, that Robert had escaped from prison. They were devastated and could not believe he got away with from a maximum-security prison where no one had ever escaped without getting caught. David asked to speak to Paul and asked him who knew they were going to Japan. "Only our immediate family, and all my staff," Paul answered. David had spoken to Jamerson, and he said he had a hunch that Robert pulled the same thing on one of Paul's staff as he did with Roland's. "Paul, he must have been in Tokyo and followed you, who else is going to shoot you," David remarked. "Oh my God!

It was him, it has to be, now what do we do since he has not been caught?" Paul asked. "As soon as you get back to the States, you need to follow-up with the police here," David answered. "I will! But one thing's for sure, Robert does not know if I am dead or alive because the doctor insisted the police not leak the story," Paul remarked. David encouraged Paul to get more security, not just at their estates. Paul agreed he would seriously think about it; especially since Robert was on the loose.

Once the Albanese family went back to their normal routines back in the States, with the children back in their schools and Paul and Jezalee at home. Paul spoke with the guards they had at their San Francisco Estate, and they agreed that each of their children should have a bodyguard, at least until Robert was captured. That was taken care of immediately! They also called Montrose at the Chateau and Franco at the villa, and they would add extra guards there.

Paul had gone to the police station, and he said Robert his obviously armed a dangerous and they would be questioning all the staff at all his businesses. They did find out that it must have been Robert that called their California Winery because one of the staff remembered telling a man where they were. It took a week for Paul to fly and have meetings with all his employees at each business, he adamantly said under no circumstances are they to ever say where he is, other than, he currently is not in the office and take their name and number and he will get back to them. Now! That was taken care of, and Paul and Jezalee knew he was dangerous, and they had to have less outings away from the home for an extended period-of time.

The police and the FBI hit a roadblock, and there were no traces of Robert anywhere. They did not have a clue on what he could be living on; unless he had a bank account under another name and changed his identity. Once Paul and Jezalee got back to normalcy in their lives, as their children did. They still-kept as low a profile as they could. The months flew by into a couple of years; and could not foresee Robert ever bothering them again.

PART EIGHT

JUNEAU, ALASKA: SEPTEMBER 1995

It had been two years since Robert successfully escaped from San
Quentin; however, everyone in Juneau, Alaska knew him as
Clarence, the recluse. He was living a quiet life and for the most
part, not too many people asked questioned. If they did, he told them
he had never been married, did not have any children that he knew of
and told them he had inherited money from his family and had
always wanted to live in Alaska. He mostly kept to himself but was
friendly when he went into town; but stayed under the radar as much
as possible. He certainly did not look like the man he was. Robert

purposely broke his nose, busted his mouth, had a deep scar on his face and chipped his upper front teeth. He had plastic surgery on his face, nose, mouth, and his teeth capped to make them larger and whiter. Robert no longer existed; Clarence was the new person who looked nothing like the old Robert, other than his height. Instead of dying his hair and eyebrows, he was now bleaching them a slight blonde color so he could grow a full beard that was lighter than his natural color of hair. He was hoping eventually his natural hair color would be white like his grandparents. When he was in the courtroom and looked over at them, first thing he noticed was their snow-capped heads; so, hopefully he would eventually not need to bleach his hair. Robert purposely gained fifty pounds and liked being heavier and rugged looking. His current wardrobe was a far cry from his Armani suits and accessories. He now wore flannel plaid shirts, usually corduroy or fleece pants, and any other Alaskan wear that kept a person warm.

Once Robert got acclimated to Juneau and its people; he purchased a fifteen hundred square foot cabin, on 10 acres of land, a few miles out of town. AHe moved into his new place, added an additional five hundred square feet on the first floor and added a second story with two thousand square feet. Robert felt good having more space, even though it was still smaller than his penthouse; but larger than his Manhattan apartment; he knew he may as well be living in a larger space to enjoy himself. He had come to terms with his life as it was; but ever-so-often he missed David, and especially Deanna and her family. He knew he would never be able to talk or see them again; that was a great void in his life. He continually had nightmares about his childhood and was occasionally fixated on Jezalee; but he knew that had to stay in his past, in-order-to keep Clarence in the present. He never wanted to go back to prison; and the only way for that to happen was stay in Alaska the rest of his life and fit in with the locals.

Clarence had become a creature of habit, he would get up at 6:00 AM, have his morning coffee and read for a couple of hours, drive down to Jellies' Café, and have breakfast with the regulars. When he first started going out in public, he had tried various, out of the way cafes but some of the regulars in a few of them appeared too nosey and he was getting uncomfortable being around them. As soon as he walked into Jellies', he knew it was the place he could come to without people getting too curious about him. He did have a story he stuck to; he was raised by a single mom, his dad got killed by a drunk driver just before he was born. His mom was from a well to do family and his mom never had to work. She home schooled him for fear something would happen to him. She died from a heart problem when he was 14, and his aunt and uncle raised him. They kept up his home schooling until he was a senior. Right after he graduated, his uncle took ill, he helped his aunt take care of him for a few years. By this time, he was 19 and his aunt wanted him to go off to college; however, she had a stroke and he watched over her for six years. Between his mother, grandparents, and aunt and uncle, there was enough money left to him for college and to live nicely for the rest of his life. Clarence ended up not going to college because he was extremely shy and had no social skills. When Robert thought up this story, he felt it sounded convincing and would be ready to tell the story if he ever had to.

He was still following the O'Malley's and Albanese's whenever they were in a magazine; it was a lot less now than before. He was extremely upset that he did not kill, Mr. Perfect Paul. He had missed Deanna; but he knew he could never keep in touch with her, after she ratted on him.

The Albanese's and O'Malley's decided to go on a long overdue vacation together. David and Paul were trying to decide where they should take their lovely wives. They had never been to Alaska and wanted to go in September; and thought it would be a great getaway. They thought it would have been nice and more comfortable if Paul could have used the private jet; but only commercial airlines could travel into Alaska. "Shall we book our flights?" David asked. "Absolutely," Paul answered.

Mallory and Jezalee had eagerly packed for Alaska and were so excited for the trip; some of their friends had gone and said how breathtaking the scenery was. Once the four of them got on the commercial jet to Juneau, it only took a little less than 6 hours. When they got to their hotel suite, the ladies had the men plan out their entire trip.

After being there for several days, they understood what all the fuss was about coming to this city with the snow-capped mountains and the brilliant blue Pacific Ocean. The girls decided to wonder off and do some shopping; but the men were right behind them, and they had no clue they were following them. They finally decided to catch up to girls and find a nice place for an early lunch, as they walked into Jellies', Clarence was sitting in the corner of this mom-and-pop restaurant, where he came almost every day for breakfast. As the vacationers sat down at a comfortable booth, Clarence first slightly panicked when he saw them; he kept staring; they looked right at him and did not recognize him. He realized it would be impossible to know it was him with his drastic new appearance. He had also started wearing dark brown contact lenses and wore non-prescription glasses. He stayed there the entire time they had their lunch; he was not about to move in case they got some vibe from the way he walked; so, he stayed put until they left. He usually stayed a couple of hours, but that day he came for breakfast, brought a book to read and got so caught up in the story, it was time for lunch. Robert waited a little longer to make sure they would not see him, then, got in his truck and rode back to his cabin. He knew the FBI was still looking for him; he was on the ten most wanted fugitives list in America, but the photo they had of him was a far cry from how he looked now. He was, enjoying life and it was a beautiful place to live. Clarence, Jim, Chris, Robert, whatever name he was or is currently, he still had one thought that he could not shake; that was of Jezalee. Clarence knew someday he would eventually get on a plane and head to San Francisco.

Made in the USA
Monee, IL
24 February 2023

98e13bf4-6a2b-446c-96b9-eca10c14d5b9R01